AN IRRESISTIBLE T...

Devon placed ... ...ead and moved his body ... that there was no chance for escape. The powerful scent of his masculinity permeated her nostrils. She could smell the saltiness from his sweat, leather from the saddles . . . and something more. There was a deeper, more personal smell that was uniquely his own and was so purely masculine it made Claire's head swim. Her legs trembled while her lungs fought for air. All her years of proper training and decent, ladylike behavior went flying out the stable doors. His sea green eyes had darkened to the sultry color of midnight, and she felt engulfed by his magnetic stare.

"What about if I tell ye how beautiful ye look right now?" he breathed into her ear. "So beautiful ye fair take my breath away."

"I . . . well . . ." It was useless to even attempt an answer, not when she could only marvel at his sleek, lean body standing in front of her, scant inches away. She felt his warm breath upon her cheek. And then his hand, strong enough to control the powerful thoroughbreds housed within the stable, was gently caressing her back. As before, his touch sent shivers coursing through her body. His gaze locked with hers for the barest of instants, then his head dipped forward to block out her view as his warm, moist lips captured hers.

She didn't realize he intended to kiss her until just before he did so. By then it was too late. She could no more have stopped him than she could have stopped a stampede. And, Lord forgive her, she didn't want to.

BOOK YOUR PLACE ON OUR WEBSITE AND MAKE THE READING CONNECTION!

We've created a customized website just for our very special readers, where you can get the inside scoop on everything that's going on with Zebra, Pinnacle and Kensington books.

When you come online, you'll have the exciting opportunity to:

- View covers of upcoming books
- Read sample chapters
- Learn about our future publishing schedule (listed by publication month *and author*)
- Find out when your favorite authors will be visiting a city near you
- Search for and order backlist books from our online catalog
- Check out author bios and background information
- Send e-mail to your favorite authors
- Meet the Kensington staff online
- Join us in weekly chats with authors, readers and other guests
- Get writing guidelines
- AND MUCH MORE!

**Visit our website at
http://www.kensingtonbooks.com**

SEASON
OF
SPLENDOR

Liz Madison

ZEBRA BOOKS
Kensington Publishing Corp.
http://www.kensingtonbooks.com

ZEBRA BOOKS are published by

Kensington Publishing Corp.
850 Third Avenue
New York, NY 10022

All Kensington titles, imprints and distributed lines are available at special quantity discounts for bulk purchases for sales promotion, premiums, fund-raising, educational or institutional use.

Special book excerpts or customized printings can also be created to fit specific needs. For details, write or phone the office of the Kensington Special Sales Manager: Kensington Publishing Corp., 850 Third Avenue, New York, NY 10022. Attn. Special Sales Department. Phone: 1-800-221-2647.

Zebra and the Z logo Reg. U.S. Pat. & TM Off.

First Printing: August 2002
10 9 8 7 6 5 4 3 2 1

Printed in the United States of America

For Jari, whose unwavering love and support inspire me every day. Kiitos, Kulta.

One

Everything around them was a saturated mess. The carriage, horses, and trunks were soaked. Deep pools of water in the roadway had caused mud to spatter in all directions, and the torrential wind made sure that anything which had somehow managed to escape the straight downpour received a thorough dousing.

"Why on earth does it always have to rain when we move?" moaned Louisa Rushmoor. "This dreadful weather makes me want to turn right around and go back to the country."

"It doesn't rain any less there," Louisa's second oldest daughter, Lavinia, wisely pointed out, "and besides, you know you'd never dream of not being in London for the season."

"I know that," Louisa huffed. "But I detest arriving in the city looking like a drenched cat."

Their relentless bickering, along with the rain, continued for the duration of the trip, until at last the carriage pulled up to No. 23 Park Lane, the stately London town home of Lord Kendal Rushmoor, Earl of Bedington, his wife, and their four daughters. At the moment his wife and daughters arrived, the downpour hit its peak of intensity, and amid the confusion of everyone trying to be the first inside, the rain managed to soak them all.

As soon as they walked through the door servants

rushed to do their bidding, supplying towels and compassion to their agitated mistresses.

"Oh, my ladies, we'll need to get you warm and dry before you catch your death," exclaimed Emma Leeds, the dutiful head housekeeper. "Doesn't it always happen that the rains come just as you do. But don't worry, I already have my girls heating up water for your baths. In no time you'll all be feeling much better."

"Thank you, Emma," replied Louisa gratefully, turning toward her daughters. "Girls, dash upstairs and have the servants help you with your baths. I don't want anyone coming down with fever. Prospective suitors don't find it attractive, and we wouldn't want that to be this year's excuse for not finding one."

All heads within hearing range turned toward Claire, the eldest of Louisa's four daughters, and unmistakably the one to whom her mother's remark was directed. An uneasy silence filled the room. Embarrassed for their sister, Lavinia and the twins did not meet her eye. The scurrying servants paused, waiting to see if this would at last be the time when Claire stood up to her mother.

Indeed, Claire was stung by the comment, but her genteel upbringing forbade a reproach. Instead she turned away and headed up the stairs.

"Mother can say such terribly mean things sometimes," Lavinia said to her sister in a conspiratorial, hushed tone once they had reached the second floor. "But she isn't truly trying to hurt you."

"I know she isn't," Claire replied. "She's just afraid that I'll wind up a spinster if I don't catch anyone's eye this year. After all, it will be my third season."

Lavinia paused before entering her bedroom. "Claire, you know I'd sooner bite my own tongue than sound like Mother," she began hesitantly. "But the problem is not that you haven't captured any man's fancy. For goodness sakes, you're beautiful enough to have whomever you want. It's just that you've let them all go." She took a deep breath as if wanting to add something else, then seemed to change her mind and asked simply, "Why?"

Claire smiled at her younger sister. "Because I haven't been in love with any of them," she explained.

"Love?" Lavinia stated the word as if it were foreign. "What does love have to do with finding a husband? You just need someone respectable with whom to bear heirs." She coyly added, "Then you can have a lover who . . ."

"Lavinia!" Claire cut her off before her sister finished the sentence. "Don't talk of such things. Respectable ladies do not have lovers. I certainly hope you haven't let the twins hear you speak that way."

Kate and Emily, the youngest sisters, were identical twins six years younger than twenty-year-old Claire. Because she was the eldest, Claire was protective of them.

"Of course I haven't," Lavinia responded, slightly rebuffed. "But it isn't like they don't know about such things. Honestly, you're the only one I've ever heard talk of trying to find a husband who you truly love."

"And I'll keep talking about it until I find him," said Claire, her voice sharp with conviction. "I want a man to sweep me off my feet, Linny. To make me feel as if I'm the only one in the world who matters to him. I want him to make me feel special."

Lavinia eyed her sister as if she were daft and slowly shook her head. "Well, when you meet that man be sure to let me know. Perhaps he'll have a brother. In the meantime, I'd advise you to consider the more down-to-earth prospects. After all, you don't want to endure Mother's needling for the entire season, do you?"

She was right about that. For the past several months Claire and her mother had clashed as badly as two cats in a bag. This was, after all, Claire's third season (as her mother never hesitated to point out), and it was *high time* she got herself married.

"It isn't like you haven't attracted respectable suitors, Claire, but you never give any of these men an opportunity."

"Because I haven't been in love with any of them, Mother."

"Love is not a consideration here; getting married is. And anyway, is spending the rest of your life as a spinster something you want?"

"It's better than being stuck with a stodgy old bore!"

And so on. As Claire walked down the east wing toward her room, she knew her mother was only doing what was socially expected of her. As she said, it wouldn't do for Claire to come out of this season mateless once again. It simply wouldn't look good for the family. And anyway, it wasn't as if she didn't want a husband. She just didn't want a boring one.

She reached her bedroom just as Marie, her serving woman, stuck her head out the door, apparently wondering what was keeping her mistress.

"Mademoiselle, *entrez, entrez!*" she insisted, worrying like a mother hen. "You will catch ze sick if you stay wet!" Claire smiled as she allowed Marie to begin peeling off her rain-soaked clothing. The kindly maid's English fluency was in direct proportion to her level of agitation. She was, however, extremely efficient, and in no time at all Claire found herself being helped into a steaming hot bath. At once Marie took up the lavender-scented soap she knew her mistress favored and spread it lavishly across her smooth, enviable skin. She then grabbed the washcloth and scrubbed until Claire felt tingles all over her body. Finally Marie took more of the soap to wash Claire's hair and topped it off with a lemon rinse.

"You feel better, *non?*" Marie asked after wrapping her mistress in a warm fluffy robe.

"Much better," Claire replied, settling into the vanity chair with a comfortable sigh. It was good to be in London again, she thought. Despite the difficulties she would soon have to face, being here in her spacious bedchamber had always made her feel protected from troubles beyond. The warm rosewood furniture, from the vanity set to the ornamented bed frame to the corner chair tucked discreetly in the intersection of the farthest walls, gave the room a cozy feel. Matching rosewood nightstands graced either side of her feather bed, and the walls were covered with cream-colored wallpaper dotted by irises.

Marie picked up the pearl-handled hairbrush and began combing out Claire's long, golden locks. The cumulative effect of her chestnut brown eyes, set off by pure white skin, full pink lips, and mounds of golden hair had been turning many a gentleman's head ever since her coming out three seasons ago. Indeed, an abundance of suitors had vied for her attention, but again and again Claire bemoaned that she felt nothing for them, and wondered whether she ever would for anyone.

The effects of the long, wet trip began taking their toll, and Claire felt her eyelids grow heavy. Just as she was contemplating the appeal of a nap, a sharp knock on the door chased away her reverie.

"Who eez it?" Marie asked.

"It's Amanda," came the prompt response. "I need to speak with Lady Claire."

"You may let her in, Marie," Claire acquiesced.

After the door swung open the young servant girl swiftly strode across the room and stood before Claire. She made a quick curtsy and then rushed through her story.

"I'm so sorry to bother you, my lady, but it seems there's a bit of a problem with your cousin."

"Lilia?" Claire raised her eyebrows in surprise. "What's she up to?"

Amanda looked down at the floor before answering, as if embarrassed about the information she was forced to deliver.

"Well, my lady, she has taken to standing about the kitchen and insisting that the staff there teach her how to cook."

"What?"

"Yes, my lady. We tried telling her that she needn't worry about such things and that we would bring her anything she wanted, but Lady Lilia told them she wants to learn."

"Good heavens," muttered Claire, already preparing to go downstairs.

"We tried looking for Lady Bella, but she and Lady Louisa are overseeing the unloading of the trunks. We were informed that you were the next one to speak to."

True enough, Claire admitted to herself. Ever since it was decided that Aunt Bella and Cousin Lilia would stay in London with Claire's family during this year's season, Claire had been denoted Lilia's unofficial caretaker. As the oldest of four sisters, Claire was the natural choice. She was poised and elegant. Her manners were impeccable. Every gesture she made, all the mannerisms she'd developed, were indications of the well-bred lady she had become. And these were all areas in which Lilia sorely needed instruction. It was thought that if Lilia attended a few social events under Claire's guidance, she would be better prepared for her official "coming out" next season.

But as she dressed to go downstairs, Claire reflected on how far Lilia's preparation had to go. The girl was ill-mannered and rambunctious, perhaps due in part to the early loss of her father. There was no steady guiding hand in Lilia's life to keep her in check, and she had long ago become too big a burden for her single mother to handle.

After Marie finished dressing her, Claire hurried downstairs with Amanda to the site of the commotion. Inside the kitchen, it was just as the young servant had described.

"Really, my lady, it isn't necessary for any of this to concern you," the head cook was trying diligently to explain. "Just tell me what you want and I will be happy to fix it."

Lilia did not move. "I understand that, Ellen, but it won't help me," she said obstinately. "I need to learn how to cook, and you're the only one who can teach me."

The cook's big bosom heaved in annoyance, and despite her better judgment, she was about to give the young chit a piece of her mind when Claire arrived, just in time.

"Lilia!" she sternly admonished. "What on earth are you doing in the kitchen?"

"Oh, Claire, I'm glad you're here," Lilia answered, doing her best to ignore her cousin's tone. "The servants are being most uncooperative. I've asked them to teach me—"

"That will be enough, Lilia. Come with me and we'll talk in the sitting room."

"But Claire, I—"

"Now, Lilia." Claire's voice was firm yet controlled, with just a gentle touch of authority. She did not wait for Lilia's acknowledgment; instead she turned briskly around and walked out the door and down the long, gilded hallway. As expected, Lilia trailed behind her.

When they arrived in the sitting room, Claire closed the door behind them and primly sat upon the large mahogany ottoman. It was an elegant piece of furniture, with a satinwood veneer and floral ornamentation carved into the reeded legs. As she sat down she folded her hands in her lap and calmly waited until Lilia did the same.

Awkwardly, Lilia did sit down, choosing one of the tripod Sheraton chairs across from Claire. Various bric-a-brac dotted the room's walls and small tables, and heavy curtains framed every window. The atmosphere in the room was dark and somber, as if reflecting Claire's apparent dissatisfaction. A majestic grandfather clock ticked the seconds away while Lilia nervously cleared her throat and waited for her older cousin to begin speaking.

"Please explain to me exactly what you were doing in the kitchen, Lilia," Claire stated without preamble.

Feeling a little less sure of herself now than in the kitchen, Lilia avoided Claire's dark scrutiny and answered, "I wanted to learn to cook." Still the stare continued, and, trying to excuse her behavior, Lilia added, "I thought it would be to my advantage when trying to attract a suitor if I possessed culinary skills."

At the absurdness of that last statement, Claire couldn't help but smile.

"Lilia, why would you possibly think such a thing when there are servants to do the cooking? A refined lady never goes into the kitchen, or anyplace where servants are, for that matter. You couldn't imagine one of the servants coming into the sitting room and bothering us, could you?" At the girl's slight head shake, Claire continued. "So why would you possibly think that they would want you in the kitchen? Remember, Lilia, we have our place, and they have theirs. The kitchen is theirs, the sitting room is ours. Do you understand?"

"Well, of course I know that. Mother has said the same."

"Then why would you act so appallingly? You know you don't need cooking skills."

Lilia said nothing at first, then suddenly rose from the chair and blew out a sigh of frustration. "Oh, I don't know, Claire," she exclaimed. "I'm just so utterly bored these days. I want some excitement in my life. I want to do something different. I'm so very tired of shopping and making calls."

Something deep, very deep in the core of Claire's soul identified with the exasperated words of her younger cousin. But Lady Claire Rushmoor, product of ingrained genteel breeding, would never consciously acknowledge that. Instead she looked smartly at Lilia and assured her that life as she knew it would change very soon.

"You'll be attending a few dances and outings this season, Lilia, and then next year you'll really be in a whirlwind. Coming out is such an exciting time. There will be an endless stream of balls, parties, dinners and breakfasts, all—"

"All for the purpose of catching a husband." Lilia made the statement with inarguable finality. Her voice then softened as she sat back down. "Let's be honest, Claire. All those engagements might be fun on the surface, but I know as well as you do that there is only one reason for attending them, and I just don't find that particularly exciting."

Lilia's honesty was unsettling, and Claire hesitated before answering her.

"Perhaps you feel that way now, but I know you'll feel differently next year. All proper women want to get married and raise families, Lilia. Are you telling me that you don't?"

"No, of course not. I want to get married and have children. It's just that, well . . ."

"Well, what? What are you trying to say?"

"It's just that I'd like to have an adventure before that part of my life begins. That's all."

For reasons unknown to her, the conversation was suddenly making Claire feel uncomfortable. She decided then and there that she'd had enough.

"Carousing with the servants is not the way to have your adventure, Lilia," she said briskly. "Ladies with our upbringing look to their husbands for adventure, and that's just what you should be doing."

"But, Claire . . ." her cousin protested.

"That's enough, Lilia. Among other things you need to learn respect for your elders. Although I'm only five years older than you, I nevertheless expect appropriate behavior."

"Yes, Claire," Lilia meekly answered.

"And now that I have you here, we might as well go over a few other rules that you must obey. Since you've never spent any real time in London, there are several things for you to be aware of in addition to refining your manners and behavior. I don't imagine this will be a problem since you are never to leave this house unescorted, but I feel I must bring it up."

"Truly? What things?"

"When you go shopping, stay within the Mayfair district on Bond and Regent Streets. There's no reason to stray farther east than Regent. Moreover, do not, for any reason, go down to the docks, particularly the area beyond the East End of the Tower."

Lilia's eyes lit up with a curiosity Claire found disconcerting as she asked, somewhat breathlessly, "Why not? What's down there?"

"Nothing but disreputable people and dishonest shopkeepers. There's no reason whatsoever for you to venture in that direction. Do not ever go anywhere near Blackwall, Wapping, East India, or any of those other docks. Is that clear?" Claire emphatically stressed the prohibition, as she did not like the intrigued gleam she spotted in her cousin's eyes.

"Yes, it's clear," Lilia acknowledged. "But just what kind of disreputable people live there?"

"Well . . ." Here Claire paused, somewhat unsure of her answer. No one really spoke of the types of people living over there, no doubt because it was such distasteful conversation.

"Mother says she's heard that East End people are migrants, mostly. People from southern and eastern England—Sussex, Kent, Hertfordshire—places like that. And then, of course, there are all those immigrants." She wrinkled her nose at that last word, as if its mere mention created a stench. "Scots. Jews. *Irish.* I've heard talk that they're all unskilled, lazy people with crude manners and even cruder speech. The blight of society, Mother says." She could see her inquisitive cousin was fascinated, too fascinated, by such talk, so she waved her arm as if to brush away the topic. "Anyway, Lilia, the sort of people over there are the type not mentioned in polite conversation."

"So you mean to say you've never been there?"

"Of course not. People like us do not go to such places."

Lilia could not resist the temptation. "But if we're not to speak with disreputable people or go to disreputable places, how does anyone really know what it's like down there?"

Her brazenness had tested the limits of Claire's patience. "We just hear things, that's all. And I know enough not to question those in charge."

The meaning of her last statement was not lost on her younger cousin, and for once Lilia realized when it was time to keep quiet.

At that moment there was a timid knock upon the door.

"Yes?"

The young serving girl Amanda poked her head

through the door. "Pardon the interruption, my lady, but we've rung the dinner bell."

"Oh my, I didn't even hear it. Thank you, Amanda," Claire responded, polite as ever. Then she turned toward her cousin and eyed her with some disdain. "In the future, Lilia, make sure you are properly dressed in time for dinner. The dress you're currently wearing is not adequate."

"Yes, Claire," Lilia responded, weary of being admonished. She rose from the chair and darted out of the sitting room, hoping to avoid further reproach.

For a moment Claire stayed where she was sitting and looked after Lilia reflectively. She didn't mean to sound so harsh with her cousin, but Lilia's behavior had always been rebellious. Claire knew her Aunt Bella had tried many times to correct Lilia's unruly demeanor, but Claire secretly thought that Bella indulged her only daughter, perhaps on an unconscious level to try making up for the loss of Lilia's father. Earl Rothman Chatterton had always been a nervous man, and had died suddenly nearly ten years ago, a victim of apoplexy. In his very unorthodox will he had left his entire estate to his wife, Bella, and, in turn, to Lilia upon his wife's demise. Lilia, therefore, would bring an enviable dowry with her to marriage, and thus had an excellent chance at commanding high peerage. She needed only refinement and politesse, as well as some pointers on proper etiquette.

Claire's mind went back again to Lilia's earlier comments, about yearning for adventure. What was it about those words which seemed to touch a chord within her? She'd never once thought of herself as an adventuress, so why did it seem that Lilia's comments made sense? Could she, too, be longing for something beyond what she had?

"Don't be silly," she muttered under her breath, telling herself that it was a ridiculous notion. True, she had been holding out on previous suitors. But that was because she hadn't found herself in love with them. Beyond that one streak of stubbornness that had so lately vexed her mother, Claire was a polite, reasonable, proper young woman. And she was content to follow the leagues of other polite, reasonable, and proper young women who had gone before her to capture well-bred husbands and raise well-bred children. Claire stubbornly insisted that she be in love with her husband, but beyond that she was content to do what had been rigidly mapped out for her even before she was born. Wasn't she?

Claire shook her head to rid herself of an aggravating uncertainty. Of course she was. And it wouldn't do at all to allow her rambunctious young cousin to instill doubt in her mind. Claire Amelia Rushmoor knew what her future looked like, and it was a respectable one. It was absurd to question her role in life, and she'd not do it again. Ever.

Two

Sharp, beady eyes peered outside the shopkeeper's door, needing to ensure that the surroundings were clear. It was a necessary precaution, for the lateness of the hour did not preclude others from being out and about. When the owner of the eyes felt confident that he and his mates would not be observed, he signaled thus with a distinctive, low whistle. Making no more noise than gently falling snow, the four men crept out the back while their partner on the lookout held open the door. As soon as they had exited, the door closed behind them with a faintly audible click.

Words were unnecessary to complete the heist. As previously arranged, the five men soundlessly crept along the unpaved walkway, keeping themselves low and as close to the adjoining buildings as they could. This was the darkest area of the street and provided the most cover until they could get underground.

In no time at all they reached the opening of the sewer. With a final look behind them to ensure they were alone, the five men unhesitatingly stepped into the sludge.

Saturating the air was the smell of human waste; its rank, putrid stench completely enveloped them. A person who had never before been assaulted by the noxious odor would have been sickened at once. But the thieves scarcely noticed it. More of a bother was the filthy, wet sewage they were forced to wade through. It penetrated their poorly constructed shoes, filling them up with a cold, wet scum.

When they had walked along far enough to be certain they were alone, the men halted their journey and soundlessly began dividing up the evening's take. It was best not to speak in moments like these. Water was an excellent sound carrier, and even in the deepest hours of the night one could never be sure who else might be there, seeking possible treasures floating in the sludge.

The pervasive darkness made it necessary to light a candle. They'd made certain to steal one, along with some matches, from the innkeeper's shop. Silently Joshua reached into his pocket and pulled the candle out, then with a quick, practiced flick of his wrist he lit a match and touched it to the candle's wick. The five of them huddled around the solitary flame, ensuring that the light was cut off from outside viewers.

Devon, their acknowledged leader, reached into his pocket and pulled out the pilfered money. It was their practice to steal only currency from those they robbed. Lifted goods would have to be sold before they were of any use to them, and the selling brought a whole host of additional problems.

Devon counted out the money they had stolen this evening. In spite of the deceitful way he made his living, Devon was honest to a fault where his friends were concerned, and he insisted on always openly counting out the take so everyone would know the money was equally divided.

" 'Tis one bob, two bob, three bob, half a crown, and a quid," he said, showing it to them all. "So, let me see. That comes out to . . . a bull and a farthing apiece!" The news was whispered with forced enthusiasm, for they all knew the amount of money they were to receive had hardly been worth the trouble they had gone through to get it.

The expressions on the men's faces were grim. They were cold, wet, poor, and hungry, with scarcely a hope of ever being different. Filth and squalor, part of their everyday existence, had forced them to adopt a lifestyle of thievery. It was a way of life they all detested, but none of them had ever known there could be anything more. Now they turned back toward the sewer's entrance. In the morning Devon would get the coins changed through his regular contact, and then dole out everyone's meager share. They'd use the money for whatever they wanted, usually food, and when it ran out the cycle would repeat itself. It was a horrific existence for anyone forced into it, but such was the way of life for many in 1808 London.

Jonathan, their lookout man, walked ahead of the group to make sure the area was clear. His small size made him the most difficult to spot, but it was his un-canny vision that earned him his post. It was said by his mates that Jonathan could see the fleas on stray dogs.

When they heard his distinctive low whistle, they moved out of the sewer and back into the street. As was their usual custom, the group immediately dispersed so as to lessen the chance of being followed. Later they would meet up at the rookery in Clerkenwell that they called home.

The commotion of a fight in progress was the first sound to greet Devon as he awoke the next morning. By the level of noise just outside his door, it seemed to be quite a terrific row. And indeed, as he stepped outside to have a look, he saw that the two brawlers had drawn a large crowd that was encouraging the scuffle. It was difficult to be certain about the age of the boys as they rolled in the street with fists flying, but to Devon they looked no older than ten. Normally he did not interfere

in the affairs of others; in his dog-eat-dog way of existence it paid only to look out for oneself. But the rude
awakening had made him irritable, and at this moment
Devon could not tolerate the impromptu commotion.

With quick, sure strides he broke through the crowd
and looked down at the fighting boys. With one powerful
hand Devon grabbed a fistful of the first boy's shirt,
hauled him off the ground, and set him on his feet. The
second boy, relieved to see that his adversary had been
pulled off him, scrambled to his feet to continue the
brawl. But Devon was not about to let that happen. While
maintaining his grip upon the first boy, he seized the
second boy's shirt and then held both of them apart from
one another at his arm's length. They attempted breaking
away but quickly realized that they'd met their match
with this man's iron strength.

The aggravated crowd bellowed their disapproval at
Devon for breaking up the fight, but his piercing stare
silenced them at once.

"What the devil's the matter with ye?" he angrily demanded. "Ain't ye bloody fools got nothing better to do
than wake people up by yelling outside their doors?" As
expected, no one said a thing. When Devon unleashed
the wrath of his anger, it was commonly met with an
uneasy silence.

"Be on yer way and don't come 'round here again.
Next time I catch any of ye outside my door, I'll knock
yer silly skulls together. Now get out of here!" No more
convincing was needed. Devon released the brawlers, and
the entire crowd ran as if fire licked their heels.

Before they were gone from sight, Devon glanced
once more at the boys who had been fighting. It was
easy to see himself in their faces. Although this year he'd
seen the passing of his twenty-eighth birthday, it seemed
not long ago that he had been one of those boys. He
remembered that virtually anything could be cause

enough for a brawl. Looking back on it, he supposed it was just boys' way to relieve the tension of their destitute lives. It also prepared them for what was to come, since fighting ability was necessary in this way of life. And Devon had obtained more than his share of preparation. The vicious teasing he had received about his mother's chosen profession resulted in almost daily rows. But the older he became the better fighter he was, and by the age of fourteen Devon no longer had to worry about coming to blows with other boys around him. None of them were brazen enough to face him.

Thinking of his mother made him remember what he needed to do this morning. Hastily he went back inside the dilapidated single room he shared with his mates and gathered up the money they had stolen last night. After donning one of the two shirts he owned, he eased back out of the room, allowing those inside to continue sleeping.

The chill of the morning was dissipating, and the day held promise of sunshine. Despite the early hour people were already swarming the streets. Those who had jobs walked or rode hastily to them, those who didn't merely stood around with dour expressions on their faces. Eventually hunger would drive them to begin begging or stealing for spare coins and scraps of food.

As Devon made his way along the unpaved walkway, a few stray dogs and cats darted between his legs. The pathetic creatures nosed their way through the refuse littering the streets, hoping to salvage something edible.

The cries of the costermongers rang in Devon's ears. "Eeeee . . . lllls! Get your eels! Cherries here! Nice ripe cherries! Apples! Oranges!" Their everyday grind often took them ten miles throughout the streets of London.

At last Devon reached his destination, No. 7 Cloak Street. Since those employed within generally worked evenings, the house was quiet at this early hour. But Devon knew that Madam Sally Landry, the establishment's owner and his mother's longtime employer, would already be working in her office, keeping the books and tallying last evening's take. He stood for a moment just inside the door, letting his eyes adjust to the room's oppressive darkness. No matter how brightly the sun shone outside, the heavy velvet curtains covering every window ensured discreet darkness for Madam Sally's wary clientele.

When his pupils had dilated sufficiently, Devon walked straight to the office with the knowledge of one who had been there many times before.

As expected, Sally was hunched over her desk, entering figures into her ledger. Devon silently stood in the doorway, waiting for her to notice him. When she at last did, her reaction was the same as always.

"Devon!" she gasped, clutching both hands to her heart as if quelling rampant palpitations. "Good Lord, ye'll scare the blooming life out of me yet, ye will. How long have ye been standing there?"

"Oh, not more than twenty minutes," he said solemnly, but the twinkle in his eye revealed his teasing.

"And I'm the king of England," she teased right back, now that her initial shock had passed.

"Then ye're the prettiest king I ever seen," said Devon, planting an affectionate kiss upon her cheek.

"Oh, my," giggled Sally like a shy schoolgirl. "With that kind of compliment ye must want something other than seeing yer mum."

"Pretty *and* smart, ye are," Devon responded, holding out the coins for her to see. "I'm just looking for some change so I can divide this among my mates."

Sally's expression turned serious. "Is that all ye were able to get last night?" she asked, knowing the money would be divided five ways.

"Aye, 'tis it, old gal. We thought we'd get us quite a

load, but when we broke inside the cash box was empty. Gareth thinks the place has been hit before, so the owner probably takes the money home with him every night if he can't get to the bank. The only reason we was able to get even this is because Joshua spotted a coin purse stuffed behind a flour barrel. We think the owner's wife kept her own secret money."

"I suppose so," Sally agreed. "The old twit probably hoards everything to himself."

"Too bad we had to take her stash. But my mates and I are hungry."

"She'll get more, ye can be sure of that," Sally said crisply. Unlike Devon, she felt not a whit sorry for the woman from whom they'd stolen. It was hard enough making ends meet, let alone dealing with guilt on top of it.

"Let's see what ye got." She swiftly counted the coins in Devon's hand and divided the total into five.

"That's a crown apiece with a pence left over," she said, knowing that Devon had already figured it out. The boy'd always had a mind for numbers.

"Nothing left over," he insisted. "A crown and a farthing apiece."

"But a copper only gets you four farthings. Are you going to draw straws to see who's left out?"

"Nay," Devon replied, and Sally knew at once who would be the one shortchanged.

"Devon," she lightly scolded. "Why're ye always doing that? Them mates of yers don't appreciate it, 'cause none of them's got a head for figures. Whenever the money don't divide out right, ye're always leaving yerself out."

Devon brushed her words aside. "Oh, what's a farthing good for, anyway? Ye can't get much with it."

"Nothing but some tea or a night's lodging," she

pointed out, despite knowing that Devon's mind was made up.

"They earned the money," he said firmly, "and I mean to give it to 'em." His tone then lightened and he rapped upon her cash box. "So how's about some change, old gal, so we poor buggers can get our day's bread."

Sally let out a resigned breath. "Very well. You win, as always." She rapidly made the change and poured the coins into Devon's waiting hand. "Now go on upstairs to see yer mum. She'll be wanting to talk to ye." She made a dismissive gesture with her hands as she looked back down at the books on her desk.

Devon smiled to himself while walking toward the staircase. He had known Sally since the day he was born, and was forever grateful for everything she had done for him. It was by no means taken for granted that when one of Sally's doxies got herself with child, the child would be allowed to live in the bawdy house. After all, it was bad for business. Callers in The Night Star did not take to having children underfoot. However, Devon's mother, May, was one of Sally's most requested ladies, and over the years the two had grown to be friends. Perhaps it was their common bond of having come over from Ireland when they were but young girls. Living in a new country, being laughed at because of their accents, both had developed willful dispositions through years of scorn and abuse. In May's case it had been even worse, for she'd come to England all alone with nary a friend or relative to help acquaint her with the new country. At least Sally had had her sister, though the poor girl had died of typhus after having been here only a year.

Two years after starting her business she met May through a common friend, and shortly after that hired her full time. When May realized she was pregnant and insisted on birthing the child, Sally had agreed that Devon could live at The Night Star provided he didn't get underfoot and May's earnings did not diminish. It was an arrangement that worked better than anyone could have anticipated. The joy of having Devon fulfilled May completely, and that joy carried over to her work. She pleased her clients with abandon, the frenetic pace of her lovemaking fueled by the thought of seeing her son the minute she was free. May brought in more money than Madam Sally could ever have dreamed, and if it was merely having her son live with her that spurred May to work so hard, far be it from Sally to cast the child out. Anyway, if the truth be told, over the years she had grown extremely fond of the boy, as had all the other ladies who worked for Sally. It was almost as though Devon became the child they all wished to have had.

In the end, it was May who ultimately decided Devon had to leave. She knew in her heart of hearts that a bordello was no place to raise a child. May knew Devon fought other boys because they teased him about his mother, and the thought was nearly more than she could bear. As long as Devon lived in a brothel, boys in the streets would tease him ruthlessly. And so, with a heart so heavy it felt filled with lead, May Blake had told her thirteen-year-old-son that he needed to find another place to live. She hoped against hope that the outside world would hold a better life for her son than it had for her.

At first it had not been so bad. One of May's regular customers was a somewhat craggy character who owned a livery just outside of town. The man made his living by boarding horses for London's elite, and one day had mentioned to May that he was looking for an extra pair of hands to help him out. It seemed that oftimes the owners left their horseflesh in the livery for so long that the animals' once lean muscles grew fat and weak. When the owners finally did pick them up they complained to the livery owner that their horses were mistreated. The accusations were untrue; nevertheless, the livery owner needed to keep his customers happy. He had thus come up with the bright idea of hiring a boy to take the horses out for daily rides and keep them exercised. May at once suggested Devon for the job. It was a decision that would always haunt her. The man hired her boy, paid him a few shillings a week, and gave him a warm place to sleep in his home. All was well at first, for riding the horses came as naturally to Devon as breathing, and he enjoyed racing the steeds across the lush English countryside. But after a time it came clear that May's regular customer had more of an interest in young boys than he ever had in her. After the third time he tried climbing into bed with Devon, her son had left the house, swearing his hatred against the vile man.

May shuddered when she remembered how shocked and furious Devon had been as he told her everything that happened. She vowed to find a way to get even with the man who had degraded her son, but they both knew deep inside that there was nothing to be done. People of their class simply had to accept that the wealthy had privileges and the poor had few rights. In the end there was nothing they could do. May was terrified to let Devon face the streets on his own, knowing that any work he might find would most likely be either illegal or demoralizing. Still, he had no chance of becoming anything if he lived in a brothel, and anyway it wasn't a place for a boy to be, especially one who was becoming a young man.

Devon promptly joined a group of Irish pickpockets and soon became the most accomplished among them. It was no trouble at all for him to quietly and inconspicuously steal handkerchiefs, pocketbooks, watches, and scarf pins. The rest of the group admired Devon's adroitness, and before long he was the unofficial leader. Together Devon and his group "graduated" to stealing higher-priced items, but soon realized that anything but money was difficult to trade. And so it was money that the group went about stealing: first from people on the streets and later from shopkeepers. Devon had countless times expressed his disgust for what he did, but the alternatives amounted to little more than killing rats or working as a mudlark and foraging through the sludge of the Thames for salable scraps of iron or coal. Both ideas were loathsome. So despite Devon's distaste for larceny, he had been a thief for more than half his life.

He cleared the memories as he approached the door to his mum's room. He put his ear against the door to make sure she was alone, and when no sound emerged from within, he rapped against the wood to let her know he was there. In seconds the door flew open and a joyous May Blake opened her arms to her son. Knowing Devon often came on Sunday morning, she had awoken early to prepare for his visit. The room she called home was small but tidy, with all her belongings neatly in place. She hugged Devon with a mother's fierce intensity, then ushered him into the room and shut the door behind them.

As they settled into their usual chairs, May noticed that Devon was looking somewhat gaunt. He'd always been thin, but his normally muscular body appeared leaner than when she'd last seen him; his clothes seemed to hang on his tall frame. His cheekbones stood out more than usual, which emphasized the scar he had along his left jaw. Locks of his long, sun-streaked chestnut hair hung in disheveled array. His piercing green eyes held an almost haunted look, and May knew at once that Devon hadn't been eating.

"Ye've lost weight," she pronounced, direct as always. "What's going on?"

Devon smiled at his mum's concern, knowing that no matter how old he became, she'd always feel the need to look out for him.

"It's nothing, Mum," he tried gently assuring her. "The takes just haven't been very good lately, that's all. Seems like nobody's making any money."

"I got me a bit," she began, rising to her feet, but Devon silenced her at once.

"Sit right back down there," he quietly commanded, and May knew better than to argue with him. Devon had long ago stopped asking his mother for support, aware of the meager earnings in her profession.

"It pains me to see ye like this, Devon," May said, her voice growing thick with worry.

"Forget it, Mum," Devon said airily, trying his best to calm her fear and steer their conversation away from him. "Tell me how ye've been doing."

May shrugged; nothing was different. "I've been feeling pretty fair. That bum shoulder o'mine . . ." Her attention was distracted. She could never think of herself when she knew her boy was having trouble. She tried talking about a few superficial things that had happened lately but eventually gave up trying.

"Devon," she said softly. "Tell yer poor mum honestly what's going on. I can't stand the thought of ye keeping me in the dark. We've always been truthful with each other. Don't shut me out just because ye think I'll worry."

Devon stared at his mother, amazed, as always, at her ability to decipher his thoughts. May continued, " 'Cause I'll worry regardless." Her last comment made him smile, and he finally decided that maybe it would be good to confide in his mother. After all, he always had.

"It's just that we've been on a bad streak lately. It takes so bleeding long to study where we'll hit next, and when we finally make the break there turns out to be nary a bob in the entire place." Devon expelled a sigh of frustration as he continued. "If this keeps up for much longer we got no choice but to start picking again, just

like the ragged little boys we once were." The shame
and disgust was evident all over his face, and May sorely
wished that there was something she could do.

"What does Joshua say about that?" she asked, knowing Devon would have expressed his feelings to his closest friend.

"Nothing ever seems to get to him. He just does whatever's necessary to get by and thinks nothing of the consequences."

" 'Tis good advice," May said sternly, knowing that
Joshua's nonchalance was a quality Devon both admired
and despised. "Besides, Devon, what other choice ye
got?"

He knew his mum was right. What did it matter if he
and the gang went back to picking pockets? If they made
money to get by he should feel grateful, not ashamed.
Anyway, the people they stole from didn't need the
money half as badly as they did. Devon felt a familiar
bitterness churn in his stomach whenever his thoughts
turned to the upper class. It wasn't envy he felt, but rather
anger at how the elitists treated people like him—poor
people, those who hadn't been born with a title to their
name and who didn't have an army of servants ready to
care for their every need. Those were Devon's people;
he identified with them. What angered him to the core
was the contempt they received from London's elite. The
callous disregard cast upon anyone lacking wealth and a
country estate. In Devon's mind the only difference between rich and poor was luck. Upper-class people were
born wealthy; lower-class people were not. Yet despite
having done nothing to attain their prominence, the upper
class made it clear that they considered themselves superior to the East End poor. They didn't look at the lower
class, certainly didn't talk to them. The day he had been
spit on by a passing dandy had sparked a flame of hatred
toward the upper class that still burned in Devon's heart.

"Ye're right, Mum," he said to his mother as he rose from his chair and prepared to leave. "Whatever it takes, eh?"

"Whatever it takes," she said solemnly, wanting to make sure her son never felt ashamed in front of her. Devon kissed his mother on both cheeks, then opened the door that led to the hallway.

"What's yer day like today?" he asked her on his way out.

May's gesture with her hands indicated nothing unusual. " 'Tis free until nine o'clock tonight," she said. "It'll be nice just to rest until then." The tone in her voice made Devon study her face more closely. For the first time in his life he noticed a weariness around his mother's eyes and mouth, and he realized that the life of a prostitute was finally taking its toll upon even his strong-willed mother. Unexpectedly Devon felt a lump in his throat, and he turned away before his mother noticed. This life was hell, he thought, making his way down the stairs. No matter how strong the person, sooner or later it gets to everyone. Feeling more depressed than he had in years, Devon quietly let himself out the door.

Three

Platter after platter of steaming hot food, artfully arranged so as to occupy every available inch of free space, made the Rushmoor table look obscenely decadent. Diners gathered around the feast and heaped mounds of assorted meats, vegetables, breads, and cheeses upon the distinctive bone china, designed exclusively for the Rushmoors by master craftsman Josiah Wedgwood before his death at the end of the last century.

A bright fire in the fireplace crackled merrily, casting a warm glow throughout the room. This was the only area of the town home that had its floor graced by thick, lush carpeting, a detail Louisa had insisted upon so as to muffle the footmen's steps, thereby increasing their low profile.

As usual, dinner conversation revolved around an upcoming event, the one currently under discussion being Lord and Lady Caswell's traditional May ball, which was always thought of as the first "important" event of the season. This was a ball not to be missed, and Louisa made sure that Claire was aware of it.

"I think you'd do well with your muted yellow silk gown, Claire," she was saying between bites of food. "After all, it goes so well with your hair."

"All right, Mother," Claire replied dutifully, not in the mood to even think about the ball, much less discuss what she would wear. The thought of having to go through another season trying to seize an available, respectable man who would win approval from both Claire's mother and Claire herself thoroughly exhausted her.

Thankfully, Lavinia's complaints about the footman's sluggish dessert service saved Claire from once again being subjected to her mother's never-ending diatribe on the virtues of snatching a titled gentleman.

At last the dinner was over, and Claire, her three sisters, and her cousin Lilia headed upstairs to retire for the evening. Since Claire and Lilia shared an adjoining room, they fell into step together as they headed for the east wing.

"Do you want to go riding tomorrow morning?" Claire asked her younger cousin.

"Oh, yes," Lilia replied, clapping her hands with enthusiasm, "and I know just the place where we could go."

"Really? Where?" Claire replied, wondering how Lilia could have become familiar with London's vast layout so quickly.

"How about a picturesque ride alongside the river Thames?" she answered, relatively certain Claire would forbid it. She was right.

With a stern look in her eyes that stifled reproach, Claire's answer was firm. "I told you, Lilia, you are never, never to go down by those docks. It's a dangerous area down there, filled with dangerous people. We want nothing to do with them or that area, and you are not to even think about going there. Do you understand?" Claire knew how mischievous her younger cousin could be, but this was one time when Lilia's curiosity could put her in a perilous situation. When Lilia hesitated before answering, Claire again asked, "Do you understand, Lilia?"

The girl exhaled a disappointed breath but assured

Claire that she understood. "It's not fair, though," she protested. "I want to explore everywhere. Why are we so limited about where we can go?"

"It's for our own protection, Lilia. Certain people are meant to be together, and therefore must stay where their own types of people are. For us it happens to be Westminster. For others, it might be Wapping. But we do not go to Wapping, and those people do not come here."

By the look on the girl's face Claire knew she had digested the information, but what was still to be determined was whether or not she accepted it.

Claire turned to go when another thought struck her. "Incidentally, Lilia. I've mentioned this to you once before, but I suppose I must say something again for it appears you did not understand me the first time."

"Oh? What's that, Claire?" her cousin innocently asked, although she had already guessed what Claire was about to say.

"I've seen you speaking to the servants on a number of occasions. Remember, the servants are here to do a job, not to waste time away in idle chatter. They spend enough time talking amongst themselves, and it is not appropriate for you to be hanging about and distracting them from their work. Please remember that."

Leaving no opportunity for rebuttal, Claire turned away and continued walking toward her bedroom. She'd have to be careful with that girl. She remembered vaguely that she, too, had been a rambunctious child. But years of proper lessons and grooming had refined Claire to the genteel woman she was today. In time, she knew, Lilia would be the same. But a minute trace of longing, like a shimmering mist, enveloped the cavern of Claire's heart, for she mourned the curiosity within herself that had forever been smothered by the restrictions of polite society.

* * *

As the late spring air gradually warmed toward summer, the next two weeks passed with relative calm. The Rushmoor women spent their time riding, making calls, having tea, and preparing for the ball. Lord Bedington held a seat in Parliament, and when it wasn't in session he passed time at the Pall Mall Club.

Midweek, before the Caswells' ball, Lord and Lady Bedington accepted an invitation to dinner at Lady Katherine Spellton's, a vastly wealthy widow whose fortune provided her with everything she could ever need. As such she had grown fond of hosting dinner parties for her equally wealthy friends. The occasions were elaborate affairs, with the dinners being some ten courses long, followed, of course, by coffee and dessert. The Rushmoor girls knew their parents would be away all evening.

Their own dinner was the customary four courses— soup, meat, fowl, and dessert—and when it was over Claire took to her room. Though the sun had set it was still early evening. Claire was not tired in the least, but she longed for the opportunity to relax alone. In the daytime the balcony off her bedroom afforded her a breathtaking view of the gardens below, as well as Hyde Park just beyond. Now she would be content just to sit and enjoy the rich floral smells perfuming the air, and the songs of the birds saying good-bye to the day.

Not surprisingly, Marie was already waiting for Claire, instinctively knowing her mistress's needs. Without a word between them she began unpinning the heavy coils of hair that had been so neatly piled atop Claire's head. When the last tendrils had fallen free, she took Claire's pearl-handled brush and smoothly swept it through her mistress's thick blond mane. Claire's hair was truly the crowning glory of her beautiful face. It flowed down to nearly the small of her back and shone like the sun reflecting off a waterfall. Yet much of its beauty was almost always hidden, for it was uncouth to be in public without one's hair neatly pinned up.

When she was finished with the brushing, Marie helped Claire change into her dressing gown and prepared to leave.

"Bon soir, my lady. Your cold water, it eez already in the bowl on ze washstand, so you should be set." It had been Claire's habit since childhood to splash her face with cold water before going to bed, for after the initial shock, she found it relaxed her.

"Bon soir, Marie. *Merci."*

The unusually warm evening was indeed beautiful. Claire flung the doors to the balcony wide open and reveled in the strong breeze that swept through the room. The balcony's large size allowed for a table with four chairs around it to occupy half the space, but it was the other side, where a small wooden high-backed bench laden with soft pillows had been placed, that was the focus of Claire's attention. It was here where she spent a great deal of time either reading, sewing, or simply relaxing.

The smells from the garden below were especially strong this evening, brought out by the breeze, and for a few moments Claire sat upon the bench with her eyes closed, intoxicated by the scent of lavender floating all around her. Moments later, however, her tranquility was interrupted by three sharp knocks upon her bedroom door.

"Mademoiselle! Mademoiselle! Come quickly!" The urgent tone in Marie's voice was alarming, and Claire ran to see what was upsetting her maid.

As soon as she swung the door open, Marie burst into the room and began frantically pacing the floor. It took

Claire over five minutes to calm her maid down and find out what was troubling her.

"It's . . . it's . . . Lady Lilia," Marie told her, and Claire's heart sank. Her first thought was that there was trouble again with the servants. But Marie's next words revealed that the situation was much more serious.

"What about her? What's happened?"

"She eez missing."

"Missing? What are you talking about, Marie? Lilia told me she had a headache and asked to be excused from dinner so she could lie down. I'm sure she's in her bedroom."

But already Marie was shaking her head, indicating that was not the case. "Dominique went to check on her after dinner, to make sure that Lady Lilia did not wish to 'ave something to eat after all. She knocked many times, but there was no answer. Dominique, she became worried that maybe Meez Lilia was really very sick, so she went inside the room to check on her. She was not there."

Claire's mind was already racing, trying to figure out where her cousin might be. "Have you checked the stables? Are any of the horses missing?"

"*Oui*, mademoiselle. It's one of the first places we looked. But all of the horses, except for the ones monsieur and madame are using for this evening, are in the stable."

That meant Lilia wanted to make sure her absence would be undiscovered for as long as possible. If she had requested one of the horses to be saddled for her, the groom would have alerted someone. Sneaking out of the house as she had indicated she had probably gone somewhere she had been warned against going. And Claire knew exactly where that someplace was.

"Tell James and Reston to have Daniel ready the carriage and be prepared to leave within five minutes. I'll join them outside the stable, and the three of us will leave together."

Marie's mouth gaped, and she stared in wonder at her suddenly commanding mistress. Refined, genteel Claire was taking charge in a way Marie had never seen before, and her wonderment caused temporary paralysis of her limbs. In seconds, Claire's sharp retort cured her. "Get moving, Marie!" she commanded, and the maid flew down the stairs with uncharacteristic speed.

It wasn't difficult to figure out where Lilia had gone, despite the fact that she'd been given several warnings against visiting those East End docks. Claire felt responsible for the safety of her cousin, and she knew that she must go after Lilia.

Changing faster than she ever had in her life, Claire pulled the dressing gown over the top of her head, donned the same gown and tunic she'd worn earlier, and laced on a pair of low-heeled slippers. Once downstairs, over the din of protests from her sisters, she ordered Marie to fetch her cloak and reticule.

"Claire, you can't mean to go out looking for Lilia at this time of night," said a worried Lavinia. "It's not safe."

"That's exactly why I do need to go. Lilia could be in danger."

"Just have the servants go, Claire," Emily piped up.

Claire shook her head firmly before addressing her younger sister. "Lilia is my responsibility, Emily, so I must be the one who goes looking for her. And anyway, it's not like I'll be going alone. I'm bringing James and Reston along for protection."

"Where do you suppose Lilia has gone?" asked Lavinia.

Claire was vague about answering, for she knew that if she confessed her fear that Lilia had gone down to the docks, such a panic would arise that her sisters might try to physically bar her from leaving.

"Oh, I'm sure she's not far. She probably just went down to the park. I'll be back as soon as I can." She quickly kissed each sister on the cheek, then turned toward Marie. "Is the carriage ready?"

"*Oui,* mademoiselle. James and Reston are already waiting for you."

"Then I'll be off." She waved to her sisters and hurried out the door. As she'd been told, the carriage awaited her, and the two burliest servants employed by the Rushmoors were poised and ready to go. James would drive, while Reston sat inside the carriage with Claire.

"Where to, my lady?" asked James in his characteristic stoic tone.

"Wapping," Claire answered, without hesitation.

A raised eyebrow was his only outward sign of surprise, but Reston felt compelled to question his mistress's direction.

"The docks, my lady? Are you sure?"

"Positive. Ride on, James." With no further questioning James grabbed hold of the reins, and the carriage lurched forward. Claire was relieved that she had managed to hide her fear and doubt about whether she should actually go. It was not without reason that warnings were given concerning the safety of the East End.

The area where Claire assumed Lilia had gone was roughly four miles due east from the Rushmoor mansion, but the street conditions grew increasingly worse the farther east they drove, and combined with the many pedestrians still lurking about, it was slow going reaching their destination. At last they passed by the imposing Tower, and Claire asked James to slow the horses down. It was somewhere around here that Lilia had gone; of that she was certain, for it was one of the areas she had direly warned her cousin against going. The horses were now at walking pace, and everyone in the trio intently scanned their surroundings.

Claire noticed the drastic differences between the area of London she had known all her life and this part of the city, only four miles away, where she had never before been. To begin with, it was eerily dark. There was absolutely no street lighting; the only illumination came from the windows of taverns and from the lanterns of some of the people walking about the docks. And the people! Never before had Claire seen the kind of human beings that populated this section of the city. Their clothes hung about them in tattered rags, and many were barefoot. Women paraded up and down the street, brazenly calling out to the men walking by. The lewdness of their comments flushed Claire's face deep red, despite the fact that she didn't understand half the words they used. It was the way they said them, accompanied by the suggestive swaying of their bodies, that had Claire staring in wide-eyed amazement. Hastily she looked away, hoping that neither Reston nor James had noticed the way she gawked.

James held his lantern out in front of him, its light valiantly trying to penetrate the inky darkness. Unfortunately, despite their effort to pass quietly by, he noticed the carriage was drawing attention. In the haste to leave James hadn't given thought to the family crest prominently displayed on the outside of the door. It was rare indeed that such a carriage would be in this neighborhood, at this time of night. James felt his body tense, for he now had two things to be on the lookout for: Lilia, and thieves.

The sound of loud-mouthed bragging caught their attention, and as Claire looked again toward the docks, it was with relief and fear that she spotted Lilia. Relief because she had found her cousin, but fear because of the situation Lilia was in. Three husky sailors had strategically placed themselves around the vulnerable girl, preventing her from walking away. They were apparently trying to woo Lilia into accompanying them to wherever they were going, and although it was obvious that Lilia had no intention of joining them, what wasn't clear was exactly how she planned on avoiding it.

James extinguished his lantern, attempting to avoid unwanted attention, then turned around to speak with Reston and Claire.

"There's no way we can overtake them by force," he said in a low voice, "so I'm afraid I must try to persuade them to let Lilia go using good old-fashioned means—money."

Claire and Reston nodded their agreement. After all, there seemed to be nothing else they could do. They decided that James would walk over there by himself while Reston stayed in the carriage to protect Claire. After handing James the money in her reticule, Claire whispered, "Good luck," and watched the faithful footman approach the sailors. His voice was now out of earshot, but after several minutes it was evident that merely offering money to the sailors was not going to be enough. Their voices grew louder, and Claire now understood why they were reluctant to part with the pretty young girl. They'd been out on the seas for over a year and had not seen a woman in all that time. It was not money these men were interested in—they had enough of that to keep them happy for a while. No, what they wanted was standing right in the middle of them, and no amount of bargaining seemed to change their minds. Soon it was obvious that James could not get Lilia back on his own.

"Go on, Reston," Claire whispered. "James needs help."

"But, my lady, I don't dare leave you here by yourself."

"I'll be fine. It's Lilia who needs help now." Claire

gave a light push to the servant, wanting to hurry him as much as possible.

Still Reston hesitated. "If you're sure, my lady . . ."

"I'm positive. Now, go. Please. James and Lilia can't do this without you." Spurred on by the unexpected compliment, Reston hastily opened the carriage door and strode over to where James and Lilia were standing. He joined the group just as the sailors' voices were reaching a crescendo. Claire stared intently at the group, trying to determine what else she could do. The fear she had felt earlier had ebbed somewhat, and she now had half a mind to go over there herself. She knew, however, that it would do no good. It was entirely possible that the sailors would grab hold of her as they had Lilia, and instead of having to get one hapless female away, Reston and James would have to rescue two.

Therefore, she sat, anxiously watching the scene unfold before her. At least the sailors' voices had calmed down once more, and it appeared they were listening to what Reston had to say. Claire strained to hear the conversation, but sounds of a scuffle on the other side of the carriage distracted her attention from the sailors.

Wondering what was the cause of the fight, Claire slid across the seat of the carriage and looked out the window on the opposite side. What she saw in the distance made her recoil in horror.

Approximately twenty yards away from where she sat in the carriage was a fight so savage it sickened her to watch. There appeared to be only two men involved, and thus far no one had shown up to stop it. Claire wondered if it was because such fights were common around here. In disbelief she watched as the apparent victor brutally, repeatedly, kicked his victim, who was down on the ground. The blows were struck all over the victim's body as he weakly tried to ward them off. Claire could hear the man groan every time his attacker's boot slammed into his body. At one point he reached up as if to try pulling the man down to the ground along with him, but he succeeded only in tearing off a piece of his attacker's shirt. Finally he was no longer able to even attempt moving away, but it wasn't until he lay completely motionless that his attacker stopped the vicious assault. Off in the distance Claire suddenly heard shouts, and it was obvious they were directed toward the assailant. Hastily the man tucked his shirt into his trousers and smoothed down his hair, a gesture that seemed almost ludicrous to Claire, considering what he had just done to the man on the ground. Then the attacker turned on his heel and promptly walked away, never once looking behind him to check on his victim. Claire followed his trail for as long as she could, the whiteness of his shirt making it possible for her to watch him, if only for a short while.

Seconds after the aggressor had left, the two men who had shouted at him came upon the fallen man. These men were much harder to see, for their clothes were dark and neither carried a lantern. Claire was only able to make out their silhouettes as they knelt before the man on the ground. She leaned her head out the window as far as she dared, straining to see what they were doing.

At that moment the door to the carriage opened, and Reston and Lilia climbed inside while James took his seat on top to drive. In her relief at seeing that her younger cousin was safe, Claire put out of her mind the fight she'd just witnessed.

"Lilia!" she exclaimed with joy as she tightly hugged her cousin while the carriage began moving. "I'm so glad you're all right."

Shaken by what she had just been through, Lilia hugged Claire back and thanked her for all she had done.

"I don't know what would have happened if you and

the men hadn't come along, Claire," she said in a trembling voice. "I . . . I . . . I was so scared and, and . . ." her voice hiccupped as she choked back a sob. "Oh Claire, I promise I won't ever do that again." Her remorse was so achingly evident that Claire decided scolding the girl would only add to her misery. It was obvious Lilia had learned her lesson.

"I'm just glad you're safe," she said in a soothing voice, trying her best to calm her cousin down.

As she continued to hold Lilia, Claire asked Reston what had happened.

"Well, it wasn't really money those men were after," Reston delicately began, "so James's offer was refused. But then I was able to convince them that Lilia was not the kind of woman who, uh, who could handle them. . . ." his voice trailed off as he wondered whether Claire understood what he meant. With a polite nod, Claire assured him that she did.

"Well, anyway, my lady," Reston hurried on, anxious to get the story over with, "I pointed out that there are places to go that are much more suitable for what they had in mind, and combined that with enough money to make their night one they wouldn't forget. That convinced them they could do better with someone else, so they let Lady Lilia go."

Claire could not hide her disgust toward the sailors, and she was relieved that the ordeal had ended. Now they would return to fashionable Park Lane, where the confines of her world did not include drunken sailors and lewd women, where people acted with decorum and everything was clean. Claire felt a pang of sympathy for the people forced to live on the East End, but then did her best to brush those feelings aside. After all, she had her own problems to worry about, such as pleasing her mother and finding a husband before the end of the season. All in all, Claire was grateful that her first visit to the East End was most certainly her last.

The carriage whisked away as soon as the three people had climbed aboard, but not before Jonathan had spotted the crest on its side.

"Ye sure ye got a good look at it?" asked Clive.

"Aye," Jonathan grimly replied. "Now go find Devon. We need his help to move Joshua's body." As Clive ran off, Jonathan looked down at their beaten friend as rage consumed him. Joshua's clothes were saturated with blood, yet the sticky clothing had not been able to completely stop the bleeding. Already a thick crimson pool had formed around Joshua's head and steadily seeped into the earth beneath him. Frantically Jonathan tore off his only shirt and began ripping it into bandagelike strips. He wrapped the cloth around Joshua wherever he noticed open wounds and at last was able to stop the bleeding.

Swiftly he took a look around him. There were few people out on the streets, and it appeared no one was going to try taking advantage of them. For that Jonathan was grateful. Again he examined Joshua's wounds to make sure none of them had reopened. The makeshift bandages appeared to be holding up, but Jonathan knew they wouldn't last long. At least Joshua was still unconscious and not yet aware of the pain he would have to endure. That is, if he lived.

At last Jonathan heard the sound of footsteps racing along the hard-packed dirt walkway, and as he turned around he saw Clive and Devon running toward him.

"Quickly!" Jonathan hissed, as if his words could make them come faster. In seconds they arrived and knelt down before their fallen comrade. Devon took one quick look at Joshua and demanded to know what had happened.

Clive shook his head before answering. "We're not sure, Devon," he said, as enraged as the rest of them. "Me and Jonathan, we was walking about the docks, planning where we should hit next. Joshua left before. Said he was going to look for some grub. So Jonathan and me, we was just walking along when all of a sudden we heard someone groaning. Jonathan could see ahead of us that someone was lying on the docks, and another man was standing over him."

Jonathan nodded and continued. "That's right. So we shouted and started running over that way. As we got closer, I saw 'twas Joshua lying on the ground."

"And ye didn't see who done this to him?"

"Nay, Devon. It was dark, and they were too far away," Jonathan answered. "By the time we was close enough to tell that it was Joshua, whoever did this was already gone."

His response to the statement was a silent, deadly stare. From his longtime friendship with Devon Blake, Jonathan knew the cause of that unsettling gaze. It happened whenever he was consumed with fury.

"Jonathan did see something, though," said Clive, reminding his friend to let their leader know about the slight glimmer of hope.

"That's right. When I was looking to see if whoever did this was still around, I saw a carriage parked in the road just a ways down from here."

"Just some hackney, most likely."

" 'Cept there ain't no hackney drivers who use a town coach."

Devon's left eyebrow shot up in surprise. "A town coach? In this end? What the devil are ye talking about?"

"I don't know what it was doing here, but I know what I saw. It was a big fancy coach set right across the street."

Devon shook his head at the ludicrous thought but encouraged Jonathan to continue.

"It was too dark to tell what color it was, but I know there was someone inside the coach because I saw light from the window."

"Well, was it a bloke or a lass?"

"I'm not sure, but I think 'twas a lass."

"Can you describe her?"

"Not exactly," Jonathan faltered.

Devon threw up his hands in defeat. "Then what bloody good does it do us?" he demanded. "If ye couldn't tell anything about who was in that carriage, how does it help us?" Devon's anger was close to boiling over, but instead of flinching Jonathan held his ground.

"Because I saw the family crest," he proclaimed triumphantly.

"Family crest?" Devon wasn't even certain he knew what such a thing was, but Jonathan was quick to explain.

"Painted on the coach was a kind of decoration," he said. "And I remember Samuel once telling me—ye know how he goes to the West End to deliver coal—that a lot of them people over there have fancy decorations painted on the outside of their coaches, and in their houses, too. A family crest, he called it."

"Family crest," Devon repeated slowly, as if restating the words would help him better understand them. "So how does that help us?"

"Samuel told me that family crests ain't alike. Every one's different from the others, and it tells something about the family. So—"

"So if ye can tell what was on that thing ye saw to Samuel, maybe he'll be able to tell us what family it belongs to."

"Right!"

For an instant Devon felt that there was a chance of

hope. If they could find out who was in the carriage, there was a possibility of learning the identity of Jonathan's attacker. But then he thought of something that extinguished his hope like a flame doused in water.

"Wait a minute. If 'twas too dark for ye to see who was in the coach, how could ye be sure that ye made out the painting on the outside?"

"By luck, I'd say. A few seconds after I saw the coach, a couple people, maybe three, came running up to it. The driver climbed on top and put his lantern down by his feet. It was right then, after he put the lantern down but before he picked it up again when the coach started moving, that the light was bright enough for me to see the outside painting."

"And ye got a good look at it?"

"I only saw it for a few seconds, but, aye, 'twas long enough."

Devon took a moment to digest the information, then made his decision. "All right. First off we get Joshua out of this filth before the rats start smelling the blood. We can't take care of him in the middle of the street, anyway. In the morning we'll talk to Samuel and see if there's any way that family crest can help us."

Clive scratched his head in confusion. "But I thought that if we could find the family, then—"

"Then what?" Devon snapped. "Then we walk over to their mansion and start having us a little chat with some snobbish, pampered chit who'd as likely prance naked in the streets of London as risk being seen talking to one of us? Think, man. Those people try their bloody hardest to pretend we don't exist. That's why I don't even know what good it will do us that Jonathan saw that coach."

Clive remained silent as he realized what Devon meant. People with family crests and fancy coaches never talked to people like him and his mates. So, like Devon, he was skeptical about whether Jonathan's identification of that family crest would help them at all. One glance at the fixed look on Devon's face, however, told Clive everything he needed to know. If there was any way in the world to speak to the girl who saw Joshua's attacker, Devon would do it. He and his mates were like brothers to one another, and exacted revenge upon anyone who dared hurt them. It had been that way since they were kids; it would continue until they walked the earth no more. In their world, it was the way of survival. Devon's icy determination and fierce fighting skills had made him the natural leader of their gang since its inception when they were boys of thirteen. And Clive knew now that those same qualities in Devon would carry over in his quest for the truth. In a small way Clive pitied the man who would ultimately be the target of Devon's wrath. That man would never be the same again. But in order to find him, Devon would first have to find the girl.

For now, however, Devon hoisted Joshua onto his shoulder, and the three men trudged toward their shanty through the unlit streets of town.

Four

Louisa's face pinched together in an unattractive grimace as she looked anxiously upward at the cloudy sky. "I do hope that rain won't spoil the ball," she fretted, wringing her hands together with uncustomary force.

Claire set down the cup of breakfast tea she had been enjoying to try calming her mother's nerves. "Now, Mother, don't worry. I'm sure those clouds won't give us any trouble."

"How can you be so certain?"

Claire gave the sky a cursory glance herself, and then answered reassuringly, "Because they don't have that heavy, gray look that rain clouds often have."

Indeed, the puffy white clouds that floated across the sky were more telling of a tranquil spring day than that of impending rain. A warm breeze accompanied the morning, and as Claire took a sip of her tea she thought how lovely it was to have breakfast in the garden.

Louisa nibbled on a plum as she considered Claire's forecast. "I truly hope you're right. After all, this evening's ball will be an opportune one for you to meet the kind of eligible gentlemen we're interested in."

Claire noted with some agitation the way her mother included herself in the search for Claire's prospective husband, but let the matter pass without comment.

"Is your dress ready?"

"Yes, it is. It's been cleaned, aired, and pressed. Marie has been working hard preparing it."

"You decided on the pale yellow silk?"

"As you suggested, Mother."

"Wonderful. It complements your hair so beautifully."

Claire finished her tea and rose from the table just as she spotted her Aunt Bella walking toward the table to join them.

"You can't be finished already, Claire?" her mother queried. "Why, you've hardly eaten anything."

"I'm not very hungry this morning, Mother." Claire brushed the crumbs off the folds of her dress with short, quick strokes.

"I think someone must be a little nervous about this evening's ball," Bella declared as she reached the table, giving Louisa a knowing smile.

"Insightful as always, Aunt Bella," Claire replied, then excused herself without further delay. As she walked up the grand staircase toward her bedroom, she breathed a sigh of relief that she had escaped another tiresome conversation regarding the virtues of a titled husband. She knew her mother would be especially mindful of Claire's behavior at the Caswells' ball, and if she did not give fair opportunity to all eligible suitors proffering interest in her direction, Louisa Rushmoor would be a most displeased parent.

Activity around the household was at an all-time high, with every available servant doing something related to preparations for attending the evening ball. Outside, the carriage was being thoroughly cleaned and the wheels greased. The horses were bathed and curried. Inside, the maids had cleaned, pressed, and aired all the ladies' gowns, and were now making sure that the accessories—fans, reticules, gloves, shawls, and lace slippers—were in order. The sight, for Claire, brought about unexpected melancholy. The start of the season was at hand, and before the close of it she would, in all likelihood, be a promised woman. But to whom would she be promised? A stuffy bore like Lord Thurston of Middlebury? A spoiled child like Lord Ardale's son Nicholas? The thought was disheartening to be sure, for despite Claire's determination to wed only someone for whom she felt unequivocal love, there was every possibility she was running out of time.

Their fashionably late arrival was perfectly timed. In private Louisa had always complained of her dislike for the opening minuet featured at every ball. Tonight that dance was just ending as the Rushmoor carriage pulled up to the driveway.

A long line of carriages already claimed precious parking spots close to the door, but no one minded the short walk. The evening was warm, but not overly so. The air was perfumed from hundreds of flowers blooming in the Caswells' garden, and the faintest trace of music could be detected from the party within. Bubbly Lilia had been the first to alight, failing to wait until Daniel stepped down from the driver's seat to assist her. Following closely behind were Lavinia, Claire, Louisa, and Kendal.

As they walked toward the townhouse, they saw Lady Caswell standing there ready to greet them, and a flurry of maids helped the ladies with their wraps as they entered the house.

"Louisa, it's so very good to see you again," Lady Caswell said. "Did you enjoy the country this year?"

"It was a delight, Eleanor, truly a delight." As if on cue, Louisa produced an enormous smile, anxious to remain in the good graces of her wealthy and respected hostess.

"And Claire. How are you, my dear?"

Claire curtsied before her hostess as she replied, "I'm very well, Lady Caswell, thank you. How are you?"

"Lovely. Please go in and make yourselves comfortable. We'll talk more later." Eleanor Caswell made a sweeping gesture with her left arm, inviting them all to proceed from the entryway into the ballroom.

As they stepped inside, Claire found herself amused by Lilia's open expression of astonishment at her first glance of the Caswell ballroom. Indeed, even Claire had to resist the urge to stop and stare, for though this was her third appearance at the annual party, the opulence of the ballroom was a sight to behold. The floor shone like an expensive jewel, its luster the result of heavy beeswax polishing. Reflecting off it was the glow from nine enormous candelabras suspended from the ceiling. Centered at the back of the massive room was the orchestra, in turn surrounded on either side by great pots of decorative spring flowers in brilliant shades of yellow, violet, and red. The scent of roses perfumed the entire mansion. On both sides of the room were refreshment tables heavily laden with wine, lemonade, and ices. Enormous ice sculptures graced the middle of each table, making impressive centerpieces.

Elegantly attired men and women glided across the dance floor or stood as couples or in small groups. Ladies with silk shawls draped around them fluttered decorative fans and emitted tinkles of laughter whenever conversation so required. The sound of chatter blended with the orchestral music, giving the whole room an ornate, fussy ambiance. Another season had begun.

"Close your mouth, Lilia," Claire advised her gaping young cousin. She noticed that her parents and sister had already gone off to begin mingling with other guests, so Claire suggested to Lilia that they do the same. "I see Lady Catherine and Lord Timothy Hughes across the room. Let us say hello and I'll introduce you to them."

Lilia nodded to indicate her agreement; it appeared she was still too overwhelmed to speak. As they walked across the room, Claire noticed out of the corner of her eye that she herself appeared to have attracted the interest of one of the guests. He was a rather short man of approximately thirty-five years in age. His narrow eyes were mere slits underneath long, bushy brows. His lips were also thin and pale, he had jet black hair, and stamped in the middle of his face was a large, hawkish nose. He was lavishly dressed in ornate clothing. His white linen shirt was heavily frilled all down the front and accented by not one but two bright silk cravats positioned on top of one another. They had been tied into overly large bows, ornamented by an even larger jeweled pin. Claire noticed that the man apparently still favored frilled shirt cuffs despite the current trend toward straight ones. His linen shirt collar was also very high, higher than the usual style, nearly reaching the middle of his ears. All this she noticed in the glance of an instant, for it would have been improper to look any longer.

With Lilia trailing obediently behind her, Claire approached Lady Catherine with a welcoming smile.

"Claire! How wonderful to see you again. It seems like such a long time since we last met."

"It was last June, at Ascot," Claire reminded her. "You were off on your honeymoon shortly after that."

"Of course. It's difficult to believe it was nearly a year ago."

"Indeed. The time has flown by. Incidentally, may I introduce my younger cousin, Lady Lilia Chatterton. Lilia, this is Lady Catherine Hughes." Claire peered down at her suddenly sheepish cousin, who until that moment had not uttered a word. Upon hearing her name, however, Lilia swung into action. Grabbing a fistful of her skirt in each hand, she performed a deep curtsy, lowering her head before Catherine and holding the curtsy for several moments before at last straightening up.

A surprised Lady Catherine nearly choked on her lemonade, and Claire felt flames of embarrassment heat her cheeks. She hadn't realized until this moment just how unfamiliar Lilia was with the world of social graces.

"I'm pleased to meet you, Lady Catherine. Claire has told me so much about you." An impish grin was plastered across Lilia's face, for she knew very well that Catherine Hughes's name had never once been mentioned in conversations between herself and Claire. Fortunately Catherine had no time to respond, for at that moment Claire's silent admirer approached the group.

"Catherine," he said smoothly, "I don't believe I've had the pleasure of meeting your friends."

Catherine turned toward their new arrival, and as she realized who it was a tentative smile crossed her face. "Philip, hello. I wasn't even aware that you were here yet."

"I opted this time to forgo my usual grand entrance for a more understated one," he replied, all the while keeping his gaze fixed on Claire.

"I see," Catherine answered. "Well, ah, let me introduce you to Lady Claire Rushmoor and her cousin, Lady Lilia Chatterton." Catherine turned to Claire with an almost apologetic look. "Claire, Lilia, this is my cousin, Philip Westbury, Marquess of Townsend."

Before Claire could utter a word, Philip swept her hand up to his mouth and boldly brushed his lips across the back of it. "It's a pleasure to meet you, Lady Rushmoor," he murmured, ignoring Lilia. "Come, we must dance."

His brazen action rendered Claire speechless, and before she knew what had happened she found herself in the middle of the room, caught up in a vigorous country dance. All couples involved were moving simultaneously, and there was no opportunity to stand by while others performed the figures. This eliminated all possibility of conversation, so although Claire found herself wondering about her companion, she was forced to withhold questions until the dance came to an end.

Twenty minutes later Lord Townsend at last guided her off the dance floor. They walked over to one of the bountiful refreshment tables, and without bothering to ask Claire what she would like, Philip planted a lemon ice between her hands.

"Thank you." Claire was growing more aggravated by his arrogance with every passing moment, but she knew that in this, her third season, she must give him a chance.

Philip had taken to lazily eyeing every inch of Claire's body, appreciating her graceful curves and lush bosom. Claire felt her cheeks flush. In an effort to stop his arrogant inspection she said, "You must be the Duke of Townsend's son, am I right?"

Philip raised an eyebrow in surprise. "How intuitive you are."

"Catherine mentioned that you and she were cousins."

"Ah, indeed she did. Then I must admit you've guessed correctly. The Duke of Townsend is my father."

Claire took a delicate spoonful of her lemon ice and let its tart flavor melt across her tongue. Despite having already acquired a dislike for this man, she knew how pleased her mother would be. Lord Townsend's social standing would be a boon for the family.

Philip suddenly gave a sniff as he noticed two new arrivals walk through the door. Claire turned in the direction where he was looking but realized she did not know the couple. However, acting as though he were a recognized authority on the *ton,* Philip gave her a private introduction.

"Do you know the LaVoies, Lady Rushmoor?" As she shook her head he continued. "Consider yourself lucky.

They're terribly ill-bred. My mother hosted the most elegant breakfast last June, and Cecile LaVoie actually showed up wearing a diamond bracelet." Philip rolled his eyes to accentuate his disgust and gave a loud snort. "Can you believe it? Diamonds at eleven in the morning? Simply appalling."

What was appalling, Claire thought, was Lord Townsend's behavior. What a condescending, self-righteous man. His gossipy conversation was too much to bear for long, and Claire's mind worked frantically for a way to make a graceful exit. She knew her efforts would be futile, however, for at that moment she saw her mother and aunt making their way over.

Struggling to suppress her irritation, Claire used their arrival as a way to change the subject. "Lord Townsend, I'd like you to meet my mother, Lady Louisa Rushmoor"—Claire gestured toward her mother—"and my Aunt Bella, Lady Chatterton." Philip donned polite behavior as introductions were exchanged. "It's a pleasure to meet you both," he said, inclining his head toward Claire's mother. "I've just been exchanging pleasantries with your lovely daughter, and I must say she's been a most intriguing conversationalist."

Louisa Rushmoor glanced at Claire, beaming with happiness. "I'm so pleased that you've been enjoying each other's company."

"Indeed we have. And I must admit I'm hoping we'll be able to continue to do so in the future."

"Of course, Lord Townsend," Louisa nearly gushed. "You are welcome to call at any time."

"Then be certain I shall take you up on your offer."

"We'll look forward to it."

Philip then nodded to all three women as he made to leave. "It's been a pleasure meeting you, and I will see you again soon."

As soon as he was out of earshot, Louisa turned to

Claire and gave her a triumphant smile. "Claire, how wonderful. A marquess."

"And such a handsome one, too," Bella chimed in.

Claire realized at that moment that she had given little thought to Philip's looks, so incensed was she by his haughty behavior.

"Mother, I don't want to disappoint you, but—"

"But what, Claire? But you're not in love with him?" Louisa's sharp tone silenced Claire's objection.

"It—it's nothing, Mother."

"Do you think he'll call?"

"Yes, I think so. He seemed to enjoy talking with me."

"Wonderful. Then we will welcome him with all the proper respect due a marquess."

Claire felt her heart sinking heavily in her chest, as if it were a balloon filled with lead. She muttered something about going to look for Lilia and walked away.

"Don't surround him too closely, lads. He needs to breathe." Four anxious faces peered down at the man upon the bed who was, at the moment, fighting for his life. Since they'd brought him back to their shanty nearly a week ago, Joshua had still not regained consciousness. His partners worked around the clock trying to heal him, but they all knew the situation was critical. They weren't able to feed him anything but broth, and the effects of malnutrition were taking its toll. Joshua's already slender frame was now frail. His ribs were painfully obvious with every shallow breath. His eyes were sunken. Purple and black bruises covered his body, and there was a deep gash in the back of his head. Fortunately they had been able to stop the bleeding, but they were still concerned with how much blood Joshua had lost. By the washed-out pallor of his skin, they knew his body had not yet replenished it. Though they had all been in fights over the years, none had ever been trounced so badly.

Rain steadily dripped from various leaks in the roof, its relentless monotone permeating the room. Devon cast a weary eye toward one particularly large gap and watched as the water streamed onto the floor. Of course, they had no physician to examine Joshua. Such luxury was reserved for the rich, as doctor's fees were costly. Joshua was wasting away, and Devon made a decision.

"We've got to move him," he announced.

His mates looked up expectantly. They knew Joshua wasn't getting any better in their cold, wet shanty, but where else could they go?

"I'm taking him to Sally's," Devon said with grim determination. "At least the roof doesn't leak there."

Clive knit his brow in confusion. "But Devon, Sally won't let us take Joshua there. 'Twould be bad for her business."

"Sally's not going to say anything about it," Devon replied, in a voice so quiet they had to strain to hear him. The quiet tone directly equated to the level of his fury. The softer he spoke, the angrier he was. And his men knew better than to challenge him.

Without another word spoken, they all worked together to prepare Joshua for the move. The old horse blankets they owned were carefully wrapped around him. Jonathan tore a strip from the shirt he had been using to make bandages and put a fresh dressing around Joshua's head. The remainder of that shirt, along with the laudanum Clive had stolen four days ago, were wrapped together in a small bundle. They waited for the rain to slacken, then picked Joshua up and headed for The Night Star.

By the time they arrived every one of them was a mud-spattered mess. Mud dripped from their clothing, their hair, their faces. Their shoes were filled with it.

Without bothering to seek permission, Devon walked straight into Sally's office and informed her that they needed a room. Her initial reaction was pure outrage, due to the muck Devon and his friends had carried into the garish waiting room. But one look at the sparks of fury in Devon's eyes quenched any protest she'd been about to issue. "Go on down to the basement," she instructed them. "It's a little cool, but there's a cot down there. I'll bring ye some more blankets so ye can keep him warm. Right now ye'd best get him out of those wet clothes."

They walked in the direction Sally had pointed and came upon a narrow, steep staircase. Slowly, carefully, they made their way into the basement, guided by light from the lantern Sally had given Clive to use. As she had promised, they found a cot, and they placed Joshua upon it.

He uttered a low groan as they set him down, and Devon took that as a hopeful sign. Perhaps, he thought to himself, if Joshua was becoming aware of how much pain he was in, that meant he was getting closer to waking up.

Creaks on the staircase indicated someone else was on the way down, and as Devon glanced over he noted that it was Sally. Despite her ample girth she was surprisingly graceful, and she walked over to where they were all gathered. She placed her hand upon Joshua's forehead and felt his temperature. The hot, dry skin told her immediately that he was feverish.

"Ye've got to cool him down, lads, or he won't be lasting long."

"Could ye lend us a sponge, Sally? And maybe a bucket of water?" Devon kept his eyes fixed on Joshua as he made his request.

Sally paused before answering, and when she finally spoke, the rigid tone in her voice garnered Devon's attention. "Aye, I'll fetch those things for ye, lad. But when I get back, you and me, we're having us a chat."

She was back in minutes, and along with the water and sponge she brought a clean undershirt. "Left here by one of the customers," she explained as she handed it to Jonathan. "Ye might as well use it for making fresh bandages."

"Thanks." Jonathan immediately began tearing the shirt into strips.

Sally glanced at Devon and cocked her head toward the staircase. "C'mon, lad," she said as she started walking away. "I'm wanting to talk to ye. Ye can leave him with the others for a minute or two."

Devon reluctantly left his post and followed Sally into her office. When he was inside Sally shut the door, then sat down behind her desk. She indicated to Devon to take a seat as well, but he shook his head.

"I'm too wound up to sit, Sally," he said.

"Then ye can stand, lad, but I'm not letting ye leave until I find out what happened to him."

Devon raised his shoulders in an angered shrug. "That's the devil of it, Sally. Nobody saw anything. Clive and Jonathan were the ones who found him, but by the time they spotted him, whoever had done this was gone."

Sally's eyebrows furrowed in disbelief as she listened to Devon's story. "Ye mean that there was nobody, no one out on the docks that night who saw anything?"

"At least no one who's talking." Devon began pacing the length of the room. "Ye know how it is. Ye look out for yerself out there. No one else matters. So even if someone did see who beat Joshua, his mouth is staying shut."

"For fear that he'll be the next one."

"Nothing worse than a rat."

Sally was not to be subdued. "I still say there's someone out there who saw it and will talk."

Just then Devon stopped pacing as he remembered what Clive and Jonathan had told him the night it happened. "Actually, there might be someone."

Sally gave a triumphant smile. "I knew it!"

"But there's no way of finding her."

The smile faded. "Why not?"

"Because we don't know who she was."

Sally slumped back in her chair. "Devon, ye're making as much sense as a snowflake in July. Now what are ye talking about?"

As Devon related details of what had happened that evening, understanding dawned in Sally's eyes. "So if ye found out who that family crest belongs to, ye'd know who was there that night," she said when he had finished.

"Exactly."

Sally eyed Devon warily. "But ye don't know how to find out whose it is, do ye?"

"Nay, 'tis not the problem. Ye know Samuel Hastings, the coal porter?" At Sally's nod, he continued. "Samuel delivers coal to a lot of West End addresses, and he'd probably know who that crest belongs to."

She could guess what was coming next. "But information like that don't come for free."

"Nothing around here does. I talked to him the day after this happened, but the damn bastard won't even open his mouth unless I have something to bargain with."

Sally considered the problem for less than a minute before making her decision. "Tell ye what, Dev. I'll give ye a bargaining tool. Tell the old whoremonger Samuel to tell ye everything he knows about that family crest. Then when he does, he can have an hour free with Meredith. She's his favorite gal. That'll get him talking."

For the first time since the beating happened, a glimmer of a smile crossed Devon's face. "Thanks, Sally."

"I'd do more if I could, lad. Now go on, get moving. Samuel's probably just getting back from his daily rounds. Ye can catch him at Otis's. It's where he hangs out 'most every night."

Devon leaned over and kissed Sally on the cheek, then without another word opened the office door and left. Sally watched his backside as he went down the basement stairs, admiring the lean, graceful way that he walked. Despite the unforgiving surroundings in which he lived his life, his mastery of thievery allowed him to scrape together enough money to sustain his existence and stave off the emaciated, gaunt appearance common among the poor. Even if it was only bread, Devon generally had something to eat every day. And with the miles that he and his mates frequently walked—targeting shops or warehouses where they'd likely find cash—came Devon's sinewy, muscular frame that turned many a female head in rapt admiration. He certainly is a handsome devil, Sally thought. Wherever he went, Devon stirred that reaction in women, yet never once had Sally seen him show more than base interest in their attention. He bore the weight of the world on his shoulders, and there was simply no room in his life for women.

As Sally had predicted, Devon and his mates spotted Samuel amid the raucous crowd gathered at Otis's. Using the last of the money that they had between them, they ordered a pint of ale and joined Samuel at his table.

"We're needing to talk to ye," Devon stated.

"Put down yer coins and maybe we'll have something to talk about."

"Are ye willing to make a trade instead?"

"Depends. What've ye got?"

"A free hour with Meredith in exchange for information."

Samuel looked suspicious until Devon added, "Guaranteed by Sally."

"The fat old whore guaranteed it, did she?" He took a long draw on his beer and smacked his lips. "Well then, lads, we got us a deal."

Devon noted with disgust Samuel's comment about Sally, but ignored it—for now. "Jonathan says ye might be able to identify a family crest for us."

"I might. What's it look like?"

Jonathan spoke up. "Straight across the top and then curved outward on either side to—"

Samuel impatiently held up his hand. "I don't mean the shape of it, ye fool. They all pretty much look like that. It's the inside what's different."

Jonathan thought for a minute before answering. "Well, on the inside bottom there was drawn two lines, what looked like an upside-down 'v.' And inside the border of that 'v' was a picture of a castle. Then on the upper left side was a picture of some plants."

Samuel narrowed his eyes. "What do you mean, plants? What kind of plants?"

"I dunno. Long plants, like grass or something."

Devon spoke up. "Anything else?"

"Well, on the right side of the crest there was a picture of some type of big field. Almost could have been a big moor, I suppose."

That last clue clinched it. "Oh, ye're talking about the Rushmoors," Samuel said. "The crest describes their name, ye bloomin' idiot. Them plants isn't grass, they're rushes. And the field is just what ye said—a moor. Rushes . . . a moor. Rushmoor. Get it?"

"The Rushmoors, eh?" Devon mused. "So then what's the castle for?"

"How the bloody hell should I know? With all their money, they probably own it."

"Ye know where they live?"

Samuel's thick lips split into a self-righteous grin. " 'Course I do. One of the wealthiest families around. I deliver to them twice a week. I'll be going there tomorrow, as a matter of fact."

Devon felt his heart race with excitement. At last they were getting somewhere. "Tomorrow? Then I'll be needing to go with ye. I have to talk to someone there. I have to—"

"Now just ye wait a minute." Samuel's eyes narrowed to spiteful slits. "Ye're not going anywhere with me. Our agreement was for information only. I'll not have the likes of ye tagging along and causing trouble."

The muscles near the back of Devon's jaw became tight with anger, and his hands automatically clenched into powerful fists. He had half a mind to smash Samuel's nose into an unrecognizable pulp, and it was only by sheer will that he held himself back. Quietly, very quietly, he said, "I need information from a lass in that family. How do you expect me to get it if I don't go with ye?"

Samuel might not have been the brightest man around, but he could sense that his physical well-being was threatened. In a calm, soothing voice he answered, "Yer anger has made ye daft, Devon. If it's information what ye need from the family, ye ain't getting it by following me anyways. I never talk to the family, and they never talk to me. It ain't easy, ye know. Ye can't just walk up to the lady of the manor and start chewing the fat. I only talk to the servants."

Devon felt his anger diminish by a fraction, and with a curt nod he said tightly, "Go on."

"If I were ye, I'd get a job there. That way ye'll be on the inside, so to speak. Then, real slow and easy like, so's ye build up their trust, ye start talking. Just a wee bit, mind ye, now and then. Ye become almost like a mate to them."

The very idea was repulsive. "I don't have that kind of time," Devon snarled.

"Then make it, ye lowly bloke. It's the only way. Them upper-class snobs hate poor bastards like ye, Devon, and they'll only start speaking to ye if they got a reason. If ye're a friendly, trusted servant, it might do the trick."

Devon was already shaking his head at the repugnant idea—he'd sooner be stricken with gout—but to his dismay his mates were in agreement with Samuel.

"It's perfect, Dev," Jonathan opined. "And with your looks and background, ye're the only one of us what's got a chance of pulling it off."

"What the devil are ye blathering about?" Devon asked, already sensing the answer. His suspicions were confirmed with Jonathan's next sentence.

"Well, Madeline Pickett, o' course," he said, noting how Gareth and Clive were nodding in agreement.

Devon allowed a minute grin to lift the corners of his mouth. Just hearing Madeline's name stirred up memories of long ago, of a relatively easy time in Devon's boyhood, before having to fend for himself, when those whom he called friends were the bawdy, funny, sometimes crude ladies employed by Sally at The Night Star. There had been one woman among Sally's group—a lady, really—who distinguished herself from the others by her past affiliation with none other than Viscount Camdon Davis. Viscount Davis was a noted authority on French port, traveled in all the best circles, and had for many years claimed the comely Madeline Pickett as his exclusive mistress. As such she had oftimes joined him at balls and dinners attended by London's exclusive elite. The gatherings had required Madeline to showcase exquisite speech and manners, behavior at which she naturally excelled, despite her modest upbringing.

After eleven lavish, whirlwind years, Viscount Davis passed away, Madeline's fortunes dried up, and she eventually found herself in Sally Landry's employ. Nevertheless, she retained her stylish way of speaking and behavior, and during the years when Devon was raised in The Night Star Madeline would often—with May's encouragement, for how could it hurt the lad?—share with him her knowledge of proper etiquette. Years later, when Devon was out on his own, his behavior more closely matched that of his street mates. Yet a small part of Madeline's teachings had stayed with Devon, causing his speech and manners to be a shade less crude than others around him. Because of that his mates now knew that if Devon were cast into the elitist ocean of London's high society, Miss Pickett's teachings would be the life raft keeping Devon afloat. But the prospect was grim. He despised those people and wanted nothing to do with them. The idea of becoming friends with someone who'd sooner spit in his face than consent to a conversation made his stomach churn.

"Hastings's plan is the only one what makes sense, Devon," Jonathan said, breaking into his thoughts. "We got no other choice. Ladies are always spinning their bloomin' heads for a look at ye. For Joshua's sake, use yer charm with the ladies to make friends with this lass and get her to talk. It's our only hope."

Still Devon resisted, repulsed by the thought of befriending the class he despised, but when he saw the grim faces of his mates mirroring Jonathan's dire prediction, he finally caved in.

"All right," he agreed, spitting the words from between gritted teeth. "I suppose it's worth a try, though I don't see an elitist princess being charmed by a thief. I got no Shakespeare quotes fallin' off the end of my tongue like them fancy sods she's used to. She'll never want to talk to me or think of me as a friend."

" 'Tain't necessarily so, laddie," Samuel said. "Sure, yer manners are a bit rough around the edges, but it don't never seem to bother the ladies none. Fact is, sometimes I think they like it." He poured more ale down his throat, then snaked his tongue around his lips to catch some errant drops. "A chit's a chit, and for reasons I'll never understand they all seem to melt before ye. Those West End snobs ain't no different. Gain her trust, use yer charm, and the combination will get her to confide in ye eventually." Samuel paused to point a chubby finger at Devon. "Just watch that bloody temper of yers. Don't let them wealthy get ye all firing mad like what usually happens when ye see 'em. Ye'll do fine. Ye'll see."

"So ye say," Devon replied. "But first tell me how I meet her in the first place."

"Why, that's the easy part, mate." Samuel grinned. "Like I said, just get yerself a job."

This time it was Jonathan who felt anger burn within him. "A job?" he scoffed. "Don't ye think that if we could've gotten us a job somewhere we would have by now? Just what do ye think they'd hire any of the lot of us for anyway?"

Samuel finished the last of his pint and rose to leave. "It ain't for me to say. Look, I'm in pretty tight with one of the housekeepers," his chest puffed up with pride, "and she owes me a favor. Tomorrow I'll ask if she thinks there's anything a sorry bummer like yerself could do. Ye never know. I also got me some connections with fake references just in case this works." Samuel's thick, shiny lips curled upward in a smile. "But now I've got me 'business' to attend to. See ye, mates."

He pushed his large bulk away from the table and headed out the door. He certainly wasn't wasting any time collecting his share of the bargain, Devon thought.

"Ye think it'll work?" asked Jonathan.

Devon shrugged. "It's worth a try. We have to find the filthy bastard who did this to Joshua no matter how long it takes, and a job would bring us money besides. I s'pose Samuel's idea could work," he admitted, though doubt laced the tone of his voice. "Anyway, it's all we got."

Five

"Does it feel all right?"

Devon looked at himself in the mirror of the servants' quarters and gave a slight shrug. "Aye, I s'pose it does," he answered, with some uncertainty. How was he to know the right way to wear a waistcoat?

The groom decided that it was a smart fit and indicated that Devon was to follow him outside.

Together they walked across the garden toward the stable, and as they did so Devon couldn't help but glare at the main house. The lavishness of it nearly sickened him. It was a three-story majestic townhouse that looked as if it were home to the king. Brick after elegant brick had been used to build this monstrosity, and Devon knew for certain that the sturdy gabled roof was not prone to leak. Lush green ivy crept up the sides of the house, and like the garden they were walking through, it had been exquisitely manicured. The windows were all meticulously bright and clean, and the flowers in the window boxes bloomed with healthy vigor. Never before had Devon seen such an outrageous display of wealth. He promised himself that as soon as he learned all he needed to, he would get away from here as fast as his heels would carry him.

Of course, he was thankful to have the opportunity to search for information. Surprisingly, the lascivious coal porter Samuel had come through for him. As promised, he had talked to the housekeeper about a job for Devon, and his timing, it turned out, could not have been better. Kendal Rushmoor, it seemed, had a passion for acquiring horses, and the small stable that was kept in the city now housed eight majestic thoroughbreds. Between taking them out for exercise, feeding and watering them and keeping the stable clean, it was more work than a single man could handle. The problem had been brought to the butler's attention only the night before Samuel had come inquiring about employment opportunities for Devon. An interview was quickly arranged, and after taking one look at Devon's muscular body, the butler was certain he could handle the job. Some extra coin in Samuel's pocket had even produced fake letters of reference. Now, two days later, here Devon was, employed at the Rushmoors' as the groom's assistant. It had all been amazingly easy.

They reached the stable, and Daniel showed Devon around once they were inside. "Back here is where all the equipment is kept." His hand made a sweeping gesture. "Curry brushes, feed sacks, saddles, reins, whips, water buckets. They're all kept in their separate places back here, so you shouldn't have trouble finding anything. Over here," he walked farther along, "is where we keep the pitchforks and hay. It's going to be your responsibility to clean the stalls out every day and make sure that the horses are watered and fed."

Daniel then gestured toward the stalls where all eight horses were sheltered. Devon noticed that they seemed to have quite a keen interest in Daniel, and it wasn't long before he learned the reason why. As he passed by the stalls and told Devon the name of each horse, Daniel reached into his pocket and took out some sugar cubes.

"Give them a few of these from time to time and you'll have friends for life," Daniel joked. Devon smiled right along with him, wanting to make a good impression. "Where do I get them?" he asked.

"From the kitchen. Just ask any of the cooks. They keep them in there for tea. I'll give you a tour of the house later on and introduce you to the rest of the staff."

Next they stepped over to where the carriages were kept. Devon noted with more than a passing interest that it must have been the larger carriage that Jonathan had seen that night. The smaller one was not adorned with the family's crest.

"After a while I'll show you how to hitch the horses. For now, though, just make sure the coaches are clean."

"This one sure is big," Devon commented offhandedly. "Does it get used much?"

"Usually only for special occasions," Daniel replied. "Although a couple weeks ago you might say it was a rescue carriage."

Devon's interest was immediately piqued. "Why is that?" he asked, doing his best not to appear overly curious. The last thing he needed was to arouse suspicion about his real motive for being here.

Daniel chuckled to himself as he told Devon of Claire's and Lilia's adventure on the docks.

"But everything turned out all right?" Devon asked when he had finished.

"Yeah, fine. Although, it's funny you should ask. Lady Claire did say that she saw a rather nasty row. Some poor bloke was beaten pretty badly." Daniel shook his head in disgust. "Wonder whatever happened to him."

"Did she see who did it?"

Daniel looked at Devon in surprise. "Well, I don't know. Personally I don't think she paid much attention to the whole thing. She was more interested in finding her cousin than watching two drunken bastards beat each other." Daniel snorted. "If you ask me, it serves them right. Two less worthless blokes in this city can only be good news, right?"

Devon's stomach soured with disgust at everything he

encountered here. Even the servants spewed forth contemptuous arrogance toward the East End poor. He had to get out of here. Nothing, not the money, the food, or the comfortable quarters would keep him here a minute longer than he absolutely had to be. At his first opportunity he'd seek out this pompous Lady Claire, find out if she had seen anything that could help him locate Joshua's attacker, and then leave the Rushmoor mansion without ever looking back.

Louisa Rushmoor felt as though she would faint. For two weeks straight, ever since the dinner party invitations had been sent, she had done nothing but prepare for the event. Every servant at her disposal had been delegated duties in anticipation of the grand occasion. All the rugs had been beaten, the floors scrubbed and waxed, the silver polished, and every piece of furniture dusted and then dusted some more. For two days the cooks had been preparing the food that would make up some eight different courses of the meal, and so far things had gone exceedingly well. Until today. Now, a mere four hours before the party would commence, Louisa received news that caused a rapid spike in her blood pressure and forced her, for the first time in two weeks, to sit down.

A concerned Emma Leeds fanned her distraught mistress and assured her in soothing tones that everything would be all right.

"How can you be so certain, Emma?" Louisa held the back of her right hand against her agitated forehead and expelled a sigh signifying the greatness of her burden.

"We have other male servants, my lady. We'll simply press one of them into service for this evening."

Instead of reassuring her, the thought put Louisa into another fit of anxiety. "Other male servants? Like the groom or the gardener, perhaps?" Her naturally high voice became shriller still. "What a disgrace to the family! I simply cannot bear the thought of all the talk that will follow."

Emma clicked her tongue at her mistress. "Now, my lady, you know that isn't true. And it's not like it's never been done before. Remember Lord and Lady Steele's party two seasons ago?" Louisa nodded. "Well, if it worked for them, it shall work for us." Emma patted her mistress's hand with confidence. "Now, it's best that I take you up to your room for a nap until it's time to get ready. Leave everything to me. I'll make certain one ill footman doesn't ruin your party."

Indeed the thought of trying to resolve the problem by herself was simply too overwhelming to dwell upon any longer. Gratefully Louisa decided that Emma was right, and she knew a nap would do her a world of good. With a nod she allowed Emma to help her upstairs and prepare her to rest.

As soon as Lady Bedington was settled in her chambers, Emma left to seek out the butler, Nigel Penworthy, and put an end to the problem that had so vexed her mistress.

She found him in the wine cellar, carefully considering his final selections for the evening.

"A word with you please, Mr. Penworthy." She walked over to where he was standing.

Nigel Penworthy peered at Emma from over the bottles of port he held up and said, in his typical droll manner, "Certainly, Mrs. Leeds. What is it?"

"You're aware that your footman James has become ill?" Nigel nodded. "Well, I fear Lady Bedington may suffer from hysteria unless I assure her that we've secured James's replacement for the party. His absence, after all, does create an odd number, and there's so much food to be brought out, what with all the courses being prepared."

Nigel was thoughtful as he considered the dilemma. "I see the problem."

"Do you suppose Daniel could be pressed into service for this one occasion?"

The butler shook his head. "No, Daniel wouldn't be right at all. He's not the proper height, and the mismatch with Grant would be an embarrassment to the family."

Emma's lips pressed tightly together as she considered other possibilities. "What about Jeffrey, the gardener?"

Again Nigel dismissed the suggestion. "He's not strong enough to carry those platters. I'd fear the cook's efforts would be found strewn across the floor instead of on the guests' plates."

The head housekeeper threw up her hands in frustration. "One of the pages, then?" The butler shook his head once more. "Well, there must be someone we can use."

Nigel Penworthy considered all possibilities before realizing he had the perfect solution. "Of course," he drawled in a triumphant, dry voice. "I know the perfect man for the job."

"Who?"

"The groom's new assistant, Devon Blake."

Emma's eyes widened in surprise. "The groom has an assistant? Since when? And why wasn't I informed?"

"Since Lord Bedington acquired those two new thoroughbreds. Daniel couldn't keep up with all the work, but just when we were preparing to send out inquiries we heard through the coal porter about someone looking for work. It all happened rather quickly."

"Oh, I do remember hearing about it. I've just thought of nothing but this party for the past fortnight."

Nigel nodded his head empathetically. "Yes, well, the fellow's only been here a little longer than that. But Daniel says he's working out splendidly. He doesn't say much, but he's nearly as strong as those horses he takes care of and seems to have his wits about him. He's also polite—who knows from whom he received his manners. I'm sure he'll do fine for one evening."

Emma snorted with mild skepticism but was relieved the problem had been solved. "Just make sure he doesn't bring the smell of the stable in with him."

"Certainly not, Mrs. Leeds," Nigel replied, miffed that she had even suggested such a thing.

"Fine. Then I'll leave everything in your capable hands, Mr. Penworthy." Emma turned on her heel and left, grateful that she now had one less thing to think about.

The guests were due to begin arriving at any minute, but still Claire found herself reluctant to leave the isolated comfort of her bedroom. Marie had finished preparing her over half an hour ago, and by all accounts Claire should have been in the drawing room with the rest of her family. Instead she sat outside on the balcony, mindful of the extra attention Marie had paid to her hair and dress. This evening she wore a flowing white muslin gown, over which was a pale green tunic. Underneath the gown her legs were bare, but dainty slippers covered her feet. For warmth, a cashmere shawl was draped over her shoulders. Marie had done her hair up in a chignon at the back of her head, but let long curls flow freely on either side. She had decorated the entire ensemble with a delicate jeweled comb and tiny white flowers. An elegant emerald necklace adorned her throat. She was a sight to behold, according to her gushing maid, but Claire could not suppress the annoyance she felt over the entire occasion. It was her mother's decision to host the dinner party, and all for the chance to invite Lord Townsend to dinner. The status of his peerage was not lost on Louisa, and she vowed to do all she could to help him maintain his interest in Claire.

A gentle breeze ruffled Claire's hair, yet she hesitated going inside despite the risk to her coiffure. The problem with having her mother entertain Lord Townsend, she thought, was that not only was she certain she could never love the man, she doubted that she could even like him. The incessant insults he'd hurled at the guests at the Caswells' ball had been insufferable.

"Mademoiselle?" Marie rapped on the door. "They're expecting you downstairs. Your mother, she eez wondering what 'as become of you."

"I'm coming, Marie. Tell everyone that I'll be right down." Claire rose and walked into her bedroom. With a final look in the mirror she smoothed her ruffled hair and went downstairs.

"There you are, Claire," Louisa said when she spotted her eldest daughter. "What's been keeping you?"

"Please forgive me, Mother. I didn't notice the time." No use confessing to her mother things she didn't want to hear.

"Very well, but be smart now. You want to continue impressing Lord Townsend, and he certainly won't be by a girl with addled wits." Louisa walked away after issuing that uplifting advice, and Claire appreciated the sympathetic look she received from Lavinia.

Moments later, the company began to arrive. Elegantly attired, artfully coiffed, the ladies and gentlemen selected as guests for the Rushmoor dinner party strolled in with majestic dignity and grace. Like the profusion of colors in an English garden, there seemed no limit to the variety of pastel shades boasted by the women's gowns. Silk and cashmere shawls accented the dresses, and the lavish jewels around their pale throats sparkled like sunlight on newly fallen snow.

After leaving their wraps with the servants, they gath-

ered in the drawing room, and conversation began. Lord
and Lady Ashton swept Claire up in an engaging discussion about a play they had recently seen. Although Claire
had always previously been intrigued by the elderly couple's lively banter, she now found herself struggling to
concentrate. She knew Lord Townsend would be along
soon, and her apprehension over his arrival disrupted her
focus. At last she excused herself to go speak to Lavinia,
but her timing could not have been worse. At the very
moment she left the Ashtons to seek out her sister, Lord
Townsend appeared at the top of the stairs. As he entered
the drawing room and spotted Claire alone, he seized the
opportunity to rush to her side and hold her hostage.

"My dear Lady Rushmoor, how lovely to see you
again." He uttered the affectionate greeting loud enough
so only Claire would hear and, as at the Caswells' party,
lifted her hand to his lips and brushed it with a kiss.

With resolve as firm as steel Claire summoned up a
modicum of politeness and welcomed the marquess in
return. "How kind of you to remember me, Lord Townsend," she said.

"Remember you, my lady?" He arched one refined
eyebrow in surprise. "How could I possibly not remember you? Your captivating brown eyes, your silky blond
hair, your creamy skin, your beautiful full lips—"

Claire cleared her throat in alarm. "You're much too
complimentary, my lord," she gently admonished him.

But instead of apologizing as she had expected, the
cavalier marquess offered no excuse for his behavior. "It
is simply the effect you have on me, Lady Rushmoor."

For once in her life Claire found herself speechless,
but as luck would have it she was saved from making a
response because at that moment Nigel announced dinner.

Lord Townsend offered Claire his arm to escort her,
leaving her no choice but to accept it. Together they went

downstairs to the dining room. Knowing in advance the seating arrangements, Claire showed Lord Townsend to his designated spot. Right next to her.

"Ah, this must be my lucky evening," he said upon realizing they were seated next to one another. "I get the pleasure of spending the entire dinner with the most enchanting, and lovely, lady at the party."

With an aversion that was difficult to conceal, Claire sat down with her disdainful companion. She failed to notice how his gaze fixated on her décolleté. Someone else, however, did not.

Two dispassionate footmen stood in the doorway, awaiting the signal to begin service. Devon was directly across the room from the flustered Lady Claire, and noted with slight surprise the leering gaze of her companion.

"Who's the woman across from us?" he whispered to his counterpart standing next to him.

"The one in green?" At Devon's nod, Grant, the other footman, replied, "That's Lady Claire Rushmoor, Lord Begington's eldest daughter. Beside her is Lord Philip Townsend. His father is the Duke of Townsend." It was clear by his tone that Grant admired their guest, but the reason for his respect was lost on Devon, who lacked full understanding of peerage.

He was, however, grateful to finally get a look at Claire. He had known since his first day of Rushmoor employment that she was the one on the docks the night Joshua was beaten, but until now had not seen her. It had been discouraging to wait so long to see her, and, despite the money he was earning, he had begun to think that Samuel's idea of working here had been a mistake. At last, the opportunity for indoor service had presented itself. As soon as Nigel had asked him, Devon had eagerly accepted the additional duty. Carrying platters of food wasn't difficult, and he'd have a chance to meet the elusive Lady Rushmoor. Or so he thought. It wasn't until Devon was given his instructions that he learned he was under no circumstances to address any of the guests, including family members. Initially Devon had seethed with anger. His anxiety to meet Claire had caused him to forget the strict social code. But then he realized that this still wasn't a pointless venture. At least he'd find out who Claire was. Finding opportunities to begin gaining her trust and friendship would have to come later.

At Nigel's discreet nod in their direction both Devon and Grant came forward with tureens of lobster bisque. As instructed, they walked to either end of the table and placed the tureens to the right of the guests seated there. The soup bowls were already in front of the guests, so it was a simple task to pick one up, ladle soup into the bowl, and set it back down in front of the guest. Although it was an entirely new experience, Devon handled himself with the ease of one who had done it many times before. And as luck would have it, his instructions were to serve the side of the table at which Claire was seated.

Although she gave a pretense of rapt attention toward Lord Townsend's prattle, Devon could tell Claire was trying to conceal complete and utter boredom with her dinner companion. She gave polite responses in places where the conversation required, but provided nothing to enhance the dialogue. No worry, however, for Lord Townsend seemed more than content to listen to the sound of his own voice.

At last he approached her, and for the first time since he'd been in the room, Claire looked into his eyes. She was startled to realize that she'd never seen this footman before, since Marie had not informed her of any new additions to the staff. But her main surprise was at how handsome he was. As proper manners dictated, Claire normally paid scant attention to the hired help. But it was impossible to give this man a mere passing glance.

There was something exotic, almost dangerous about him. His hair was light brown, shot through with streaks of blond. His eyes were sea green, fringed by impossibly long, dark lashes. His lips were full, but not overly so, with the bottom one being slightly more so than the top. Unlike most Englishmen with whom Claire came in contact, this man's complexion was not pasty white but instead rather tan. And across his left jawline he sported a distinct scar.

There was something unnerving about him, and as soon as she realized she'd been staring, Claire hastily looked away. To her relief, Philip seemed not to have noticed. He waited until both their bowls were filled with the thick, creamy soup, then disregarded the footman as one would a fly. But Claire could not resist another glance as the servant walked away, and as she watched him, to her horror, a flash of desire surged through her blood. Immediately her eyes flew to her bowl of soup, and she began eating with the intensity of a starving person. Philip sniffed in her direction as though appalled by her manners, and it was only her years of etiquette training that enabled Claire to compose herself. She looked up at Philip with an engaging smile and asked if he was enjoying his soup.

"Very tasty," he replied, still wondering about the reason behind her strange behavior. She now seemed to be back to normal, so Philip attributed Claire's minor aberration to female quirkiness.

For the rest of the meal Claire exercised a mighty will to singularly concentrate on Philip Westbury's interminable chatter. Between courses of fish, game, and fowl, he monopolized her attention and spoke incessantly of plays he had seen in which the acting was deplorable, concerts he had heard where the musicians were flat, and the latest gossip that had been forced upon him. Mind you, *he* never took part in spreading heinous rumors, but alas, it was so difficult not to hear the talk, what with all the social obligations he had. Claire wondered if it ever occurred to Philip that by repeating to her all the gossip he had heard, he was doing the very thing he so fervently claimed to despise.

At long last the meal came to an end, and as was the custom, the ladies of the room excused themselves and headed back to the drawing room, leaving the men to drink port and smoke.

As Claire walked through the door she sensed that eyes were upon her, but not wanting to discover that it was the mysterious footman who held her in his gaze, she made her departure as quickly as possible without looking back.

When she entered the drawing room Claire caught Lavinia's eye, and before anyone else could broach a conversation with her she whisked her sister away to a corner of the room.

"Claire!" Lavinia hissed at her sister as discreetly as possible. "Whatever are you doing? We're supposed to be entertaining our guests, not ignoring them."

"I know, I know. But I only want to speak with you for a moment."

Lavinia hastily looked around to make sure their mother wasn't glaring with disapproval; luckily, she appeared to be thoroughly engrossed in conversation with Lady Ashton.

"All right, Claire. It seems to be fine—for now. But, really, we mustn't stand here excluding our guests."

Claire raced to the point. "What do you know about the new footman who was serving dinner this evening?"

Lavinia's brows drew together in careful concentration, but after several moments she shook her head. "I don't know what you mean, Claire. What's there to know about a footman?"

"Well, it's just that I've not seen him before, and . . . well . . ."

Lavinia was alarmed at once. "What is it? Was he rude to you or any of our guests? If so, instruct Nigel to dismiss him at once."

Claire vigorously shook her head. "No, no. It's not that at all. I was only wondering if you knew where he came from."

Her sister peered at Claire as if she'd grown a second head. "Why are you taking such an inordinate interest in the servants? I've no idea where he came from. If you must know, I suppose the best person to ask would be Nigel, or Mrs. Leeds. But what's this all about, Claire?"

Flames of embarrassment began licking Claire's cheeks. Lavinia was right. Why was she so interested in knowing about a common footman? Lord Townsend's wearisome conversation must have been even more drab than she realized for it to have inspired such curiosity toward the hired help. Claire decided that her best recourse now was to brush off the entire incident and begin mingling with the other ladies before she said something she'd regret. "Oh really, it's nothing. I just thought I'd mention his fine work this evening to Nigel. You know how we want to keep the servants happy. It makes the entire household run more efficiently."

Lavinia remained skeptical, but there was no time to discuss the matter further. "Very well, Claire. I need to speak with Mrs. Leeds this evening after the party. Why don't I ask her to mention your compliment to Nigel? No doubt he'll be pleased."

"Of course. That would be fine. Thanks, Linny." Claire smiled affectionately at her sister and then went to speak with the other guests.

A half hour later the gentlemen entered the drawing room to resume socializing with the ladies. Lord Townsend wasted no time in monopolizing Claire's attention.

"What a delightful little party this has been," he stated with a priggish smile. "It was especially pleasurable seeing you again, Lady Rushmoor."

Claire smiled demurely. "You are too kind, Lord Townsend. Thank you so much for coming."

Encouraged by her positive comments, Lord Townsend leaned close to Claire and whispered, "I would so enjoy continuing the discussion we were having about the appalling theater of late in Covent Garden. Would you be free to go riding tomorrow?"

Not only was he arrogant, but terribly rude as well, Claire thought. Imagine asking if she were available to call on the very next day. "I'm afraid I am engaged tomorrow, Lord Townsend. Perhaps if you sent your card I could . . ."

Townsend almost looked as if he would yawn. "Oh, Lady Rushmoor. Why bother with such inconvenient formalities when we can plan everything right now? If you're unavailable tomorrow, then perhaps the day after would be more suitable?"

Of all the unchivalrous nerve! Claire knew she must get away from this man as soon as possible, but one glance across the room at the beaming look on her mother's face emphasized the necessity of allowing Lord Townsend to come calling. "Very well," she replied. "The day after tomorrow would be suitable. I shall look forward to it."

"Splendid!" With brazen carelessness, he allowed his hand to brush a bare spot on her shoulder from where her shawl had slipped away. "However, the pleasure of your company shall be sorely missed until then. I fear the slow passing time until we meet again."

He lifted her hand to touch his dry lips. "Good-bye, Lady Rushmoor. Thank you again for such a marvelous evening." He peered deeply into Claire's eyes as he uttered his parting words, but rather than leaving her breathless with anticipation, he left her instead with a feeling of nausea.

The others were also preparing to leave, so she excused herself from Philip and bade good-bye to the remaining guests. Only when the Rushmoors had their house alone to themselves could Claire say good night to her family and excuse herself for the evening. Marie was already waiting for her in the bedroom. But instead of engaging Claire in the usual chitchat, she sensed something was bothering her mistress and maintained a respectful silence. As was her custom, Claire splashed cold water on her face to help her relax. Then, with a sigh of gratitude, she climbed into her luxurious bed as Marie left the room, shutting the door behind her.

Moonlight shone through the open French doors, bathing Claire's room in a soft mellow glow. From outside she could hear the sounds of thousands of chirping crickets, accompanied by the occasional croak of a frog. There were many of them in the garden's pond. Claire settled into her huge feather bed and pulled the coverlet up around her. The curtains softly fluttered as a breeze swirled into the room. But instead of being lulled to sleep by the nocturnal chorus outside, Claire found herself wide awake and unexplainably distracted. Surely the reason was that imperious Lord Townsend. He had galled her every insufferable minute he was around. But there was something else on Claire's mind this early June evening. Or rather, someone. Someone with the most intriguing scar across his left jawline.

Devon rolled over on his simple servant's cot and kicked away the thin bedcover. It was not an overly warm evening, yet his body felt heated. He reached his arms overhead, stretching and flexing his muscles, trying to relax. The attempt was futile. There were too many thoughts invading his mind and prohibiting sleep. As always, he thought of Joshua. Reports on his progress were received via Samuel on his twice-weekly coal deliveries. So far it wasn't looking good. Joshua was healing slower than they had hoped; in fact, he still wasn't able to get out of bed. It pained Devon not to see his friend, but he knew the others were doing the best they could. Certainly the money he'd been sending them had helped ease their physical suffering, though it had done nothing for the emotional anguish. Devon knew he had to find out who had done this, then make the bastard pay. He looked forward to getting a day off soon. Daniel had promised it to Devon after the extra work he did for the party, but just when he would get the reprieve was not yet clear.

At least he had made progress here—that is, if you could call seeing the person with whom you wanted to speak progress. Devon sighed in frustration. She'd been just as he'd expected—aloof, sanctimonious, full of herself. He saw the way she had stared at him during dinner, as if she were shocked that a man such as he had dared to enter her dining room. She was just like all the other wealthy people he'd seen. Or was she? Of course, if he was honest with himself he'd at least have to admit that she was quite a beauty. When she'd first looked at him he'd been startled by the intensity of her eyes. The color was such a rare chestnut brown, especially for someone with golden blond hair. And her creamy white skin was devoid of imperfection. As Devon lay on his cot recalling the plunging décolleté of Claire's dress, he couldn't help but imagine what it would be like for his mouth to sample the exquisite softness of her breasts. He was certain her pampered body would be softer than anything he'd ever experienced. And he was equally certain of how much she would enjoy his kiss. But despite his vivid imagination, the thought filled him with the same contempt he always had toward the wealthy. Claire Rushmoor would sooner allow the touch of a python than she would a wretch like Devon. His heart burned with anger. If not for Joshua he would leave this minute. Instead he would do what he must in order to speak to Claire, then forever dismiss the Rushmoors and their fancy house from his mind.

Six

For the third time in as many minutes, Claire peered at her reflection in the mirror to check on her riding outfit. Unfortunately, nothing was out of place. There were no last-minute tears to be fixed, missing buttons to be sewn, or wayward ribbons that needed adjustment. Nothing that would take any time away from her riding engagement with Lord Philip Townsend, who, at this moment, was awaiting her downstairs. Claire also had no luck in acquiring a sudden cold or even a headache that could have served as an excuse to cancel. Of course, she could have faked a headache, but Claire knew that she'd have to be a pretty good actress to put that over on her mother. No, it was impossible to get out of this. She was going to have to be brave and face the situation straight on.

As she walked downstairs she spotted Philip in the drawing room speaking with her mother. His clothes were as outlandish as always. He wore tight black riding breeches, one of the overly frilled shirts he so favored, and a double-breasted purple waistcoat with exceedingly large revers and six yellow buttons down the front. Atop his head rested a fawn beaver tophat. Claire shuddered at the sight, but continued descending the stairs to face her caller.

"Lady Rushmoor, what a pleasure to see you again," Philip said with glee when he saw her, as if they were old friends reuniting after several years instead of distant acquaintances meeting again after two days.

"I've been looking forward to our ride," Claire responded with a smile, unable in good consciousness to say she was delighted to see him again.

"My horse is tied out front, but I understand yours is still being saddled. Shall we wait here until it's brought 'round the front?"

"We could continue our discussion of Beethoven's piano concertos in the meantime," Claire's mother chimed in.

Suddenly Claire felt as if she were being suffocated, and she longed more than anything to get some air outside. "Actually, Lord Townsend, Mother," Claire acknowledged them both, "I'd enjoy waiting outdoors for my horse to be brought out. It's such a lovely day."

"Whatever my lady wishes," Philip said with a gallant smile, then turned to Louisa. "Let's do continue that conversation at another time. I find your musical knowledge to be so very enlightening." Louisa blushed crimson at Lord Townsend's flattery, but Claire nearly choked with laughter at his transparent attempts to get on her good side. Louisa Rushmoor had never been a lover of music, and knew as much about Beethoven as Claire knew about manufacturing a plough.

They waited outside for only a minute before her horse was led to her. But instead of it being Daniel who brought out her favorite gelding, Claire was startled by the sight of the handsome footman. What in the world was a footman doing working in the stables? Oh, if only she'd had that conversation with Mrs. Leeds about who he was. But fearing the same reaction from the head housekeeper as she'd received from Lavinia, Claire had opted to say nothing. Now here she was again, facing a man she'd believed to be a footman, and still knowing nothing about him.

"Yèr horse, m'lady." He spoke in a quiet, respectful tone, yet Claire had the distinct feeling that he bore no respect for her at all. Just why she should have that feeling she had no idea; yet, there it was. "Thank you, er . . . ?"

"Devon, m'lady. Devon Blake." His eyes captured hers for one brief moment, and once again, the effect was unnerving. She was the one who broke the stare, unwilling to become hypnotized by the gaze of a servant. However, there was still the task of mounting her horse. Devon stepped forward and held out his hand, patiently waiting to assist Claire. She extended her hand in response, determined to think nothing more of this servant. But when their fingertips touched, it was as though a current shot through her. Her heart beat like the excited wings of a bird, and without warning her palms felt moist.

Thankfully, she maintained her composure and released his hand as quickly as she was able. Hastily she looked away from Devon, slapped the reins of her horse, and rode away with Lord Townsend in tow, feeling sea green eyes burning into her back.

They rode through the park, with Lord Townsend droning on incessantly. Claire paid only scant attention to his rambling until he offhandedly brought up the subject of Devon.

"I beg your pardon, Lord Townsend. My mind wandered for a moment. What is it you were saying?"

"I said that you ought to dismiss that insolent servant of yours at once."

"Insolent servant? Has one of the staff been rude to you, my lord?"

"Not to me, my lady. To you."

"Me? Whatever are you talking about?"

Philip sighed at Claire's seeming naïveté. "That presumptive Irish footman, or whatever he is. The one who brought your horse to you just now."

"Oh, yes. I know the one. I believe he's new. Was he rude?"

"Was he rude? My lady, is the sky blue? Is the grass green? That servant stared insolently at you and ought to be dismissed at once."

"Forgive me, my lord, but I did not feel he stared insolently, or at all, really. I'm afraid you have a rather spirited imagination."

Philip tsk-tsked at Claire as if she were a child. "Lady Rushmoor, please do not make the mistake of defending their kind. The pathetic wretches do not deserve your sympathy. At the very least you must punish that man for his behavior at once lest he becomes accustomed to acting in that manner and is never properly trained on how to treat his superiors."

Claire could not believe what she was hearing. "Properly trained, my lord?"

"That's right."

"But you're acting as if our servants are nothing more than animals."

"Well they are, essentially. People in the lower classes are so far below us that they're really closer to animals than people, and ought to be treated as such."

"Lord Townsend!" Claire was shocked by his outrageous attitude. "I'm sure that you're entitled to your opinion, but I feel I must disagree with you on this point. Servants are certainly not closer to animals than people. They are merely different people, that is all."

Philip could see by the bright spots of color on Claire's cheeks that she had become quite angry, and he decided not to push her any further. One day she'd realize that everything he said was right, but for now he'd change the subject. He didn't want to get on her bad side, after all, not with that huge dowry she had.

"I see this conversation is upsetting you, my lady, so why don't we speak of more pleasant things than common servants, hmm? A change of topic would do us good."

Claire still bristled at his pompousness, but decided he was right about changing the subject. "Very well, my lord. What shall we talk about?"

"Ah, here's a fascinating idea." Philip puckered his lips together in anticipation of his engrossing topic proposal. "Tell me what you thought about the way people were dressed at your dinner party. Frankly, I thought Cecil Preston's frock coat was abominable. Why, that dull pea-green color made him look as dour as a January day, and that awful cravat he wore . . ." The sound of his voice faded into the background, and once again Claire let her thoughts wander from the interminable chatter of Lord Philip Townsend.

"It's been over a week since he last called, Claire. Explain what you've done to turn him away."

Louisa and Aunt Bella hovered over Claire with scowls on their faces, waiting for an explanation of Philip Westbury's recent absence.

"I haven't done a thing, Mother, honestly I haven't." Claire tried her best to remain composed, despite feeling like a trapped animal.

"Then why do you suppose he hasn't been here lately? Have you received word that he took ill?" The sarcasm in her mother's voice was clear.

"He is a busy man, Mother. I'm certain he simply has other obligations to attend."

Claire's explanation did not suit her mother. Louisa had gone through two previous seasons in which, for one reason or another, Claire disregarded all whom Louisa had deemed outstanding suitors. She was not about to let that happen again.

"If you were conducting yourself properly, his primary obligation would be to you."

Suddenly the accusations were more than Claire could stand. She resented being treated like a child who had misbehaved, particularly when the issue they were discussing was her own future. "I'm sorry you feel that way, Mother," she said through gritted teeth. "But I can assure you that I said nothing to dissuade Lord Townsend from calling." Although her outward appearance remained calm, inwardly she seethed. Her behavior had always been beyond reproach. How unfair of her mother to imply that she had purposely sent Lord Townsend packing. True, she was none too fond of the man; however, to hint that she had acted inappropriately in order to keep him away, well, it simply wasn't true.

"Of course, it may be all those insipid gowns you've taken to wearing lately."

"Pardon me, Mother? Whatever do you mean?"

Louisa heaved a sigh of annoyance. "Claire, you know exactly what I'm talking about." She added cream to her afternoon tea and took up the dainty silver spoon with which to stir it before continuing. "Sometimes I've thought you're doing it just to spite me. You disapprove of my suggestions for your future husband, and you're making sure I know it by donning those dreadful, colorless frocks which are sure to turn away every prospective suitor. You've always had that rebellious streak in you, ever since you were a young girl. I think you get it from your father. Wouldn't you say, Bella?"

"Absolutely," Bella concurred, nodding in solemn agreement.

"Sometimes I just don't know what to do with you, Claire. Between your stubbornness and the dreadful weather we've been having lately, it's a wonder I don't faint dead away." Louisa fanned herself as if her own dire prediction were on the verge of coming true before another thought seized her mind and turned it elsewhere. "And, Bella, do you know what I heard the other day about Caroline Trellis? Why the nerve of that tawdry woman . . ."

The scolding and complaining infused the parlor like toxic smoke, and suddenly Claire knew that she had to get away. She rose from her chair and marched toward the door. "Just where do you suppose you're going?" her mother demanded in a shrill voice.

"I need some air, Mother. I'm going riding."

"Riding! Alone? Claire Rushmoor, you're absolutely not doing that! Imagine the talk, the gossip, when people hear about . . ."

But that's exactly what she did. Even her mother's demanding tone did nothing to halt her, for Claire felt at that moment that if she didn't get away from the house she would fall apart. It wasn't just anger that drove her down the cobbled drive toward the stables. Her mother's insistence that Philip Westbury would be Claire's future husband also evoked emotions of loneliness and despair. Never mind any possibility of falling in love with him, but to envision the years ahead of her as devoted wife to that priggish man, enduring his insufferable gossip while pretending to be vastly interested in his every word, left her with a feeling of utter hopelessness.

It was with the burden of her emotional baggage that she entered the stable. She scanned the area, looking for Daniel, but it seemed he was nowhere to be found.

"Daniel?" she called out, slight alarm tingeing her voice. Where was he?

Seconds later someone appeared, but it was not who Claire expected.

"He's not here. It's his day off."

She whirled around. "Oh. It's you."

His answer to that statement was a silent stare.

Feeling curiously unnerved by the sight of Devon Blake, her instructions were curt. "Well, don't just stand there. I need my horse saddled."

He did not seem surprised by her impudence; it was almost as though he'd expected it. In minutes her horse was prepared and Devon stood alongside it as he waited to help her up.

She recalled what had happened the last time their fingers touched, and the memory stirred something in her, deep down inside. But just as quickly as it had come, she brushed the thought away and approached her horse.

Without a word he helped her up, and Claire refused to even acknowledge the strange tingling she once again felt as he clasped his powerful hand around hers. The contact lasted mere seconds, yet as soon as she could Claire yanked her hand away. She dug her heels against her horse's flank and thundered out of the stable.

Devon watched her until she turned the corner and was out of sight. He was not caught off guard by her disdain toward him, despite the praise the other servants had given her. They'd do or say anything to keep their jobs. In truth, Lady Claire Rushmoor had been exactly as he knew all wealthy people to be—rude, condescending, and scornful of anyone outside of their class. She was no different than all the others, Devon thought. The only curious thing was why he found that realization oddly disappointing.

Hyde Park was, on that particular late afternoon, largely unoccupied. Claire rode in peace through the thousands of lush green trees that made up the vast park in the heart of central London. A chorus of chirping birds kept her company, along with squirrels and moles scurrying across the ground. She even spotted a hedgehog rolled into a protective, prickly ball. She'd no doubt covered several miles on her ride, and the distance and time away from home had eased away the anger that had led to her solitary outing. Claire knew she should not allow herself to be angry with her mother. Louisa only wanted what she thought was best for Claire, and should not be blamed for failing to realize that mother and daughter had very different ideas on what kind of man made the ideal husband. Louisa's only demands were that Claire's prospective husband hail from a respected family, be a member of peerage, and have enough money to maintain her daughter's established position in society. Claire herself desired such qualities—after all, didn't every woman?—but she also longed for a man who was kind, generous, honest, perhaps even funny, all qualities that Louisa deemed "frivolous and unnecessary." But for Claire they were the qualities that mattered most, and she imagined a dismal life with a man who lacked them.

Unexpectedly, thoughts of Devon Blake entered her mind. She remembered how he had stood in the stable, silently reacting to the commands she'd barked at him. Of course, Claire mused, that's what servants were supposed to do—serve. Still, it wasn't necessary for her to have been so petulant toward him. He, after all, was not the reason for her anger. For a moment Claire entertained the notion of apologizing to him, but really, why should she? On the rare occasions when she had become angry with Marie, she had never asked for the servant's forgiveness. What was it about Devon that made her even entertain such a thought, much less seriously think about acting on it?

On the other hand, she was appalled to realize that her thoughts were along the same line as Philip Westbury's. Now there was a man who would never stoop so low as to even speak to a servant, other than his valet, much less apologize to him. And because Claire had grown to abhor everything Philip stood for, on impulse she decided to do just what he wouldn't.

Immediately she turned her horse around and took the straightest route toward home. Within fifteen minutes she had arrived, and just as a good groom was expected to do, Devon was waiting to assist her. Ignoring the familiar tingle she felt when he helped her down, Claire forged ahead with what she wanted to say.

"Ah, Mr. Blake, there is something I need to mention to you."

Devon's left eyebrow slowly arched upward, the only indication of his surprise. He leveled his gaze on her upturned face and waited for her to speak.

His stare left her momentarily speechless, and for the briefest of seconds Claire forgot what she'd wanted to say. She found it necessary to look away from his hypnotic eyes, so instead of speaking directly to him, she found her words aimed at her horse.

"I . . . well, I believe . . . that is, when I came into the stable to have you saddle my horse, I perhaps acted somewhat less than polite."

"Yes." It was impossible to tell if he was agreeing with her, or merely encouraging her to continue. She decided it had to be the latter.

"So anyway, I suppose that it would be fitting of me to offer an, well, an apology."

Her effort was rewarded with complete silence.

"Do you have nothing to say in response?" Had she somehow not realized that he was a simpleton?

He remained silent, as if considering the words she had just spoken. His unwavering gaze seemed to bore through her restrictive clothing. For several moments he leisurely inspected every inch of Claire's body, and she instinctively crossed her arms in front of her, as if to shield the very thing his roving eyes sought. Then, apparently deciding there was no need to look any further, he murmured in a low, magnetic voice, "Ye can do better than that."

Had she heard him correctly? "I beg your pardon?"

"Ye heard what I said, m'lady."

Claire was dumbfounded. "But what exactly does that mean?"

Rather than answer, Devon took a step forward and narrowed the gap between their bodies. The widening of Claire's eyes and soft pout of her lips betrayed her attempt at nonchalance toward his actions. She'd not met men like him before, and it was obvious that she was both frightened and enthralled. He stood so close to her that she could feel his warm breath caress her ear as he whispered, "It means that ye're a crafty lass, capable of doing better than the babble ye gave me just now."

He towered above her, forcing her to look directly in his eyes. But instead of being fearful, she felt elated. Her senses came vibrantly alive. The heady aroma of his raw masculinity perfumed the air around her, and she could feel the heat radiating from his body. He was no priggish dandy trying to charm her with clever wit, but instead the very essence of pure male power. Without realizing it, she'd momentarily stopped breathing, but that did nothing to calm her racing heart. For one wild moment she wondered if he was going to kiss her, but then, just as suddenly as he'd walked toward her, he abruptly did an about-face and walked away, leaving her with unfulfilled desire.

Without thinking, Claire began to follow him. "Where are you going?" she asked, not realizing until she spoke that she needed to catch her breath.

He turned back around but stood planted where he'd stopped. "Yer apologies need improvement, m'lady," he said. "After ye've taken some lessons, ye know where to find me."

Claire was so struck by Devon's audacity that for several moments she stood rooted to the ground, unable to comprehend just exactly what had happened. Had he really said what she thought he did? Lessons?! Of all the rude, insulting, unforgivable nerve! Her fury made her actually stomp the ground, and punctuate the gesture with an audible, "Oh!" She spun around and stormed out of the stable, mentally kicking herself for being such a fool. How could she possibly have thought that apologizing to a servant was appropriate behavior? There was good reason why his class and her class were worlds apart, and there was no way she'd ever again try bridging the gap.

Claire charged into the house and up the stairs to her room, feeling just as infuriated as she had when she'd left. Although the sun had not yet set, rooms in the east wing were already growing dark. As Claire opened her bedroom door, she paused to light a match and touch it to the table lamp. A soft glow immediately filled the room with warmth, but the illumination did nothing to lighten Claire's spirits.

She flung open the French doors that led to the balcony and basked in the cool wind that ruffled through her hair and cleansed her spirit. If the horrible truth were told, she admitted, taking a seat outdoors, despite everything Devon had said the thought of his kisses sent her pulse racing. He was so unlike any man she'd ever met. He was uncultivated and rude, with an aura of danger lingering about him. Indeed, Claire realized, Devon was dangerous. Dangerous because, unlikely as it seemed, she was attracted to him. She had wanted him to kiss her, to take her into his arms and hold her against his muscled chest. The thought of it even now sent shivers down her spine, and in that moment Claire understood that she had to make certain to smother that attraction for good. How could she focus on finding a

suitor by the end of the season if her attention was
distracted by a willful servant?

Claire made her decision. She would go to the stables
tomorrow morning, right after breakfast, and speak with
Devon. It was essential that he know his place—her future depended on it.

The horses were fed, fresh hay lined their stalls, and
everything within the stable was neat and organized. Everything, that was, aside from Devon's muddled thoughts.
Having finished his chores and without anyone requiring
his service, he had ample time to review the earlier conversation between himself and Claire. That is, if one
could even call it a conversation. She'd fumbled around,
clearly awkward and in unfamiliar territory, trying to offer him an apology. Even the memory of it made him
cringe. How beneath her it had been. What effort it must
have taken for the haughty princess to make amends with
the lowly toad. No small wonder, Devon reassured himself, that he had, at that moment, abandoned his mission
of befriending her. Instead he had responded in anger.
That age-old anger still seething within him whenever
he felt belittled by the upper class.

Yet . . . was that really what Claire had done? Had
she been purposely trying to insult him? Yes! his mind
shouted. But a small part of Devon remained uncon-
vinced. Looked at in a different light, at least the lass
had made the attempt to apologize. Whether her words
and attitude met with Devon's approval were another
matter entirely.

He rose from the wooden crate on which he'd been
sitting to stretch his long legs and try clearing his head.
No use in trying to make sense out of something beyond
his understanding. Who knew what went on in the mind
of the pampered upper class? Certainly not Devon Blake,

he admitted with a wry grin. The best thing for him to do was to remember Joshua and his whole reason for being here. If he wanted Claire to begin trusting and confiding in him, he'd better bear his mates' instructions in mind to be polite and charming, ingratiate himself into the household, and by all means keep his anger under control.

An unpleasant scowl was etched across his face; his stubborn posture dared her to repeat what she had said. But that defiant sneer of his was merely the icing on the cake to a situation that had gone from bad to worse.

After what had happened the day before, she had been nervous about seeing him again. But the more she told herself she was doing the right thing, the more determined she became about doing it. This morning she awoke early, rushed through a quick breakfast before anyone else was even out of bed, gotten dressed by herself (Marie was among those still sleeping), and come to the stable. There she'd found him, doing morning chores. And although she had several times gone over in her mind what she wanted to say, when she saw him putting fresh hay in the horses' stalls, she momentarily forgot every word.

He wore tight black buckskin trousers that perfectly complemented his muscular legs. On his feet were sturdy leather boots. He had yet to put on the vertically striped waistcoat that was standard uniform for all grooms; instead, he wore only a sleeveless white cotton shirt. And it was the shirt that had Claire so reluctantly fascinated. Although it was early the day had already grown warm. That, combined with strenuous physical labor, had produced a fine sheen of sweat that glistened all over Devon's hard-working body. His shirt's lack of sleeves exposed his tan, muscular forearms. And the sweat had caused the back of his shirt to cling to his damp skin, outlining rippling muscles. Again and again he used his pitchfork to scoop up the straw and toss it into the stalls. And every time he repeated the motion, Claire helplessly marveled at his perfect physique.

She would have thought she'd be repulsed by the sight of a profusely sweating servant. Instead, she was captivated. It was pure male power in its rawest form, an exhibition for her eyes only. As she watched him her mouth went dry, while a curious, unexplainable warmth flushed through her body. When Claire realized that the warmth originated from between her legs, she felt her cheeks become inflamed. And she was in that mortified state when Devon became aware of her presence and turned around.

Her embarrassment could not have been more acute. As she did her best to compose herself, to her complete horror she caught a glimpse of a smile touch the right corner of Devon's lips. Was he laughing at her? The thought brought with it a pinch of anger, and for that Claire was grateful, for it helped her collect her nerves.

"I've come to have a word with you," she informed him.

His response was his usual stare, but because she expected it she was not taken aback. At least he appeared to be listening.

"I realize that you're new here, brought in at the last minute as I understand. And it appears you have not been properly informed of the rules of correct behavior among servants and masters and mistresses of the house. Thus I have decided that I will not dismiss you for your impertinent behavior, but instead will grant you a chance to redeem yourself."

It was here where the scowl had begun. His eyebrows came together as they lowered on his face. His eyes narrowed; his jaw grew tense. He cleared his throat, then said to her in a quiet, even tone, "Redeem myself?"

His reaction was so menacing that it caused her to take an uncertain step backward. "Well, yes. I am giving you the chance to learn your rightful place so that what occurred yesterday will not happen again."

Now the scowl was full-blown, and it almost seemed as though he sneered at her. He tossed the pitchfork aside and leaned against the wall. He crossed his arms against his chest and cocked his head to one side as he peered at her through narrowed eyes. Clearly, he did not agree that redemption was needed. "I'm surprised to hear that," he said.

"Hear what?" Claire answered, already nervous about his answer.

He pushed himself away from the wall and took a step toward her. "That ye want me to stop something ye so obviously enjoyed."

What an audacious, self-centered, insolent knave! Claire sputtered with fury at his blatant disrespect, simultaneously horrified that she had been so transparent. A dozen remonstrances sprang to her lips, but as he came toward her once again she found that the words were hopelessly stuck. Again he moved forward, forcing Claire to step back. Her mind was quick to point out that now, without question, he must be dismissed, but her audacious body rebelled against the thought. As before, his nearness made her heart beat at twice its normal speed, and thoughts normally clear in her mind suddenly became muddled.

He took another step forward; she countered by moving back. He moved toward her again; she took two steps in the opposite direction. His stalking continued and she had just decided that it would be in her best interest to turn around and run, when the unthinkable happened. Her foot reached behind her to move farther away from his insistent advances when the small of her back came in contact with something very hard and unyielding—the wall. She was trapped.

Realizing his unexpected luck, Devon moved forward to seize the opportunity. He placed his hands on either side of her head and moved his body so close that there was no chance for escape. The powerful scent of his masculinity permeated her nostrils. She could smell the saltiness from his sweat, leather from the saddles . . . and something more. There was a deeper, more personal smell that was uniquely his own and was so purely masculine it made Claire's head swim. Her legs trembled while her lungs fought for air. All her years of proper training and decent, ladylike behavior went flying out the stable doors. His sea green eyes had darkened to the sultry color of midnight, and she felt engulfed by his magnetic stare.

"What about if I tell ye how beautiful ye look right now?" he breathed into her ear. "So beautiful ye fair take my breath away. Would I then be redeeming myself?"

"I . . . well . . ." It was useless to even attempt an answer, not when she could only marvel at his sleek, lean body standing in front of her, scant inches away. She felt his warm breath upon her cheek. And then his hand, strong enough to control the powerful thoroughbreds housed within the stable, was gently caressing her back. As before, his touch sent shivers coursing through her body. His gaze locked with hers for the barest of instants, then his head dipped forward to block out her view as his warm, moist lips captured hers.

She didn't realize he intended to kiss her until just before he did so. By then it was too late. She could no more have stopped him than she could have stopped a stampede. And, Lord forgive her, she didn't want to.

The instant his mouth made contact with hers, the rigidity in Claire's body evaporated. His lips were soft, softer than she could have ever expected, and the lightness with which he placed them against hers dissolved any strength that her legs might have had. His intoxicating smell invaded her senses. Her eyes fluttered shut as she sank against his body, and she was both startled and grateful for the hardness of his muscles. In a dreamy haze, she placed her arms around him. He used the opportunity to draw her even closer and then deepened the kiss. With his tongue he gently pried her lips apart, then sensuously tasted the inside of her mouth. Claire faltered for only a moment, but was helpless to resist the waves of sensation crashing through her body. This wasn't right, and it was by no means proper, but oh! how those thoughts seemed so meaningless right now. Her tongue willingly met his in a lustful duel, and the feeling was so exquisite that she could not suppress the small cry that escaped her lips.

Devon's left hand continued its exploration of the sensual curves along Claire's back, while his right hand caressed her face. His thumb traced a path along her delicate jawline, then he tipped her head backward so he could savor the creamy softness of her long, elegant neck. He kissed her chin, then the base of her throat. Her racing pulse excited him. She seemed lost in the pleasures she received from his touch, and her innocent responsiveness spurred him on. His kisses along her neck continued, and his mouth was approaching the beginning rise of her breasts. His left hand came around to caress her side, as his mouth descended lower, and lower still. At that point, the warning bells clanged.

The sudden realization of what she was doing caused Claire first to stiffen, then pull away from Devon's body as if she'd been burned. For a moment she stood, not saying a word, her startled expression framed by the tendrils of blond hair pulled free from Devon's embrace.

With short, quick strokes she straightened her dress and smoothed down her hair, then turned and ran from the stable. She didn't stop running until she stood before her bedroom door, despite the looks of curiosity she received from the servants. Frantically she turned the doorknob and locked the door behind her. She leaned against the bedpost to calm her breathing before allowing herself to think about what had just happened. What in the world had overcome her? How could she have allowed him to do that? Her mind was whirling like a dervish as she tried to figure it out, but there seemed to be no logical explanation. For some reason, unbeknownst to her, she had allowed herself to be seduced by a servant.

She placed her hand upon her heart to assure herself that she was indeed calming down, then sat upon her bed. She longed to go out on the balcony but did not want to risk being seen by anyone until she had her wits about her.

You stupid, stupid girl, she chided herself. What you've just done was pure folly, truly an act of temporary madness. You will never, *ever* do such a thing again. You will avoid him at all costs. You will not speak to him, and you will certainly not allow yourself to be alone with him. Hope that no one saw you, Claire Rushmoor, and do not ever be such a fool again. Then, not quite knowing what else to do, Claire knelt down on her knees, clasped her hands together, and in a rare moment of religious fervor, prayed for strength.

Seven

"He's a complete bore, isn't he?"

"Lilia!" Claire took a last swallow of her morning tea and then rose from the breakfast table as she cast a sharp eye toward her wayward cousin. "I've told you before that such talk is not appropriate. Please restrain yourself from making impolite comments about people."

"Even Lord Townsend?"

"Especially Lord Townsend. After all, he's been very kind to the family." Her attention became distracted. "Now where did Marie put my riding bonnet?"

Lilia couldn't hide the mischievous look in her eyes. "But Devon says men like Lord Townsend could bore a statue to sleep."

Claire whirled around to face her cousin, horror filling the caverns of her chest. Good Lord above, had Lilia seen her? "Devon?" she blurted out, unable to camouflage the fright in her voice. "And just what would you know about a servant's opinion?"

"He and I were talking about Lord Townsend, only a couple of days ago. He poked fun at Lord Townsend's outrageous clothes," Lilia said, the memory delighting her, "and about the way he points his nose up into the air. As if he's always sniffing something distasteful."

"Lilia!" Despite an insane urge to laugh from both mirth and relief, Claire maintained her composure, even managing to cloud her face with anger. "I have told you

time and again not to speak with the servants. Now
you're telling me that you have gone out and done exactly what I warned you against?"

A quiet nod was her answer. "Kindly explain what
made you do such a thing."

Lilia laid down the spoon she'd been holding with
frustration. "I don't have anyone to talk to, Claire. You
told me I can't talk to the servants, but there's no one
else around but them. You're always going out calling,
and it's fine when I can come along, but more often than
not I'm told to stay home. I get so utterly bored here."
Were those tears forming in Lilia's eyes? "One day I
decided I wanted to go riding. I went to the stable to
fetch a horse, and Devon was in there, feeding them. I
told him what I wanted . . ."

Claire braced herself for the worse. Now she'd hear
that Lilia had been going out riding. "But Devon
wouldn't let me."

"Wouldn't let you?"

Lilia sniffed. "That's right. He said I'd get in trouble
for doing something I knew I shouldn't. At first I was
angry, but then we started talking and he was so very
funny, so I've gone to talk to him sometimes." Now Lilia
appeared a little meek. "That's all."

Claire shook her head in disbelief. Lilia's tale was
almost impossible to accept. Especially the part about
Devon having a sense of humor. He's about as funny
as Philip Westbury, she thought. Then again, what did
she know? As much as she did not wish to admit it,
his observations about Philip had amused her. And she
never really talked with Devon. Their only conversation,
if it could be labeled as such, was when she'd stormed
into the stable last week to explain to him his rightful
place within the household. Remembering how that had
turned out, she pushed the memory aside. No need for
her to be dwelling on inappropriate thoughts of Devon's

kisses when she was in the midst of disciplining her wayward cousin.

"Listen, Lilia. I'm sorry that we've been excluding you. I'll speak with Aunt Louisa and see what we can do about taking you along with us more often." A triumphant smile crossed Lilia's face, but Claire remained stern. "In the meantime, you are not to be hanging about the stable chatting with Mr. Blake. Not only is he a servant, but he is a male servant," as if Lilia hadn't noticed, "and it isn't right for you to be alone with him. Decorum, Lilia. Remember decorum."

Her cousin happily nodded, and Claire felt it appropriate to resume the search for her missing riding bonnet. After all, Philip was expected to arrive at any minute.

If Philip was anything, it was prompt. Precisely at 11:00, his expected arrival time, Claire heard the door chimes ring and knew that her riding companion awaited her. At least she had located her bonnet. Now she tied it smartly under her chin and walked into the parlor where, as always, Philip was doing his best to be charming and witty to her mother. Louisa devoured his every word, growing more intrigued with him every time they met.

Resisting the urge to roll her eyes, Claire waited for a pause in Philip's animated story to greet him a pleasant morning.

He turned to her with a gigantic smile. "And good morning to you, Lady Rushmoor. You're looking radiant."

Good heavens. "Thank you, Lord Townsend. Shall we go?"

Louisa was less than successful at hiding her disappointment. "Claire, Lord Townsend was in the middle of telling me a fascinating story about his latest sojourn to Drury Lane."

"Oh, Lady Bedington, you are so kind to honor me

with interest in my trite little adventures. But perhaps we shall suspend the intrigue until next time we meet, hmm?"

Louisa acquiesced with an easy nod. "I'm already looking forward to it."

Grateful that she could leave this conversation, which had become unbearable, Claire led Philip out the front door. Thinking that they were going for a carriage ride, Claire was surprised to see Philip's white stallion tied up alone.

"Oh, Lady Rushmoor. Please forgive me for not bringing my chaise. The brakes do not seem to be working properly and I feared for your safety."

Claire ignored his obvious attempt at chivalry. "Very well. I'll have one of the horses saddled and we'll go riding instead of driving."

An appreciative smile cracked Philip's thin lips. "I knew you'd be accommodating."

Philip took hold of Claire's arm as he escorted her over to the stable. As was his custom, he began chattering about one thing or another that he'd been doing since they last saw each other, and as was her custom, Claire, for the most part, surreptitiously ignored him.

As they entered the stable, she was surprised to see her favorite horse, Raphael, already prepared. And standing beside the horse and holding the reins was Devon. Clearly, he'd been expecting her.

In light of the fact that she had gone to great measure to avoid him since their previous encounter, Claire did not anticipate conversation between them. Thus she was surprised when Devon began speaking.

"Marie came out a few minutes ago and told me to saddle yer horse." So that's how he knew she was coming. His voice then dropped to a low pitch, intending that only Claire should hear his next words. "The sunlight in yer hair right sparkles like a jewel. Ye look even more fetching outside than ye did in the stable."

Claire's cheeks burned like the sunshine to which he had referred, and his words stopped her dead in her tracks. His behavior was beyond scandalous, yet Claire was intrigued by Devon's audacity. Never before had she met a man like him. He defied the restricted boundaries of polite behavior, and he was brazen enough not to care. An utter enigma. Philip, meanwhile, who'd not heard Devon's words but had observed him speaking to Claire, had feelings of an entirely different sort.

"Why, you disrespectful, insolent clod!" he hissed through gritted teeth. "How dare you presume to speak directly with Lady Rushmoor and demand her attention. Have you any idea how preposterous you are? Have you? Have you!" The veins in Philip's neck stood out like binding cord, and his face had turned an alarming shade of purple. Claire knew she must take hold of the situation at once.

"Lord Townsend," she spoke his name in a soothing tone. "I'm sure Mr. Blake meant no disrespect. He was merely warning me that Raphael appeared skittish this morning so that I would take caution when riding him. 'Twas nothing more than that."

The fact that Claire appeared to be taking Devon's side did nothing to placate Philip; nevertheless, remembering the sizable dowry she held, he clamped his tongue shut from further comment. He mounted his horse and waited while Devon assisted Claire onto Raphael. As soon as she was settled she slapped the horse's reins and was gone, hurrying from the mansion as if competing in a race. Devon watched her rush away, sensing the reason for her haste. A ghost of a smile crossed his lips.

As Claire and Lord Townsend entered the park, Claire remained silent as she pondered what had happened. At once she felt ashamed by both her reaction to Devon's flattery and her own lies to Philip on Devon's behalf. Imagine her, steeped in years of genteel upbringing, becoming flustered by the groom's assistant! On the surface the idea was preposterous. But, her mind insisted, there was more to Devon than what showed on the surface. There was something about him, something that seemed to keep affecting Claire whenever she was near him. Well, whatever it was, she would just have to ignore it. Anyway, the most likely explanation was that Devon was merely different from other men she'd met. He had a crude way of speaking. He almost never used the proper form of address. His behavior bordered on discourteous, and he rudely stared. But for all the negatives, she found his differences oddly refreshing.

Feeling satisfied with her self-analysis, she glanced over at Philip. She hoped he had calmed down by now. Unfortunately, it was not to be.

"Of all the inexcusable, impertinent behavior I have ever seen in my life!" he began sputtering. "It's just like those filthy Irish to be so—"

"Lord Townsend, please. Don't upset yourself so. I want us to enjoy our ride."

Her request fell on deaf ears as Philip's tirade continued.

"Frankly, Lady Rushmoor, I am astounded that you would lower yourself to even employing a wretch such as that stable boy, much less speaking to him!"

"It's not necessary to insult him so."

Philip's eyes widened with horror. "Don't tell me that you're now defending him? Good heavens, Lady Rushmoor, pardon me, but have you lost your mind? The conduct of that servant was utterly atrocious, and you're sitting there supporting it?" A purple hue was returning to his face.

"No, I'm not supporting it, I just—"

"Then tell me you dismissed him immediately."

"No, I didn't dismiss him. I did not feel—"

"Of course! Your gentle manners wouldn't stand for such a distasteful job. When we return I'll do it for you."

Talk about impertinence! Claire fumed inwardly. "Lord Townsend, please. You're letting this matter upset you too much, and I fear you're not enjoying our ride. Now, please. Don't give it another thought. It's not worth your time."

Philip seemed to consider her words, and Claire punctuated them by flashing him her most charming smile. "I insist."

He relented. "Very well. How can I refuse a request coming from such a beautiful mouth?"

She resisted a shiver. "You're much too kind."

"Never, for you, Lady Rushmoor." He gave her a look that Claire assumed was meant to be endearing. She found it repugnant.

"Besides, you're right. Why would I want to spend even one more second of our precious time together dwelling upon someone lower than a snake's belly?"

He appears to have his old charm back, Claire thought wryly. She tried ignoring Philip's last comment, telling herself that she shouldn't feel offended by his assessment of a servant, no matter how uncouth it sounded. Why should she care? But, unexplainable as it was, she did.

After weeks of continuous working, Devon at last had his first day off. He wasted no time in changing back to the clothes he had worn on that first day, then left the stately Rushmoor mansion for the more familiar grounds of the impoverished East End. Although his pockets were filled with more coins than he'd ever had at one time, Devon still resisted hiring a hackney to take him home. It seemed such a foolish waste. Instead he walked down Piccadilly as fast as he could, down Regent, and over to

Pall Mall. Once he hit Charring Cross, he felt more comfortable.

Although he'd been away for a time, the sights he knew hadn't changed a bit. Costermongers were everywhere, announcing to everyone what they had for sale. Barefoot children ran through the unpaved streets, splashing mud wherever they stepped. Filthy matchgirls and orange girls occupied every corner, playing with mangy stray dogs. Having been recently surrounded in luxury, Devon now saw the sights before him with brand-new eyes. And although he'd always been disgusted by the filth in which he lived, it was more apparent to him now than ever before.

He didn't dwell on the bitterness that threatened to overcome him. Instead he strode forward until he came to No. 7 Cloak Street, address of The Night Star. He took the stairs two at a time and pushed the door open. The inside darkness demanded that he halt for a moment to let his eyes adjust, but as soon as they did Devon headed for the basement.

The sight that greeted him was much the same as when he had left. Joshua was still lying motionless on the cot, and Jonathan was keeping watch. When his friend noticed he'd entered the room, he rose to greet him.

"Devon." Jonathan clapped him on the back by way of a greeting, then quickly led him to Joshua's bedside.

Devon was shocked by his best friend's appearance. Although the bruises on his face were now nearly faded, Joshua seemed to have lost at least a stone since Devon had last seen him. His cheeks and eyes were sunken; his skin was ghostly pale. Despite obvious shivering, a thin sheen of sweat covered his entire body.

"Has he been unconscious the whole time?"

Jonathan nodded solemnly. "Almost. He wakes up now and again, but he don't seem to know what's going on. We been feeding him the broth that Sally brings down, but it's bloody hard to get him to swallow it." Jonathan paused, then said what was foremost on his mind. "I don't think our bloke's gonna make it, Devon."

It was confirmation of Devon's worst fears. Still, he could not accept the words. "Ye're speaking filthy lies to me."

"Nay. Ye know I'm not." Devon shook his head to refute what Jonathan was saying, but his friend pressed on. "C'mon, man. Look at him. He's been lying on that stinking cot for over a month, and in all that time he's never really woke up. He just groans once in awhile, and he's lost a bloody lot of weight. He's starting to get sores on his body, and some of them are already infected." Jonathan waved his hands in the air. "I think it's the damn flies what's doing it."

He's probably right, Devon thought. The filthy things were everywhere, and they seemed to have a particular attraction for Joshua's open sores. He walked over to the cot and brushed them away, but after circling awhile they were right back where they had been. Devon's heart clenched in grief at the sight of his best friend, but his overwhelming emotion was anger. Anger that they were forced to stand helplessly by while infected bedsores rotted Joshua's body. Anger that whoever had done this to him was still walking the streets. Anger that no one but him and his friends seemed to care. Devon slammed his fist against the cot's hard wooden frame, searching for a way to release his pent-up rage.

Jonathan stood quietly by, understanding what his friend was feeling, then pulled on his shirtsleeve to draw Devon away. "Listen, mate. We found something in Joshua's shirt pocket that might help us find whoever did this to him."

"What is it?"

Jonathan opened his hand to reveal what looked to be

the button from a man's shirt. Devon picked it up. Clearly, it was no ordinary button. Even in the dim light of the basement its rich luster shone. It was most certainly made entirely of gold, then polished to be as reflective as a mirror. The most distinctive marking was the engraved front. With infinite patience a master craftsman had painstakingly etched onto the button's tiny surface a detailed scene depicting the Parliament building. It was almost a piece of art, this button, yet what kind of man would wear such a thing? Surely someone who enjoyed attention, for the button's flashiness would have made it a conversation piece. And definitely someone very wealthy. The button alone probably cost more than what Devon's mother made in an entire year.

He turned toward Jonathan. "Tell me again where ye found this."

"It was in Joshua's shirt pocket. He must have torn it off the bastard during the fight and then put it in his pocket. Maybe he was hoping it would help us find whoever did this." Devon's only response was a quick nod.

"Clive was the one who noticed it," Jonathan continued. "We had turned Joshua over, and he kept groaning like he had pains. At first we didn't pay no attention, 'cause he's always groaning. But he kept it up and kept it up, and when Clive went over to have himself a look, he noticed a bump in Joshua's pocket. Turns out it was this button what made him groan like that. 'Twas pressing into his chest."

Ironic, Devon thought. The rotten cur had continued to hurt Joshua even after he had beat him. "I'm not sure what good it'll do us."

Jonathan was surprised. "Why not? There's not a lot who can afford buttons like this, and they all live in the area where ye're working. Ye just have to keep yer eyes open, mate."

Devon shook his head. "Nay. Whoever wore this had it made for him."

"At one of those fancy shops on the West End, I'll wager."

"Aye. Just the kind of places where we'd never be allowed in."

Jonathan's eyes widened with an idea. "But wait a minute, Devon. Ye got them new clothes with this job o' yours. Wouldn't they work for getting ye in? That way ye could talk to the tailors and find out which one of 'em made that button."

"Not in a million years. The only new clothes I got are for a bloody servant. Them tailors would know it in a minute and kick me right out on my arse. Anyway, who's to say the buttons were made here? The bastard might've even had them imported." Jonathan said nothing, angered by the obstacles they faced.

"The buttons like this one are probably only on the shirt he wore that night, and he's not going to go around with a torn shirt. He's thrown it out by now."

Jonathan looked dejected as he silently agreed that their once promising lead didn't look quite as good as it first had. Devon, too, was quiet. The muscles in the back of his jaw tensed, the only visible sign of his fury. There had to be a way to find the wretch, and he would do whatever it took.

Jonathan's voice finally broke the silence. "What have ye found out at the house?"

"Nothing." The dejection in his voice was not easily missed. "In all this time I haven't even spoken to her about that night."

"But ye know who it is?"

"Aye. But that's all I know. They have their rules, ye see. The kings and queens of the palace don't speak to the lowly servants, and we don't speak to them."

Jonathan was surprised at Devon's bitter tone. "Well,

of course, man. Like Samuel said, it'll take time. What did ye think? That ye'd just walk in the place, have a seat in the library, and tell the butler that ye're needing to see the lady of the house?"

The last remark made Devon smile. With that simple statement, Jonathan had managed to put everything in perspective. He was right. Perhaps in his anxiousness to get back to Joshua, Devon had had unrealistic expectations about the ease of getting the information he wanted. Of course, dealing with that irritating, perplexing Claire Rushmoor hadn't made things any easier.

"Ye're right. I was just hoping she'd be easier to deal with, I guess."

"A real priss, eh?"

"Nay, not a priss exactly." Bloody hell, was he defending her? "She just isn't around much."

Jonathan flashed a knowing grin. "Well, ye'll find a way. Ye know ye've always had luck where the wenches are concerned."

His friend's use of the crude term to describe Claire strangely irritated Devon, but he ignored the feeling. Instead he spoke a few words to Joshua, hoping against hope that his friend actually heard them, then went upstairs to see his mum.

Eight

The coast was clear. As silently as she could manage while wearing heeled riding boots, Lilia Chatterton crept through the darkened hallways and eased her way downstairs. It was still early, so she anticipated a clean getaway. Still, one could never be too sure. She took a hasty look around to assure that she was still alone, then crept through the foyer and went out the front door.

Normally she would have gone out the back door, which was closer to the stable, but she knew the cooks would already be up, and there was a greater chance of being discovered by them near the back. Of course, she wouldn't even be doing what she was doing if Cousin Claire had kept to her promise and made sure that Lilia was taken along to more events. Perhaps there was something on Claire's mind, Lilia thought, for her cousin had been acting a little out of character lately. She seemed much more introspective, as if something was bothering her. Still, to Lilia's way of thinking that didn't mean Claire should back out on her promise. She'd told Lilia that she'd speak with Aunt Louisa and make sure Lilia wasn't left at home by herself too often. But by the way things had been going lately, Lilia knew Claire had yet to do so. And that made her just a little bit mad. Maybe if she saw Lilia doing something she had warned her against, Claire would keep her promise.

And so her logic, misplaced though it might be, had

brought Lilia into the stable this fine early morning. She was determined to go for a short ride by herself. If anything, at least that action would get her attention, something that Lilia felt she had sorely lacked.

Inside the stable the air was still and the horses were quiet. So far, so good. She stepped carefully over to Claire's favorite horse, Raphael, and led the animal out of his stall. Next Lilia went over to where the saddles were kept. There were so many different kinds hanging along the wall that she felt slightly intimidated by the sight. Nevertheless, undaunted, she chose the saddle that looked the smallest, and therefore lightest, and pulled it off the wall. It was still quite heavy, and its unexpected weight caught Lilia by surprise. She dropped the saddle into the closest pile of hay. Luckily the noise she made was minimal and did not appear to have awakened anyone.

After resting a moment Lilia drew a footstool up to the horse, climbed atop it, then heaved the saddle onto the animal's broad back. The exertion caused moisture to form across her forehead, but Lilia refused to give up. She stepped down from the footstool, grabbed the girth, pulled it under Raphael's belly and tightly buckled it on the other side. Lilia stood back to examine her work, and noticed that the saddle did not look quite the same as when the grooms readied the horses. Oh well. Perhaps they'd simply used a different saddle. Surely that had to be it. Lilia then turned her attention to the bridle. As with the saddles, there were a number to choose from, but the series of leather straps that composed the bridle looked far more complicated than Lilia had anticipated. Deciding she could just as easily hold on to Raphael's mane, she opted to forgo further complications.

Suddenly there were sounds of stirring. Knowing she must get moving or her efforts would be halted, Lilia jumped onto Raphael's back with the help of the footstool. She jammed her feet into the stirrups and slapped her knees against the horse's side to get the animal moving. Raphael exhaled an agitated whinny, but nevertheless obeyed Lilia's command. The horse began walking out the stable door, but unexpectedly his own movements seemed to agitate him. He skittishly trotted around in no particular direction, and it took all of Lilia's efforts just to aim Raphael in the direction of the park. With uncertain steps, the horse moved forward.

After an entire night spent sleeping only fitfully, Devon finally decided to give up the effort. He knew himself too well, and it was no use trying any longer. Although the sun was just barely peaking above the horizon, he decided to get an early start on his chores. By the time breakfast was ready, he thought, he'd be halfway finished.

He stepped outside and took half a minute to enjoy the peace and quiet. At this hour the only ones awake were the cooks; otherwise, the place was still. Or, was it? Devon cocked an ear toward the stable and listened. Was someone up and about already? If so, he'd better hurry, because no doubt they were needing his services.

As he entered the stable his keen eyes took a quick sweep of the area, and at once he noticed that Raphael was missing. Had there been a thief? He was instantly on guard and raced to the stable's back door to see if he could spot anyone. There, heading toward the park, was Raphael. Even at this distance he could tell the horse was provoked. Was the rider abusing him? He could not tell who sat atop the horse, but spent no time in speculation. Without hesitation Devon grabbed a saddle, bit, and bridle and sprinted to Kendal Rushmoor's fastest horse, Lightning. In seconds the horse was ready, and Devon expertly leaped atop him and sped toward the would-be thief. In no time he came upon the horse and rider, only to discover that the suspected thief was not a thief at all, but instead, Lilia. Certainly she should not have been out here, riding alone. He had warned her against it once, but the little rebel evidently decided to do it anyway. Now she seemed to be not only disobeying rules, but agitating the horse as well. Again and again Raphael whinnied and bucked, apparently trying to rid himself of the pint-sized rider. It was easy to see why. In her inexperience with horses Lilia had neglected to place a saddle blanket between Raphael's sensitive skin and the rough leather of the new saddle. It was chafing Raphael's skin, and the horse was doing everything he could to rid himself of the irritant.

Devon drew himself alongside Lilia and called her name. When she saw who it was, Lilia gratefully called back to him. "Devon! I'm glad you're here. I wanted to take a ride, but I guess Raphael doesn't like mornings. He's been fighting me ever since I—"

Everything happened at once. By jostling Lilia around, Raphael caused the girl's heeled boot to repeatedly slap against his tender flanks. The last time it happened the boot had managed to tear the horse's skin, and the pain became unbearable. With a thunderous whinny Raphael kicked up his back heels and galloped away with blinding speed. The horse was out of control, and it was only with her fierce tenacity that Lilia managed to hang on. With all her might she gripped Raphael's mane as screams of terror ripped from her throat.

Horse and rider raced haphazardly through the park, barely avoiding the clusters of trees that threatened to stop them at every turn. Raphael's eyes were wild and unfocused, and Lilia knew in her heart that disaster was imminent. Over and over she screamed Devon's name.

As soon as he saw Raphael take off, Devon and Lightning immediately followed. It was no problem for Lightning to catch up, but Raphael's chaotic rampage made it difficult to run alongside him. "Hang on, Lilia!" Devon yelled, doing his best to calm her down. But she was too frightened to be placated. Devon could see the tears of fear streaming down Lilia's face, and his mission took on a new sense of urgency.

Both horses finally came upon a relative clearing, and for a few seconds Raphael headed in a more or less straight direction. Ahead of them, however, were fresh clusters of trees, and Raphael was headed straight toward them. Devon seized his chance. He pressed Lightning forward until the horse was directly alongside Raphael. Then Devon's left hand let go of its rein as he reached out and grabbed Lilia off her runaway horse.

The rescue came none too soon. Raphael did keep racing in the direction of the trees, and although he managed to avoid running directly into one, a low-hanging branch would have easily knocked Lilia straight to the ground.

Devon pulled Lightning to a quick halt, needing to assure Lilia that all was right. Her face was puffy from crying, her nose was running, and she uttered soft hiccups as she tried to calm down. When she realized that the horse had stopped running, she took a bewildered look around her and started crying all over again. "Oh, Devon!" she wailed. "I didn't mean for this to happen. I never meant to cause trouble." A fresh burst of tears robbed her of speech, and for over ten minutes Lilia sobbed.

When she was finally able to control the tears, she looked at Devon with adoration that was almost reverential. "You saved my life," she said softly, tears shining in her eyes. "And I'm going to let everyone know about it."

"Don't be doing any such thing, lass. Just forget this ever happened. If ye go around telling people, ye'll just get yourself in trouble for doing this in the first place."

Lilia's determination was not to be stymied. "I don't

care about me," she said with conviction. "Anyway, I deserve to get in trouble for this. If anything, it's taught me a lesson. But I wouldn't have been around to even learn the lesson if it hadn't been for you."

Although Devon had to admit that her words were flattering, he still thought it best if she kept quiet about the entire incident.

"I'm glad ye learned yer lesson, and that's all that matters. Now how about if we agree not to tell anyone what just happened, eh?"

The girl shook her head. "No. I'm telling."

Stubborn. Bossy. Just like her cousin. But Devon knew there was no arguing. Although he had done her an enormous favor, the hierarchy remained the same, and her word outweighed his.

It took only a few minutes to find Raphael. Once free of the extra burden, the saddle was no longer quite so uncomfortable, and he had stopped running. Devon found the horse grazing in the park, and an hour later he was bathed, curried, and settled in his own stall.

He again tried asking Lilia not to mention what had happened, but again she refused to change her mind. Instead she walked immediately into the house and spilled out the tale to the entire family, who were assembled for breakfast.

As expected, she received a fierce tongue-lashing from her aunt, mother, and Cousin Claire. But Uncle Kendal remained thoughtful throughout the telling of Lilia's adventure, and by the time she finished it appeared he had come to a decision.

"You know," he began, "that man has impressed me every time I see him. He's more responsible than many of the servants we've hired."

"Kendal, ought we to be speaking of servants at the breakfast table?" Louisa questioned. Secretly she thought her husband could sometimes be a touch uncouth.

In normal circumstances quiet, unassuming Kendal Rushmoor would have agreed with his wife and turned the conversation elsewhere. But today he was feeling spirited.

"It's fine, Louisa. This discussion stays among us and no one will be the wiser." The surprising act of his contradiction silenced Louisa at once. The young twins smiled at one another, and Claire and Lavinia bowed their heads to retain composure.

"Anyway," he addressed the entire table, "are you all aware that Christopher has left us?" Six heads simultaneously nodded. "Well, I believe that I'll replace him with Devon."

Louisa was the first to react. "Oh, Kendal. You can't bring an outside servant indoors. Think of the talk."

The thought of having to see Devon on a daily basis caused Claire to panic, and in a rare moment of agreement she backed up her mother. "Yes, Father, I think Mother is right. After all, what does a groom's assistant know about inside duties?"

The Earl of Bedington held his ground. "He's a smart man, certainly responsible, and a quick learner. I'm sure he'll do fine. And there will be no talk, Louisa. None of our friends are even aware that Devon works in the stable, so they'll not know that he was formerly an outdoor servant." Louisa remained skeptical until Kendal added, "Besides, his height perfectly matches Grant's." That convinced his wife. It was imperative in the best of circles that footmen equaled each other in height. Mismatched footmen were a social disaster and would not be allowed in the Rushmoor home. But a perfectly matching pair? Now there was a feather in Louisa's social cap. She consented to her husband's recommendation. "Very well, my lord. I'm sure you're right."

Conversation passed uninterrupted from husband to wife, but the anxiety whirling in Claire's mind blocked out the sound of their talk. The unthinkable was happening. Devon would be among the indoor servants. Claire would probably see him every day. How dreadful, she thought, ignoring the part of herself that was blithely, unashamedly cheering her father's decision.

Of course, she was grateful to Devon for what he had done. He'd saved the life of the cousin whom she had been unofficially in charge of. That was twice now that Lilia had gotten away from Claire, and she admitted that she felt rather foolish. Both times she'd been lucky, but she could take no credit for the second instance. This time, Lilia's safety was entirely due to Devon. As Lilia's guardian, Claire felt compelled to thank him. Of course, that would mean speaking directly with him, and Claire cringed as she remembered what had happened the last time they'd been together in the stable. But she then shook her head to clear the memory. His misbehavior had been a mere fluke, probably because he'd been new to his position. And anyway, what did she know of his background? In all likelihood he'd been raised without the refined tutoring Claire had known all her life. She was certain that if she approached him properly, nothing of the sort would happen again. Besides, she had Lilia to think of now. His act of bravery that surely saved her cousin's life should not go unrecognized. Thanking Devon was the fitting thing to do.

After breakfast, she excused herself and went upstairs to . . . what? Primp? Before she even reached her bedroom Claire realized that primping was exactly what she'd been planning to do. As if she needed to ready herself to speak to a servant. What was she thinking? Deciding her action was merely from habit and not for another reason best not dwelled upon, she turned back around and headed for the stable.

She found him where she had the last time, pitching

hay into the stalls and feeding the horses. But instead of allowing herself to gaze upon the enticing sight of his body, she purposely made noise so he'd notice her presence.

As though knowing who stood behind him, Devon hesitated before turning around. He finished what he'd been in the middle of doing before he faced her.

"If ye're going riding, take another horse besides Raphael. He needs some time to heal," he said.

"Heal? I thought he had been only frightened."

Devon rested his hands on the top of the pitchfork and took some time examining her before he answered. Claire felt her cheeks warm under the scrutiny, but because she felt he was purposely trying to embarrass her for her behavior last time, she withstood his piercing gaze. Finally he replied, "Yer cousin put no saddle blanket on the horse before she put the saddle on. That was the reason Raphael went wild. He was pained by the leather rubbing his skin. Then when Lilia sat on top of him, he couldn't bear it and ran."

Claire walked over to examine her horse. "Do you have some sugar cubes?"

Devon reached into his pocket and grabbed a handful, then gave them to Claire.

Claire took the sugar, stroked her horse's muzzle, and fed him the tiny cubes. She noticed that the standard healing salve that was always kept on hand, consisting of calendula petals, comfrey leaves, plantain leaves, and beeswax, had already been applied to the horse's sores, and she was inclined to agree with what her father had said earlier. Devon was indeed a responsible man.

She spoke to Raphael while the horse gobbled up the sugar, but knew that she was only stalling for time. What's the matter with you? her inner voice chided. Just say what you've come here for and get on with it. Why are you hesitating? Come on, Claire. He's only a servant.

Funny how those last words seemed less and less important every time she thought them. Still, Claire knew what she had come here to do, and there was no sense in delaying it any longer.

She walked back to where Devon was still standing, waiting to see what she wanted. She approached him slowly, ignoring the irrational, infuriating way her heartbeat sped up. She held her head high—remember your superior social status, Claire—but could not bring herself to look directly into his eyes. She felt the way he was looking at her, the way his unwavering gaze intently studied her. But of course he would stare, she thought. After all, imagine his upbringing. She cleared her throat.

"I came here to thank you for what you did this morning."

If he was surprised, he did not show it. " 'Twasn't anything."

"Oh, but yes, it was. I'm certain you saved Lilia's life, or at least spared her from a horrible accident."

"Ye don't have to thank me for that. It's what we servants are paid to do."

Her nervousness prevented Claire from catching his sarcasm. "No, Mr. Blake. You've gone beyond your duties here. You are paid to look after the horses, not save willful young ladies from breaking their necks. So I really must thank you."

"Like I said, 'twas nothing."

"Yes, well . . ." Claire's voice trailed off. "I know she's been spending time in here disrupting you, but you can be assured that I've put a stop to it. She won't be bothering you any longer."

Devon wondered when Claire would be putting that policy into effect. Based on the continued frequency of Lilia's visits, it hadn't happened yet. "The lass don't disturb me. It's nice having someone to talk to."

"But difficult to get any work done, I'm sure."

The implication in those words was unmistakable. "Maybe."

"Then you don't have to worry anymore about it. I'll make certain that Lilia stays out of your way." Claire clapped her hands together as if to brush them off after completing a task. "Now," she said briskly, "is there anything else I can do for you?"

A gleam sparked within Devon's green eyes. At last! This was his chance. "Since ye mentioned it, there is something I've been meaning to ask ye about."

Claire didn't know why she was surprised by that. Nothing Devon ever did was in line with conventional protocol. "All right. What is it?"

"I've heard talk that ye were over in the East End some weeks back, and I—"

"And what a dreadful place it was, too." Claire's nose wrinkled in disgust. "You'd do best to stay away from there."

Devon furiously suppressed what he wanted to say. "Well, it's not really the East End I was wanting to talk to ye about. It's more what happened to ye whilst ye was there."

Claire was amazed that he had heard about it. "Servants really do gossip, don't they?" she observed. "Well, I suppose that's to be expected. Why do you want to know what happened?"

"As ye said yerself, ye know how servants can gossip. I've heard so many different versions of the story that I'm wondering what the true one is."

Unexpectedly, Claire felt flattered by what she perceived to be his concern. Still, she had to remember their respective places. He shouldn't be asking such personal questions. "Let's simply say that I once again let Lilia get away from me and I had to go fetch her."

He couldn't let this chance escape him. "So ye chased her down to the East End, eh?"

"I had to. I couldn't let her be alone all by herself. After all, such dreadful things can happen there."

"The servants say ye saw something . . . ?"

Claire waved her hand as if wanting to brush aside the entire incident. "There was some sort of row going on, that's all."

Devon held his breath, hoping for more, but exhaled as he realized she was keeping quiet. "And, did ye see it?"

"Yes, yes, I saw it. But I can't say I wish to relive the incident. It was all rather deplorable, really. Imagine, two grown men behaving like children."

Imagine that one of those "children" nearly had the life beaten out of him, Devon thought angrily. Against his better judgment, he continued to press. "Did ye happen to see their faces?"

Claire's brown eyes filled with suspicion. "And why would you be so interested?"

He couldn't tell her the truth. If she found out he came from the East End, there was no guarantee he'd keep this job. The little princess's disgust for everything and everyone in the East End might very well lead to his termination if she found out the truth about him. Gone would be any hope of becoming the trusted servant whom Claire confided in, and with it the only opportunity he had for finding out the identity of Joshua's attacker. As Samuel had predicted before Devon took this job, Claire was becoming suspicious from all the questions. Devon knew that, despite how desperately he wanted the information, he'd do best to let the subject drop. For now.

"I don't know. Like I said, I was wondering if what the servants was saying is true, 'tis all."

"The value of servants' gossip is determined only by those who bother listening to it."

"So it's worth nothing, eh?"

"As far as I'm concerned."

"Yet ye're standing here talking to a servant."

Indeed, he was right. "Yes, well. That's only because I wanted to thank you, as I mentioned at the beginning of this conversation."

"So if ye hadn't wanted to thank me, we wouldn't be talking right now."

Something nagged at her. Something, like a tiny, unplaceable itch, told her that this conversation was headed toward dangerous waters. But for the life of her she couldn't figure out why. Nervously, the tip of her tongue flicked across her upper lip to moisten it. "Of course not. It's not proper."

For some reason, her absolute, unquestionable conviction served more for his amusement than irritation. Perhaps it was the sight of her now moist lips. Perhaps it was the way she grasped and regrasped one small, delicate hand with the other. Perhaps it was simply that he hadn't had a woman for a very long time.

"Not proper, is it?" Claire shook her head, then swallowed hard as she watched him lay the pitchfork aside. "Then I suppose I'm a little confused about those proper rules ye're always harping on about. I should think mere talking would be all right."

His magnetic eyes, his sculpted body, the pure masculine aura about him drew Claire toward him with the power of quicksand. Memories of how he had held her and kissed her and made her feel like the most beautiful woman on earth flashed through her mind. And if she did nothing to stop him this very instant her overwhelming desire would be to allow his seduction of her to triumph once again. Already he was advancing on her, ready to sweep her into his irresistible arms and plunder her very soul. *Get away from him!* her genteel mind screamed, at last managing to break the hypnotic spell that Devon had woven around her. Without thinking for another second, Claire grabbed up her skirts and fled, running as though her life depended on it.

Nine

It seemed like easy enough work. Devon repeated the instructions back to Nigel Penworthy. "I think I have it. Cut the wicks, pour the paraffin oil, fill the lamps, clean the lamp chimneys, snuff the candles, readjust the wicks, and clean the wax from the candelabra and the extinguishers. Is that right?"

Nigel was impressed. "That's the lot of it. Lord Bedington was correct when he said you have your wits about you. I think you'll turn out to be even better than Christopher."

Devon smiled, not because he was intent on being the best footman there ever was, but because Nigel's pleasure insured his position here for as long as he wanted. And being inside offered a much better opportunity for speaking with Claire. Damn her. Her evasiveness on the subject of that night in the East End was what kept him here, forced into service for the people he loathed.

"Remember you are to be seen and heard as little as possible, so adjust where you're working with that in mind."

"Aye, I'll do that."

"Good. Well, get on with it, then." Nigel gave Devon a short, crisp nod, then left the room. No sooner had he done so than an unexpected visitor arrived. It was Lilia.

"Devon!" she smiled as she spotted him working. "I heard you would be transferred inside."

"Ye heard right, lass."

"I'm glad. It will be easier to talk to you when you're in here."

Devon began snipping wicks. "I'm not so sure that's a good idea. Ye're not supposed to be talking to the servants."

Lilia snorted as she flopped into one of the room's oversized chairs. "I don't see why not. And anyway, I like talking to you."

Too bad Claire didn't share her cousin's opinion, Devon thought. "I like talking to ye, too, but we'd best keep our conversations secret. I don't want ye catching trouble from yer mum."

"I won't. She never pays attention to me, anyway." Lilia rose from her chair. "I'll come visit you later, all right?"

Devon faltered before answering. He didn't want to do anything to risk his position here. Still, it was pretty hard to squash the girl's enthusiasm. "All right, lass. But remember—'tis our secret."

Claire warily descended the staircase, making sure to avoid a run-in with a certain newly appointed footman. So far she had been successful. Devon had been working inside for nearly a week now, and except for when he assisted Grant to serve dinner, she had not seen him. It was all for the best. His magnetism made her as skittish as an unbroken colt around him. She found that she could scarcely look him in the eyes. The appalling thing was that whenever she did manage to steal a glance in his direction, that now familiar warmth still flooded her body. She was loath to admit her attraction toward him. It was absolutely unthinkable. Thus she did the next best thing to try taking her mind off Devon. She began seeing Philip Westbury in earnest.

They had been to two balls, a breakfast, three luncheons, and on a carriage ride together in the week since she and Devon had had their unfortunate meeting. She was determined to prove to herself that she was not, could not, would not ever be attracted to Devon. After all, it was preposterous. She had been brought up knowing that she would marry a great, noble man. Thus, great, noble men were the ones she should be attracted to. With determination Claire pursued this assumption, and it was for that reason Philip Westbury had again entered the picture.

She stole a quick glance down the hallway, making sure it was clear, then began walking toward the parlor. She and Philip had planned another ride together. As usual, he awaited her entrance by regaling Louisa with tales of fashion faux pas he had recently witnessed.

". . . and there she was, boldly wearing that outdated waist as if it were the latest trend." Amidst their peals of laughter, Claire summoned up her stamina and entered.

Philip immediately took hold of her hand. "There's no one who can wear pale yellow as beautifully as you, Claire," he murmured while planting a kiss on the back of her hand. "It's such a complement to your hair."

Ignoring his casual use of her first name, she chose to continue using his title to maintain distance between them. "Thank you, Lord Townsend. Shall we go?" If her mother was embarrassed by Claire's shortness she managed to keep it to herself.

They walked into the entryway and headed toward the front door, where they unexpectedly ran into exactly the person Claire had so fervently tried to avoid—Devon.

He was cleaning the lamp in the main entryway, perhaps not realizing that the parlor had been occupied. Then again, how could he not? Louisa had been laughing so loudly that Claire wouldn't have been surprised if the cooks had heard her. Before she had time to wonder if Devon had let himself be seen on purpose, Philip began shouting.

"Why, it's you!" he declared while pointing a finger in Devon's direction. "You're that good-for-nothing Irish cad who had the impropriety to address Lady Rushmoor in the stable. What are you doing in here? Shouldn't you be out in the stable where your equine stench won't be quite so offensive?"

The anger on Devon's face was obvious, but composed silence was his only response.

"Father has appointed Mr. Blake as the new footman, Lord Townsend," Claire informed him, hoping to avert further hostility.

"Then the earl doesn't know what happened in the stable, does he?" Philip demanded. No, Claire thought. Her father did not know what had happened in the stable. On either occasion.

"I'll have a word with Lord Bedington," Philip said. "It's imperative that he know about this cad before he shames his entire family."

It was a struggle to maintain her composure in the face of Philip's arrogance. "Lord Townsend," Claire fumed, "I believe you should show my father a little more respect. He has thus far managed to run a capable household without your direction."

Her comment caused Philip to look a little sheepish, but he did not immediately back off.

"Of course, Lady Rushmoor. Your father is highly respected. But without the knowledge that I have of this man, he cannot make an informed decision."

"I believe he is well satisfied with his appointment of Mr. Blake as the new footman." Claire couldn't help one last jab. "And he certainly looks imposing enough for a footman, doesn't he?" Compared with Devon's six-foot frame, Philip was positively dwarfed.

He coughed to divert attention from his reddening cheeks. "Yes, well. Height is not everything, you know." Claire kept her silence. "We had best be off." Philip held Claire's arm as he escorted her out the door, instinctively knowing that Devon would not like it.

He was right. As he watched them leave Devon was aware of the anger coursing through his veins, stirred up by Westbury's repeated insults. The bastard even had enough nerve to lay his hands on Claire as if she were a personal possession. Had Devon not known better, he would have acknowledged his jealousy, but he was positive that Westbury's words, not his actions, were the sole cause of his ire. Grudgingly, though, he'd formed a new sense of admiration toward Claire. Her defense of Devon—in front of Westbury!—had taken courage. In his time with the Rushmoor family Devon had come to better understand the firmly entrenched rules by which their lives were governed. And whether or not those rules made any sense, they were obeyed without question. Claire's refusal to agree with Westbury's assessment of him earned her his surprised respect.

Outside, in yet another interminable carriage ride through the park, Philip's rant against Devon continued unabated.

"That worthless, appalling, disgusting servant being allowed in the household is utterly beyond reason. When your father finds out what I know about that cad, I'm sure he'll have him dismissed at once."

Claire expelled a long sigh. "Lord Townsend, as I told you before, Father is content with his decision."

Philip placed his hand atop hers and gave it a light squeeze. "Oh, Claire. Do call me Philip when we're not in front of others. It's so lovely hearing my name spoken by your gentle lips."

Never mind that he'd dropped her title when speaking to her mother, Claire thought, though she stifled the memory and agreed to Philip's request. "Very well. Philip."

"Wonderful." His lips split into a smug grin as if delighted by her obedience. "Returning to our conversation, however, I must say that I fail to understand what could have possibly possessed your father to bring that wretched man indoors."

"It was prompted by an incident involving Lilia."

Philip looked nonplussed. "Lilia? What has she to do with anything?"

Claire explained the story.

"So because of that your father hails this horse-smelling scoundrel as a hero and decides he's destined for bigger and better things, is that it?"

Claire gritted her teeth. "Surely you don't mean to sound as though you're insulting my father, do you?" she asked sweetly.

"Of course not. You know I would never do such a thing. I only want what's best for you and your family."

And my dowry. "Then please let's stop discussing the servants, shall we? After all, it only seems to result in upsetting you."

"Very well. You're right, of course." Claire breathed a sigh of relief. Too soon.

"But I do need to add one thing. I must confess that I'm disturbed by the way you tend to rush to the defense of your servants, and in particular, that stable boy. Remember, servants are only there for one reason, and that's to serve you."

"What other reason is there?"

"None, of course. Which is why I confess to being a bit concerned about your attitude. Never grow too attached to your servants, Claire. You always want to be able to dismiss them at will, and developing fondness for any of them will prevent that."

Such a benevolent man. "Of course you're right,

Philip. Thank you for your insight. I would never grow attached to any servant."

Philip's inflated opinion of the wisdom he had just bestowed upon Claire caused him to miss her jab of sarcasm. Instead he placed a hand lightly atop her shoulder and turned to face her. "I knew you'd understand," he said.

Lilia clapped her hands together with delight. "One more time, Devon," she exclaimed. "Show it to me one more time."

Her enthusiasm was contagious, and Devon couldn't help but grant her request. "All right, then. But this will be the last of it for ye, lass. I'll be getting into trouble if I don't get back to work soon." He looked her over. "Now, have ye got the pin fastened to yer scarf?"

"It's fastened. And this time, I'm sure I'll notice what you're doing."

Devon's smile was his only response, but he knew he'd prove her wrong.

"Now, pretend like ye're a right proper lass, walking along the street minding yer own business." Lilia moved forward at a leisurely pace, as if out shopping. Devon began walking alongside her, but appeared to be paying her no attention. In one hand he held a handkerchief as he pretended to be wiping his nose. The other hand was underneath his arm and concealed from sight. With that hand he stealthily placed it within the folds of Lilia's gown and snatched away the pin. In mere seconds his pace quickened and he was ahead of her.

Lilia mouth dropped open in surprise. "Don't tell me you've already done it again!"

Devon mischievously grinned as he displayed the ill-gotten scarf pin. "It only takes a couple of seconds, lass."

"But I didn't feel a thing!"

"O' course not. This is how thieves make their living, so they're pretty good at it."

"But you're not a thief, so how were you able to do it?"

Devon was prepared for her question. "A friend of mine came onto some hard times a while back and he was forced to either steal or starve. I figured it would be good for him to show me how he did it so I would know if someone was trying to do it to me."

Lilia made no attempt at hiding her adoration. "What a good idea. You're so clever, Devon."

He laughed. "Not so very clever that I'll keep my job without doing the work. Now get on with ye."

She took back the pin he held out for her. "I guess I won't see you until tomorrow, then. We've got the Chelton ball tonight, and I finally get to go." Devon was disappointed to hear that, since once again Claire would be gone and unavailable to try talking to. "Have fun, lass."

With a cheerful wave Lilia walked out of the room. What a fun man he is, she thought. Strange how Claire seems to have such a dislike toward him. Maybe it's because she doesn't really know him. Yes, she thought. That most certainly is the reason. Claire simply doesn't know what a fun man Devon can be, and that's why she's been so unfriendly toward him. With a young girl's innocence, she decided then and there that she would tell Claire about the fun things Devon had been showing her. Then maybe Claire would understand why Lilia liked talking to him so much and wouldn't be upset about it.

Later that evening she found Claire in her bedroom, dressed in the pale lavender lawn she would wear to the evening's ball. She sat at her mirrored dressing table while Marie patiently worked on perfecting the cascade of blond curls that hung down her mistress's back.

"I 'ave a new style that will look *très belle* on you, mademoiselle. Shall I try it?"

Claire looked at her serving girl with boredom and sighed. "Whatever you like, Marie. This ball is really nothing special."

"Not special? But I thought Monsieur Westbury would be there."

Claire could barely refrain from rolling her eyes. "Yes, of course he'll be there. He would never pass up an opportunity to gossip."

Marie giggled. "Oh, mademoiselle. Surely you do not mean that?"

"I'm sorry. It is terribly rude of me to say so, I know. But unfortunately I'm beginning to feel that it's the truth."

Marie continued to fuss with the curls. "Well, *peut-être* there will be a new 'andsome man for you to meet."

Claire squashed the image of Devon that immediately popped into mind. "Perhaps."

At that minute there was a series of quick raps upon the door which could only mean Lilia. "Come in. The door's not locked."

It was evident that the maids had also fretted over Lilia, because for the first time ever she actually looked like a young woman approaching her coming-out season. She wore a white silk gown over which was a rose tunic trimmed with silver thread. The bottom of the gown swept gracefully over the floor, hiding the soft kid slippers laced upon her feet. Patterns of roses were appliquéd at the tunic's hem. Draped over her bare shoulders was a cashmere shawl. Her hair was swept up in a loose chignon, decorated with pearl combs. At her throat was a ruby-studded choker, and on her face was a gigantic smile.

"I've been looking for you all day, Claire."

"Oh, I thought I mentioned to you that Mother and I

were out making calls. We've gotten a little lax in our social obligations, and Mother thought we'd better get caught up so that we're not ostracized at the ball this evening."

Lilia's face lit up in surprise. "Do you think that would actually happen?"

"No, of course not. But you know how Mother is. Anyway, you look beautiful, Lilia. Are you excited?"

Her younger cousin's inability to stand still betrayed her feelings. "Oh yes. Very excited! I just hope I don't do anything atrocious as I did at the Caswells'."

Claire assured her that wouldn't happen, with a shake of her head. "Not to worry. You'll do fine. In any case, was there something you needed?"

The question reminded Lilia of the purpose for her visit. "Oh, no. Nothing. But I did want to tell you something."

"And what's that?"

"I learned a new trick today that I think you should know about, too. It will help us both."

Claire was intrigued. "Oh?"

"You won't ever again have to worry about getting your scarf pins stolen by pickpockets."

At once Claire guessed from whom Lilia had gained this great knowledge, but she had to ask to be sure.

"Who taught you this?"

"Devon. He knows lots of interesting things."

Anger swept through Claire's body, wave after furious wave. "Lilia, haven't I told you time and again what the rules of this household are?"

"But, Claire, don't you understand? This will help us."

Claire rose to her feet. "I'm afraid you're the one who doesn't understand, Lilia. But I am going to put a stop to this at once." She stormed to the door and called back to her maid as she exited, "Wait right here for me, Marie. I won't be gone long."

How dare he! Claire charged down the wide hallway, shadows from the lamp she carried racing ahead of her steps. She descended the mahogany staircase, fuming. How could Devon? Filling Lilia's mind with thoughts about thieves and pickpockets. Teaching her about them, no less. Well, she'd see the end of it, once and for all. If Lilia refused to understand whom she could and could not talk to in this household, then Claire would make certain that at least the servants did.

As she reached the bottom of the stairs she took a hasty look around, but Devon was nowhere in sight. The first servant who crossed her path happened to be Dominique. "Tell me where Mr. Blake is, Dominique. I wish to have a word with him."

It was obvious that the harsh tone in Claire's voice had intimidated the shy servant, so she did her best to soften her features so the girl wouldn't turn and run in fear. "Last time I saw him he was in the library, my lady. Filling the lamps."

"*Merci*, Dominique." Without another word Claire turned away and stormed toward the library.

As the young servant had said, Devon was there. He looked entranced by what he was doing, and the slam of the library door startled him. His head whirled around in the direction of the noise, but when he saw it was Claire he relaxed.

"Here for a social visit?" he drawled, knowing by her dark scowl that it was not the case.

"I've come to have a word with you."

"Again?"

"Do not be impertinent, Mr. Blake. This is a matter of grave importance."

He set down the bottle of paraffin oil upon the desk where he'd been working and crossed his arms in front of him. "Grave importance, eh?" He was trying not to smile.

"Lilia says that you've been talking to her, and I want to know if it's true."

Her brown eyes snapped with anger and her pink lips were pressed tightly together. She stood there with small, delicate hands balled into fists, determined to let him know that she demanded a truthful answer. As when she had defended Devon in front of Philip Westbury, Claire again stood against the tide of correct societal behavior. She was so much a lady, yet her unorthodox spirit spurred her toward battle with someone twice her size. The effect, to Devon, was captivating.

Trying his best to behave like a demure servant, Devon adopted an obsequious demeanor. "My apologies for offending ye, m'lady, but I didn't wish to disrespect yer cousin."

Claire looked at him suspiciously. "What do you mean 'disrespect'?"

" 'Tis true that the lass is always coming to talk to me, and I thought it disrespectful if I ignored her." He couldn't resist a jab. "We servants would never want to show disrespect, m'lady."

His sarcasm was not lost on Claire, and although he ought to be disciplined, her overwhelming thought was just to get away. All at once, his presence enveloped her. His scent, his smile, that incredibly handsome face. He was too close, and they were alone.

"Very good, Mr. Blake. You're right, servants always need to show respect. Therefore, if my cousin should happen to come talk to you again, you are to remind her that such behavior is improper and that she must leave you at once."

Ridiculously expecting that he would comply without question, Claire was both startled and aggravated to see Devon pondering her order instead of immediately accepting it.

"I suppose I could consider doing that if ye'll tell me one thing."

What an infuriating man! She tapped her foot with impatience. "Very well. What is it?"

"I want to know exactly why talking to yer cousin is considered improper."

Was that all? "As I've told you, Mr. Blake, you are a servant, and Lilia lives here. Therefore, the two of you should not be talking to one another, except in reference to matters of business."

"Ye haven't answered my question, m'lady."

"I most certainly have.

"Nay, lady. I beg to differ. Ye've only told me that I must not speak to yer cousin because it's improper. Ye haven't explained to me *why* it's improper."

He caught her by surprise, particularly because what he'd just said was true. She had to admit he had a quick mind. And before she had a chance to reply, he suggested an answer. "I suspect that the real reason is because ye feel I'm inferior to her. Because I come from a lower class than yer cousin."

She argued against the truth. "That is most definitely not the reason, Mr. Blake. Although there are some who may subscribe to such divisions, I can assure you that the Rushmoors are not among them. It is simply that we have hired the servants to work, and they cannot accomplish their daily tasks if family members are disturbing them."

Her blatant lies were maddening, but rather than being angered by her pompous airs, he felt himself becoming aroused. She personified the elitist mentality he had always despised, yet he also saw the side of her that defied convention. She had shown it when she stood up for him in front of Westbury. She was showing it now.

"Is that so?"

"Yes, it is. And to prove my point, I will be leaving now so as to let you resume your duties."

He ignored her. "Is that the reason ye ran out of the stable? To let me get back to work?"

How dreadful of him to bring that up! She did her best to maintain dignity. "Of course. What other reason would there be?" As soon as the words left her mouth she regretted it, for she knew he'd have an answer.

His sharp eyes remained focused on her, but he didn't immediately respond. Instead he began walking toward the library door. Was he planning to leave? That hardly seemed his style. The doors were still closed; her firm slam had ensured that. But no, he wasn't trying to leave. Instead he stood in front of the doors making certain that she were staying put as well. "Ye ran away because ye think I'm a lowly servant not good enough for ye. That's the reason."

His accuracy was distressing. "That's not true at all," she insisted.

He was not to be swayed. "It's not, eh? Well, sorry to say, m'lady, but I'm not believing ye."

Claire bristled. "What on earth—"

"If ye're telling the truth, then I think ye should prove it to me."

Was he mad? "I don't have to prove anything to you."

"If ye don't, then I'll know ye're lying."

"Well, well—then how should I prove such a thing?"

Traces of a grin slashed across his face. "By kissing me."

"Kissing you!" Claire sputtered.

"Appalled, m'lady?" Devon asked mildly. "Must be the thought of kissing a lowly servant such as myself. Just as I suspected."

His vile crudeness inflamed her. She trembled with outrage and wanted to scream at him to cease his preposterous accusations. "May I remind you, Mr. Blake," she seethed through gritted teeth, "of the rules of polite society, in which a gentleman would never in his wildest dreams speak to a lady such as myself in the way you have just spoken to me."

In four long steps he stood in front of her, seizing both of her arms in an unyielding, iron grip. "And may I remind ye, m'lady," he said as he towered above her, "that since I am very far from being a gentleman, those rules do not apply to me." And before allowing her to utter an objection, his lips came crashing down upon hers.

She vehemently protested against the assault. Although he held her upper arms, her fists were free, and she used every ounce of strength she had to repeatedly pummel his rock-hard chest. She might as well have used a feather for all the good it did. Instead of propelling him away as she wished, he drew her closer against him.

She was petrified by the thought of being discovered, but as her body made contact with his, the onslaught of desire coursing through her veins replaced the fear of moments before. All thoughts of opposing him were abandoned. She felt her body relax and let the feelings he aroused in her come achingly alive. His lips hotly scorched hers; he drove his tongue into her mouth and plundered the depths as if tasting a rare elixir. Now that she had stopped fighting him, he used his hands to explore her soft, feminine curves. He held her face and caressed the satiny skin. With his other hand he stroked the length of her back, and pressed her firmly against him.

Her pelvis made contact with his aroused manhood, and she heard a low groan escape his lips. Before she knew what was happening, he swept her into the air and carried her over to the nearby sofa. "Devon, no," she feebly protested, but he paid her no heed. Very gently he set her down, then eased himself on top of her. The

feel of his weight sent new waves of desire racing
through her body. His hands were everywhere, touching
her shoulders, her arms, sending shivers of delight up
and down her spine. He tore his mouth from hers and
kissed a trail of fire down her neck. She was helpless to
do anything; newly awakened feelings had made her
captive prisoner. When his hands stroked her lush, full
breasts, she instinctively arched against them, moaning
at his strength. "How soft," he murmured between
kisses. His mouth then moved over the filmy material of
her lavender lawn ball gown. He kissed and teased her
swollen, aroused nipples through the thin fabric, creating
carnal sensations in Claire like none she had ever experienced. Instinctively she thrust her hands through his
thick, sun-streaked hair, pulling him even firmer against
her, kissing his neck. Still, he kept teasing, not pushing
the fabric aside, wanting her to plead for more.

The excitement was maddening. Silently she implored
him to pull the dress away, but he refused. Gently his
teeth nipped at her tender flesh, driving her desire further
and further, until at last she could be silent no more.
"Please," she frantically whispered. He needed nothing
more. In one swift movement he forced her dress down
and freed the creamy mounds beneath. At once his
tongue lathed her velvet skin and suckled the perfect
swollen rosebuds. They hardened in his mouth as he did
so.

Without realizing it, her body rhythmically moved
against his, and the provocative motion excited them
both. Devon continued to alternately kiss and lick her
delicate breasts, but his hand probed farther down her
body. He caressed her beautiful flat stomach, then her
firm abdomen. As he touched her there he heard a small
catch of her breath, but continued his exploration unabated. His hand dipped down to caress the mound between her legs, but the erotic touch overwhelmed Claire.

Her senses rushed to her rescue, and at last she stopped the forbidden assault.

In one swift move she pushed Devon aside and rushed from the divan to escape the confines of his erotic prison. Horrified by what had happened and needing to assure Devon it never would again, she smoothed her hair while waiting to catch her breath. Finally, when she felt her heartbeat approach its normal rhythm, she looked Devon squarely in the eye and stated, "This matter is not to be discussed. Ever. I trust you will heed my advice and stay away from Lilia; therefore, there is no need for further conversation between you and me." On legs as wobbly as a rickety chair's, she walked to the door, gave herself a glance in the wall mirror to be sure her hair and gown were in order, then quietly left the room.

For several minutes Devon continued to sit on the divan and stare at the door through which Claire had just walked. Turbulent thoughts raced through his mind. He needed to establish a trusting relationship between himself and Claire so he could ask her about Joshua, but was this really the way to do it? He shook his head as if to clear the confusion. He allowed himself to admit that he found her beautiful, but why couldn't he muster the hatred toward her that he expected himself to have? It wasn't just his physical attraction to her that stymied those negative thoughts. She was different from all other upper-class people he'd met. Or, he should say, from the upper-class people he'd observed before he came to the Rushmoors'. If truth were told, he had never actually met a single one of the upper class before. It hadn't been possible till now. But he'd formed an opinion based on those he had seen, and Claire's behavior challenged his preconceived notions. And then there was Lilia. The lass seemed drawn to him like bears to honey regardless of his position in the household. She had shared stories with him, they had laughed together . . .

Had he rushed to judgment on those people? Dam
it, of course not! Westbury was a typical example. Cor
descending, rude. Lilia was young, and lonely, a lass s
desperate for company that she'd talk to anyone—eve
the hired help. As for Claire, she was only a touch ur
conventional from time to time. That was it. No need t
pretend she was strikingly different from the rest of he
pompous class. A reproach for his behavior toward Lili
was what brought her here in the first place, Devon re
minded himself.

Anyway, what did it all matter? Another opportunit
alone with Claire and he was no closer to getting mor
information from her. But a fact even more disturbin
was beginning to emerge: information from her was n
longer all he wanted.

Ten

"Ah, but you're a fine, fleshy wench," Philip Westbury growled as he slapped the buttocks of his willing whore. She responded with unabated energy and forcefully ground her body against his. She knew the ending would not take long. It never did. In seconds the marquis's body began to shake, signifying his approaching culmination. He drove his body against hers and grunted once, twice, then collapsed in a spent heap.

She carefully pried herself out from underneath the panting man and began to massage his back. "Ye've outdone yerself again, my fine, noble stallion. I could scarcely keep pace with ye." She purred the lies with the finely honed skill of one who has uttered them many times before.

Philip gave her a wolfish grin, believing her words and feeling manly because of them.

"Ye know," she continued, "I'm glad ye were able to come today."

"Yeah? And why's that?"

"Because today marks two years since ye first walked through my door."

He turned over on his back. "Two years? Already?"

She gave him a small smile as she continued the ministrations on his chest. "Time will quickly pass if ye but let it," she replied. "Although I still remember how flattered I was when ye came walking through that door."

In spite of himself, Philip had to smile. "And just what did you think?"

Her eyes held a faraway look as she reminisced. "Ye have a way about ye, Philip. A—a noble way. I knew the minute I saw ye that ye weren't from this side o' town."

Her massages were beginning to warm his blood once again, and his hands reached up to play with her large, low-hanging globes.

"How did you know?"

"Oh, 'twas easy enough to tell. Ye held yer head up high like a fine, proud peacock. When ye spoke I knew yer voice had schooling behind it. And of course, ye wore the finest clothes mine eyes have ever seen."

He was fully aroused once again, and he pulled her atop his body and instructed her to mount. As she settled herself down and began to rock back and forth, she expelled a deep sigh. "Oh, how I do love the shirts ye wear, with those beautiful, fancy buttons."

Her chatter was distracting him. "Enough, wench. Now serve me." She complied immediately, knowing that in less than five minutes she could begin anew where she'd just left off.

His relief came quickly, and once again he relaxed upon her bed. He took up the conversation. "So you like my buttons, eh?"

"In all my days I've never seen anything like them. But the ones I like best are on the shirt ye wore last time ye were here."

He cocked an eye in her direction. "Yeah? And which ones are those?"

She smiled at the memory. "Each one is engraved with the tiniest picture of the parliament building. I don't understand how a body could carve such wee pictures." She turned to face Philip. "Oh, m'lord. It's been o'er three months since ye were here and wore that shirt. Do ye think ye could wear it again next time ye come?"

Philip inwardly recoiled at that thought. There was no way he'd ever be wearing *that* shirt again, but he'd have to give her a reason why. "Now, May," he said playfully while rolling off the bed and collecting his clothes. "I couldn't possibly wear that old shirt again. After all, it's the start of the new season, and that calls for new clothing."

May Blake did not understand how someone could discard a perfectly good shirt simply because of the passing months, but she knew it was not her place to argue. Besides, if Philip said he couldn't wear it anymore, well, he knew his business better than she.

"Besides," he continued, "next time I see you I'll be wearing something you're sure to love. Now, enough talk of shirts. Tell me how your son is."

The mere mention of Devon brought a smile to May's face. "Oh, me boy's great," she said. "He got himself an honest job."

Philip's inquiry about May's son was done purely for politeness' sake; he'd never met the rogue, whoever he was, and couldn't care less about him. But May's incredible skills between the sheets made Philip want to remain in her good graces.

"I'm glad to hear it," he said while buttoning his breeches.

"I am, too, although I don't get to see him as often as before."

"Oh, and why's that?"

"Because he's working for a family over by the park."

"The park? What is he doing over there?"

May beamed. "Well, he started out as an assistant to the groom. But the family liked him so well that they made him a footman. And paying him forty pounds a year, they are! Now he's got a whole passel o' things to do, including tending the candles and filling all the lamps with oil. Oh, I'm so proud of my boy!"

As realization of the meaning of her words swept through him, every hair on Philip's body stood rigidly on end. He could feel his muscles tense, and his fists balled tightly together. A wicked smile crossed his face, and a sudden feeling of euphoria transformed his entire spirit. Imagine the luck! No more would he wonder whether Claire was secretly attracted to the family's new servant. He was the son of a whore! As soon as he told Claire she would promptly lose the girlish interest she seemed to have for Devon, and . . . wait a minute. A new thought suddenly struck him. How foolish he was! He couldn't tell Claire, or anyone, what he'd found out about Devon, for the first thing they'd want to know is how he'd learned it. How would a man of his noble stature have come across background knowledge of a servant? He obviously couldn't let the answer be known. Damn! It had seemed so perfect just a moment ago. Philip finished tying his cravat and eyed himself in the mirror. Perfection, as always. He allowed himself another smile. After all, although he couldn't outright use his knowledge about Devon against the disgusting cur, it was surely nice to know it. Philip tucked away that intriguing bit of information for possible future use. One never knew what opportunities will arise.

He left May's payment on her nightstand as usual, only this time he added an extra crown for a bonus. "I'm happy for you and your fine son, May," he said benevolently. "Now on account of our 'anniversary,' you take this coin and tuck it safely in your bosom, far from Sally's prying eyes. It's for you and you alone, May."

It was evident how pleased she was. "Ye know how it's appreciated, Philip," she said. "Now don't ye be taking too long before coming back."

You don't have to worry about that, my delicious

whore, Philip thought as he softly closed the door behind him. I'll be back before you know it.

The carriage was waiting outside, and Louisa was already seated impatiently in it. Claire knew if she didn't hurry that her mother would send one of the servants to fetch her. She took a last glance in the looking mirror, adjusted the hat bow underneath her chin, and reached for the reticule Marie was so patiently holding. "You are looking *parfait,* mademoiselle, as always," she said to her mistress.

"Thank you, Marie. Now I had best be going before Mother starts causing a fuss."

"I am confused why you have ze hesitation to begin with."

Claire waved her hand as if to dismiss the question. "Oh, it's nothing, really," she replied to her maid. "It's just that Eugenia Twine, the Earl of Barisford's wife, to whom we are paying a call, can be somewhat overbearing at times."

Since she was unfamiliar with the word "overbearing," a cloud of confusion covered Marie's face, but at the sound of another servant mounting the stairs, Claire knew there was no time for further explanations.

"Oh, dear. That must be Emma. I must get out there before Mother becomes overbearing too."

Meeting Emma halfway down the stairs, Claire assured her that she was on her way. "Be quick, my lady. Your mum's starting to get impatient." Claire was sitting in the carriage before fifteen more seconds had passed, but her rush had not placated her mother's nerves. "Good heavens, Claire, what on earth took you so long? We have a lot of calls to make this afternoon, and by getting a late start we . . ." Her voice droned off into the background of Claire's mind. She settled into her seat and instead of listening concentrated on enjoying the passing view of the beautiful summer day. Flowers had exploded into full bloom over the past several weeks, and their vibrant colors were everywhere while their perfume camouflaged what could sometimes be rather noxious odors in the city. Claire heard the chirping of hundreds of birds as they drove along Hyde Park, and she reflected on the beautiful idyllic scene before her. Despite her mother's continued reprimanding, Claire was enjoying the ride. At least she was out of the house and away from Devon. Since their last encounter, she had avoided him like the plague and had vowed to herself that she would never, never again be caught alone with him. The improper, unseemly way she had conducted herself in the library with him brought a flush of shame to her face. Imagine her, Lady Claire Rushmoor, eldest daughter of Lord Kendal Rushmoor, the Earl of Bedington, conducting herself like a low-down, good-for-nothing strumpet. Truly she was appalled. But worst of all, what made her cringe deep down inside when she could stand to admit it, was that she had enjoyed the things Devon had done to her. She closed her eyes from shame at her behavior, all the while remembering how wonderful he had made her feel. No man had ever kissed her that way. That deep, soul-searing way that Devon had. His mouth had captured her lips as if staking claim on them. Her body warmed at the thought. She remembered the way his hands had glided over her skin, and how he had complimented the satiny feel of it. Even now, in her mind, she could hear the sensual way he had said it, and some sinful part of her felt flattered by his words.

Ah! She shook her head to clear the thought. There was no earthly reason she should be thinking about such things. What was the matter with her? She should be giving no more thought to the new footman than she would any other servant. Less, for that matter, for she did hold fondness toward Marie. But as for herself, why surely she should be thinking about Lord Philip Townsend. He, after all, was a man she would be spending a great deal of time with. Try as she might, however, it was difficult to muster up any enthusiasm for the idea.

At last the carriage pulled up to the stately town home of Lady Eugenia Barisford. Claire and her mother ascended the few stairs that led up to the doorway and rang the bell. In seconds the Barisfords' smug butler, Rutherford Tate, had answered the bell and led them inside to the parlor.

"Lady Barisford will join you shortly," he announced, then without further delay turned and closed the door behind him.

Claire and her mother seated themselves on matching dogwood chairs and idly glanced around the room. "Eugenia's taste has certainly become oppressive," Louisa commented, and Claire was inclined to agree. Dark red velvet curtains shut out every ray of light from entering the parlor, and matching burgundy-colored wallpaper added to the gloom. Eugenia's taste in furniture was every bit as heavy as the room's atmosphere. She favored dark dogwood Chippendale with its characteristic claw-and-ball feet, despite the fact, as Louisa swiftly pointed out, that it was rather out of date. In contrast with her antiquated furniture, however, Lady Barisford's parlor was one of the few furnished with that up-and-coming interior accessory—carpeting. From wall to wall, a thick burgundy and gold covering was laid across the entire length of the floor. The Rushmoor dining room was now also adorned with carpeting, but Louisa sniffed as if to state that it mattered not that Eugenia had been the first to get it. However, Claire knew her mother hated to be bested by her old friend and sometime rival and that inwardly Louisa fumed.

At last Eugenia entered the parlor to greet them.

"Louisa, Claire, it's been so long," she gushed, kissing both women in turn on the cheek. "I'm so pleased that you've been able to come for tea." At that moment they all heard another ring at the door. "Oh, that must be Lady Clemonsford," Eugenia said. "I hope you don't mind the imposition, but I've asked her to join us."

Louisa beamed through gritted teeth, for Priscilla Hartwell, the Baroness of Clemonsford, was not her favorite person. As far as she was concerned, the snide old widow could be a downright bore. "It's not an imposition at all, Eugenia," she said. "It will be a pleasure to see Priscilla again." She gave Claire an exasperated glance, knowing her daughter would understand how she felt.

"The Dowager Lady Clemonsford," Mr. Tate announced as Priscilla tottered through the door.

"Thank you, Mr. Tate," Eugenia responded. "And please let Sylvie know that we're ready for tea."

"Very good, my lady," the butler answered as he exited the room.

Never one to hold her tongue, Lady Clemonsford instantly announced her dislike for Mr. Tate. "Really, Eugenia," she said in a huff, "I don't see why you continue to employ that man. He is the rudest, most inconsiderate butler I've ever dealt with."

Eugenia was embarrassed but withstood the assault with well-tempered grace. "I'm very sorry, Priscilla, but Mr. Tate's been with the family for years and we've never had a problem with him."

"You've got a problem now," Priscilla said sharply. "Do you realize that the dolt kept me waiting in the hall for the better part of a minute before escorting me into the drawing room. As if I were some common tradesman come calling!"

The ensuing conversation seemed so absurd that Claire could not restrain the smile that insisted upon showing itself. She bowed her head to hide the improper grin, but not soon enough to escape Lady Clemonsford's shrewd eyes.

"And just what is it that you find so amusing, child?" she asked in a haughty tone.

Claire felt her face flush with embarrassment, but she was determined not to let this cranky widow get the best of her. "Pardon me, my lady," Claire said while holding her head up high, "but I think you're being somewhat harsh on Lady Barisford. After all, if she had a problem with her servants, then surely she would have figured it out on her own. And since, as she said, Mr. Tate has served the family well for many years, then there is probably a perfectly good explanation for his delay in bringing you to the parlor."

Louisa Rushmoor normally might have reprimanded Claire for speaking so candidly, but she had to admit that her daughter was right, and perhaps Priscilla needed to be taught some manners. Lady Clemonsford, however, did not share Louisa's opinion. "Is that so?" she bristled. "Well, it seems there must be truth to those rumors I've heard about you after all."

Louisa turned pale. "Rumors? About Claire?"

Priscilla gave them both a coy smile. "Apparently not just rumors, either," she said snidely. "I have it on good authority that Claire was out traipsing along the East End docks not long ago. And it seems that her little escapade has turned her into a champion of servants!"

As Louisa had never been informed of the events of that evening, she looked at Claire with horrified, questioning eyes. "Claire," she said, in a voice barely above a whisper, "is it true? Could what Priscilla is saying possibly be true?"

The silence in the room was as heavy as the furniture as all three women waited for Claire's answer. But despite Priscilla's smugness and her mother's acute embarrassment, Claire refused to allow herself to feel ashamed.

"Yes, Mother, it's true that I was down in the East End," she began, "but it's not how Lady Clemonsford is trying to make it sound. I was not 'traipsing' down there; rather, I had gone to fetch Lilia."

"Lilia!" Louisa exclaimed. "And just what was she doing down there?"

"I had warned her on several occasions not to go, but her curiosity overcame her, and she wanted to see what it was like. I feared for her safety, and since no one else was home that evening, I felt obligated to find her myself."

"Wasn't that noble of you."

"For heaven's sake, Priscilla." Eugenia turned toward her friend. "What's the matter with you? Claire doesn't associate with the people down there. But she felt she had to go that one time to retrieve her younger cousin. I think she showed an incredible amount of courage. As for me, I'm not sure I would have had the nerve to face that area, no matter what the circumstances." Eugenia shuddered, the mere thought of walking along the East End docks sending a chill along her spine.

"Nevertheless," Priscilla was not to be defeated, "it doesn't mean that Claire should suddenly come to the defense of the domestics, particularly when they aren't her own."

The conversation was silenced as Eugenia's housekeeper entered the room with tea and cakes for all. Louisa remarked how lovely the flowers were that composed the centerpiece on the tea tray, and flowers became the next topic of discussion.

But Claire's thoughts remained on the remarks Dowager Clemonsford had made. Was she really becoming a 'champion of servants'? She had been taking more notice of them lately, particularly to one very handsome footman. But Devon had said Claire acted superior to him, as though she were better than he. But wasn't she? It was the way she had always been taught. "Servants are from one class," her mother had informed Claire and her sisters, "and we're from another." The two classes did not mix. Servants were to be seen and not heard. And, although it had never been said outright, it became clear to Claire at an early age that the class she and her sisters were in was better and more desirable than that of the servants'. After all, the servants were the ones who did all the work, who attended to all the needs of their employers. Claire and her sisters had been well-fed and pampered their entire lives, never doing an ounce of physical labor from the day they were born. Instead, her time as a young girl had been spent on etiquette training, private tutoring in literature, art, history, music, and languages, and riding horses. She had never considered whether class separation was right or wrong; it simply was. It wasn't until that day in the library when Devon had insisted that she felt superior to him because of their class distinction that she gave more than a passing thought to the idea. She knew that she felt uncomfortable when Philip Westbury berated the servants as he did, but until now she had never thought about the reason why. Perhaps Devon was right. Perhaps she had thought that servants were lowlier than she. It hadn't seemed to matter before, but when she heard the scathing words of Lady Priscilla Clemonsford, she realized how horrid they sounded.

As she had done when Philip was particularly nasty about the servants, Claire had tried defending the butler against Lady Clemonsford's remarks. But as with Philip, she had gotten nowhere. Anger toward both of them rose within her, while part of her insisted they were right. Claire closed her eyes as an internal moral war raged inside her head. Devon had awakened her to principles of ethics she'd have never even thought of before, yet the very consideration of those ideals meant betraying her own identity—an identity forged upon the notion of class distinction.

Claire shook her head against the confusion and nibbled on a honeyed tea cake. She wished there were something she could do, perhaps a book she could read, that would help her better understand the lower classes. Her tutors had always stressed that true knowledge comes only from understanding. Of course, she could always talk to Devon. Certainly his background must be completely different from her own. But as soon as the idea entered her mind she promptly banished it. Remembrance of their encounter in the library was reason enough for her to dismiss that idea. But what to do? Suddenly Claire remembered an article she'd once read in the *London Times* about local parishes scattered about the East End that helped those with little or no money get at least something to eat. Since she had never in her life known what it was like to be hungry and without food, Claire decided that she would go to one of those places and volunteer her services. She remembered the article named one place in particular—St. Matthew's Salvation—as being especially busy. It was on the corner of Cloak Lane and Dowgate, and it was there she would go. Tomorrow.

It had taken a great deal of covert arrangement, but at last Claire was on her way. She had opted not to take either of the carriages because both were far too ornate for the area and would draw attention. She was dressed from head to toe in plain gray clothing that Marie had secretly borrowed from one of the kitchen maids. Her hair was pinned back in a simple coif; she wore no jewelry of any kind. Before leaving she had sworn her maid to secrecy. The only other person who knew of her departure was Daniel, and if he had any thought as to the reason behind her clothing or where she was going, he knew better than to open his mouth.

She had noted on the map where Cloak Lane was located, and estimated it would take her about twenty minutes to get there. In truth the ride was closer to half an hour, for the lack of paved roads on the East End made the going a little slower.

As she neared her destination Claire was struck by the filth and poverty of the area. They had not been so apparent when she was here last because it had been at night and the streets had been dark. Now, however, she had a clear, unobstructed view of the utter desolation. Small children, no older than four or five years old, were peddling goods. She spotted little girls, barefoot and wearing what amounted to rags, selling oranges and matches to whoever passed by. She was at first surprised by the number of pedestrians swarming the sweets, until she realized that the majority of them couldn't afford coaches or even a single steed. Despite her best efforts she still drew attention to herself, for there was nothing that could have been done to hide the fine horseflesh on which she rode. Her heart hammered wildly in her chest, and for one fleeting moment she felt like turning her stallion around and charging back to the comfort of home. But no, she wouldn't do it. She had come here to help the people who called this devastation home, and help them she would.

With more determination than ever, she continued riding toward her destination. She didn't feel comfortable asking anyone for directions; instead she consulted her map until at last she reached St. Matthew's Salvation.

She had expected swarms of people to be lined up outside, but there was no one in sight. Fearing that the place might not be in operation, she warily tethered her horse and climbed the steps to the front door. For a few moments, she hesitated. It would be so easy to untie her horse and bolt back to the comfort of home without ever looking back. Could she really do this? Well, she thought, there's only one way to find out. She balled her right hand into a fist and pounded on the door.

Seconds passed, then a minute. She pounded again. Still nothing. This time she pounded with both hands and used all her might. At last she heard what sounded like footsteps, and seconds later the door cracked open and a weary eye peeped out at her.

"Wha' do ye wan', missy?" a gruff female voice asked. "Ye know we ain't servin' for ano'er two 'ours."

"I'm looking for work," Claire quickly explained.

The gruff voice cackled like that of an overly amused witch. "Work? Ha, ha! That's a good one! If it's work ye're lookin' for missy, ye're better off selling eels on the streets. Now get along with ye, 'fore I lose me good humor."

The door began to close, and Claire knew she had but one more chance to get what she wanted. "Wait! Please! I'm not looking to get paid. I only want to help you." She pounded on the door. "Please!"

For a long time there was no reaction, and Claire thought she'd ruined her chance. Slowly she turned around and began walking down the steps, when the door unexpectedly opened up again.

"Ye wan' to help, do ye?"

At the sound of the voice she spun around. "Oh, yes. I just want to offer my help. I'm not looking for a wage, truly I'm not."

Her brown eyes peered intently at the tiny crack in the door, and the woman on the other side finally relented. She opened it wide. "Well, if ye really wan' to help, then come on in. We got us plenty o' work to do, missy, and we could use an extra set of hands."

Without further ado Claire was ushered inside. She was greeted by a room filled with activity. Everywhere she looked someone was chopping, stirring, ladling water, adding salt. Giant vats filled with watery soup were simmering over open fires. The intense heat from those fires made her start sweating profusely, and she offered up a silent prayer of thanks that her dress was made of cotton.

"There's a pump out back where we're bringin' in the water," the gruff-voiced woman said, who had introduced herself as Hildie. "Go relieve Mary and tell her to come on inside." Then without further explanation, Hildie charged away to attend to other things. Claire was left feeling lonely and confused, but determined to do what she'd come here for.

The first thing, she told herself, is to find out who Mary is. Amid the noise and confusion, proper ladylike manners seemed impractical. Instead, Claire took a deep breath and blurted out as loud as she could, "Which one of you is Mary?"

Instead of everyone stopping and staring at her bois- terous bellow, Claire was ignored by all but the one she sought. "Back here," someone yelled as loudly as Claire, and as she turned to look, a disheveled woman with dirty blond hair identified herself. "I'm Mary," she said while continuing to work. "Wha' do ye wan'?"

Claire hurried over to where the young woman was feverishly working the pump and informed her of Hildie's instructions. "You're to go inside while I pump," she told her, and without pause the woman abandoned her post and did as she was instructed. No time for fur- ther discussion, Claire noted. So, like Mary, she promptly began to do as she was told.

Over ten hours later, with aching arms, legs, back, neck, and shoulders, Claire wearily walked out of St. Matthew's Salvation. The other women who worked there showered Claire with thanks for all her help, but it was her inner satisfaction that made the experience worthwhile. For the first time in her life Claire had been the one doing the feeding instead of being fed, and it had been immensely gratifying. Hundreds of people lined up for the thin watery soup that was ladled into the containers they brought. Every age group was represented, from the wee ones Claire had seen as she rode over, to the very frail and elderly who had hobbled up to the counter. All had looked at Claire with pleading, hopeless eyes, and it had taken her the better part of an hour to bring her emotions under control. Never in her life had she seen such suffering. Never before had she even known it existed. As she left she pressed over twenty pounds into Hildie's calloused palm, and told her she'd send more in the future. Tears of joy had softened the gruff woman's eyes, and she thanked Claire from the bottom of her heart. "Oh, sweet lady," she said while wiping her nose. "Ye've no idea how much soup this will buy for us."

Claire's eyes also misted over as she gave Hildie a hug good-bye. "I'm so happy I could help," was all she could say, then she turned around and went out the door.

The day's events had taken their toll, and she needed a moment to compose herself. Before untethering her horse she leaned against the animal's strong flanks and inhaled deep gulps of air. As she stood there she noticed that the sun was sinking low in the sky. Evening would soon be upon them. The streets were even busier than when she had come in the morning, and the house across the street seemed to hold a special fascination, particularly with men. Probably a pub or gambling house, Claire mused. Or possibly a men's club. Whatever the attraction, there were a good number of gentlemen walking to and from the house. Idly she observed the passers-by, then, just as she was about to look away, her eye rested on a familiar face. Who would I possibly know here? she thought, continuing to look at the man. Moments before he had walked out of the busy house across the street and was now going toward where his horse was tethered. That horse looks familiar, too, Claire thought, and it was at that moment she realized the man was Philip Westbury.

Believing that surely her eyes played tricks on her, Claire stepped behind her own horse so she could observe the man without appearing to stare. Sure enough, it was Philip. There was no mistaking his ostentatious clothing and his distinctive white stallion. Praying he wouldn't look her way and perhaps recognize her horse, Claire continued to hide and watch what Philip did. Actually, she thought, he appears to have no interest in his surroundings. In fact, he seemed to be in somewhat of a hurry. With quick efficiency he untied his horse, mounted the steed, and rode away, never once looking around to see if he were being observed.

When he was gone from sight Claire came out from her hiding place and began untying her own horse. How very peculiar that he should be here, she thought, particularly when Philip was so vocal about his dislike for the poor. What earthly reason would bring him to this part of town? Did he know someone here? Was there business he conducted? Both ideas seemed impossible. But she couldn't come right out and ask him to state his business; after all, he'd want to know the same of her. For now his reason would remain a mystery to her, although its memory was securely locked in her mind.

Eleven

As she slipped through her bedroom door, Claire breathed a sigh of deep relief. No one had seen her return. With haste she shut the door behind her and then rang for Marie. When the dutiful servant appeared Claire ordered a bath to be brought up to her room, and told Marie to inform the family that she had a headache and would not be joining them for dinner.

As Marie left to begin the bath preparations, Claire took off her drab clothing and donned a thick robe. She was glad to be rid of the gray dress, for it held an array of noticeable aromas—from pea soup to horse manure— that would inspire an explosion of questions from her mother about what she had been doing and why she was wearing that dress. It was best to forgo the entire scenario by begging off dinner to clean herself up.

When the bath was readied she excused Marie, and although the servant's eyes held questions about the events of the day, she held her tongue. Grateful to be alone, Claire sank into the steaming hot tub, whose water had been perfumed with lavender-scented oil. For several long minutes she languished there, reveling in the feel of the silky hot water covering her body and the rising steam that misted her face. Eventually, with reluctance, she sponged her body clean and rose from the tub. Grabbing the towel that Marie had placed on a nearby chair, she rubbed her body dry and wrapped herself in her thick burgundy robe. Just as she finished tying the belt, she looked up in surprise at the sound of the doorknob turning. Suppressing mild annoyance at Marie's intrusion when she had asked to be alone, Claire suddenly realized that it was not her lady's maid entering the room. It was Devon.

Uttering a shriek of embarrassment, she clutched the ends of her robe together and flew around to the far side of her bed. Crouching down to conceal herself as much as possible, she furiously demanded an explanation.

"God's nightshirt!" she cried. "What are you doing in here?"

Devon's surprised reaction was much the same as Claire's, although it lacked the embarrassment that had so overwhelmed her. Instead he noted the tub of water on the floor, the scent of lavender in the air, and the rosy glow on Claire's freshly scrubbed face. Obviously she had just finished taking a bath. With disappointment he realized the sight he had missed by not entering a few moments earlier. He felt himself becoming aroused, but rid his mind of the lustful ideas.

"I beg yer pardon," he said, "but I had no idea ye were here."

"No idea?" Claire sputtered. "Despite the fact that this happens to be my bedroom?"

He ignored her sarcasm. "With all due respect, I thought ye were eating downstairs with the rest of the family. I need to trim the wicks in here and thought this would be a good time to do it."

Had she been in a calmer frame of mind, his explanation would have seemed plausible. But her current embarrassment would not allow her anger to be soothed.

"Nevertheless, perhaps if you were mindful of the rules of correct behavior, it would have occurred to you to knock before entering."

The snide remark instantly caused his familiar feelings

of hostility toward the wealthy to well up. And her words had an even greater sting because he had begun to feel, rightly or not, that perhaps she was different. He could feel the anger racing through his veins. His back teeth clenched together and his hands balled into irate fists. He would never hurt a woman with physical force, but he longed to hurt Claire with a verbal assault.

"Proper behavior, eh?" he said slowly, while raising an eyebrow. "Well, mayhap that's something I ought to learn about. That is, if I ever have time."

At Claire's questioning look, he continued. "Ye see, m'lady, we lowly servants are bloody busy and don't have a lot of time to ourselves. After all, we have important things to attend to. We have to keep the place sparkling clean at all times, especially when important guests arrive. It wouldn't do for an old hag's rump to get mussed by sitting in a dusty chair, now would it? What a social disgrace that would be." His voice was steadily becoming more and more quiet.

"But we also have to shovel coal, clean out dustbins, scrub the lamps, scrub the floors, cook the food, wash the clothes—and what a lot of clothes there are between changing from morning dress to walking dress to tea gown to ball gown. Every bloody day the girls are tearing their hands apart from the hot water and lye they use to clean yer dresses. But of course we don't mind. Not at all. How could we face the day knowin' my lady was forced to wear the same blue gown as she had a week ago? What a bloody horror that would be!"

Devon was speaking so softly now that she had to strain to hear him. But she could tell by the corded veins on his neck that he was seething with rage.

"So, m'lady, if it should come a time when I'm finding myself without a bleedin' thing to do, then mayhap I'll take a minute and learn about this 'correct behavior' that ye seem to feel is so deathly important."

His words incensed her. "You are the rudest, vilest, most disrespectful man I have ever met!" she spat. "Perhaps what everyone has told me all along is true. I should have nothing to do with the poor because you're all ignorant, vulgar beggars!"

He couldn't believe what he was hearing. For the first time in recent memory he was so infuriated that his cool exterior exploded, and before he realized what was happening he was shouting back at her.

"Ye speak of things ye know nothing about! Yer privileged world leaves ye with nothing better to do than ride around Hyde Park, gossip about some old bugger wearing the wrong hat and gorge yourself on enormous dinners every night. Don't even begin to pretend that ye have any idea of life outside your protected boundaries!"

If she'd had something in her hand, she would have hurled it at him. But her sharp tongue was the only weapon she possessed, and she would use it to its fullest potential.

"As everyone says, a typical Irish simpleton, like the rest of your kind. Had you but a drop of common sense, you'd realize the foolishness of your words. I have traveled to the wretched part of town which seems to hold such a cherished place in your heart, although for the life of me I can't imagine why."

His quiet tone had returned, though the anger remained as strong as before. "Ye're even dimmer than the rest of 'em if ye believe for one minute that staring out the window of a luxurious carriage gives ye a feel for life outside those padded walls."

She hadn't wanted to tell him. She hadn't wanted him to know about the interest she had taken in his background. But his biting mockery of her forced the words out.

"Is that so? Well perhaps working to feed the poor would give me the opportunity to see how they live."

He sneered at her. "What would ye know about it?"

Her voice was nearly triumphant. "Because that's exactly what I was doing today, which is why I needed a bath!"

Her eyes flew in the direction of the drab, gray dress that she had lain across the chair, and as Devon's head turned to follow her gaze, he knew in that instant she was telling the truth.

Silence engulfed the air. Devon was stunned at her revelation. Still angry, he strode across the room to examine the dress, then smelling the familiar aroma of parish soup, he asked her to tell him where she had been.

"What does it matter to you? The point is I was there."

"But where was it?" he persisted.

Claire sighed. "If you must know, it was St. Matthew's Salvation, on Cloak Street, across from what I can only conclude is a club for men."

A club for men indeed, Devon thought, as he realized where she had been. It was true what she said, though. She had gone down to the East End. In that instant he felt a tinge of remorse for the accusations he had hurled at her. But pride and anger would not allow him to retract the words. So she had gone down there once, had she? That still didn't mean the noble Lady Rushmoor understood anything about Devon's way of life. After all was said and done, she had spent a few hours in the bad part of town, then beat a hasty retreat back to her sheltered, pampered life. Let her walk a month in the battered desolation of a matchgirl's steps, Devon thought with bitterness. Then mayhap Claire would truly understand.

He dropped a sarcastic bow before her. "Have me notified when it will be a more suitable time to trim these lamps." Then, without looking back, he left.

As the door latched behind him, Claire stood transfixed and thought about what had just happened. She was struck by the hostility Devon held against her. Or rather, against her and everyone like her. Where did the anger come from, she wondered. Had he undergone bad experiences that had shaped his opinion? It occurred to her then that she really didn't know anything about Devon. He had alluded to his less than affluent upbringing, but she knew nothing concrete. Who were his parents, for example? Was his father a tradesman of some sort? What about siblings? Perhaps if she learned something of his past, she could find the reason why he harbored such anger.

But wait a minute, Claire, her aristocratic mind called out. What does it matter why he's angry? Why should you care one whit about his feelings? He's a servant, you dolt! Besides, you know better than to concern yourself with him. It's far too dangerous.

It seemed to Claire that she should listen to her logical side, that there really was no reason for her interest in Devon's background. But there was another side to her brain, a side that called out for her to get to know Devon better. And she rationalized her interest by telling herself that if she learned why Devon was so angry and convinced him that not all upper-class people bore resemblance to the image he held in his mind, perhaps he'd become a happier person and thus a better footman. Indeed, that seemed to be a good reason. At any rate, it was a reason she could convince herself of.

"I don't want to manipulate him, Mother. It's not right."

Louisa huffed in exasperation at her obstinate daughter. For the past hour they'd been having this same conversation, and Claire was no closer to changing her mind now than she was when they began.

Aunt Bella piped up with a suggestion. "You mustn't think that it's manipulation, Claire dear. It's merely giving Lord Townsend incentive to propose. After all, you know what jealous clods men can be. The threat of another man spurs them into action."

"I don't see the difference," Claire insisted. "There is no other man in my life, so to lead Lord Townsend into thinking thusly would be to manipulate him."

Louisa and her sister exchanged weary looks. Claire could be so distressingly stubborn. Cousin Lilia, who made up the fourth person at the outdoor tea table around which they sat, suddenly felt the need to voice her own opinion.

"Why don't you just propose to Lord Townsend yourself, Claire?" she asked with a grin. "That would speed things along."

"Lilia!" Louisa gasped, mortified by her niece's obscene suggestion. "Has Claire taught you nothing about manners and decorum? My word, to even hint at such a thing. Sometimes you're an incorrigible goose."

Unfazed by the hurt that crossed Lilia's face, Louisa turned her attention back toward Claire.

"Look at it this way," she said. "You're correct—there is no other man. However, there is every chance that there could be. Take the attitude of going to the ball this evening to meet other men. Dance and converse with all suitable prospects, and if one of them fancies you, and you fancy him, well then, there's your other man."

"But I thought you wanted me to go to this ball to encourage Lord Townsend to propose."

"We do, Claire," Bella replied. "But if, for whatever reason, the marquess fails to do so, at least you'll have another suitor lined up."

"Remember, Claire," Louisa's voice became hard, "you will not let a third season go by without becoming engaged."

"But I—"

"And don't talk to me of love. I'll hear nothing of it.

You'll find yourself a husband, regardless of whether you harbor love for the man. I'll not have a spinster for my eldest daughter and risk shaming the entire family."

At her daughter's dour expression Louisa attempted lightening her tone. "Anyway, Claire, as long as the man you marry comes from a respectable bloodline, you're bound to at least admire him, if not fall head over heels in love."

"Love is the stuff of foolish novels and poetry," Bella informed her niece.

Claire knew when to hold her tongue. Her mother and aunt, well-meaning as they were, would never know just how she felt. Head over heels in love? Would she ever know the feeling? An unexpected image of Devon materialized just then, momentarily startling, but as quickly as it came Claire shoved it aside. Now what had brought that on? Perhaps it was just that their last argument was still on her mind. Or better still, that she was simply tired.

Rising from the table, Claire indicated an end to the conversation. "Very well, Mother, Aunt Bella. I'll do as you say and keep my eyes open for 'suitable prospects.' "

The two older women nodded their satisfaction. "In the meantime," Claire concluded, "I'm retiring to my room to rest."

"Make sure Marie has you ready by eight," Louisa reminded her, as if Claire were a forgetful child.

Without another word she turned and left the room. Once outside, on her blossom-perfumed balcony, she was able to ease away the harsh words and sobering warnings of impending spinsterhood. If only I could stay out here forever, she thought, knowing it was an idle fantasy. She didn't really want to be sheltered away, bereft of human company. She just wished she could wholly embrace her mother's dreams that she seek out and marry a wealthy, titled nobleman, with no desire for that elusive emotion called love that so lately vexed her thoughts.

A series of gentle knocks upon her bedroom door focused her attention on reality. Assuming it was Marie coming to discuss the evening's attire, she was surprised when instead it was Lilia who entered the room.

"I came to keep you company, Claire," she announced, sauntering toward the balcony in her usual buoyant style. Dropping into a seat alongside her cousin, Lilia shook her head and declared, "I don't know how you put up with those two. And to think I need to learn proper behavior?" She huffed. "Seems to me that there's someone else who should be sitting in on those lessons."

Instead of automatically reprimanding her for disrespect, Claire let the comments slide by unreproached. If truth were told, Lilia's honesty was refreshing. After all, Aunt Bella and her mother, especially her mother, had been decidedly rude.

A peaceful silence fell between the two cousins until it was Claire who broke it by impulsively confessing, "Sometimes I just feel like I'm at my wit's end, Lilia. Like I should give up trying to please Aunt Louisa, because no matter what I do it's not what she wants."

Lilia nodded, understanding what Claire meant. But she could not refrain from asking, "Why not just do whatever she wants? That way you know you'll make her happy."

Claire raised a bemused eyebrow in her cousin's direction. "Just like how you always do whatever I want to please me?"

Lilia slumped back in her chair, realizing Claire spoke the truth. It was difficult going against what your heart, soul, and mind wanted to do. After a moment's pause, Lilia spoke up once again. "I understand your predicament, Claire," she stated, sounding wise beyond her years. "Lord Townsend is such an insipid bore compared to Devon."

The mere mention of his name perked up Claire's ears, yet she would not allow Lilia to draw her into a discussion of Devon. "Anyone would be better than Lord Townsend," she said.

"But no one would be better than Devon," Lilia insisted, again inserting his name into the conversation.

Realizing it was useless to steer the conversation away from where Lilia insisted it should go, Claire stayed silent. For a moment.

"Maybe you should marry Devon," Lilia suddenly declared, an impish grin plastered across her face.

Claire bristled with disapproval at her cousin's suggestion, an automatic, trained reaction whenever something scandalous reached her ears. Yet Lilia's words could not be shaken loose. They stayed entrenched within her mind, defying reason, logic, years of cultured grooming. They went against the grain of everything Claire believed. Had believed. Thought she believed. She shook her head to clear the confusion, but the gesture was useless. In just a few short months her well-ordered world had been turned on its ear. Seemingly gone were the days when Claire accepted without question social standing and class division. Where once she had not doubted—never for a moment—that she and her family were superior to the working class, now she wondered whether those distinctions were actually quite so clear. She sighed as she turned to address Lilia. If only she could be sure.

Lilia flinched just a little, no doubt expecting a sharp reprimand for her outlandish suggestion. Instead Claire responded in a subdued voice, "I must be quite a dreadful teacher."

Lilia's eyes widened in surprise at her cousin's unexpected statement, and she rushed to her defense. "That's not true at all. You're wonderful," she countered.

"But to make a suggestion like that, to even think something so outrageous . . ." Claire's voice trailed off.

Suddenly Lilia rose from her chair, confused by the peculiar way in which her cousin was behaving. "Are you . . . is . . . is something the matter, Claire? You're acting kind of strange."

Claire glanced over at her young cousin as if seeing for the first time the mature lady she was becoming instead of the awkward girl she had been. Perhaps Claire's teaching was paying off. Lilia, after all, was the only one who had pointed out the obvious—Claire was acting strange. But who could blame her? She felt as if her life had been thrust before a twisted mirror, reflecting a distorted image of the world that had once been so clear and familiar to her. How she longed for that seemingly simple time again.

"Forgive me, Lilia. I've just had a lot on my mind lately."

"About getting married, you mean."

Ever the pragmatist, Claire thought. "Yes, that. And other things as well."

Lilia again took a seat beside her cousin, but for once she held her tongue, sensing there was more Claire wanted to say. She was right.

"I used to think I knew exactly what I wanted," Claire confessed. "That all I had to do to satisfy Mother was choose among the men in our class who came calling on me. I assumed that sooner or later I'd fall in love with one of them. But it hasn't turned out to be quite that easy."

"Is it so important, then, to love someone in our class?"

"That's just the way it always goes. You remember what I've taught you. Classes never mix."

Lilia persisted. "But is it important?"

The seemingly innocuous question lay before her, innocent yet harmful, daring Claire to respond. She hesitated, knowing full well that concealed within her answer was the very essence of what she had struggled with since Devon Blake had entered her life. She knew Lilia was waiting, wanting to hear what she would say. But this time Claire could not even pretend that she held the answer. Shrugging her shoulders, she admitted in a quiet voice, "I really don't know."

Twelve

A sea of swirling skirts flooded the expansive ball-room, as dozens of couples took part in the country dance. Light from the great candelabras overhead sparkled in every corner of the room, as if handfuls of jewels had been scattered about. Those not dancing talked with friends and acquaintances, and peals of laughter rang throughout the room. Everywhere servants were bustling to make certain no one was without refreshment. Curls of pipe smoke created a sharp, yet pleasant smell, and mixed with the heady odor of expensive perfume.

Minutes after arriving, Claire was coaxed into joining the dancing by a handsome yet shy Lord David Ashton. She accepted the invitation at once, especially in light of the conversation she had had with her mother just this afternoon. Louisa had again reminded Claire, as they rode in the sleek town carriage toward the party, that the seasonal clock was ticking and that she must be engaged before they returned to the country. Claire promised that she would socialize with other men at the evening's party. Whatever the outcome, Claire thought, she would do as her mother asked, if only to grant herself a reprieve from her constant needling.

She and Lord Ashton positioned themselves for the start of the next dance, but as Claire waited for the music to begin, she suddenly felt red-hot pain sizzling into the back of her hand. She yelped with a cry of anguish and noticed that a great ball of hot wax had dripped from the overhead candelabra onto her hand. The pain was instantaneous and burned like fire. At once she left David and stepped out of line to walk as fast as dignity would allow over to her mother. When she showed Louisa the burn both mother and daughter worked swiftly to get the wax off of Claire's hand. But the damage had already been done, and removing the wax did nothing to give Claire relief.

"I want to leave, Mother. It's very painful."

Louisa looked at her daughter with genuine concern, but a small part of her was distressed about the lost opportunity. This, after all, was a major affair; all the best people in the city were in attendance, and they had only been here an hour.

"Are you sure you don't simply want to borrow my gloves and stay a little longer?" she asked, and Claire knew what her answer had to be.

"Very well, Mother," she bravely answered. "I'll give it a try."

At that moment Philip Westbury, who had witnessed the entire incident, hurried over. "Is everything all right?" he asked, concern etched across his forehead.

Louisa smiled and answered for her daughter. "Fine, fine. Just a little dripped wax."

Claire smiled through the pain right along with her mother. "Just some wax," she echoed.

Philip looked skeptical about their answer, but decided that their truthfulness was of no concern to him. "I'm certainly glad to hear that," he said, "because I'd like to ask Lady Claire for a dance."

She had no choice but to grant his request, so off she went for yet another swirl across the floor.

Louisa's suggestion to cover Claire's hand with a glove only made the injury worse. The material rubbed across the wound every time Claire raised or lowered her hand, causing the tender skin to become even redder and more irritated. The pain was immense, and at last she could stand it no longer.

"I'm terribly sorry, Philip," she said as they walked off the floor, "but I'm afraid I'm going to have to leave."

"Leave?" he asked, with a frown upon his lips. "But you've only just arrived."

"Yes, I know. But this burn seems to be worse than I originally thought. I must get home and have my maid attend to it."

"Your mother and aunt aren't going to be happy," Philip noted.

And wouldn't that be a tragedy, Claire thought with irritation, but then shrugged away her sarcastic musings. The burn was making her peevish.

"I'm sure they won't, but unfortunately there is nothing to be done. We all came together, and I can't leave them here."

Her words triggered an idea in Philip's mind. "Why don't I take you home?" he suggested. "My coach is right outside, and that way your mother and aunt can stay a little longer."

Claire swiftly declined his invitation. "Oh, that's very kind of you to offer, Philip," she said, "but I really don't feel it's proper."

Philip's condescending laugh maddened her to the bone. "Oh, Claire. Don't be so concerned about impropriety. I'll simply take you back, then return to the dance. People will know I've done nothing more than make sure a dear friend has arrived safely home."

It seemed like a solution to a touchy situation, and when Philip proposed the idea to Louisa, she agreed.

"I'm sorry your hand isn't better, Claire," she said, "but isn't it wonderful to have such kind friends to help us?"

"Indeed, Mother. Good night," Claire replied as Philip took her arm and led her away.

His team of horses were among the finest anywhere, and after what seemed to be only a few minutes they pulled up to the town house's front door. Without hesitation Claire readied herself to leave the carriage, but Philip placed a hand on her shoulder as restraint. "I know how much you're in pain, Claire," he said while mustering up an appropriate amount of sympathy, "but I must speak with you for just a moment."

"Philip, please, I—"

"Just a moment, my love."

Claire noticed his use of the endearing words, but decided to ignore him. Her hand was throbbing too much to take the time to protest.

"We really haven't seen much of each other lately, which is why I'm grateful for the opportunity to escort you home."

She managed a smile.

"I'm afraid my calendar is very full this upcoming week, but we simply must see each other again. I do believe I have a few spare hours on Wednesday. May I pick you up to go riding?"

At that point she would have agreed to go spear fishing. Anything, just so he'd allow her to leave. "Wednesday would be lovely, Philip. But now I'm afraid I really must go and attend to this burn. Thank you for a wonderful evening." She was nearly out of the carriage and running as she said those last words. Without a backward glance or a wave good-bye, she hurried up the steps and rushed inside the front door.

The entryway was unusually quiet, and Claire realized that most of the indoor servants were probably in their quarters. Marie wouldn't be expecting her for several more hours, and she likely was spending time gossiping with the other maids. Well, no matter. Claire could attend to the burn herself. She knew that Emma kept healing herbs in the kitchen, for it was there where most of the accidents occurred. Although Claire wasn't sure exactly what she should use, she hoped to find something that would work.

As she approached the kitchen, she noticed light coming from within. Were the cooks making preparations for tomorrow's meals? As she walked inside she realized the light's source came not from the cooks, but from Devon. Several lamps were set upon a worktable, and he was carefully filling them with paraffin oil. He looked up when he heard her enter.

"Evening," he said, without halting his work.

"Good evening," Claire cautiously responded, remembering the harsh words exchanged last time they'd spoken to one another. She looked around the kitchen. "I was hoping to find out where Emma keeps the herbs in here."

He set the container of oil down on the table and looked up sharply. "Why? What's wrong?"

If not for the pain, Claire would have recognized the note of concern in his voice. She held up her hand. "I'm afraid I've burned myself on some wax," she began to explain, but her words were halted when Devon rushed over and grabbed her around the waist. "Come on," was all he said while nearly carrying her out of the kitchen.

"What are you doing?" she gasped in surprise, but the determination on his face allowed for no questions.

In seconds they were up the stairs and inside Claire's bedroom. Without wasting time lighting a lamp, Devon instead pulled Claire over to her bedside table and plunged her hand into the pan of cold water that Marie always prepared for her to wash her face.

The relief was instantaneous. Suddenly the awful throbbing subsided as the cold water washed over the burn.

Devon had been holding his hand around her wrist,

but when he realized that she would keep her hand in the water, he let it go.

Several minutes passed without either of them saying anything, until Claire finally confessed that although the pain was much better, she could no longer stand the cold.

Devon held a towel out toward her. "Set yer hand lightly on top of this," he instructed, "but do not rub it across the towel." She did exactly as he commanded, and when she placed her hand upon the soft material, Devon took up the ends of the towel and gently blotted most of the water away. He was careful to avoid touching the actual burn, but dried the skin around it. It wasn't until he'd completed the ministrations that either of them realized the intimate setting they were in. Although there were no lamps lit, light from the full moon outdoors streamed into the bedroom, casting a soft glow. Claire looked up and noticed how intently Devon gazed at her. The silence between them continued, until at last he asked, "Does it feel better?"

"Yes, thank you. Much better."

"Where I grew up we had no herbal medicine, but it only takes cold water to relieve pain from a burn."

She smiled in appreciation at him, at his benevolence and selflessness; and the way her beautiful face lit up as she did so proved to be his undoing. Without thinking he lifted her still wet wrist to his lips and tenderly placed a kiss upon it. His tongue worked gently to lick away the few remaining drops of water, and the sensation caused Claire's pulse to go wild.

Their eyes met as he looked up, and without further words Devon swept Claire into his arms and kissed her with such force and passion it took away her very breath. She answered the kiss with equal fervor and before she realized what was happening he had drawn her onto the bed and lay his body on top of hers.

He covered her like a warm, unyielding blanket, and

the weight of his body pressed them deep into the mattress. His mouth glided over her skin; his kisses were everywhere—her lips, her cheeks, the base of her throat. He murmured again and again how lovely she was, as if the beauty was something he cherished, like a rare, precious jewel. His words instilled a passion within her that she had never before known, and she responded in kind. She thrust her hands through his lush hair, and frenetically caressed his arms and shoulders. Wantonly she wished that he wore no shirt, for she longed to feel his smooth, manly skin.

His mouth burned a trail of fire along her throat, and as his hands sensually stroked the creamy mounds of her breasts, the sensation was so great that she softly cried out his name. "Devon."

It was just a word, just his name, but when Claire heard the depth of emotion in her voice as she said it, she knew they must stop.

She pushed her arms against his shoulders to allow room to escape, and because he had not been expecting it, he was not quick enough to stop her.

"No, it will never work," she cried out, before realizing what she said.

For several long moments Devon stared at her, baffled by her reaction, mystified by her words.

Trying to pretend nothing had happened, Claire straightened her hair and dress, then looked around for a lamp. "Isn't it best that you leave?" she asked, though her tone implied it was not a question at all.

He was not to be put off. Not again. "What did ye mean, 'it will never work'?" he said, ignoring her request to be alone.

She tried to evade the issue by again suggesting that he leave, but Devon was insistent.

"Ye said, 'It will never work.' What did ye mean by that?"

His persistence was aggravating. She hadn't meant to utter the words; they had simply come out before she could stop them. And anyway, they meant nothing. They had to mean nothing.

"I was simply stating that you must leave before we get caught," she insisted, though she could feel her face flush with embarrassment.

"So ye meant that we could go elsewhere, someplace more private, where it would work?" he asked crudely, knowing it was untrue.

"Remember your position, Devon."

As she'd intended, the words stung him. But she had failed to anticipate exactly how deeply.

He flew off the bed as if prodded by a hot poker. With short, angry gestures he tucked in his shirt, then turned to walk out the door. Before leaving, he threw a hurtful barb at her as well.

"Just when I started to think that ye might be different from all the others, ye've proven me wrong. For that, I thank ye. 'Twould be a shame for me to go 'round thinking ye were anything but the arrogant, self-serving, spoiled brat that ye are."

Before she had a chance to reply, he stormed out the door and slammed it shut behind him. Claire stood transfixed for a moment, then two, knowing that everything he'd said was the truth. Shortly after that, a single large tear rolled slowly down her cheek.

With a roar of fury, his emotions erupted. He slammed his fist into the wall; he upturned the cot; he hurled the bedpan across the room, all the while crying "No!" again and again. Finally his body wearied of the physical exertion, and he collapsed upon the floor, burying his face in his hands.

Jonathan came over to comfort him. " 'Tis best that

he's gone, mate," he told Devon. "Toward the end, he was crazed with the fever."

Clive spoke up. "Sally said it was infection from all the cuts what finally did him in."

It was devastating news. After three months of lying in the filthy basement upon an even filthier cot, Joshua had died the day before. Devon had not had a chance to say good-bye, for Sally had insisted the body be buried immediately.

"It'll just start to rot down here with this hot weather," she had said, and Devon's old gang members had all agreed. After all, they couldn't have known that he would be there the very next day. So, when night fell, they wrapped Joshua in the bedsheet from the cot, sneaked into the cemetery, and dug him an unmarked grave. Jonathan had warned that if they dare try to mark the plot the body snatchers could easily dig it up and would sell Joshua's cadaver to unscrupulous surgeons for a couple of guineas.

"But I can show ye about where it is," he had told Devon, wanting to say anything to help ease his friend's pain.

Devon waved the idea away. "Nay, I don't have time for that," he said. "I only have today off, and I still haven't seen my mum."

Jonathan, Clive, and Gareth said nothing. They knew how upset Devon was to learn of Joshua's death, and they gave him the silence he seemed to need.

Finally Devon heaved a great sigh and looked at the three faces so patiently watching him. They were great friends, he thought. They had all known one another for so many years, and the loyalty they held for each other could never be broken, no matter what devastation they had to face. And they had faced a lot of it.

"Anyone up for a pint at The Snarlin' Dog?" he asked,

and was pleased to see the grins that cracked his friends' solemn faces.

Despite the crowded tables, unruly customers, and occasional fights, the old hangout comforted Devon. Perhaps it was simply the familiarity of it all. Luck was with them as they walked through the door. A group of drunken sailors had just negotiated payment terms with a surly young prostitute, and as they left to conduct business with her, they made available a corner table. Devon and his mates took advantage of the unexpected room, sat themselves down, and ordered pints of thick black ale. They drank the first round in pensive silence, but after ordering their second pints, Jonathan spoke up.

"We got to find out who did this to Joshua," he said to no one in particular, but Devon felt the statement was directed toward him.

"And don't think I'll ever stop looking until I find out who it is," he assured his friends. "The bastard is going to pay for what he did." He raised his glass solemnly and proposed a toast. "To Joshua," he said, and they all banged their mugs together in a salute for their departed friend.

Sample stitching had forever proven to be an infuriating task for Claire, but on this day the job was next to impossible.

"Something on your mind, dear?" her mother asked.

"No, nothing."

"But you've been working on that same pattern for over three hours," Bella observed.

Claire nearly threw down her needles in utter frustration. "You know I've never been fond of sampling," she said to them both.

"It's really something you ought to get over," Louisa

said, as if her daughter's aversion to sampling were something like a cold.

"Where's Devon?" Lilia piped up, and although that was something else Claire found infuriating, she was thankful for the subject change.

"It's his day off," she answered, straining the emotion from her voice.

"I wonder what he does on his day off," Lilia asked aloud.

"That's not something you should be thinking about," Claire pointed out. "The servants' affairs outside of this home are none of our business."

Lilia exhaled a small huff of frustration. "I know, I know. But I still wonder what he does. Do you suppose he's courting anyone?"

"Lilia!" Claire exclaimed. "You are not to be saying such things. Haven't I taught you anything while you've been here?"

The sharp tone of her voice caused both her mother and aunt to look up in surprise, and Claire offered a retreat. "I didn't mean to be so harsh," she said. "But it's not right for Lilia to be speculating on the outside activities of the servants."

Louisa nodded in agreement and eyed her young niece. "Listen to your cousin, Lilia," she said. "Not only should you not be voicing such thoughts aloud, but you shouldn't be having those thoughts in the first place."

"I'm sorry, Aunt Louisa," Lilia said primly, and Claire was grateful that for once her mother had stood behind her.

Silently they all went back to her work, but Claire's mind was whirling with the questions Lilia had posed. What did he do on his day off, anyway? Was it possible, as Lilia had suggested, that he was courting someone? With irritation, Claire realized that the idea made her uncomfortably jealous. She tried telling herself that she

Take 4 FREE Books!

We created our convenient Home Subscription Service so you'll be sure to have the hottest new romances delivered each month right to your doorstep — usually before they are available in book stores. Just to show you how convenient Zebra Home Subscription Service is, we would like to send you 4 Kensington Choice Historical Romance as a FREE gift. You receive a gift worth up to $23.96 — absolutely FREE. You only pay for shipping and handlin There's no obligation to buy anything - ever!

Save Up To 30% On Home Delivery!

Accept your FREE gift and each month we'll deliver 4 brar new titles as soon as they are published. They'll be yours to examine FREE for 10 days. Then if you decide to keep the books, you'll pay the preferred subscriber's price. That all 4 books for a savings of up to 30% off the cover price! Just add the cost of shipping and handling. Remember, yc are under no obligation to buy any of these books at any time! If you are not delighted with them, simply return the and owe nothing. But if you enjoy Kensington Choice Historical Romances as much as we think you will, pay th special preferred subscriber rate and save over $7.00 off tl bookstore price!

couldn't care less whom Devon saw while away from here, but she knew deep down inside that it was far from the truth. Still, it was insane to feel anything for a man like Devon. Think of his background. Think of his lack of social standing. The irony of the situation was that the more she reminded herself of how socially wrong Devon was for her, the less it really seemed to matter.

Thirteen

It had been a week since she'd seen him last, but the time apart had failed to whet her enthusiasm for seeing him again. And as the carriage rolled along, imitating the droning sound of Philip Westbury's voice, Claire suddenly realized why.

"So as I turned around to see who the newcomer was, I couldn't believe my eyes when Laura Tistwell entered." Philip glanced over to assure himself that Claire was sufficiently impressed, then continued on and on, until Claire was unable to focus on what he was saying. It all seemed so unimportant. What was happening to her? Four months ago she would have thought Philip's snide comments appropriate. But now everything he was saying seemed foolish. When had this change happened?

It took only seconds for her to realize the answer. It had happened with Devon's arrival, of course. He had a way of poking fun at the very issues Philip Westbury was now discussing—who wore what to a ball, what color their frocks were, how many wore hats. Though Claire herself thought Philip a gossiping bore since the day they first met, Devon nevertheless used to anger her, for she felt he was criticizing things that shouldn't be poked fun at. Now, however, it was slowly occurring to her that maybe Devon was right. Did it really matter that Sir Geoffrey Welton was still sporting a pigtail despite it going out of style last year? Perhaps, just perhaps, it didn't.

Suddenly one of Philip's comments caught her attention. ". . . and after all was said and done, I really felt that she was acting just like one of those strumpets on Cloak Street. Imagine having her ankles exposed!"

Cloak Street? That name sounded so familiar, but yet . . . yes! Claire had her answer. Cloak was the name of the street where St. Matthew's Salvation was. And it was also where she'd spotted Philip that day, coming out of that gentlemen's club. Claire shook her head. None of this made any sense. Philip expressed such disdain toward the underprivileged, yet she'd seen him walking about that area. Suddenly she could no longer resist the urge to question him about it.

"I'm sorry, Philip," she interrupted, "but I'm afraid I'm quite confused about your last comment." She gave him a sideways glance to be sure he was listening, then added, "Where in the world is Cloak Street?"

She beamed a sweet smile, knowing the question had made him uncomfortable.

"Cloak Street?" he asked, eyebrows knitting in confusion. "What are you talking about?"

"It wasn't me, but you, who mentioned it just now. You said, 'I really felt she was acting like one of those strumpets on Cloak Street.' But I'm afraid, Philip, that I've no idea where or what Cloak Street is, so I'm asking you to explain it to me."

She noticed the almost imperceptible way his hands tightened around the reins, signifying his discomfort. Still, Philip Westbury was a gentleman, and it would take more than a few unexpected questions for him to lose his composure.

"Oh, well, it's just a name I made up," he laughed, "as a euphemism for that nasty side of town that's best not talked about."

"Made it up just now, did you?" Claire pressed.

"Why yes, I did. I thought 'cloak' would be an appropriate name because it has an aura of darkness and danger, much like that part of town."

She knew he was lying, but how to get the truth out of him without revealing what she herself had been doing there?

She gave him a coquettish smile and lightly touched his arm. "Oh, Philip, come now. I believe you've much more knowledge than you're letting on, but you're simply trying too hard to protect me. Now tell me how you really know about Cloak Street."

Her question was unsettling for it was so very unlike her. Still, Philip knew he was backed into a corner, and his mind was overwrought trying to come up with an acceptable answer to still her tongue. At last he replied, "Well, if you must know, one day I was down at the club on Pall Mall and there were some rather abhorrent men, whose names I won't mention, discussing the differences between the East and West Ends. Now don't ask me how they knew it, Claire, but it was mentioned during this appalling conversation that one of the best places to meet East End ladies of a less respectable nature was on Cloak Street."

He desperately hoped his answer would quiet her prodding, but one glance in her direction told him it was not to be.

"But why would anyone ever go there to find such things out?"

He was beginning to get angry. "How would I know, Claire? I only overheard the conversation; I was not part of it. And I dare say I would never think of doing such a thing myself. It was just something I heard being discussed."

He was lying, but there was no way to prove it. His presence there was not something he would admit to, least not to her. But why? She tried telling herself that perhaps he had simply attended to a business transaction there, but she knew it could not be the answer. There was no reason to ever venture east of Regent Street. So what was Philip doing there? The question turned incessantly in her mind like the wheels of a perpetual clock, yet her curiosity, for now, remained unsated.

Although feeling a mild twinge of guilt, Claire nevertheless took a second biscuit and liberally spread it with butter and marmalade. She sighed as she bit into the warm bread, relishing not only the gastronomic enjoyment, but her rare moment of solitude at the breakfast table. She'd risen early this morning, after a fitful sleep puzzling over Philip Westbury's lies. Perhaps he had a perfectly plausible reason for being on the East End, as she did, but did not feel like discussing it. Yet Claire knew, deep down inside, that it was not the case. Philip had been obviously uncomfortable as he fought to think up a quick lie to her question, and his past denouncements of the area belied any proper reason for him being there.

Her musings were interrupted when she heard the sound of someone clearing his throat. As she turned toward the source of the noise she was surprised to see Devon standing in the room.

"Oh!" she said, startled by his presence.

"Sorry for the interruption." His voice was low.

"It's quite all right," she answered, having composed herself once again, "but mayhap next time you could make a little more noise when you enter a room." She said this with a smile, letting him know she was not angry.

"I must speak with ye as soon as possible," he stated, ignoring her attempt at levity. "In private."

Gone was the normally serene look on his face, replaced by tightly controlled anger and despair. Could it be from their previous argument? Yet that seemed unlikely, especially considering that they argued nearly every time they were together, and it had never before taken a toll on him. There was some other reason for his request, and Claire felt herself both concerned and intrigued.

"Are ye able to meet me in the stable tonight at eleven?" he continued. "I know Daniel won't be there for 'tis his night off, and Thomas, his assistant, is always in the servants' quarters by half past ten."

She was aware that her heartbeat accelerated at the thought of being alone with him, and knew for that reason that she must deny his request.

"I'm afraid it's impossible tonight. I've other engagements."

He was not to be dissuaded. "Ye'll be pardoning my frankness, but I know that's not true. Yer maid told me ye were free tonight, and there's been no messenger this morning carrying news of another ball to attend. In fact I understand it will be an early evening for the entire family, which is why ye'll be able to go outside to the stable undetected."

She was embarrassed that he'd caught her in a lie, but it was nothing compared to the realization that he knew why she'd told it.

"I'll not try ravaging your body, so ye needn't worry about letting yerself get out of control."

Dear Lord, if it were possible for the very earth to open and swallow her whole she'd welcome it right now. She felt flames of mortification shoot down to her toes. She knew her face matched the color of a full-blooming rose, yet was helpless to do anything about it. Best to simply agree to his request and get him out of the room.

"Very well, then. I'll meet you in the stable at eleven

tonight." She inspected her biscuit while saying so, unable to meet his eyes.

Devon turned and left the breakfast nook without saying another word. Despite the seriousness of the situation, he could not erase the grin that insisted on cracking his lips. For the first time in his life, he was flattered.

Bolts of the finest fabrics—silk, linen, cashmere, velvet—were spread before them like the colorful fan of a peacock's feathers. In front of each lady was a delicate bone china teacup resting atop its matching saucer. Small plates of sweets flanked the sides of each cup.

The tinkle of ladies' chatter echoed within the papered walls of the dressmaker's shop as seamstresses flitted back and forth to fetch still more bolts of fabric from Hattie Wellington's stock in the back room. It was a busy atmosphere, no different from that of any dressmaker's store, and for the ladies who shopped there it was nearly always an enjoyable experience. Nearly.

Louisa glanced over at her eldest daughter and frowned. "Really, Claire. How do you expect to get any new dresses when you're staring out the window instead of at the fabrics? Now stop this foolishness and pay attention. Hattie's bringing us more material, and we're not leaving the shop today before you're measured for five new gowns."

"Yes, Mother," Claire responded automatically. She turned away from the window to examine the luxurious bolts of cloth being displayed on a nearby table, though she could not prevent her thoughts from drifting back to the person on whom they'd been all day—Devon. Despite telling herself that it was preposterous nonsense to spend so much time thinking about him, she could no more stop her daydreaming than she could halt an advancing war battalion. It was his enigmatic request of this morning that had fueled her fantasies like an out-of-control wildfire. Why did he want to meet her? What would they talk about? Did he have in mind something beyond talking? *I'll not try ravaging your body.* She colored even from the memory of those words, but yet . . .

Stop it! Stop! her mind shouted, but the warning was ignored. There was something so different, so mysterious, so enticing about Devon that Claire was helpless to stop the longing for him that grew more powerful every day. He was so unlike the boring trail of men she'd been exposed to all her life. His questioning of class structure shook the foundation of her world and brought forth emotions Claire never knew she had. Being around him, even if in the midst of an angry row, fired within her a new zest for life.

In more self-indulgent moments, when she allowed her thoughts to drift where they might, she had even envisioned a life with Devon. But then she brushed those fantasies aside like so much worthless dust. They were as real as the legendary unicorn, and far more foolish.

Still, the burgeoning desire for him remained, and she could not ignore the tiny flutter in her heart as she wondered what would happen in the night ahead.

"You must be very tired this evening, my lady, for you are going to sleep so early." Marie busily worked getting Claire ready for bed, as her mistress had advised her of unusual weariness.

"Yes, I don't know what it is, Marie, but I don't seem to have any energy tonight. I think I just need some extra sleep." Claire felt bad about lying to her faithful maid, but she wasn't about to let Marie know what she was up to.

"Well, it seems you are not alone. Ze whole family

is going to bed soon. *Mais oui,* I am sure it was ze sauce that Ellen made tonight. It was too strong!" Marie pronounced her decision with finality, signifying she expected no argument.

For her part, Claire had no wish to give her one. Whether or not the sauce was too strong was not something she could have commented on, for she hadn't tasted a thing. Despite trying to convince herself of the contrary, she could no longer ignore her nervousness about this secret meeting with Devon. What could he possibly want to talk to her about? She'd tried coming up with an answer all day, but to no avail. Her apprehension about the reason behind it all, combined with the knowledge that she'd once again be alone with him, had made eating dinner an absolute impossibility.

Following the meal, Claire had requested a bath be brought up to her room. She thought it might help her relax. Marie had insured that the water was hot and generously perfumed with lavender oil, insisting it was just what her lady needed to help her fall asleep. To be sure, Claire was relaxed from the bath, but she was as far from feeling sleepy as one could possibly be.

"On your table I 'ave a basket of fruit for you, my lady," said Marie. "You ate nothing at dinner, and I think maybe you will wake up very hungry." She fussed over Claire as she said this, brushing Claire's long, golden locks before pulling them all together into one large braid. She tied the end with a piece of red ribbon and helped Claire into her sleeping gown. Once snuggled under the covers, Claire asked Marie in an offhanded way, "It seems so very early to be going to bed, though—what time is it, anyway?"

Marie stepped out of the bedroom to glance at the grandfather clock steadily ticking in the hallway. "It's nearly ten o'clock, my lady. It's not too early for sleeping. You're just used to all those parties, and not getting home until well past midnight." There was no trace of accusation in her maid's voice, but Claire knew Marie was no enthusiast of having to wait up night after night for her to return home.

"You'd best get yourself some sleep, then," she instructed Marie.

"*Oui*, I'm going right now. *Bon soir,* my lady."

"*Bon soir.*"

The door clicked shut behind her as Marie left the room. Claire continued to lie under the covers, listening for any sounds of people moving about within the house. She estimated it was approximately a half hour later when everything around her seemed perfectly still. Indeed, it appeared the entire household had retired early. As quietly as she could she climbed out of bed and walked outside onto the balcony.

The evening air was balmy, yet a refreshing breeze stirred the trees. As always, the scent of the flowers in the garden below perfumed the air. Claire sat down upon the bench to wait until the appointed meeting hour.

The time seemed to pass with immeasurable slowness, but at last she heard eleven steady chimes from the grandfather clock. She waited until the noise was stilled for one last check of any perceptible motion. Carefully she opened her bedroom door, then paused just outside to take a look around.

Up and down the hallway there was no one in sight, so with the grace of a ballerina she delicately closed the door behind her and crept down the stairway.

She had dared not light a lamp for fear of its glow attracting attention, so it was the beam of the moon that illuminated her way. Deftly she crept out the back and stole her way to the stable.

Once inside she relaxed, until she became aware of Devon's presence. He was waiting for her in the back of the stable, farthest away from the house.

"You're here already," she whispered, easing toward him.

" 'Tis easier for me to get here than it is for ye," he said. "I didn't have to sneak past my family."

At last she arrived to where he was already sitting, and although it was quite dark, her eyes had become adjusted and she could make out his shadowy figure.

"Sit down," he said, indicating an upturned crate across from him.

She hesitantly took his suggestion—the seat seemed awfully close—but knew that they had to keep a tight distance between them so that their voices wouldn't awaken anyone.

When she was settled onto the crate, Devon at once began to explain why he had asked her there.

"I thank ye for coming, especially considering our last conversation. But what I'm needing to speak with ye about can't wait any longer, and I'm running out of time."

She couldn't help but be intrigued. "What is it, Devon? What's the matter?"

He launched into his story, detailing everything he knew about what had happened to Joshua. She was attentive all the while he spoke, never once interrupting, never seeming to get bored. His explanation brought with it limited details of what his life had been before he came to the Rushmoors', yet he neglected to give her a full-fledged account of what he did to make money. He only alluded to that life, without furnishing particulars. Instead he focused on that night, and all that had subsequently led up to his being employed by Claire's family.

"So it was Jonathan who spotted the coat of arms on the carriage?" she asked when he concluded his tale.

"Aye, which is how we found out who the carriage belonged to," he replied. "If it hadn't been for that emblem, we never would've known."

Claire was silent for a few moments while she thought back on that evening, but then she shook her head.

"I'm so sorry, Devon, but you've been wasting your time here. I really didn't see anything that night. It was so dark, and my concern was really for Lilia . . ." Her voice trailed away with regret.

"Think about it a little longer, Claire. Think," he pressed. "There may be something ye saw, something ye remember that doesn't seem to matter. Just tell me everything."

His concern for his friend touched a special place within her heart. "You're very loyal to him," she said.

Devon nodded his head in agreement. "Aye, I am," he said. "He was like a brother, and I'd do anything for him, as he would have for me."

It was rare to hear of such devotion, and Claire was touched with admiration for Devon because of how much he cared for those he loved. She knew it was a scarce characteristic among the wealthy to care so much for someone because of what they were. The upper class devoted themselves to people according to where they were ranked in the *ton*'s hierarchy. Never mind if a person they admired was smug, rude, and pretentious. It mattered only that he or she had plenty of wealth and an impressive title. Again she realized how misguided it all seemed.

She closed her eyes and tried to visualize what had happened that evening. "I remember there appeared to be two men fighting," she said slowly, while her mind's eye replayed the event. "And one of them was on the ground. He was being kicked, repeatedly, by the man standing up." Her face reflected the horror of what she had witnessed. "I think the fight had been in progress for some time before I saw anything, because it seemed like it was almost over by the time I first noticed it."

"Why do ye say that?" Devon asked anxiously.

"Because the weaker man was already on the ground, and he wasn't fighting back very much. The man kicking him was so savage, which was why it was strange."

"Strange?"

Claire opened her eyes and nodded. "Yes. After I had watched for a while, I heard shouts off in the distance. Apparently they were directed toward the attacker. As I look back on it now, I remember thinking how odd it was that the man actually stopped to smooth down his hair and tuck in his shirt before walking away. I would have thought he'd have left immediately if he thought someone were chasing him, yet he took the time to groom himself first."

Every word she said etched itself in his memory, as he tried piecing the sketchy details together. "Did ye see which way he ran off?" he asked.

Again, Claire nodded. "Yes, actually I did. He ran away from the docks, headed northwest. I didn't see anything of the people who ran up to the man on the ground, but I remember that it was easy to follow which way the attacker ran off because he was wearing a very light-colored shirt, probably white."

She nonchalantly mentioned that last detail, not realizing the importance of what she'd just said. But Devon's heart raced as he heard it. Criminals in the East End knew better than to wear light-colored clothing, for the very reason Claire had just stated. It stood out too much. You could be spotted. And for those who made their living by illegal means, the more concealed they were, the better. Devon instantly knew that the man who had murdered Joshua was not from the East End.

He encouraged Claire to continue her story, but at last she could say no more. "That's all I remember, Devon. Truly. Nothing else comes to my mind."

He accepted her statement with thanks. "Ye've done

more than ye know," he said. "Thanks for taking the risk o' being seen with me."

She looked up sharply at his last statement, thinking he was being sarcastic. But one look in his eyes told her the truth. He knew how difficult it had been for her to meet him here, and his gratitude was sincere.

His gaze returned her own, but no words were spoken between them. Suddenly the room overflowed with tension; it came as quickly as if a switch were turned on. In that instant Claire was aware of how intimate the situation was. She wore no more than a thin summer gown and robe. It was very late, and she was alone with Devon. A shiver crept its way down her spine, but she knew it was not from the cold.

He continued to look at her, unable to take his eyes off her beauty. She was unaware of how the moonlight streaming in from behind her made her gown translucent. Every shapely curve of her body was outlined, from the graceful slope of her calves to the arch of her breasts. She was unintentionally on display before him, and his body was aroused as it had never been before.

He felt his breath catch in his throat; knew his heartbeat was at twice its normal speed. Still, he made no move toward her.

It had grown quiet in the room, and it appeared their conversation had come to an end. Claire tried telling herself to get up from the crate and go back to the house. There was no more reason for her to be in the stable, alone with Devon. What if they were caught, for heaven's sake? The longer she stayed in here, the better she increased her chances for the unthinkable to happen. Still, her mind's arguments were feeble, for her body refused to obey the commands. Her lips had turned dry, and her small tongue darted out to uneasily lick them. Try as she might, she could not keep from staring at Devon's lean, muscular body. He wore loose-fitting breeches, as if for bed, which gracefully fell against the tops of his thighs, tracing the outline of the taut muscles beneath. His white cotton shirt was open halfway, and it was impossible to overlook his exposed masculine chest.

He was like the fabled Adonis sitting before her in the moonlight, and she could no longer ignore how much she longed for him to kiss her. Please, please! her mind cried out, feverishly hoping he'd hear her plea.

Without thinking, she leaned forward, almost imperceptibly so, but enough for Devon to notice the movement. Yet with an iron will he resisted her reaction, averse to being scorned again. His fists clenched, causing his bronzed forearm muscles to flex tauntingly.

She sensed his agitation and knew in her heart that she was the cause of it. Devon wanted her; that much was clear. But he hesitated now because of what had happened in the past. She had allowed him, mayhap even encouraged him, to bestow his passions upon her, only to flee when her societal consciousness deemed his actions inappropriate. Would she have been so averse had "Earl," "Duke," or "Lord" preceded his name? Had she been doing the very thing for which she criticized others?

Abruptly, he stood up, signaling an end to their meeting. "Ye'd best get back before yer absence is noticed," he said tightly, struggling against the desire he felt for her.

It was all too much. Discarding the years of proper breeding that had taught her to ignore everyone like Devon, Claire rose as well, but it was in an effort to block his way.

"No one knows I'm here," she said slowly, carefully. "They're all asleep."

The invitation was put forth. Unknowingly, Claire held her breath, already feeling flustered by her brazen behavior. Would he reject her now as she had done to him in the past?

His gaze pierced her soul as he studied her, looking to find falseness in the words she'd just spoken. He took a step toward her so their bodies were only inches apart. Slowly his hand slid around the back of her neck, and Claire gratefully closed her eyes as she awaited his kiss. She tipped her head back, feeling his warm breath upon her cheek. She waited . . . and waited.

With surprise and confusion her eyes reluctantly opened, only to see Devon scowling upon her.

"Ye're not wise enough in the ways of the world to play these kind of games with me," he sneered, then brushed her aside as he turned to leave.

If she'd been thinking clearly, shame and mortification would have dominated her thoughts, but in that moment it was blind emotion rushing forth, causing her to call out, "No, Devon! Wait!"

He had not expected to hear protest, so it was with more than a little surprise that he stopped in his tracks and turned around.

She was a forlorn figure standing there in the moonlight, dressed in nothing more than a thin robe and gown. But it was her words and not the image she presented that cracked through his emotional barrier.

"I play no games with you, Devon."

Could she be telling the truth? Did he even care? What the hell was happening to him? He'd come to this household to gain her trust, not a place in her bed. He despised her class and all who belonged to it. But at this moment those feelings seemed hollow, as if based on unproven assumptions. Hadn't she defied those very stereotypes by coming here tonight?

His thoughts whirled about, a maelstrom of confusion, but the desire he felt for her raged stronger than ever. He hesitated only slightly, but when she innocently, yet seductively, pulled at the drawstring on the top of her robe, Devon could no longer fight his unbridled need.

Before she could even finish the movement he stood before her, catching the hand that tugged at her robe.

"Let me do it," was the last thing he said before his lips descended upon hers.

His passion exploded when the contact was made, and he feverishly explored every crevice of her body. Fiercely his lips ground against hers, engulfing her senses. Without delay she succumbed to his hunger, feeling every bit as starved as he. Never before had she felt like giving of herself so completely, and it was this submission that heightened the experience.

She opened her mouth to the insistent probing of his tongue, then copied his actions with equal fervor. His right hand caressed her face, while his left arm wrapped around the small of her back, pressing her body firmly against his. She felt the hardening of his manhood against her leg, and was secretly elated, knowing she excited him.

His lips and tongue moved away from her mouth to trace a hot, wet path to the base of her throat. With blind abandon she tipped her head back, exposing the creamy white skin. He continued kissing her neck and throat, while steadily moving lower toward the beginning mound of her breast. His arms still caressed her face and back, so it was with his teeth that he grabbed hold of the drawstring on her robe and pulled it open.

The light, diaphanous fabric floated away from her body, but still she wore the sleeping gown. It was of no consequence to Devon, for his lips and tongue traveled over the material and began lathing at her nipple as if the skin were laid bare.

The sensation was thrilling, maddening, and suddenly Claire knew her legs could not support her. They began buckling under her in response to Devon's caresses, but no sooner did she feel she was falling than she was swept up in his powerful arms.

Without breaking the attention he lavished upon her breasts, he walked to the far corner of the room and laid Claire upon a mountainous stack of hay.

In one fluid motion he placed his hands underneath her sleeping gown and pulled it over the top of her head. She was now completely undressed, on display before him. He sucked in his breath as he surveyed her spectacular beauty. Never before had he seen a more exquisite woman. Her pale, creamy flesh was a splendor to behold, with nary a flaw to mar its perfection. Her breasts bore the pertness of youth, while at the same time showing the development of womanhood. His eyes traveled down to the flatness of her belly, then lower still to where the golden triangle of hair met at the apex of her firm, shapely legs.

"Never in my life have I seen such beauty," was all he could say before resuming his lavish attention upon her body.

Claire was keenly aware that she wore not a stitch of clothing while Devon was still fully dressed, but instead of that shaming her, she felt roused by the notion. His words, his actions, brought out a wantonness in her that she had never known existed. As his mouth gently suckled on her inflamed buds, she arched up against him to heighten her pleasure. She became aware of a low moaning noise arising in the barn, and was startled to realize that she was the source of it.

Devon's body lay on top of hers, as if to shield it from outside harm. His hand now caressed the same breast where his mouth had been only moments before. His tongue traced a path along her firm stomach, marveling at the softness of her skin. As he approached the initial crest of her mons, he briefly sat up to remove his shirt. With quick, nimble fingers he opened the few buttons that were still fastened, then tossed aside the offending garment.

He was a study in perfection; every inch of his shoulders, arms, and torso rippled with taut muscles. He moved with a fluidity more befitting a cat, as he dipped his head down to nestle between her legs.

She resisted at first, not knowing the pleasures that awaited, but when he whispered that she must trust him, her compliance was immediate. In seconds she felt transported to heaven, for she had been unaware of such earthly stimulation. He kissed and licked at the velvety skin on the inner thigh of each leg, then continued the ministrations on the core of her womanhood.

At first his touch was so gentle she almost didn't feel it, but soon carnal sensations went sweeping through her body, all originating from the secret place between her legs. Her heart hammered wildly as her blood roared in her eardrums, and without warning she sensed there was something more to come.

"Devon!" she cried out, unsure why her body trembled and shook, yearning for something she did not know existed.

His answer was to place his hands on either side of her hips, and pull her body toward him to intensify the contact he made. Again and again his tongue relentlessly teased her tiny button of pleasure, knowing it was her source of sensual delight. Suddenly Claire felt rolling spasms shake her body, and again she cried out Devon's name.

When the waves of her pleasure subsided at last, he knew the time had come to claim her as his own. His manhood was as hard as iron, and he ached to bury himself deep within her.

He removed the loose trousers he'd been wearing, and knew from Claire's reaction that it was her first sight of an unclothed man.

She said not a word as he kneeled between her legs, but he could sense her fear.

"Don't be afraid, beautiful one," he whispered. "I'll give ye more pleasure than ye've had thus far in yer lifetime."

"Is that possible?" she asked, doubt lacing her tone.

"Aye, it is. But there's a bit of pain at first."

Her dark eyes widened with fear and she made a feeble effort to push him away. "Pain? What do you mean?"

He was so consumed with his need for her that speaking became difficult. "Shhh," he cooed. "Let me teach ye."

Up until now he'd given her no reason not to trust him, and as she looked into his eyes and saw how they burned with desire for her, she felt an overwhelming need to please him despite any predictions that she might be hurt.

Silently she gave her consent, and with a look comprising both gratitude and passion, he buried himself within her in one, forceful thrust.

Her eyes popped open in both surprise and panic. Despite Devon's forewarning, she had not expected such pain, and she put forth her best effort to rid herself of its source.

He was actually grateful for her weak pummels upon his chest, for they provided a moment of distraction from the supreme pleasure of being enveloped in her womanly sheath. In response to her beatings he laid kisses upon her face and neck, all the while assuring her the pain would subside.

Even as he spoke the words Claire realized they were true, and in place of the pain she felt an increasing warmth. Soon Devon began to move slowly inside of her, and Claire automatically responded in kind.

His initial subtle movements changed to smooth, powerful strokes, and soon Devon was groaning from the overwhelming ecstasy that fired his body. His motion became faster, then faster still, and he knew he wouldn't be able to hold off much longer. He could tell by the way Claire was breathing that her peak was very near. Her body writhed in passion, and her skin glowed from the efforts of her exertion. In lustful desperation she clung to Devon's body, anticipating the climax that hovered near them both. At last the pent-up desire exploded within her body, and as Devon felt her cries from the release, he, too, succumbed to the culmination of their sensual mating dance.

For long moments they lay quietly together, the only sound being their rapid breathing. When at last Claire knew she must get back to the house, it was with reluctance that she reassembled her clothing.

Silently Devon watched her dress, wary of speaking lest the spell be broken. When she rose from the haystack he stood to join her, and by the longing in her eyes he knew she did not regret what had happened between them. Without saying a word she reached her hand up to stroke his face, then placed both arms around his neck to pull him toward her in a parting embrace.

The gesture was a tender one, and appropriate for the moment. Both reveled in the glory they had shared as one, but both also realized it was only temporary joy.

As the kiss ended Claire gave Devon's hand a goodbye squeeze, then turned and left the barn without looking back. Her body and mind had been opened by a breathtaking experience, but as she stole through the garden one thought dominated her consciousness: where would it lead?

Fourteen

She awoke waiting for mortification to consume her, but it never came. As she lay in bed remembering the beautiful experience she'd shared with Devon the night before, the only feeling she had was a longing to see him again. On this day, however, she knew it was not to be, for she'd already made plans to spend the day with Philip.

A sense of gloom washed over her, as if a dark cloud had instantly blocked out the sunshine streaming through her window. Still, Claire knew she mustn't feel that way. Seeing Philip made her mother and Aunt Bella very happy, and he was, after all, more than appropriate for marriage. He ranked high in society, was accepted in all circles—why, what more could she hope for? A tiny voice inside her shouted out *Love!* but it seemed that notion would never materialize. Her matrimonial clock was ticking loudly, and Claire knew her mother would be mortified if she failed to find a husband by the end of this season. And that time was fast approaching. It was now less than four weeks until the grouse-hunting season opened, and then everyone who was anyone would retreat to the country. It was unheard of to remain in London beyond August 12, and Claire knew that day would come sooner than she wanted.

She closed her eyes as if to bar the dark thoughts that were threatening to overtake her. Better to attempt enjoying her day with Philip and not dwell on thoughts that were better left alone.

Minutes later Marie rapped upon the door, and the next half hour was spent enjoying the rapid chatter of her delightful maid, whose nonstop talking was a welcome distraction.

As usual, Philip was prompt, and when the clock struck 10:00 he was ringing the bell. Claire was dressed in one of her favorite gowns, an off-white muslin over which lay a pale pink satin tunic with beaded accents on the hem and sleeves. She forced a big smile upon her face as she walked into the parlor where Philip awaited her.

"Good morning," she said merrily, last evening's memories impressing themselves in her tone of voice.

"Good morning to you, Claire," Philip answered, pleased to see her in such good humor.

They took off without haste, for their plan was to have a picnic in the country, at a favorite destination of Philip's more than two hours away. The ride began as others always did, with Philip prattling on about the latest gossip, and Claire feigning interested responses.

"So whatever did he do?" she now asked, intent on proving she'd been paying attention.

"Dismissed him, of course," Philip answered. "After all, you can't have a manservant showing disrespect."

Mention of servants conjured up images of Devon, and without considering whether or not Philip would be interested, Claire at once brought up his name.

"I'm glad such troubles have not occurred within our staff," she said, unaware of the sated look that crossed her face. "In fact our newest footman, Devon Blake, has proven to be especially fitting. He's taken on his position with an enthusiasm that even Father appreciates."

"Is that so?" Philip managed to utter, annoyed by how blissful Claire seemed.

"Indeed. In fact, I don't ever remember Father even mentioning any of the servants before, but he has openly expressed his appreciation of Devon's good work."

Philip eyed his companion with growing annoyance. "You know, Claire," he said, in an I'm-going-to-set-things-straight-for-you tone, "it's really very unbecoming of you to prattle on about the domestics, no matter how good they are. After all, they're supposed to be good, and if they're not they are dismissed. It confounds me to understand why you're taking such an interest in them, and frankly, I'm surprised by your behavior. It's so uncharacteristic."

His admonition stilled her tongue, and for that Philip was grateful. Nevertheless, it was easy to sense a certain fondness she seemed to hold toward the servant, no matter how ludicrous the notion. For that reason Philip decided the time had come. He had courted Claire long enough, and in order to secure that dowry before the chit did something foolish, today was the day when he'd insist that she marry him.

The grassy clearing where they were to have their picnic was everything Philip had described to Claire, and more. Acres of lush grass spread out before them like a giant green welcome mat. Willow trees graced the landscape, their boughs gently sweeping the ground. Alongside the clearing was the most charming lake, its clear blue water rippled by the whisper of breeze stirring the air.

Claire dismounted from the carriage, awed by the beauty surrounding her. The tranquil setting, the fragrance in the air, could only be made more perfect by—by what? an inner voice demanded. A different companion? Perhaps one with a lean, muscular build, startling green eyes, and a scar running along his left jawline? Perhaps someone fiercely loyal to his friends, no matter what their social standing? Perhaps someone whose name happens to be Devon and with whom you are falling in love?

She stood rooted to the ground. Falling in love? Did she just think that? Of all the crazy, outrageous, inane ideas! Claire shook her head to clear the notion, lest it accidentally take root. She'd always dreamed of falling in love, of course, but with a servant? A mere commoner? The scandal was unthinkable. Besides, she'd been taught from early childhood to associate with only those people who could perpetuate or improve the family's social standing. In love with a servant? Preposterous.

Thankfully, Philip interrupted her self-imposed outrage by asking her to have a seat upon the blanket he had laid out. At that moment, Claire realized that she'd been idly standing by with her ludicrous thoughts while allowing Philip to do all the work. To make up for it, she gushed with gratitude over his efforts.

"Oh, Philip, how wonderful!" she exclaimed as she eyed the feast spread upon the blanket. His cook had gone through a good deal of extra effort to prepare all the food Philip had brought with them. A giant platter filled with various cold meats and fish was the picnic's centerpiece, and surrounding it were baguettes of crusty bread, hard-boiled eggs, beetroot salad, olives, assorted cheeses, a basket of fresh fruit, and a jug of sweet wine.

"Come, sit down, and let's enjoy this wonderful meal," Philip said, sweeping his arm out in an invitational gesture.

As soon as they were seated he poured them each a glass of wine and said he wanted to propose a toast. "To the most charming, beautiful woman that I could ever hope to be in the company of," he said, looking deeply into Claire's eyes. His intimate gesture made her feel uncomfortable, so to break the moment she took an unladylike gulp of her wine.

"Good to see you're enjoying it," was all Philip said

as he started dishing out the food. For several long minutes they ate in silence, both of them savoring the delicious fare. Then, as Claire was contemplating a second helping of the smoked salmon, Philip laid his plate down, then took hold of Claire's and did the same.

Surprised and mildly annoyed at having her food taken away, Claire was about to issue a composed retort when she realized that Philip had moved unexpectedly close to her. Her immediate instinct was to put some distance between them, but he halted her effort with the gentle but firm placement of his hand upon her shoulder.

"I've been wanting to speak with you for some time now," he began, "and I've decided that I can wait no longer." He grabbed hold of her hand and pressed it firmly against his lips, then, adopting his most passionate expression, looked deeply into her bewildered eyes and said, "The time has come when I must express my deepest, truest feelings for you and ask that you honor me by becoming my wife."

If he had punched her in the stomach Claire would have been less surprised. All the life drained from her in that one dreadful moment, because she knew she had no choice but to accept Philip's offer. The dreams she had clung to about falling in love, about being swept off her feet by a man who treasured her, were now wrenched away with that one horrid sentence—the very sentence she had hoped to one day hear from a man she loved. No time to seek out someone who would make her feel she was the single most important thing to him. No time to fall in love, no time to be swept away. Her time had run out.

Still, she could not bring herself to accept her inevitable fate. For just a while longer, she felt compelled to stall.

"Why, Philip, I . . . I don't know what to say."

He smiled broadly. "Just say the words we both want

to hear—that you agree to become Lady Philip Townsend."

What *you* want to hear, she corrected him in her mind.

"It's . . . it's such a big decision." She smiled sweetly. "Please, I must have just a little time to consider your proposal."

"But why?" he pressed. "You know it's what we both want, what we're both destined for. Claire, I'm not a man to openly show his true feelings, but you must realize how deeply I've loved you these past several months."

You mean how deeply you love my money, Claire nearly snorted, but kept the retort to herself. After all, what choice did she have? She knew Philip was no more in love with her than she with him, but what did it matter? He more than met her family's approval, and Claire was no longer a blushing girl of sixteen. Why, later this year she'd see her twenty-first birthday, and with fears of "spinster" being whispered about her, she had best seal her fate as quickly as possible.

"I'm just so overwhelmed. I really must have time to sort out my feelings."

He moved even closer to her, if that were possible. "Very well, darling," he breathed against her ear, "you go on and take whatever time you need. I know you'll realize that you feel the same about me as I do about you, and I only ask that you don't keep me waiting too long, for what we both know the destined answer will be."

"I'll be as quick as I can," she promised, fervently wishing he'd give her room to breathe. Instead, she was forced to deal with yet another unpleasant matter, for Philip decided at that moment that he wanted to kiss her.

With all the romance he was capable of mustering, he used one hand to tip her head up—"push" up was perhaps the more appropriate word—then eased himself forward and plopped his lips upon her own.

For long moments he did nothing else, merely rested his mouth atop hers like a cold, slick eel settling upon a berth. Then, crudely, he forced his tongue into her mouth and grunted upon discovering how warm and soft it was. So repulsed was Claire by his unexpected affection that for a minute she was shocked into stillness. But when she felt his left hand traveling dangerously low down her neck, her immobility vanished.

With a start she jumped away from him and crossed her arms against her chest. "Lord Townsend," she said formally, "no matter what our eventual relationship may be, your actions are inexcusable. I demand that you take me home this minute."

"Oh, Claire, I'm so sorry," he said in his most humble voice, "but my feelings for you went temporarily out of control. I assure you, it will never happen again."

She breathed a huff of disgust. "Your apology is noted. Nevertheless, I would like to leave."

"As you wish. Allow me a moment to put our things together and we'll be off."

Deciding he deserved to clear their picnic by himself, Claire walked toward the lake as she waited for him to finish the job. Where in the world had Philip learned to be so crude? she wondered. In her opinion, admittedly an inexperienced one, she felt as though he'd treated her like a common doxy. His kiss had been so passionless, so thoroughly unarousing, quite unlike . . . She tried clearing the thought, but the inevitable comparison emerged. Philip's kiss had been the exact opposite of Devon's. Where Philip's was cold and slimy, Devon's had been hot and full of desire; where Philip was motionless, Devon had moved seductively. She knew she shouldn't be thinking like that, but the sensible side of her mind consistently lost out to the emotional one. Accept your fate, Claire, she kept hearing. Still, it was difficult, and at that moment the only thing she knew for sure was that she wanted that dreadful afternoon to end.

The drive back home was primarily in silence, as both passengers were absorbed in their private thoughts. Despite her initial stalling, Philip was confident of Claire's eventual acceptance. Before this year was over he would claim her as his lawful wife, and every pound of the dowry that came with it. All in all he felt quite satisfied, and knew at once where he'd go to celebrate. It was a sweet victory, indeed, over that slovenly servant Claire seemed to hold in such esteem. Not only was he losing the one upper-class woman who had ever paid him mind, but his mother would soon be servicing the man who'd made it happen. Philip nearly laughed aloud with glee at the irony, and hurried the horses along so he could get an early start on the evening.

For her part, Claire was moody and despondent. Philip's proposal had solidified a notion that previously had merely been a possibility. Her life was suddenly, irrevocably altered, and the only thing she wanted was time for a good cry.

At long last they arrived back on Park Lane, and Philip helped her down from the carriage and walked with her to the door.

"Now remember, my darling," he said with a smile, "don't keep me waiting too long for your answer. After all, we both know what it will be."

She resisted the urge she had to slap the smug grin off his face. Instead she replied coolly, "We'll be in touch," then withdrew her hand from his grip, walked inside the house, and went straight up to her bedroom. The emotional turmoil of the day had exhausted her, and in seconds she was sound asleep.

Three hours later, she awoke with a start from a dream she'd been having. In it was Philip, now her husband, sitting across from her at an impossibly long table. They were having dinner, the two of them, but in the dream she had never felt more alone. The distance she felt toward Philip was represented by the length of the table at which they sat, and in a high, distinct voice, Philip was laughing at her. The sound was menacing, taunting, for Philip knew he was victorious in getting everything he wanted, entirely at her expense, while she was left with nothing.

As she sat in the darkness the dream faded away, but not the lonely feeling it had brought. A surge of desire to see Devon suddenly seized her, and realizing that she was still dressed, she swung her legs over her bed and left the room to seek him out.

Except for the servants, the house was empty. "At a dinner party," was the explanation Claire received in regard to the family's absence. Throughout the household, servants were making early preparations for their work tomorrow. As she spotted Emma walking down the stairs, her huge key ring slapping her thigh, she hurried to catch up with her and inquire about Devon.

"Last I saw him, my lady, he was in the basement filling the coal bin," the head housekeeper informed Claire in her crisp, efficient manner.

With a quick word of thanks Claire left to seek him out, feeling secure in the knowledge that no matter what Emma Leeds might think of Claire's inquiry, she was one of the few household servants who knew how to hold her tongue.

Carefully holding a lamp in one hand, she grasped the railing leading into the basement with the other and descended the narrow, steep stairway.

As Emma had said, Devon was down there, and as Claire watched his lean, taut body, now covered with sweat and soot, gracefully shoveling coal into the bin, she knew she had never seen a more fascinating man.

A slight noise, the shuffle of her foot upon the ground, was enough to alert him of her presence. He looked up immediately, straight into her eyes, and at once became aware of the hunger lurking within the liquid brown depths.

He tossed aside the shovel and walked steadily toward her. Neither of them said a word. It was hot in the room—very hot. Fire roared from the coal stoves, and the heat had long ago forced Devon to remove his shirt. As he drew closer Claire could see his muscles slickly outlined by the sheen of sweat that covered his body. He crossed the room as gracefully as a panther, and she was captivated by the way his body moved. He was like a study of masculine perfection. When at last he stood before her, she shook with desire.

Soundlessly, he gathered her in his arms and pressed his lips against hers. She melted against him, molding the length of her body against his unyielding male strength. Her instant compliance seized his desire, making his senses race. He deepened their kiss, exploring every corner of her soft, pliant mouth. Her response was a lustful moan. He thrust both hands into her thick, golden mane, then pulled her head back to expose her neck. Instantly he traced his tongue across her smooth, creamy skin, following every lick with fiery kisses.

He could taste the saltiness of the sweat that had begun forming on her skin, and Devon knew he had never wanted anything as much as freeing Claire's body from the restrictive clothing. He tore his mouth away only long enough to undo the fastenings and reach under her dress to pull the entire gown over the top of her head. Carelessly he tossed it aside, and for one fleeting moment Claire knew how dirty it would be lying amidst the soot. But when she felt Devon's tongue plunge into her ear, any thoughts other than the sensations racing through her body vanished at once.

With only a couple of additional moves he had removed every item of her clothing, and now she wantonly pressed herself against him, reveling in the exquisite feeling of his smooth, hot skin making contact with hers. He rubbed himself against her, hardening her nipples until the feeling was almost painful. He slid both hands across her luscious mounds, then took one nipple deeply into his mouth. Over and over his tongue bathed the swollen areola, until it was so sensitized that Claire cried out his name.

"Oh, Devon, Devon!" she moaned repeatedly. Hearing her say his name that way hardened him more than he had ever been, yet he put off their mating, wanting to prolong it for as long as possible.

He lifted her onto a nearby table, then began to kiss the length of her body. As he neared the apex of her femininity, she trustingly spread her legs before him. He was stirred by her passion, and bent his head between her thighs to satisfy her need.

As his tongue began to work magic, Claire sighed with unrestrained pleasure. She felt as though she were floating, that a great weight had been lifted from her body and she was free from all that troubled her. She closed her eyes and allowed her head to fall back, focusing only on the pleasure Devon brought her. She could feel the sweat pouring from her body, knew that it streamed down paths between her breasts. Yet it didn't matter. She knew Devon didn't care, was in fact aroused by the slickness of her body, and the thought made her feel uninhibited. There was no need for pretenses with him—he accepted her for what she was.

Soon she felt a tightness between her legs, waiting to explode. Her breath came quicker now, in shallower gasps. She was close, so close. Devon sensed her impending release and responded in kind. All his attention was centered on the core of her pleasure. His tongue swished relentlessly back and forth with quick, firm strokes. He felt her body tremble, then shake. She again cried out his name and clamped her thighs against his head. Still he continued his assault upon her senses, and in seconds she reached her peak once again, only this time with more force than before.

The impact of her unrestrained passion stirred him to near madness. He stood and pulled her toward him, plunging his tongue into her mouth as he readied her to receive him. But to his astonishment she forbade his entrance—for a moment.

With the grace of an oak leaf floating to the ground, Claire slid off the table and went down onto her knees. She burned to couple with Devon. Every nerve in her body cried out for him. But she would hold off their union for a few minutes more, long enough to give him the same pleasure he'd just given her. She wanted to kiss him, to touch him, to taste him—everywhere. So instead of allowing him to bury his manhood within her sheath, she knelt before him, wrapped her arms around his hips, then drew him into her mouth.

"Claire, what—"

His confusion turned to moans of desire as her moist, soft lips enveloped him. She was gentle at first but became bolder, more confident, as she heard his reaction. He thrust both hands into the silky locks of her hair and rocked his hips against her. He could hear his blood roaring in his eardrums, was aware of the furious pounding of his heart. He felt her wet tongue sliding along his manhood, stroking his rigid flesh until he teetered on the verge of insanity. Suddenly he couldn't wait another second to sheath himself within her warm femininity. In one sweeping gesture he lifted her onto the table, positioned himself between her long, slender thighs, and drove himself inside her.

He filled her completely, and was amazed at how right it felt to be there. Their bodies fit together as if created from a single mold. Knowing instinctively what she would want, he varied his movement within her; sometimes fast, sometimes slower, teasing her until she longed for fulfillment, then giving her everything she desired. He pulled her even tighter against him, their slick skin making contact, and seared her mouth with a kiss as hot as the room in which they mated.

It took only minutes for them both to reach their peaks, so aroused were they by their hunger for one another. Claire felt searing heat coiling within her groin, then suddenly it was like a wild animal bursting out of its cage. The fury with which the climax greeted her was so strong she nearly fainted afterward, but Devon held her in his arms until she regained her senses, planting gentle kisses upon the top of her head.

They sat together on the table for several long minutes, neither saying a word, not wishing to break the spell they had woven.

Finally Claire knew they must return to reality, and she moved from the table to begin assembling her clothes. As she had thought when Devon tossed them aside, they were covered from top to bottom with soot and ash. Oddly, the thought of explaining the reason for her garments' condition did not distress her in the least. More disturbing to her now was remembering what had happened this afternoon. So far she'd kept the event bottled up, but the one person to whom she suddenly wanted to relay the conversation was sitting beside her. Not pausing to ask herself why she felt compelled to tell him, Claire heard herself say, "Lord Townsend proposed to me this afternoon."

Devon's green eyes clouded over like the sea before

a storm, and he remained eerily quiet in response to her announcement. Claire was not to know that his calm exterior was indicative of inner turmoil; in this case, the piercing stab of jealousy as he pictured her with another man.

"I haven't accepted his offer yet . . ." She purposely left the statement hanging, as if the outcome were up to Devon. What she dared not tell him is that she was stalling to accept Westbury's proposal because she hoped, despite how ludicrous the idea, that Devon might give her one of his own. It was crazy, irrational, and completely unacceptable, but the notion refused to disappear. By bringing up the conversation with Westbury, she longed to hear Devon tell her not to accept the proposal, or at least give her some indication to put off the marriage. He remained silent.

Hadn't accepted the offer yet? A glimmer of hope illuminated Devon's soul. Could it be that she was suspending her decision because she felt something for him? Had he finally been proven wrong in his hatred toward the upper class and found someone who disregarded the societal pecking order? Perhaps Claire really was different. If only she'd tell him why she was not yet officially engaged. It seemed apparent that the Marquess of Townsend intended to make Claire his wife, so why the delay? Why wouldn't she tell him more?

His silence was his answer, Claire realized, and instantly felt silly for even entertaining the idea that he would want anything to do with her. He'd always made it clear how he felt toward people of her class; why would she possibly think she were any different? Her embarrassment was acute, and she hastily donned her tarnished garments. She wanted nothing more than to get away from him. So acute was her disappointment that she turned bitterly angry, and a need to hurt him welled up inside her.

"I have to tell you how grateful I am for the time we've spent together," she said flippantly. "You've taught me well, and I'm sure I'll have no trouble pleasing my new husband."

Had she buried a knife in his heart he would have felt less pain. The idea of another man even glancing her way set his blood boiling, but far be it for him to show outward signs of jealousy. She'd all but said outright that she wanted to marry Westbury. He was an idiot to think she'd consider marrying below her class.

"Think nothing of it," he said with a quiet sneer. "Ye're a quick learner, though I don't remember showing ye everything ye seem to know. Perhaps it's to another teacher ye owe the real gratitude."

His comment enraged her, and in a white-hot fury she drew back her arm and slapped him soundly across the face. "I should have expected such a crude, foul thing to come from you," she spat.

"And why not?" he shot right back. "Ye've always been good at reminding me where I come from, making sure the line between us stays firmly in place. It's not like men from my background are ones ye'd consider marrying, so why should I feel like treating ye special?"

"Who said anything about marrying?" Claire nearly shouted, trying to control the shaking of her voice.

" 'Twas ye who did," Devon said evenly, "the minute ye brought up the subject of Westbury."

He was right, of course, and she had no response to what he'd just said, nor any desire to shoot back a retort. Instead she was riveted to the spot where she stood, hearing over and over one of the statements he'd just made: ". . . it's not like men from my background are ones ye'd consider marrying." So that's what he thought, did he? That she'd never consider marrying someone like him? On the surface, he was right. Men like him were not marriage material. After all, he had no wealth, he had no title, he had no connections. Did he even know who his family was? He'd never mentioned his parents. Perhaps he didn't know them. The thought acutely saddened her, speculating on what his upbringing must have been. But it was that one statement that held her transfixed. Was he suggesting, as wild as it seemed, that if she'd let him know about the feelings she held for him, that he wouldn't reject her as she had assumed, but instead would admit to sharing those same feelings himself?

She heard a creak upon the stairs and realized that Devon had dressed himself and stood on the staircase, preparing to leave. But before doing so, he growled, "Have a nice life, princess." Then he vaulted up the steps, leaving her coldly alone in the hot, sooty basement.

Fifteen

With complex emotions swirling within his head, Devon welcomed the chance to put aside his worries and spend time with the one pillar of sanity he could always count on—his mum.

She could read her son as easily as others read pages in a book, and Devon longed for the comfort and understanding she gave him. He'd received no protest when asking for the day off—in fact Nigel apologized for not giving it to him sooner.

As he walked the familiar streets of London's East End, he spotted a surprising face among the crowd. It was Philip Westbury, just leaving The Night Star. What a hypocritical sot he is, Devon thought. He snubbed Devon in front of Claire, but patronized the East End whores. No doubt in secret, for he would just as soon walk the streets naked rather than openly admit his presence here.

Ducking behind a building to avoid confrontation, Devon waited until Westbury mounted his horse and rode off before making his way inside The Night Star. Absently, he wondered who Westbury had been with, but the sight of Sally's big grinning face obliterated the thought.

"Now here's a sight for sore eyes if ever I did see one," she said while walking toward him with outstretched arms. Devon gave her the biggest bear hug he was capable of giving and held her until Sally squeaked in protest.

"My, lad, ye'll be breaking me bones with a greeting like that! Now step back and let us have a good look at ye." Her eyes roamed the length of Devon's body, and when she was finished she gave an appreciative whistle. "Ye've gotten a mite bit stronger than when I saw ye last, boy. And I can't say I ever remember ye looking quite so good."

Her candid talk was a welcome change from the subtle innuendoes he'd grown used to at the Rushmoors'. Maybe Sally wasn't ladylike, as Claire would say, but it was refreshing to know exactly what a person thought.

And thinking of Claire . . . no. He dashed the thought from his mind as quickly as it had taken root. He was here to forget his current worries, not dwell on them.

"Eating hot meals does a body good," Devon admitted, then changed the subject. "Is Mum available?"

"Just finished up with a client, as a matter of fact," Sally nodded. "Ye go on up and see her. I know she'll be happy."

"I won't leave without saying good-bye," he promised Sally as he bounded up the stairs.

"Not if ye know what's good for ye," she joked.

In seconds he stood in front of his mother's door and rapped upon it. May opened the door expecting it to be one of the other girls, and when she saw it was Devon she squealed with joy.

"Finally!" she yelped as she embraced her son. "I was wondering when ye'd ever get another day off."

She ushered him into the room and plopped him into his favorite chair. "Oh, darling, I was hoping it wouldn't be too much longer before I saw my favorite boy again." She beamed with happiness.

"Ye know I'll always come when I can," Devon said.

"But 'tis not too often that the newer servants get days off."

"They been working ye hard, have they?" May asked, concern replacing her smile.

Devon patted his mother's hand. "Now, Mum, don't ye be worrying about me." He stood up and turned around. "Can't ye tell that I'm eating better?"

May nodded with appreciation as she noticed the firm, strong muscles that graced his physique. "They just don't get better looking than my son," she said with a chuckle.

"Ye'll have me blushing like a bloomin' maid if ye keep that talk up."

He sat back down again, and the conversation became sober. "Sally says ye just finished with a client."

Oddly, his mother smiled. "He left about five minutes before ye came."

"Ye like this man, do ye, Mum?" Devon asked, puzzled by his mother's expression.

May waved aside her son's question. "I don't like him, if that's what ye're thinking. It's just that he's a noble man, and always gives me a right handsome tip."

Noble man? And he'd just seen Westbury leave. Oh, Lord, Devon thought, his stomach making a sickening flip, please don't let it be . . .

"What's his name, Mum?" he asked, loathing to ask but needing to confirm his suspicions.

"Now, Devon, ye know that's confidential. Sally'd kill me if she was knowing I talked about any of the clients."

"Who's gonna know, Mum?" Devon pressed. "I promise I won't tell anyone."

May hesitated. "Still, I really shouldn't . . ."

Devon heard the doubt in her voice and knew he'd won her over. "Oh, c'mon. If he makes ye happy with a big fancy tip, then I want to know who the bloke is."

May smiled in defeat. "Very well. Ye're right, o' course. I know ye wouldn't tell Sally."

"Not in a million years."

May leaned toward her son with a conspiratorial air, then confessed in a low voice, "His name is Lord Philip Townsend, and he's a bloomin' marquess!"

Despite being prepared for it, hearing the name spoken aloud nauseated Devon. His stomach clenched, and he felt sour bile rising up, threatening to spill forth. He doubled over with his hands across his abdomen, mentally forcing his stomach to settle. May was made frantic by her son's response and rushed forward to help him. She asked him what was wrong, but Devon blocked everything out until he felt calm enough to speak.

When the nausea finally passed, he leaned back in his chair to look his mother straight in the eyes. "Ye'll not see that man again," he commanded in a calm, eerie tone.

May was appalled. "Not see him? Ye're crazy! He's my best customer! I've been seeing him for over two years now. What's the matter with ye, Devon? Why are ye acting like this?"

Devon ignored all her questions and instead repeated his order. "Just listen to me, Mum, and don't see him ever again."

May knew Devon would never say anything without having good cause, but the thought of losing the marquess's money was almost more than she could bear.

"Oh, Dev, why're ye doing this to yer poor mum? I don't want to stop seeing him. He's the only client I have who ain't a smelly sod from around these parts. I like his fancy smells and his fancy clothes. He always wears the nicest shirts, as white as snow, with buttons like ye've never seen before."

Shirts . . . white as snow? There was something about that, something that seemed to trigger his memory. . . . Devon sat as still as a vulture, letting the meaning of his mum's words fully penetrate his mind. Of course! That was it. The white shirt. Claire had mentioned how easy it had been to watch Joshua's murderer slip away because of his "light-colored" or white shirt. Devon had known then that the man he sought was not from the East End. His mother's description of Lord Townsend solidified his suspicion. The fancy white shirt. With fancy buttons . . .

He jammed his hand into his right pocket, where he'd been carrying a certain fancy button ever since the day Jonathan had given it to him. He pulled it out and shoved it under his mother's nose. "Have ye ever seen this button before, Mum?"

She recognized it immediately. "It's the marquess's!" she said, not yet understanding what it all meant. " 'Tis from my favorite shirt of his."

"Ye're sure?"

"Positive. I'd recognize this anywhere. Have ye ever seen such a button like it? A wee picture of the parliament building carved on every one of them." May frowned as she thought of the shirt. "Of course, he never wears that shirt anymore."

Devon's hand tightened around the button. "Why not?"

"Oh, ye know those rich folks, Devon. He says he can't wear it anymore because 'tis old and past the season." May sighed with exasperation. "I'm telling ye, if I had the money to buy just one of those shirts I'd retire for a year."

Past the season? Missing a customized button and torn beyond repair was more likely the reason, Devon thought bitterly. Rage boiled in his veins as he knew beyond a doubt that Lord Philip Townsend had murdered his best friend. His mind whirled with the realization, with the startling clarity of truth.

His eyes bore into his mother's as he searched for the words to tell her what he knew. She'd been chattering steadily along about Westbury's shirts but at last noticed her son was paying not the least bit of attention to her. She also knew what his silence meant.

"What's wrong, Devon? Ye haven't heard a word I been saying."

"It's him, Mum. It's Westbury."

May shook her head, not understanding. "Lord Townsend? What about him?"

"Don't ye see? Don't ye know what's going on here? Westbury's the one who killed Joshua!"

If the situation hadn't been so serious, May's expression of horror might have seemed almost comical. Her eyes widened into twin saucers, her mouth formed a silent "o," and her hands clutched her heart as if in response to an attack. "Ye can't be serious!" she exclaimed, rebelling against the truth.

But Devon grew more emphatic with every passing minute. "There's no denying it, Mum. Look at everything that's happened. First, ye said he's been a regular customer for over two years, so we know he often comes over to this side of town."

May nodded, acknowledging what Devon said but still not wanting to believe it.

"Ye also said he wears white shirts, 'snow white,' ye called 'em. With fancy buttons unlike any ye've seen before."

May expelled a heavy sigh and indicated that Devon should keep talking.

"Claire Rushmoor, the lass who saw the fight that evening, told me that it was easy to watch the attacker leave the docks, because of the white shirt he wore."

"That still don't mean 'twas him. White's not an uncommon color, and besides—"

"Aye, 'tis uncommon around here, Mum, and ye know it. It's too easy to spot, so no one wears white. And besides, white doesn't stay 'snow white' for too long around here. With all the mud and soot, a white shirt would be gray in a couple of hours. Unless, of course, ye've got enough pounds to keep an ample supply of white shirts on hand."

Devon took a deep breath, then continued. "Finally, Mum, and this is the most important thing. Westbury wears custom buttons on his shirts. While he was being attacked, Joshua pulled a button off the shirt of the cad who was beating him. This is the button, the one I'm holding in my hand. And ye just told me who it belongs to."

The indisputable evidence stared May in the face, and she finally acknowledged what Devon had been so adamantly trying to tell her. "All right, ye've convinced me. It seems it couldn't be no one else but the marquess." Unexpectedly, May buried her face between her hands and began to sob.

"Mum?" Devon said, startled by her breakdown. "What is it? What's wrong?" He rose to put his arms around his mother's shoulders, but the comforting gesture only seemed to agitate her further.

"Everything's wrong, Devon. Everything. Just when I think I've gotten used to this miserable life and nothing can hurt me, I hear something like this. My life consists of sleeping with strangers—pathetic, dirty men with stinking bodies and even fouler breath. And the one man who's clean and neat and treats me with at least a drop of respect turns out to be the worst of the bloody lot." Tears rushed down her face and dripped out between her splayed fingers. The sight of her despair made Devon's heart clench with sadness. He longed to do something to ease his mother's pain, but he knew it was a futile wish.

Suddenly May's tears stopped and dried up as quickly as they'd come. "I'm not seeing him anymore, of course. Not ever again. I won't be letting any murderers through my door."

Something about that last statement didn't sit right with Devon. "On second thought, Mum, that's not a good idea."

"Not a good idea?" May was incredulous. "Ye've got to be joking. Why wouldn't it be good to send a murderer packing?"

"It will arouse his suspicion, that's why. Have ye ever told Westbury that ye can't see him?"

"Of course not. But that was before—"

"It don't matter, Mum. He doesn't know what ye know. And ye don't want him to."

"Because he might leave?"

"Or worse, he might try to pin the murder on someone else. Maybe even me."

"But that's not true! And we've got the evidence to prove it."

"Nay, we don't have it yet, Mum. Remember all the money Westbury has. And all the friends he has. The two combined can get ye almost anything. Westbury could pay people to say they never seen him wearing a shirt with those buttons. They'd probably even say that I stole the button from his shirt in order to pin the murder on him."

"The rich are thieves just like the poor, only instead of scraps o' food, they steal people's lives."

"They'll do bloody anything, Mum. Westbury's a marquess; we's just poor buggers from the East End. Ye got no idea how upper-class people defend each other." He bitterly spat the words out as if they tasted foul.

"So what do we do?"

Devon stood and paced the room for several minutes, trying to answer his mother's question.

"For now, nothing. Just go on as if ye don't know nothing about Joshua, or the murder. Accept Westbury whenever he comes, just like ye do now. It's important that he doesn't find out what we know before I can figure out a way to prove him guilty."

" 'Tis so unfair," May lamented, and Devon said nothing in response to her statement. He would be hard-pressed to argue with the truth.

Sixteen

"Don't you think it sounds splendid, Claire?"

Hearing her name spoken aloud chased the daydreams away. "Pardon me?"

"Claire," her mother spoke the word with sharp exasperation in her voice, "why aren't you paying attention? We're speaking of the Eton/Harrow cricket contest this weekend. Philip has proposed that we all drive up to Lord's to see it. Don't you think it sounds like fun?"

Oh, of course it does, Claire thought sarcastically. Watching twenty-two grown men running around an open field to bat balls between wickets is always enormous fun.

"It would be wonderful, Mother. We missed last year; it would be a shame to miss it again."

"Exactly my thinking. Why don't you tell him this evening that we accept his invitation. You two are going to the theater, aren't you?"

"Yes. Philip will be here at seven to pick me up." She managed to keep the despondency from her voice, then slyly resumed watching Devon, as she had been doing for several minutes. If she leaned ever so slightly to the left in her chair, she had a direct view into the library across the hall. Devon was in there, trimming wicks and filling lamps, but his back was to the door. He couldn't know that she was watching him, and if she didn't lean too far in her chair, neither would her family. Or so she thought.

A light raspberry sorbet was the luncheon dessert, and as soon as it was eaten, Kendal excused himself. "I must be getting back to Parliament," he said with a nod toward them all.

"Very well, but don't be late this evening," Louisa instructed her husband. "We're having dinner with the Canes."

"What a novelty," Lord Bedington muttered below his breath, not meaning for anyone to hear him. But Claire had been positioned in just the right way for her sharp ears to pick up his words. And for the first time in her life, she realized that her father disliked the social whirl of the season as much as she did. She took comfort in that knowledge, for it made her feel that she was not quite as alone as she had always thought. At least there was one other person who could identify with the way she felt.

"I'll be going up to rest," Claire announced, more out of a desire for solitude than a need for slumber.

"A word with you first, Claire?" Lavinia asked. Surprised by the request, Claire turned toward her sister. "Is something the matter?"

"No, no. Not at all. Shall we go upstairs?" Lavinia steered the both of them into Claire's room, then firmly latched the door behind them.

Her sister's actions were a departure from the usual, and made Claire uneasy, for she suspected the reason.

"I have to admit, he is very handsome," Lavinia stated.

Claire's mouth was suddenly dry, as if gale winds had just blown through it, extracting all the moisture. Lavinia must have caught her staring at Devon during lunch. But, good heavens, did she know anything else? Had she caught Claire with him any of those times in the stable?

Embarrassment flooded her face red as she realized all Lavinia could have seen. But had she?

"I can see from the look on your face that you agree."

Claire rolled her eyes and decided to play the innocent. "For goodness' sake, Linny, what are you talking about?"

"Don't play games with me, Claire. It's not *what* I'm talking about. It's *who*. The footman, Devon. He's caught your fancy. I've seen you looking at him several times, when you thought no one was paying attention. You should see the expression on your face, Claire. Your eyes light up, a little smile touches the corner of your lips."

"Lavinia, please . . ."

"You're in love with him."

Her first impulse was to shout out words of denial. To adamantly, fervently denounce Lavinia's statement. But somehow the words wouldn't come out; the contradiction died on her lips. And Claire knew, in that moment of revelation, that she couldn't deny what Lavinia said, because her sister spoke the truth. She was in love with Devon.

She sat down heavily upon her bed. "It wasn't supposed to happen."

"You're right about that."

Claire chewed her lower lip as she thought about how to respond. She sensed Lavinia didn't mean to be cruel by confronting her; still, she knew her sister was asking for an explanation.

"I . . . I'm not sure where to start."

Lavinia pulled up a nearby chair. "You don't have to tell me anything, Claire. Whatever has gone on between you two is private. But what I want to know is what you're going to do about it. You know you can't be with him."

Truer words were never spoken, Claire thought bitterly. No, she could never be with him, even if Devon wanted to be with her. And remembering the last words he'd spoken to her, she doubted that. So what to do? In all likelihood, nothing.

"Of course I know that. That's why there's nothing to do. I'll marry Philip, just as Mother wants."

"Has he proposed to you?"

"Yes, last week. I just haven't given him my answer yet."

"What are you waiting for? He's a marquess, Claire. You'd be marrying above. And Westbury's one of the wealthiest men available."

"Yes. That's all true."

The dejected look on Claire's face told the whole story. "But you're not in love with him, are you? And that's what you've always wanted, what you've always talked about. You want to be in love with your husband."

Claire tried a wan smile. "I see that my preaching has finally sunk in."

"Oh, I heard you, Claire, loud and clear. And I always thought you were being silly, because I assumed that if you found a husband like Lord Townsend you'd forever be happy. But when I look at you watching Devon, I know now what the difference is, and I know what you were looking for."

"He's not like anyone I've ever met. He has qualities I never even knew people had." Claire turned toward her sister to emphasize her point. "At first I thought maybe it was only a superficial, physical attraction that drew me toward him. But I've come to realize that it's far beyond that. I have true feelings for him, Linny. An admiration and respect that I've never felt for another man, especially not the pretentious knaves Mother is so enamored with."

She looked her sister straight in the eye, wanting, needing her to understand. "He cares about his friends, Linny," she continued. "Not because of how much money they have or who their parents are, but just because he likes them. He doesn't berate someone because they're wearing the wrong shoes, or lecture about the proper etiquette when attending the races. He just accepts his friends for who they are, he—"

"Claire, stop."

The words were as effective as a bucket of water dumped on her head. She was silenced immediately.

"Listen to yourself," Lavinia continued. "You're talking foolishness. You're praising someone who can never be anything to you. As far as you're concerned he doesn't exist. Whatever you feel for him, Claire, you've got to let it go."

The truth of her sister's words was like a punch to the stomach. She felt empty, deflated. As crazy as the thought was, she'd been hoping all this time that she and Devon could somehow be together. That despite the difference in their backgrounds and class standing, they could find a way to make it work. But Lavinia was right. She had to forget him.

Small tears welled up in the corner of each eye, and before she could stop them they spilled down her cheeks. "But that's impossible," she said softly.

Lavinia rose from the chair and sat beside her sister on the bed. She put one arm across Claire's shoulders and pulled her against her bosom. The unexpected tenderness was overwhelming, and as if a dam had broken loose, her tears poured forth.

She rested her head against Lavinia's shoulder while sobs consumed her body. She felt as though she were receiving a life sentence for a crime not committed. She was condemned to marry a man she could never love, while the one to whom her heart belonged was prohibited from ever having it.

When the sobs had finally reduced to a trickle, Lavinia

pulled herself away from Claire to look directly into her sister's face.

"Claire, I don't want to sound heartless. I've never seen you like this, so I can only imagine what you're feeling. But you're in an impossible situation, and the sooner you get out of it, the better off you'll be."

"How can you say that, Linny?" Claire asked. "How would I be better off married to a man for whom I feel nothing?"

"Because the alternative would shame the family. And you. You're a member of the peerage; thus, you must marry into peerage. You cannot forsake your destiny because of misguided emotions."

It all sounded so practical and right. Lavinia's words made sense, and besides, from the day she was first able to understand it, Claire had known what her life's mission was. But what of those "misguided emotions"? Where did they fit in? She heaved a sigh. Seemingly nowhere, was the dismal answer.

"You're right, of course. I must marry Philip. It's what I'm meant to do."

"Yes, it is. But remember, there's nothing that says you can't take up with a lover. . . ."

"Lavinia! And you talk about shaming the family."

"Oh, Claire. Don't be so old-fashioned. Everyone does it, so where's the harm? Just be careful about babies."

Red color again graced Claire's cheeks as she realized that her younger sister was no longer so young.

"Maybe I am old-fashioned, but I don't believe in adultery."

Lavinia clicked her tongue. "You know Philip will take up with someone, especially during the years when you're fat with child."

Claire stood up abruptly and began removing the pins from her hair. "This conversation has gone far enough.

I'm going to rest now, and I suggest you do the same. Aren't you joining Mother and Father for dinner at the Canes?"

Lavinia knew when she was being dismissed, but still she hesitated before leaving her sister alone. "Will you be all right?"

Claire looked up from the nightstand mirror and gave Lavinia a reassuring smile. "I'll be fine. Thanks, Linny."

"You know I won't say a word about our conversation."

"I know you won't."

Without another word, Lavinia left and shut the door behind her, then Claire went over and latched it to prevent any of the servants from entering. She took up her favorite brush and began stroking it through her hair. Lavinia's suggestion of Claire breaching the contract of marriage had temporarily taken her mind off Devon. But now that she was once again alone with only her thoughts, naturally they turned toward him. Admitting her love for Devon had felt good, despite how unorthodox it was. But the fact that she could do nothing about it filled her with a despair that was nearly debilitating. Again she felt tears threatening to surface, but with a mighty will she prevented their escape. What was the use? She was trapped in a predestined situation. Oh, perhaps the names of the players were not firmly engraved in stone, but the rules were. Claire would marry a member of the peerage in order for her family to maintain its long-standing, noble reputation. And now that it was known exactly who was her husband to be, all that was left was for the marriage to take place. Then she'd become Lady Philip Townsend, and all would remain as it should, with the cogs and wheels of life grinding along in their proper and expected manner. The only flaw in the scenario was her utter devastation.

Seventeen

The hypnotic clip-clop of the horses' hooves against the street was a thankful distraction against Philip Westbury's droning voice, fussing over the seating arrangements at the dinner party they had just left. The stream of words exiting his mouth never ceased, but Claire found that by focusing her attention on the sound of the horses' hooves, she was nearly able to block out Philip's endless chatter.

"What could she have been thinking," he demanded of Claire, "seating me next to Patricia Wallesford? Why, the old bat can hardly see, much less hear, and I'm supposed to make lively conversation with her?" He loudly clucked his tongue at what he deemed a major social faux pas. "As far as I'm concerned, it's a small coup on our part to leave Lady Claudia with two empty seats. Naturally I'm sorry you're feeling ill," he glanced over at Claire with his best attempt at showing sympathy for her plight, "but it serves her right having to rearrange everyone."

Guiltily Claire glanced down in her lap. She was as far from being ill as Philip was from being a gracious dinner guest, but moments before they were to be seated for the meal she suddenly knew she could not tolerate being there. She had been overwhelmed by the litany of Philip's sarcastic comments, and found herself comparing his every gesture and word to Devon's. Devon wouldn't do that, she'd think, or he would do that. Whatever it was—a movement of the hand, a comment about a dress—Claire compared what Philip did to what she imagined Devon would do. Not surprisingly, Devon always came out on top, and that realization had spun Claire into a lonely depression. Since that day over a week ago when she'd admitted her true feelings for Devon, she'd done nothing but think about him. It was as if telling Lavinia how she felt had lifted her self-imposed ban, and it was suddenly acceptable to let her thoughts roam as they may.

At last Philip's carriage pulled up in front of the town home, and Claire prepared to alight. Philip rushed out of the carriage and ran around to help her out. As if she were crippled, he helped her down the steps, then placed his right arm around her back while his left arm clutched hold of her elbow. Matching every step with hers, he walked her to the front door and then inside the house.

Before going upstairs Claire glanced over her shoulder. "Good night, Philip. And thank you."

Elegantly Philip bowed toward his intended fiancée. "Sleep well," he said, then turned to leave.

Disappointed that another engagement with Claire had ended without her consent to be his bride, Philip decided he needed a distraction. He climbed inside his carriage and was about to instruct his driver to head east when the sound of his name claimed his attention. Glancing toward the right-hand window, he saw who it was. Devon Blake.

Annoyed at the man's impertinence but nonetheless curious about what he wanted, Philip leaned across his seat. "What in the world are you doing?" he sneered.

Undaunted by the tone of Philip's voice, Devon coolly answered him, "I got me some information ye might want to hear." Then, without waiting for an invitation, he opened the carriage door and slid in beside Philip.

Angered by Devon's lack of subservience, Philip started to protest, but with a simple hand gesture Devon stopped him.

"Listen to what I have to say, and don't be raising yer voice," he commanded. "Three months ago a friend of mine was in a row down by the Wapping docks. He had the bloody life kicked out of him, literally. He died some weeks later."

Something about the story was vaguely familiar, but Philip showed no sign of recognizing it. Instead he covered himself by sneering, "What should I care about your low-life friends?"

"My mates and me," Devon continued, ignoring Philip's barb, "we did a lot of looking to see if we could find the filthy snake who done this. We talked to a lot of people, asked a lot of questions. Turns out there was an eyewitness to the crime who gave some details. But our best lead was something the killer left behind." Reaching into his pocket, Devon pulled out the button, placed it in the palm of his hand, and slowly showed it to Philip. "Look familiar?"

After the shock had passed, Philip lunged toward Devon to seize the evidence, but he was much too slow. Quicker than the eye could follow, Devon shoved the button back into his pocket, and with the other hand blocked Philip's movement.

"Without saying a word ye've admitted yer guilt."

The declaration effectively stopped him. Sitting back in his seat, Philip glared at his opponent while sizing up the best way to defeat him.

"I've admitted nothing," he finally said, "and I can already tell you that you'll regret ever having uttered these stinking, vile lies. Who do you think you are, anyway? Are you under the false impression that someone is going to care about what you say? The whole reason for your pathetic existence," he poked a finger toward Devon, "is to serve the rest of us who are above you."

Devon could feel the familiar hatred churning in his stomach like so much bile, but for the moment he held his tongue while Westbury ranted.

"The only reason I don't have you dismissed this instant is because of Claire. The chit's got a tender heart, and in her innocence believes servants should be treated with respect. She's going to become my bride very soon, but because I'm still waiting for her 'official' word, I don't want to anger her by getting rid of you this second like you deserve."

"Ye're an even bigger coward than I thought," Devon replied. "Using a woman as yer excuse not to have me dismissed when ye know there'd be questions to answer if ye ever tried doing it. Why can't ye just be a man and admit what ye did? I thought about going to the police, but knowing what a 'gentleman' ye are, I thought ye'd be happy I'm coming to ye first."

The implication that he was anything less than the dashing hero he fancied himself to be infuriated Philip. Immediately he launched into a biting tirade, eager to cut Devon to the quick.

"You no-good, filthy sneak," he growled. "Have you actually deluded yourself into thinking that someone would pay attention to what you have to say? Do you pretend that anyone would believe your word over mine? Just try going to the police with your foul lies and see who they believe: a common footman, whose baneful existence depends upon the good graces of others, or a wealthy, titled, respected marquess, whose unblemished lineage can be traced back to the fourteenth century. Use whatever speck of brain you might have stored in the empty space between your ears and figure it out. You've no chance against me, Blake, and don't ever forget it. Now get out of my coach."

Devon needed no further prompting. Blinding fury roared through his veins, and the thought of killing Philip right in his own carriage seemed dangerously appealing. With steely determination he held himself back. Murdering someone, no matter how wretched the individual, was not in Devon's nature, and he would never let himself sink to Westbury's level. In the end, it would lead to no good. For all of Westbury's pompous arrogance, he had been right about one thing. No one would believe Devon's word over his.

As soon as Devon had shut the door, Philip rapped upon the carriage and the driver pulled away. As Devon stood in the driveway watching them go, despair washed over him. How was he ever going to prove that Philip Westbury was a murderer? It was clear that walking up to a constable and telling him the story would most likely result in his spending time in a prison cell. What he needed was someone of Philip's class on his side. Someone like Claire? No. Devon dismissed that idea as quickly as it came, though it wasn't the first time today that she'd entered his mind. More like the hundredth, he thought with a grimace. Despite his best effort to forget everything about her, it was virtually impossible. There were practical reasons, of course. He worked in her home; they were bound to see one another. But it was not only the geography that prevented him from freeing his mind of her. Since the last time they'd spoken he'd done nothing but think of her, and lately he'd come to the reluctant conclusion that she had carved a place for herself in his heart. It was the closest he had come to admitting he had feelings for her, although he did not allow himself to dwell on the exact nature of those feelings. It would be a pointless indulgence.

Devon shrugged away his vague disappointment as he walked toward the servants' quarters. In regard to Claire's witnessing Joshua's beating, he knew he'd gotten all the

information from her that he was going to get. She had
told him all she knew. Except for the money, there was
no further reason for him to stay there. He had come to
speak with her about what she saw, and now he had. It
was time for this chapter of his life to end. He would
finish the week out, then proffer his resignation.

Again, thoughts of Claire surfaced, but as usual, he
brushed them aside. It was senseless to think of her, and
the sooner he left this place the sooner he could banish
her from his life. Forever.

Sharp, impatient raps upon the door invaded the calm
of her garden balcony. With a sigh of annoyance, Claire
set down the book of poems she'd been reading and acknowledged whoever was behind the door.

"You may enter."

A second later the door sprang open and Marie rushed
inside.

"Mademoiselle, I'm so sorry to disturb you, but Monsieur Westbury is downstairs waiting to see you."

"Philip?" Claire's eyebrows wrinkled with perplexity.
"But I wasn't expecting him today."

"He said as much, mademoiselle; yet he insists on
seeing you."

"How impertinent of him," Claire muttered under her
breath as she strode toward her vanity mirror. "Very well,
Marie. You may tell Lord Townsend that I will be down
to see him in just a few minutes."

"Keep him waiting, mademoiselle," Marie said softly
as she left the room. Claire smiled at how easily her
maid understood what she was feeling, but the smile
faded as her thoughts turned to Philip. What was he doing here? Certainly it was expected that she would one
day be his wife, but until then he should not have taken

the liberty of calling unannounced, and it rankled her that he had done so.

She glanced into the mirror to check her appearance, then headed downstairs to where her visitor awaited.

"Claire, thank you so much for seeing me without notice," he said, bowing with a flourish and taking her hand to plant a kiss upon it.

"It's quite all right, Philip," she answered. "But naturally I'm concerned about the reason for your unexpected visit."

Philip looked around as if checking for eavesdroppers, then said in a quiet voice, "Perhaps we could have some privacy?"

Though he wanted to close the parlor doors, it was a request Claire had no intention of granting. "That's not necessary, Philip," she replied. "The servants are not in the habit of listening by the door."

A slight nod of his head showed he acquiesced to her decision. "Very well, then. Shall we sit?" Without waiting for her permission he led them both to the two chairs farthest back in the long room, where his request for privacy was accommodated. From the parlor door, it was impossible for anyone to see who might be inside without actually stepping into the room.

Claire knew at once what he had done, and could not hide her irritation. "Philip," she admonished, "you'll not embarrass me in my own home. It's not proper for us to be hiding in the back of the room like two illicit lovers. Now tell me at once why you're here, and then be on your way."

"Oh my, Claire. Do not be angry with me. I mean nothing indecent by my visit here today. It's just that, well . . ."

His voice trailed off as if to add more emotion to the already anguished plea.

"Well what? Get on with it, Philip."

Slowly, deliberately, he gazed into Claire's eyes. "I feel ashamed for having to do this, but I can no longer stop myself."

He had sapped her patience. "Do what, Philip? What are you talking about?"

"It's been three weeks since I asked you, and you've not yet given me your answer. Therefore, I feel obliged to ask you once again for your hand in marriage."

Oh. That. Could it really be the sole reason that brought him here without notice? Philip was ordinarily the very definition of proper behavior, so it was perplexing indeed that he was acting this way. Did he truly have such feelings for her as to shame himself by proposing twice? She doubted it.

"Philip," she said, clearing her throat, "I'm flattered by your persistence, but I must insist that you give me more time. I do not take the matter of marriage lightly, and when I decide upon my bridegroom, I want to feel confident with the decision I've made."

"Does . . . does that mean there are others?"

"That's really none of your concern. Now, however, I think it's time for you to leave."

He did his best to appear humble. "Very well. I shall simply wait on pins and needles until I hear from you." He picked up his hat, and together they walked toward the door. "Thank you again for seeing me, Claire. I truly hope there are no misgivings."

"I'll see you soon, Philip," she responded, not assuring him, as he had thought she might, of her forgiving nature.

"Are you still planning on attending the Holdens' ball?"

"Yes, of course. The whole family, except for Kate and Emily, will be there."

"Fine, fine. Then I'll see you this evening."

As soon as he was down the front steps, Claire shut

the door behind him. Philip didn't mind her irritation, however, for he'd gotten what he wanted. To be sure, his hand reached inside the pocket of his overcoat and wrapped around the valuable crystal figurine he'd taken from the knickknack shelves in the parlor. Feigning impatience for her answer had been the perfect excuse to come calling today. It pressed Claire to hurry with her answer (although from speaking with her mother, he knew she'd dare not refuse him) so as to hasten the moment when he'd get his hands on her money, and it had also allowed him time alone in the parlor to steal the figurine.

It felt good having the object in his hands. Louisa often spoke of how she treasured the thing, emphasizing repeatedly of how her father had brought it back from a long-ago excursion to Austria. Philip laughed aloud. It would break Louisa's heart when she discovered it was missing. Luckily for her, Philip would know exactly on whom to place the blame.

His smile became dark, menacing. Before too long he'd have that filthy troublemaker out of his life. For good.

Eighteen

"Missing, you say?" Philip wrinkled his brows together in a show of concern. "For how long?"

"Hard to say, really. We only noticed it was gone this evening, just before we left."

"Kendal's right," Louisa agreed in an anguished voice. "And the most dreadful part is that it means there's a thief amongst our staff. The figurine could have been taken as many as three days ago. That's the last time Ellen dusted in there. If it had been gone then, she would have noticed."

"I see. So since it's been cleaned, who's been in there?"

Kendal and Louisa glanced toward one another in silent consultation before answering the question. "No one, as far as we know," Louisa finally said. "Why?"

Philip glanced away, as if embarrassed to reveal what knowledge he possessed of the incident. And for the moment, he was relieved of having to do so, for Claire and Lavinia walked up to the group.

"Good evening, Lord Townsend," Lavinia greeted the Marquess. Claire merely nodded.

"We were discussing the missing crystal," Louisa said, filling them in on the conversation.

"Isn't it the oddest thing?" Lavinia said. "Our servants have always been so loyal. But I suppose someone must have taken it."

It was time, Philip decided. With them all gathered about him in rapt attention, there couldn't be a more perfect opportunity.

"I'm afraid I have an idea about who your thief may be," he said, bringing about immediate curiosity, "but I'm not sure you want to hear it."

"By all means, man, if you know something, come out with it," Kendal urged.

"Well," Philip looked at them all, his glance lingering the longest on Claire, "I suspect that the one who took that figurine is none other than your footman, Devon Blake."

There was a quiet moment of shock in the group, none feeling it more than the unsuspecting Claire. How could Philip do this? she fumed. How could he go about making false accusations against Devon? He had no proof!

It was Kendal who found his voice first. "Devon?" he questioned, the doubt clear in his voice. "What makes you say that?"

"I'm afraid there's more to Mr. Blake than any of you suspect," Philip said, with a conscious effort to dampen his delight. "You see," he stared Claire directly in the eye, "Devon Blake is nothing more than a two-bit, pickpocket bastard, raised in a brothel by a prostitute mother."

If he'd used a fire poker to trounce her the blow would have been less painful than the words he'd just spoken. Claire felt as if the very life had been sucked out of her. She no longer possessed the ability to breathe, or move, or speak. She was riveted to the floor by the heinous lies Philip had dared utter, and knew instinctively that she could not rush to Devon's defense. Philip was a titled lord; Devon was a servant. Or worse.

"Bloody hell, Westbury! Those are some strong accusations you're making," Kendal said. "How can you be sure of what you're saying?"

"My husband is right, Lord Townsend. We've all come to appreciate the work Mr. Blake has done for us."

Her mother's kind words finally gave Claire the voice to speak. "And where in the world would you have found all this out?" she quietly demanded.

Their reactions were even better than he'd hoped. Already Philip sensed the doubt laced around the edges of Kendal's outraged voice. And weak-livered Louisa would go along with whatever her husband decided. As for Claire, well, she'd come around. It was just her schoolgirl fascination with the servant's rugged good looks that upheld her false sense of loyalty toward him. Of that he was certain. Oh, this was perfect! Were it possible, he would have rubbed his hands together with glee.

"First off, let me confess straight away that I did some checking into Mr. Blake's background. I felt it only prudent."

"What in the world for?" Lavinia asked.

"It just struck me as so odd that a groom's assistant would suddenly have the qualifications of a footman. And because of my deep caring for not only Claire," he lovingly glanced her way, "but for the entire Rushmoor family, I felt obliged to ask a few questions."

"That's noble of you, Westbury," Kendal said, "but I was aware that Mr. Blake had not had previous experience. However, based on what he did for Lilia, and the fine reports I'd received from Mr. Penworthy, I decided to go ahead with the appointment."

Philip held his palms up toward Kendal, as if warding off an oncoming blow. "Please don't take my actions as anything other than what they were—a simple show of concern for this family. I merely wanted to be certain you were getting nothing less than what you deserve—the best."

I'll just bet you did, Claire silently huffed. And how

convenient that you happened to uncover Devon's sordid past.

"Of whom did you ask these questions?" she said, raising an eyebrow.

"It wasn't difficult," Philip replied vaguely. "When you know as many people as I've come to know, you're bound to find whatever you need."

"So through your connections it was revealed to you that Mr. Blake was a pickpocket?"

"Not only a mere pickpocket, Louisa, but the leader of a gang of thieves. And apparently they were quite adept at stealing whatever they needed, from whomever they wanted."

Louisa's eyes widened with horror. "How dreadful," she breathed.

Philip turned to face them all. "The main point is this: you've never had a problem with thievery before this incident. Mr. Blake is new to the household staff, and it's known he was a pickpocket in the past. Now something is missing. It seems to me an obvious solution."

Claire could hold back no longer. "I don't believe you," she stated. "You have no proof that Mr. Blake took the figurine."

"Claire," Philip chided, as if scolding a naïve child, "you have no proof that he didn't take it. And based on his past livelihood, I have to say that I think my accusation holds quite a bit of weight."

Based on the looks of those gathered about him, they agreed. Philip knew he'd planted enough doubt to finally have Devon dismissed and out of his life for good.

"There's just one more thing," he said. "Devon Blake was and is a thief, and as such should not only be dismissed, but properly punished as well."

His strong words convinced Louisa. "He's right, Kendal," she maintained.

"But Mother," Claire protested, raw panic surging

through every vein, "shouldn't we at least give him the chance to speak for himself?"

"I don't see why that would be necessary, Claire. Lord Townsend is right. All the evidence points to Devon."

"What evidence?" she nearly shouted in frustration. "Accusations don't equal proof." She turned toward the only one she felt would listen to reason. "Father?"

But for the first time in his life, Kendal had to disappoint his eldest daughter. "As much as I've grown to like Mr. Blake, I'm afraid I must side with your mother on this, Claire. If we're lenient on thievery this time, who knows what will happen in the future? As unfortunate as it may seem, Mr. Blake will be used as an example to curtail any further problems with the staff."

"But that's so unfair!"

"Good heavens, Claire!" Louisa admonished her daughter. "What's come over you? It's only a footman we're talking about. What difference does it make? It's not as if we're threatening to dismiss your personal maid."

No, only the man I love, she thought, but she knew there was nothing more she could say. Any further objections on her part would only result in a barrage of potentially embarrassing questions. What difference, indeed. Over the past several months her stable, calm, well-planned-out world had been turned upside down. Ownership of her heart had been relinquished to an enigmatic, devastatingly handsome, not-so-common servant, who was about to be ejected from her life by her well-meaning but misguided father. And all because of one man.

With emotion nearly akin to hatred she turned dark eyes upon her nemesis. He was now laughing heartily at something her mother had just said, working to secure his place in the Rushmoor family. With a laugh here, a light touch there, he was charming her mother as she'd not been since her courtship with Kendal had ended. Louisa was smitten by Philip Westbury, and it was all but official that he would soon join the family ranks as eldest son-in-law. He would then have everything he wanted: inheritance of a large dowry and a proper, titled wife. In return, Claire would receive a lifetime sentence of boredom and heartache.

The sound of Lavinia's voice dispersed her reverie, but though her musings had been woeful, they were nothing compared to the devastation she felt upon hearing Lavinia's news.

"Come, Claire. We're leaving. Since Father is convinced that Devon is the one who took the figurine, he's agreed to dismiss him this evening at Mother's insistence. Philip's already left to get the constable."

Pure dread seized hold of her body, and her heart pounded within her chest as if she'd just completed a foot race. Bracing herself against the answer she already knew, she managed to utter, "The constable? But why?"

Lavinia brought her voice down low. "Get hold of yourself, Claire, but they're going to have Devon arrested."

No! she wanted to scream at the top of her lungs. It couldn't be true! This had to be a nightmare from which she would soon awake. It was simply too awful to accept as reality.

"For the love of God, Linny, why? Why don't they simply dismiss him?"

"Shhh!" Lavinia warned her sister. "Keep your voice down. The last thing you need is to draw attention to yourself. You've already raised eyebrows by the way you seem to hold Devon in higher esteem than Philip. Remember your dignity."

Fear and confusion forced Claire to acquiesce. "Very well. I know you're right, Linny. But why is Father having Devon arrested?"

"Because Philip thinks it would be a good idea. He told Father that if he only releases Devon from service he will be putting a thief back upon the streets. 'For the good of the people of London,' Westbury said, 'you must make sure this man is secured in a jail cell so he won't cause the upheaval in anyone else's life that he has brought to yours.' "

Claire conquered an impulse to hurl herself at Philip and scratch his lying eyes out.

"I must do something to stop this," she whispered urgently to her sister. "I can't let this go on any longer."

She started to rush over to speak with her father, but Lavinia managed to restrain her. "Don't even think about it, Claire," she insisted. "There's nothing you can do. Are you willing to stain the family's reputation by your deluded fascination for Devon? No matter what you feel for him, you simply cannot let it go any further."

If her sister's words sounded so right, why did they feel so wrong? Against her better judgment, Claire acquiesced.

"Fine. Now go get your wrap. I'm sure the carriage is waiting by now."

The ride back home was both the fastest and the longest Claire had ever endured. Her heart beat with sorrow and fury, and she was helpless to act on either emotion. She felt as if she were being whisked toward an execution, so heavy was the feeling of doom that enveloped her.

When they finally pulled up in front of the house, Philip was already there, waiting with the constable, who had been roused from his bed.

"Good evening, Constable," Kendal said as he alighted from the carriage. "Thank you for coming."

"You're welcome, Lord Bedington," the constable answered, "though I don't see why this couldn't have waited 'til morning."

"It's on account of my wife, sir," Kendal said in a low voice. "It seems one of our servants is a thief, and my wife does not feel comfortable having the man in the house. Really, you can hardly blame her."

The constable sighed. "I suppose you're right, Lord Bedington. Well, let's go get him."

The entire family ascended the stairs and went inside, and after Emma recovered from her fright at seeing a man of the law inside the home, she rushed off to find Devon.

In a last attempt to put off the inevitable, Claire moved to speak with the constable. "Sir," she said politely, though her status outranked his, "isn't it a matter of course for suspected thieves to have their cases heard before the magistrate?"

The portly constable peered down at her. "Of course, Lady Rushmoor. Why?"

At that moment Lavinia rushed forward. "My sister has an unusual interest in legal proceedings, sir. That's all." She tugged on Claire's arm to indicate an immediate halt to her questions. Further prompting, however, proved unnecessary, for at that moment Emma returned with Devon in tow.

"Ye wanted to see me, Lord Bedington?" Devon inquired of Kendal.

Gruffly, Kendal cleared his throat. Though he believed Devon to be the thief, the moment was uncomfortable because he'd grown to like him.

"I'm afraid we have some serious questions for you, Devon," he began. "Questions to which I hope you have an explanation."

Though the tone of Kendal's voice conveyed the seriousness of the matter, Devon's expression remained calm. "I'll answer whatever ye like, m'lord."

"Then let's not waste any time. Are you familiar with

a crystal figurine that sits on the shelves in the back of the parlor?"

"In the shape of a swan?"

"Yes, that's the one."

Philip looked positively triumphant, as if Devon's admission that he knew of the piece confirmed he had taken it.

"Bit strange for a bloke like you to notice knick-knacks, isn't it?" he said.

Devon turned toward Philip, his expression calm. "Ye're right about that. I wouldn't never notice such things, 'cept the one Lord Bedington speaks of sits right next to a lamp that I regularly tend. I always move it when I trim the lamp's wick for fear of breaking it. 'Tis why I know it."

"Then you'd also know how valuable it is," Philip accused.

Devon nodded in agreement. "Aye. Right near everything in this house is valuable, so I'd be assuming the crystal swan is as well."

Claire felt unexpected pride swell within her breast, for Devon had scored a victory in the early round.

"You're right, Mr. Blake. It is valuable," said Claire's father. "And now it's missing."

For the first time since this exchange had begun, Devon looked surprised. "Missing, m'lord?"

"That's right. It's gone, not to be found anywhere. And we have reason to believe you might know something about it."

In that instant Devon knew who was behind these trumped-up charges. Philip had sworn revenge when he'd been confronted with the truth about what he had done to Joshua, and this was his way of fighting back.

Before answering Kendal, Devon looked long and hard at Philip, silently conveying to the group that he knew who his accuser was. "I'm afraid I can't help ye,

Lord Bedington," he answered steadily, "for I wasn't even aware that 'twas gone."

The constable spoke up. "Then you maintain, before all the witnesses present here this evening, that you had nothing to do with the theft of that figurine?"

Devon stared him straight in the eye. "Nothing at all."

There was a moment of confused silence among the group, for the quiet intensity with which Devon asserted his innocence had caught both Kendal and Philip momentarily off guard. Philip, however, was the first to recover.

"You're lying," he declared. "Your background is all the proof we need."

To this Devon raised a questioning eyebrow, but remained silent.

"We know about the way you used to lead a gang of thieves all over the East End," Philip continued. "You're nothing but a low-down pickpocket, which is why we know you're the only one who would take that knickknack."

"And my past is proof for this crime ye now accuse me of?" he asked, to no one in particular.

Stated in those terms, it did seem like rather thin evidence. But Philip was adamant. "Listen to the way he runs at the mouth!" he sneered. "Trying to make us all look like fools. Of course that's all the proof we need. There was no problem with theft before you came here, and now some valuable crystal is missing. What would you have us think, Blake? That one of the other servants, who have shown their loyalty time and again over the years, would suddenly get an urge to give up their positions in a respected household, and risk a public hanging, for a knickknack?" His words were taking effect, and Philip knew that he once again had the backing of Kendal and Louisa. "It doesn't make any sense. But what does is the coincidental timing of your arrival in this household with the disappearance of that crystal swan."

The constable spoke up. "It makes sense to me as well, Mr. Blake. Now come along. You can tell your story to the magistrate. For now you'll go with me." He placed both hands around Devon's left arm, but Devon refused to move.

"I'm warning you, Mr. Blake. You can either come quietly or you can put up a fight, but either way you'll be leaving. The only thing I can tell you is that the more you resist me, the worse you'll look before the magistrate."

The wealthy. The bloody, hateful, stinking wealthy. Devon was so outraged that for a moment he couldn't see straight. But when his vision cleared, he looked directly at Claire. And it was that look, that brief stare into her heart, that would haunt her every waking second. For it was in that silent plea that Devon lowered his pride and asked for her help, and it was her refusal to speak out that sealed his fate.

Certainly there was no one else who'd speak on his behalf. Not Claire's father or mother, not Lavinia; certainly not Philip. Devon was being accused of a crime Claire was certain he did not commit, and she was the only one who could speak on his behalf. So what had halted her words? What had frozen the protest on her lips? She was in love with this man, so why wouldn't she fight for him?

The thoughts reeled through her mind in scant seconds, but in the end Devon was led out the door, and out of her life.

Nineteen

The days that followed were a study in hell. Automatically, like a well-trained animal, Claire went through the motions of everyday life. Her outward appearance gave no one pause for thought. She made calls. She attended every social engagement to which she was invited. She spent time with her family and ate every meal. No one save Lavinia knew her inner turmoil, and as Linny felt the situation could not be changed, she thought it best not to bring up the subject so as to let Claire get on with her life.

And Claire did get on with her life. Still, when she found herself with a moment alone, inevitably her calm exterior would crumble into a mass of tears—not the kind of tears that one sheds over a tragic play or the sounds of sweet music, but tears that seemed to rip the life from her soul. These were tears of raw emotion, relentless sorrow. Tears that symbolized Claire's utter devastation.

There had yet to be a trial, and Claire heard from her father that ofttimes the poor lingered in jail for months, even years, before receiving one. And the horror story hadn't stopped there. Marie confessed to her mistress that once, long ago, she'd taken a lover who had spent time in Newgate. "Ze stories what he told me were 'orrible, mademoiselle! Hugo said he 'ad no room to 'imself, but instead shared it with at least four other men. They slept on mats made of rope with nothing but a dirty stable blanket for cover. Prisoners often beat one another trying to get a place to sleep, or some food, which was almost impossible to eat. Sometimes insects or worms crawled over it. And ze rats! Oh la la! Rats, they were every-where!" Claire had finally commanded her maid to stop, unable to hear even one more word about it. But by then she'd been so grief-stricken that she was inconsolable. Of course, no one knew that. As she'd been taught to do her entire life, she remained calm and ladylike upon hearing Marie's tale. No one knew that her mind had gone into shock, her body had become numb. And no one knew that after everyone had gone to bed, Claire spent the night muffling the tears that ripped apart her soul.

It had now been a week since that heinous night, a week spent trying to cope with everyday life; a week that included long moments of quiet introspection. And it was during that time that Claire came to the undeniable realization that no matter how unorthodox, how uncon-ventional, how irrational it seemed, she could not live life without Devon.

But what to do? Making the decision in her mind and taking action upon it were two entirely different matters. And what of Devon? After the way she had kept silent when his eyes had asked for her help, would he even want anything to do with her? If only there were some-one she could talk to. If only there were someone who knew Devon and who could help her understand and learn more about him.

If only . . . her thoughts were abruptly interrupted. But of course! There was someone to whom she could speak—Devon's mother! If anyone knew him, it would be her. Even if Devon were not close to her, Claire still firmly believed that his mother would be able to shed some light on the complexities of her son.

But how to find her? Where did she live? Was she even still alive? The surge of inspiration Claire felt was dampened as the questions arose. Despair threatened to wipe away her hope, but with irritation she brushed it aside. She'd succumbed to enough tears over the past week to last her a lifetime. Now was not the time for more misery.

With determination she reviewed every conversation she'd had with Devon, trying to remember if he had ever mentioned anything about his mother. Sadly, she could remember nothing. It was as if the woman didn't exist. But that couldn't be, not when Philip had announced to everyone his knowledge that Devon's mother was a whore. . . .

New ideas were flashing through her mind so quickly she almost couldn't grasp them. But just as clouds move away after a storm and the clear blue sky appears, her swirling thoughts were giving way to concrete impressions. Her mind flashed back to the time when she saw Philip coming out of that building across the street from St. Matthew's. At the time she had assumed it was a pub or gambling house. But remembering all the men who'd been going in and out of it, including Philip, and realizing that there had to be a way he knew about Devon's mother, Claire realized that the "gambling house" was more likely a brothel. And likely Mrs. Blake's place of employment.

But could she, Claire Rushmoor, eldest daughter of the highly respected Earl of Bedington, dare venture into a den of iniquity? What if someone saw her? Her reputation would be ruined. She'd disgrace the family. The talk would be ruthless. She'd be ostracized from social circles. But did it matter? Certainly her life would be different. No more dinners, dances, or ladies' teas. No more calls to make. No more cricket matches. But instead of mourning the loss of what she had, she found

her spirit elevated by what she'd be free of. Despite the
risk of social ostracizing, Claire caught herself smiling
at the idea of a new and different life, one built around
the man she so desperately loved.

Would he have her? There was only one way to find
out. She would go to the East End and pay a visit to his
mother.

Twenty

As the sun blazed over the horizon to welcome a new day, Claire set out on her journey. To avoid standing out, she'd again donned the dress she'd worn that day in the mission house. Her hair was done up in a simple bun, and she rode twelve-year-old Rachel, the oldest of the Rushmoor steeds. Rachel was still a magnificent horse, but time had slightly dulled the glossy sheen of her coat, creating a less than stellar appearance.

Getting out of the house had been fairly easy. Upon waking she had Marie dress her as she normally would. Then she'd gone outside and instructed the groom to saddle up Rachel, telling him she'd decided to go for a leisurely ride and wanted Rachel to get the exercise. She did tell Daniel that she wasn't quite sure what time she'd be leaving so it wasn't necessary for him to wait for her. Simply saddle the horse, she'd said, and then tie her to the post outside the stable's front entrance. It had worked perfectly. Claire had then gone back inside and changed into the gray dress, and when she was certain no one was outside the stable, she'd mounted Rachel and rode off. So far, so good.

Upon nearing the East End, however, sadness and doubt replaced earlier feelings of euphoria. Sadness at seeing the pitiful conditions people were living in, and doubt as to whether she was really doing the right thing. After all, the entire trip was based on suppositions. She was assuming Devon's mother worked across from St. Matthew's, but what if she didn't? And even if she did, what if she wanted nothing to do with Claire? Those from the West End looked down their noses at people from across town, so perhaps the reverse was true as well? Perhaps Devon's mother would refuse to see her. What then?

Still, she pressed on, all the while admonishing herself for having fears. Don't be such a ninny, she chided. You've always done without question what others have told you, so why be so dubious of what you're telling yourself?

The questions whirled about her mind like leaves in a windstorm, until at last she reached her destination. Quickly she dismounted and secured Rachel, but as she turned toward The Night Star her footsteps halted.

She'd come here almost on a whim, feeling as though there were no other alternative. And though part of her was dogged in her resolution to go through with it, the other part was begging for a return to the old Claire. But the old Claire was not really a person. She was the product of a well-worn mold that had turned out others like her for centuries past. This new Claire, the one who had admitted her love for an outcast rogue, was an independent person exercising free will. Taking a deep breath, she walked up the stairs and entered The Night Star.

As she shut the door behind her, she realized she couldn't take another step forward until her eyes adjusted to the pervasive darkness. Not a crack of light passed through the heavy velvet curtains, and it took several minutes before Claire was able to see anything.

Once she could make out her surroundings, she looked around for some sign of activity, but all was quiet. Had she come too early? she wondered. But the door had been open. Surely if the place was closed it would have been locked. Was there a bell she was supposed to ring? There didn't appear to be anything in sight. What next?

Fortunately she was spared from deciding, for a large woman finally entered the room. Or rather, Claire's mind corrected itself, an enormous woman.

Despite the plush carpeting, the floorboards underneath creaked and groaned with the weight of the newcomer. She took several steps toward Claire before pausing to scrutinize her.

As the huge woman looked Claire up and down, Claire felt her face burn from the appraisal, particularly when the woman's gaze paused upon her chest. She seemed pleased with what she saw, however, for she smiled after the examination was complete.

"I take it ye're here for a job," she stated.

Job? Suddenly Claire's cheeks burned fire red. Surely the woman didn't mean . . . ? "Oh, heaven's no," Claire stammered, shamed by the thought. "I'm not here for a job. I . . . I . . . was hoping I could see someone."

The woman hesitated before answering, but then her eyes lit up with a wicked gleam while her mouth unrolled a knowing smirk. "See someone?" she laughed. "Well, honey, I suppose there's one woman who would take ye on. It's gonna cost ye, but by the look of yer face ye've got the money." She inspected Claire up and down, then appeared to come to a decision. "All right, honey, how much time are we talking about?"

The woman may as well have spoken Chinese for as much as Claire understood her. "I'm terribly sorry," she said, "but I don't think I know what you're talking about, so perhaps I could try to explain myself better. I'm looking for a Mrs. Blake, and it's my understanding that I might find her here."

The woman's face clouded with suspicion. "I don't know any Mrs. Blake," she stated firmly, defying Claire to challenge her.

But there was no challenge upon the young girl's face, for she was positively crestfallen. "I see," she said, turning to leave. "Well, thank you so much for your time. You've been very kind."

There was something about her impeccable manners and elegant politeness that gave Sally pause. Who was this girl, and why did she want to see May? Oh, it was probably none of her business, and she almost let the girl go. But at the last second, as the girl placed her small hand upon the doorknob and gave it a clockwise turn, Sally stopped her.

"Wait a minute, honey," she said, placing a restraining hand upon Claire's shoulder. "Why don't ye come into my office and we can talk about why ye're here. I might be able to help ye after all."

"Really?" A grateful smiled stretched across Claire's face. "That would be wonderful."

Sally ushered them both into her office and shut the door behind them. When they were seated, she asked to know exactly who Claire was and what she wanted.

"My name is Claire Rushmoor. I am the eldest daughter of Kendal Rushmoor, Earl of Bedington."

"Ye don't say," Sally uttered, impressed by the prestige of her visitor.

"A Mr. Devon Blake has been employed by our family for the past several months," Claire continued, "and it has come to my understanding that I might find his mother here."

"And what might ye be needing to speak with his mum about?"

Claire was grateful to realize that the woman knew who Devon was. "I'm afraid Mr. Blake is in a bit of trouble," she relented, "though it was through no fault of his own."

For a moment Sally buried her face in her hands. "Oh,

my," she whispered, almost to herself. "I don't know if May will be able to handle this again."

May? Was that Devon's mother's name? "I'm sorry. Did you say 'again'? Has Mr. Blake been in trouble many times?"

Sally was immediately on guard, thinking that Claire was here to gather information on Devon. But when she searched the girl's eyes she saw them filled with compassion and concern. Truly they were not the eyes of someone who harbored ill intentions toward May's boy.

She abruptly stood. "I think I'll let May explain it all to ye, lass."

Claire followed Sally's lead. "Then you know where I can find her?"

"Sure. She's up one floor, at the top of the stairs, first door on yer right."

"Then it's all right if I see her?"

"I'm afraid that's for May to answer, lass. But ye're welcome to go see for yerself."

Claire smiled in appreciation. "Thank you, er . . . ?"

"Oh! I never did introduce myself, now did I?" Sally's laugh reverberated throughout the room. "I'm Sally Landry, proud owner of The Night Star. Pleased to meet you, lass."

Sally led the way out of the office and again directed Claire toward May's room. As she ascended the curved staircase Claire again felt anxiety take a tight grip of her. The meeting with Sally had gone well, but what of May? Would she be so welcoming, especially after Claire confessed her responsibility for landing Devon in jail?

At the top of the stairs she turned right and in just a few footsteps stood in front of May's door. She took a deep breath, then rapped her knuckles against the hard wood.

There was a pause, and within the room Claire could hear someone fumbling around. It hadn't occurred to her that perhaps Devon's mother was a late sleeper and Claire's arrival was waking her, but before those thoughts could take hold, the door swung open and May Blake stood before her.

Claire's first thought was the remarkable resemblance Devon bore to his mother. It was easy to see where he'd gotten his green eyes. May's were a deep sea green, perhaps even greener than Devon's. She'd also passed along the chestnut hair color, though her hair lacked the blond streaks that highlighted Devon's. Probably because she has to spend so much time indoors, Claire thought.

May was surprised by her unknown female visitor, but nevertheless her demeanor was warm. "May I help you, miss?" she inquired.

"May Blake?" Claire asked, and when she received an affirmative nod, added, "I've come to speak with you about your son, Devon. May I come in?"

"Ye know me boy? Well, o' course, lass. Come on." May ushered her in and directed Claire to a nearby seat. "So, lass. What's yer business?"

"I . . ." Claire took a deep breath. "Perhaps I should begin by introducing myself. My name is Claire Rushmoor, and—"

"Rushmoor? The same Rushmoors where Devon works?"

"Yes, the same ones."

May jumped up and reached out to grasp Claire's hand. She enthusiastically pumped it up and down, exclaiming, "It's so nice to meet you, lass! Ye've no idea what ye've done for my boy. He finally got some coins in his pocket, and is earning 'em right proper."

Claire smiled. "He's a fine worker, and we're happy to have him."

May noted the subdued tone in Claire's voice and caught on immediately. "But ye ain't here to talk about that, are ye?"

"I'm afraid not, Mrs. Blake."

"It's May, lass. Call me May."

"As you wish." Claire unclasped and clasped her hands as she thought how to begin. "I'm not sure how to tell you this, Mrs. Blake, but I'm afraid your son's in jail."

May clutched her hands to her heart and threw her head back. For a moment Claire thought she was suffering an attack upon hearing the devastating news, until she heard what sounded like a sigh of relief. "Oh, mercy! Is that all? Is that all ye came here to tell me?" Claire nodded as May added, "Thank the good Lord above. For a minute I thought ye came to tell me he was dead."

"Dead? No, no. I'm so sorry I gave you that impression. How frightened you must have been."

"Aye, ye had me going, lass. But it's a relief to hear it's only jail."

Only jail? "But you don't understand. I'm responsible for his being in jail."

Instead of the scorn Claire expected to receive, she was answered by May's hooting laughter. "Ye're responsible, lass? Now there's something I don't believe for a second. If ye had anything to do with my boy being in jail, I don't think ye'd be here to tell me about it."

"But it's true," Claire persisted. "And I'm here because I want to do something about it. You see, I . . . I'm in love with your son."

The laughter abruptly halted, replaced by disbelief and confusion. "What? In love with Devon? Do ye know what ye're saying, lass? Do ye understand where he comes from?"

She shook her head. "No, I don't. I know nothing about him, except that he's the most honest, caring, wonderful person I've ever met, and now I've gone and put him in jail."

Good heavens, May thought. The girl looks like she

actually might start shedding tears. It was time to find out what was going on. "Perhaps ye'd best start at the beginning, lass."

And so she did. For over an hour Claire spun the tale of everything that had happened since Devon Blake entered her life. She told her what he'd selflessly done for Lilia, and how her father had been so impressed with his service that he made him a footman. She told how Devon had come to her for help to find his friend's murderer. She explained the way Philip Westbury had treated Devon. In her concentration to remember every detail, she failed to notice May's subtle reaction upon hearing Philip's name. Claire outlined the beginnings of her attraction toward Devon, how it had blossomed into respect and admiration and pride as she came to know him better day by day. And how every time they were together the attraction grew stronger. Though her face burned red she told May everything, even admitting to their lovemaking. May did not appear shocked in any way, but merely nodded as the story went along, allowing Claire to continue uninterrupted.

When Claire began speaking of the missing crystal swan and the accusations Philip made against Devon, her voice became noticeably shaky.

"Calm down, lass," May urged.

But Claire was not to be comforted. "I can't calm down. Don't you see? I know Devon didn't steal that swan, but I held my tongue. I didn't defend him. And that's why he's in jail."

May clucked her tongue at the younger girl's foolishness. "I'm afraid that's where ye're wrong, lass. My boy's not in jail because ye said nothing. He's in jail because of what Philip did."

Claire looked at May with surprise. "You sound as if you are acquainted with Lord Townsend."

May nodded, but only said, "Ye could say I'm acquainted with him."

"Then you might know how insensitive he can be to people he feels are 'beneath' him."

"Aye, I know."

"He was the one, after all, who accused Devon of stealing that figurine. I know Devon didn't do it, but I didn't defend him. He asked for my help, and I stayed silent, fearful of betraying my family. Now I realize I betrayed him."

Two large tears rolled down Claire's face; she was helpless to stop them. She wiped them away, not wanting Devon's mother to see her weakness, but she was too late. May had seen the tears, and walked over to place a comforting arm upon Claire's shoulders. "If ye've come to ask for my forgiveness, ye've got it, lass. I know ye were only doing what ye've been taught."

"But what I've been taught is so wrong!" Claire cried. "I've been taught to ignore others who are not like me. I've been taught not to even speak with people who don't have a title after their names. I've been taught to be unkind to people like you."

Her sadness was profound, and May was touched. "Don't be thinking it's yer fault about Devon, lass. I know ye meant no wrong."

How could anyone be so forgiving? How could anyone be so kind? Never before had Claire known such genuine compassion for others as what she felt from May Blake. No wonder Devon harbored such bitterness toward the wealthy. There was not one among them who would be as gracious.

"Still, I want to make up for what I've done. I'll do whatever I can to get Devon out of jail."

"I'm sure he'll get out of there with or without yer help, lass. He always has in the past. Not that I'm not worried, mind ye. A mother always worries about her babes. But Devon's got his wits about him, and he'll get out."

"Still . . ."

"As a matter of fact, the more ye were talking, the more I thought ye'd come to speak with me about Joshua's murder."

"Joshua? Devon's friend?"

"Not just a friend. They were more like brothers, were the two of them. They grew up together, looked out for each other. When Joshua was killed I saw some of the life snuffed out of my boy's eyes. It was only looking for the killer what made Devon keep on going."

For the first time since they'd met, Claire saw fear surface on May's face. "He asked me what I had seen that night."

"Aye, I know."

"But I really couldn't tell him anything. I didn't see the person's face, and at the time I was really more concerned . . ." She halted abruptly, realizing that once again her motivations had been selfish. Despite the fact that a man was being kicked to death, Claire had only been concerned for Lilia's safety, who hadn't been in nearly as much danger. She groaned aloud, and wished the earth would swallow her whole.

"Ye don't have to explain, lass. Devon told me the whole story of what ye were doing down there in the first place. And I admire ye for looking out for yer own kind. That's all anyone can do, after all." Her words appeared to have no impact on Claire, so May lifted Claire's face and peered straight into her eyes. "Listen to me, lass," she said. "Ye did all anyone would have done in yer shoes. Ye couldn't have known what ye were seeing. I'm sure to ye 'twould look like nothing more than a drunken brawl. Stop acting like ye did something wrong."

"I just wish I could have done more to help Devon."

"Ye spoke with him, lass. I'm afraid that's more than some folks like ye would have done."

Although she knew May meant nothing cruel by the remark, Claire was nevertheless ashamed and felt compelled to change the subject.

"Has there been any progress on finding out who did this to Joshua? Devon's said nothing to me about it since I told him what I knew."

May cocked an eyebrow. "Nothing? Then he hasn't told ye about the button."

"Button? What button?"

"Strange that he kept ye in the dark about this," May mused. Then she was struck by a thought. "Are ye good friends with Lord Townsend, by any chance?"

It was nearly impossible not to roll her eyes in disgust upon hearing Philip's name, but Claire maintained her composure. "I don't know whether you could say we're good friends. But . . . well, it seems Lord Townsend is to become my fiancé."

"I see," May said slowly.

"That is, unless I turn down his proposal of marriage."

"And Devon knows that Philip asked ye?"

Claire nodded. "He knows."

"Well, that's it, then."

"I beg your pardon? What's it?"

When May failed to answer right away, Claire became more adamant. "What's it? Please, what are you talking about?"

"I have a funny feeling about this, lass. I don't think I should be talking about it."

"If you don't talk about it I fear I shall have to be institutionalized," Claire said in exasperation. "Now, please. Say whatever's on your mind."

"Very well. I'll tell ye all about Philip Westbury and his magnificent button."

For the next fifteen minutes Claire sat in rapt attention,

clinging to every word May uttered, riveted by what she was learning about Philip. She felt both nauseated by what he had done, and euphoric knowing she was free of the obligation to marry him. There was no way even Louisa would insist upon Claire's marriage to Philip after finding out what he'd done.

"So ye see, unless there's another man wearing the same custom button that Philip wore, he's the one who beat Joshua to death."

It was all so unbelievable. "I suppose it's possible for someone else to have those kinds of buttons," she said lamely, knowing even as the words left her mouth that the notion was pure folly.

"Anything's possible, lass. But think about it. Philip definitely had a shirt with those buttons, a shirt which he now refuses to wear. He says it's because it's out of season, but we know that Joshua ripped the button off the killer's shirt the night he was beaten. Seems more likely to me that Philip won't wear that shirt because it's been torn."

"And has a missing button," Claire added, sickened by what Philip had done.

"Exactly."

In agitation Claire rose from her chair and began pacing around the room. "Then why hasn't Devon had Philip arrested?" she demanded, as if the fault were May's.

"Who would believe him, lass?" May asked. "Do ye think the magistrate would take a poor thieving law-breaker's word against a rich, titled marquess?"

"But it's not just his word," Claire protested. "Devon has proof!"

"No proof as far as the law is concerned," May informed her. "Remember, no one actually saw Philip do it. The fact that Devon has the button could be explained away by saying Devon broke into Philip's home and ripped it off the shirt himself."

"It's not true!"

"Of course it's not true, lass. But ye have to realize, Devon himself is a lawbreaker. What's to make the magistrate think he didn't kill Joshua himself and is trying to cover up the crime by framing Philip?"

She heard the devastating words, but refused to believe them. How could anything be so unfair? No wonder Devon felt embittered toward the wealthy. She was beginning to share those feelings herself.

"There has to be something we can do," she said, more as a question than a statement.

"Aye, there is, lass," May sagely informed her. "Ye can charge Philip with the crime yerself."

"Me?" The idea shocked her.

"And why not? Ye seemed convinced enough a minute ago. And ye've got the power to do it."

"Well, I . . . I'm not sure."

Familiar doubts began rearing their heads. What was she doing, really, getting involved in this situation? Shouldn't she be at home, receiving callers, and finding herself a socially acceptable husband? What was she doing entertaining the crazy idea of having Devon Blake as her future spouse? It wasn't even possible, was it?

Perhaps. Perhaps not. Everything was so confusing right now. But one thing Claire knew for sure. No matter what happened, no matter if she and Devon never saw one another again after this whole mess was over, she knew she could not go through the rest of her life knowing she'd been responsible for putting the man she loved in prison. And she'd do whatever was in her power to get him out.

"Not sure, lass?" May could not hide her disappointment.

"No. That's not true. I am sure. Devon's been falsely

imprisoned, and I'm to blame. I'll do whatever I can to get him out."

"Lord praise ye, lass."

Claire held up her hand toward May, as if to block her words. "Please, such kindness is not necessary, or even appropriate. I'm only trying to correct a wrong I've done."

"There aren't many like ye, lass, and I'm grateful, no matter how much ye protest."

She was touched by May's honesty, and vowed not to let her down.

"I'll do what I can; I promise." She paused then, wanting to make a last request, but unsure whether May would honor it. She knew the lady's first loyalty was to her son; still, Claire felt she had to try.

"May, I—"

When she failed to go on, May gave her encouragement. "I think after the conversation we've just had ye can ask me anything."

Claire smiled; she was right. "It's just that I'd like you to keep the conversation a secret," she said. "I'm not sure how Devon feels about me. I may never know. And for that reason, I'd prefer that he doesn't find out I was here."

May's cheerful expression momentarily faltered. "Not know, lass? But why?"

Claire shrugged. "I'm not sure, really. But Devon is such a private man that he may feel I've violated that privacy by coming to speak with you."

"Oh, lass, I don't think—"

"Please. Please don't tell him. I just don't want him to know."

Claire was distressed by the thought of Devon knowing what she'd done, and May was fairly certain she knew the reason why. So, not wanting to cause the lass any more stress, she gave her promise.

Silence fell between the two women, and there appeared to be nothing more to say. Claire took the opportunity to ready herself to leave.

"It's been a right pleasure meeting ye, but I won't be saying good-bye. Hopefully we'll soon be seeing much more of each other."

"It's my hope as well. Thank you for everything, May."

" 'Twas nothing."

Claire gave her a final smile and opened the door.

"Say, lass. One more thing before ye leave." May leaned closer toward her, making certain she would not be overheard. "Devon always carried with him the button that Joshua ripped off Philip's shirt. He probably had it when the constable took him in."

Claire immediately understood where May's thoughts were going. "So they may have it with his other things down at the jail."

May nodded. "Exactly. So if ye could get hold of the shirt Lord Townsend wore, and show the prison officials that it matches the button Devon had on him, ye'd have more power on yer side."

Claire nodded agreement; her mind was already working to devise a plan.

"Ye're a smart one, lass. Best of luck to ye."

Claire gave her a final wave and left the room. As noiselessly as possible she made her way down the stairs and outside The Night Star.

Thanks to the drab gown and unflattering coiffure, no one paid a whit of attention to her, and the ride back home was cathartic for clearing her head. She was able to restrain the anger toward Philip that kept threatening to resurface, and instead directed the energy toward vindicating Devon. She was filled with the certainty that she could do it; more importantly, she was convinced she wanted to. Gone were the doubts as to whether she should get further involved or simply leave Devon's plight in the hands of fate. Gone, too, was the decision to marry Philip Westbury. He was a horrid, wretched, self-absorbed knave who filled her with more loathing than she ever thought possible. To imagine spending even one more minute with him caused waves of nausea to surge through her body. She must control that reaction, however, for spend more time with him she would. Enough time to gather evidence against him and secure his rightful place in the world—locked up in prison.

Twenty-one

So far it had all gone easier than expected. She'd made arrangements to meet with Philip for dinner, and he was available the next night. Claire was certain that when he had received her letter he'd been curious about why she suddenly had the urge to see him, but he had probably assumed she wanted to accept his marriage proposal. His response had been immediate, and his suggestion that she come to his place for dinner had been perfect. It would give her an opportunity to look around for his shirt, and the crystal swan, which she was now convinced he'd taken to frame Devon. If someone were rash enough to kill another human being, stealing a family heirloom wouldn't warrant a second thought.

Though she refused to dwell on Devon's fate, deep in her heart she knew his life was threatened. If her family chose to pursue the matter to the fullest extent, it was possible he could spend the rest of his life in jail. And a short life it would be, with the inhumane way prisoners were treated.

With haste she closed her eyes to block out the frightful image of Devon's imprisonment. It's your fault, it's your fault, her mind kept shouting at her, relentlessly reminding her of her role in this debacle. But plotting how she would help him kept her sanity intact.

As distasteful as it had seemed when the idea initially came to her, Claire had now decided that the best way to get what she wanted from Philip would be through the age-old art of seduction. She had to do something that would put him off guard, and playing a flirtatious young chit was the last thing he would expect from her. Prim, proper Claire Rushmoor would never do such a thing, would she? Of course, little did he know of the passion and emotion she had experienced with Devon. And, Claire mused, he probably never would. Philip was a cold, self-serving fish, incapable of giving of himself to anyone and thus never receiving anything in return.

But, she allowed, his baser instincts would surely respond to her coquettish behavior, which was exactly what she wanted. Proper Lady Rushmoor would be momentarily retired, for tomorrow night she would be the most surprising, enchanting temptress Philip had ever met. And she harbored no doubts as to whether or not she could pull it off. Though she was far, far from ever being considered a femme fatale, she had figured out a way to successfully play the part. She had only to remember how she felt and acted the times she had lain in Devon's arms, and all the passion and sensuality she would ever need was instantly brought forth. For the first time in many days, Claire smiled.

"Lord Townsend doesn't deserve such a beautiful woman as you, mademoiselle. I think he does not appreciate you."

"That's not a very nice thing to say about your future master, Marie," Claire admonished her maid.

"*Oui,* it is not nice, but it is ze truth."

"Well, with the beautiful work you're doing on my hair, I think he'll notice tonight."

"Hmmmph. If he's smart he'll notice."

It was useless to keep correcting her maid when she was in one of her moods, and if truth be told, Claire was perfectly content to let her go on. Marie never hesitated to speak her mind, at least not in front of Claire, and the fact that she was berating Philip didn't bother Claire in the least.

"There!" Marie pronounced triumphantly. *"Finalement,* it is finished."

She took up the looking glass and held it behind her mistress's head so Claire could admire her maid's handiwork. Indeed, Marie had done a beautiful job. Mounds of curled blond locks were loosely piled atop her head in a carefully arranged coiffure. Woven throughout the hair was a green and silver satin ribbon. A few loose strands were purposely left free to frame Claire's face. It was tastefully elegant, yet slightly daring—exactly the effect Claire had asked for.

She'd had the green and silver gown she would wear taken in several inches at the high waist, calling extra attention to her bosom. The front of the gown plunged daringly low, certainly much lower than what was currently in style. Still, she reminded herself, she was playing a seductress, and had to look, as much as act, the part.

"I still don't know why you look so beautiful for him, mademoiselle, but I 'ave done my best."

"Your best is perfect, Marie. *Merci.* Now I must go. Is the carriage waiting?"

"Oui, mademoiselle. It has been ready for ze past hour."

"Then I'm off. Hand me my shawl, please."

Her maid brought forth the diaphanous emerald shawl that was the final complement to her ensemble. Carefully Claire draped it over her shoulders, then gave herself a final check in the mirror before departing. She smiled in spite of herself, for the effect she had created was a definite departure from the way she usually looked. At her insistence, she'd even had Marie apply some sparing cosmetics. A touch of pink along each cheekbone, a dab of color on her lips. She couldn't help but wonder if Devon would like "temptress Claire," but brushed aside the thought before her eyes welled up with unwanted tears. No time now for crying over his desolation; it was time instead to do something about it.

She was successful in leaving the house without anyone seeing her. She'd purposefully arranged to meet Philip rather late, knowing that everyone else would have left for the evening and she could get away unobserved. Apart from Marie, everyone else in the family thought Claire would be spending the evening with an old family friend who had recently become bedridden with gout. Claire had said she would likely be arriving home late, as she anticipated entertaining the dear lady by catching her up on the latest gossip and reading her poetry. The only reason Marie had been informed of the truth was that Claire would have been hard-pressed explaining her need for seductive dress if she were truly just keeping a friend company. But Claire had also taken the rare step of threatening Marie with termination if she breathed one word of the truth to anyone. As distasteful as it had been for her to do so, it was imperative that no one find out what she was doing.

After settling into her seat, she rapped upon the door, and the carriage was off, swiftly carrying her to Philip's lavish town home. She'd been there only once before, at a party he had thrown at the end of last season. She hoped her unfamiliarity with the surroundings wouldn't hamper her efforts too much, but she was prepared for the possibility that it might take longer than she wished to accomplish her goals.

In no time they were pulling up in front of Philip's home. Daniel jumped down to help Claire out of the carriage, and before she knew it she was standing by the front door. She took a final deep breath, then rang the bell.

Within seconds Philip's butler, Albert, swung the door open and ushered Claire inside.

"So good to see you again, my lady," he said, in a respectful monotone. "May I take your wrap?"

"Thank you, Albert," Claire said, her tone one of gushing gratitude. Best to get into the mood right away, she thought.

"My lord will be down momentarily, but he has given me instructions to make you comfortable within the parlor and offer you an aperitif."

"That sounds wonderful." Claire bit down gently on her lower lip as she pondered what would be an appropriate drink for a budding temptress. Finally she said, "I believe I'll have a glass of sherry. Dry, if you please."

Although he showed no outward sign of it, Claire was certain the butler was surprised by her acceptance of something alcoholic to drink. But Claire knew that if she were going to do this, she'd better do it right.

When Albert had left the room she took as much time as she dared to check the room for the remote possibility that Philip had put the crystal swan on his own parlor shelves. Not surprisingly, it was nowhere to be found. But Claire did not despair. After all, it would have been extraordinary sloppiness for Philip to let his deception be so easily uncovered after going through the trouble of taking the swan and using the theft to frame Devon.

She seated herself on the divan not a minute too soon, for Albert entered the room bearing the requested glass of sherry, and right after he left, Philip made his appearance.

He swept into the room with all the grandeur he could muster, wearing his typical tasteless outfit. This time he was adorned in yellow broadcloth breeches, so snug against his legs they fit like a second skin. He wore a shockingly bright blue waistcoat, over which was a black coat. The open buttons at the top of the waistcoat revealed a blindingly white, frilled shirt underneath. The collar was upright, held stiffly in place by two lawn cravats, one yellow, the other blue. If she hadn't been there to lure him to distraction through seductive charm, Claire would have laughed out loud.

"How lovely you look this evening, my dear," Philip said by way of a greeting.

"And you as well, Philip." She rose with a smile. As usual he captured her hand and raised it to his lips, but instead of pulling away as quickly as possible, she allowed his lips to linger upon her hand, even closing her eyes as if savoring the feel of his kiss.

He was surprised by her action, but more importantly, he was also pleased.

"Come, let's sit," he invited, guiding her back to the divan.

Once they were both seated he rang for Albert and requested his own aperitif. "I'll join the lady in a glass of sherry," he instructed the butler.

When Albert had left, Claire moved just a little closer to Philip, then cozily informed him, "I'm glad you were able to accommodate my request to see you."

Surprised by the way she was acting but rapidly warming to it, he replied, "But of course, Claire. You know I'd cancel plans to see you whenever possible. You're always my first priority," he paused to take a sip of sherry that Albert placed in his hand, "and besides, I have been expecting a certain answer from you . . . ?"

In response, she gave a little laugh and placed one hand atop his arm. "I haven't forgotten, and it's something we'll be talking about before the night is over." Boldly she looked him in the eyes, putting him on notice that tonight would be different from others he had spent with her. Only she knew exactly how.

"You've . . . you've come to a decision, have you?"

With a small seductive smile, she again slid closer to Philip and captured his attention with a flutter of her eyelashes. "I have most definitely come to a decision. But let's get to that later, hmm?"

Aroused, Philip wondered what was going on. Claire had never acted this way toward him before. Why, she was flirting! At once his naturally suspicious nature reared its inquiring head. Her behavior was so out of character that she must have come here for something. But what? Had that bastard Devon Blake filled her silly head with lies about him? Was she on some sort of mission on his behalf? But that couldn't be. Whatever strange attraction she may have felt for the servant boy, she would no more shame her family by allying with him than she'd take up smoking cigars. So what reason could there be for her wanton behavior? He'd certainly find out—by giving her a taste of her own medicine.

Taking up her lead, Philip set his glass down to free both hands. Then, without uttering a word, he placed one hand against her creamy cheek, and the other behind her back. Firmly but gently he drew her forward, disregarding her resistance.

"Oh, my lovely," he murmured in her ear, then pressed his tongue against her earlobe to lap along the delicate edge. Immediately Claire's entire body stiffened, and she pulled her head away. Philip appeared to have anticipated her action, as he used the hand that had caressed her cheek to hold her head against his mouth.

"Philip!" Claire exclaimed, alarmed by his behavior. "Stop that at once!"

Her words went unheeded as he continued his assault. He plunged his tongue within her ear, licking with the gusto of an affectionate puppy.

"You needn't feign impropriety, my dear," he breathed. "As I'm certain you've consented to be my wife, let us both enjoy this celebration of our love. After all, it's what you want, isn't it?"

So that explained it. He was testing her. Her behavior was so out of character that he failed to completely accept it, and he was calling her bluff to see what she was up to. Well, Claire thought, score one for Philip. He'd most definitely won that round. But it would be his last victory. She was here for Devon, and would do whatever it took to clear his name.

Swallowing all semblance of pride, Claire leaned against Philip, pretending to enjoy his attention, before gently pulling away. "I was ashamed to show my feelings for you," she lied, "thinking you'd view me as some sort of . . . tramp."

He noticed the gentle shrug of her shoulders, the way she ran her tongue across her bottom lip, and her lowered eyelids. They could all signify her nervous confession of the truth, or her attempt at concealing a well-constructed lie. He was still unsure which one it was.

He lowered his head and pressed her tender lips against his unrelenting mouth. He was purposely forceful, insistent upon knowing the truth behind her visit. To his amazement, she was neither hesitant nor unyielding. Instead, she deepened the kiss and stretched its duration. When at last they parted, it was he who decided they'd continue later.

"As much as it pains me to tear us apart, I want to ensure we both have our strength for this evening." There was no mistaking the meaning behind that sentence. "Come, let us go to the dining room. The cooks have prepared us a feast."

Gratefully, Claire accepted his invitation, fighting back the nausea that threatened to blow her cover. His kiss had been sickening, causing her to doubt her ability to go through with the evening. But as her mind's eye conjured up images of Devon being led away to Newgate, she felt the love she held for him course through her veins, rejuvenate her spirit, strengthen her resolve. She'd never been more sure than at that moment of the depth of passion and love she held for him. Whatever happened in the future was not to be speculated upon. She would live for now, this moment, made stronger by the acceptance of her love for Devon that burned so brightly in her heart.

Philip led them both to his massive dining room, of which a table large enough to serve fourteen was the main centerpiece. But now a cozy dinner for two was the event at hand. Philip sat at his usual spot at the head of the table, and just to his right was where he seated Claire.

Despite the intimate number of diners, the table was set as majestically as it would be for a party of kings. A great epergne graced the center of the table, surrounded by the finest silver and bone china that money could buy. Crystal champagne flutes and wine goblets were also on hand, and Philip's footmen made certain they were always kept full.

As the soup was served and the meal began, Claire made certain to keep up a constant banter of flirtatious conversation, determined to remove any doubts about her visit that may have lingered in Philip's mind. Throughout the meal she batted her eyelashes, made a point of touching his hand or arm whenever she could, and laughed if he said something even remotely amusing. And her efforts, combined with the enormous amount of wine Philip was consuming, were beginning to pay off. He was thoroughly enjoying himself, relishing how manly Claire made him feel. To her advantage, he did not notice how little champagne she drank. Many times she raised the flute against her mouth, but actually consumed almost nothing. Philip's drunken mind failed to make the connection that her glass should have been emptied several times over. The unfortunate thing was that the drunker he became, the more lewd and repugnant were his actions. Thus it was increasingly difficult for Claire to feign attraction to him. And no matter how good an imagination she had, it was impossible to pretend that she was dining with Devon. The differences between the two men were inconceivably vast, and her mind simply could not replace the repulsive buffoon before her with an image of the dashing, courageous man who held claim to her heart. Still, her efforts to fool Philip were now working without a fault.

Ices and walnuts were finally brought around, signifying an end to the very long meal. Claire had successfully managed to eat very little without drawing Philip's attention. The last thing she needed was to dull her wits with the discomfort of a full belly.

"Will you require anything else, my lord?" Albert quietly asked as Philip smacked his lips with pleasure.

"Nothing for now, Mr. Cane," Philip replied, stifling a belch as he did so.

Claire waited until Albert retired from the room, then coyly said to Philip, "You mentioned something about us continuing where we left off."

Lust lit a fire behind his glazed eyes, and he responded by planting a sottish kiss upon her lips. His sour breath made Claire's head reel, but she somehow hid her disgust. The bigger test came, however, when Philip's hand rose up to roughly knead her right breast. With steel determination she managed not to pull away.

"Is this what you had in mind?" Philip grunted when he broke the kiss to expel another belch.

"Unless you don't want to . . . ?"

"Ah ha! So you're a teasing wench as well!" Philip proclaimed, pleased by the perceived change in Claire's personality. "I knew that prim ladylike role you always put on was a farce. You're as lusty as a bitch in heat when you want to be. Just like the rest of us!"

Claire had little idea who the "rest" of them were, but she knew she had no desire to find out. Philip's abhorrent behavior shocked her. Never had she imagined him uttering the filth that now easily flowed from his mouth. He was always so insistent upon absolute propriety, pretending to be disgraced when she had spoken with Devon, a "common" servant. He had lectured her endlessly on the rules of refined etiquette, yet now he was acting as if "decorum" were a foreign word.

Another horrifying realization suddenly seized her. If Philip could easily change from prudish socialite to filth from the streets, all the more reason to believe him capable of beating a man to death. Claire knew with undisputed certainty that Philip's whole demeanor was nothing but pretense. The real Lord Townsend had emerged from his shell.

With much fanfare Philip rose from his seat, then swept over to where Claire was sitting and nearly pulled her out of the chair.

"I know just the place where we'll be completely alone," he bragged, hoping to impress Claire with this privileged information. "In the parlor!"

That's the last place she wanted to be, for she had already determined that the crystal wasn't in there; neither would be the shirt, if it still existed. Thinking fast, Claire summoned up her best seductive smile and combated Philip's suggestion with one of her own.

"If it's all the same to you," she said, lowering her voice for a sultry effect, "I'd rather go upstairs and do it properly."

Surprisingly, he balked at her suggestion. Trying to keep something covered? Claire wondered.

"No, no. Not upstairs," Philip slurred. "That's reserved for our wedding night."

A pathetic excuse, taking his behavior into account. "Oh, please," Claire feigned annoyance, "don't go turning proper on me, Philip. What's the difference whether we're there now or later?" She wrapped her fingers around his arm, sensually caressing his pulpy biceps.

The seduction worked; Philip was hooked. He was like a boy headed to a candy shop as he eagerly pulled Claire upstairs toward his bedroom. Once they reached the door, however, he did not immediately lead her inside.

"Just wait out here a moment." He smiled wolfishly. "I want to prepare myself."

More likely prepare the room, Claire thought, but nodded her consent. Philip stumbled inside and shut the door behind him, leaving her standing in the hallway for nearly ten minutes. Just when Claire was beginning to wonder whether Philip had fallen asleep, his garbled voice summoned her within.

She pushed open the door and stepped inside, then had to pause as her eyes adjusted to the darkness. Just like The Night Star, she thought, then realized that Philip was probably trying to recreate the atmosphere of the place he so adored. Too bad, because it would be an extra deterrent when she searched for the torn shirt and crystal swan.

"Come here, you bawdy wench," he commanded, drooling as a dog would before devouring his meal.

Again the nausea surfaced; again Claire tamped it down. Remember Devon, her mind chanted as she walked toward the imposing bed. As she neared it she saw that Philip had tossed his clothing aside and was clad only in a thin silk robe. He now languished atop the bed in what he likely deemed an inviting pose, though to Claire he resembled an overfed goose. The unhealthy pallor of his skin was showcased on his feet, which had probably never seen the light of day. Stuffed as they usually were in his garish, buckled shoes, his toes now wiggled like so many worms, freed from the captivity of their underground prison. He lay on his left side, propping his head up on one hand. As Claire approached the bed he untied the drawstrings around his robe, purposely letting the material fall away.

"Like what you see?" He leered, and at her mute nod of affirmation, continued, "Because it's all for you."

It was suddenly too much. Claire felt her head begin to swim with the first signs of a dizzying faint. Black spots appeared before her eyes; the blood washed from her face. Philip was like a horrifying dream brought into reality. He was not only physically appalling, but crude and filthy in his entire demeanor. She'd made a vow to do whatever it took, but her body was rebelling against the wishes of her mind. Frantically sending up a silent prayer for strength, Claire steadied herself by clutching onto the bedpost and waited until the dizzying waves washed away.

She needed more time; she simply had to have more time. But how? She was finally where she wanted to be—in Philip's bedroom. The only problem was, he was here, too. She had to get him out long enough to check the room for the shirt and crystal swan. If she didn't find them by the time he returned, she could plead cold feet and beg him to delay their union for just a little longer. Of course, he'd be furious, particularly since he was convinced she wanted him as much as he seemed to want her. But with a little luck Claire could get him to drink so much—that was it! The solution to her problem.

As provocatively as she knew how, she placed one hand between her breasts. "Philip," she purred, knowing she was in command of his attention, "I can't believe you brought me up here empty-handed."

"I . . . what? What do you mean?"

She giggled. "I mean, silly boy, that you don't expect me to spend an entire evening here without any wine, do you? It's terribly hot in this room, and I'm very thirsty."

"I'm a bumbling idiot," Philip chuckled aloud. "Please accept my apologies, my lady. I shall ring for the wine immediately."

Claire took a sharp breath inward, shocked by his suggestion. "Ring for it!" she exclaimed. "And ruin my reputation by letting your servants know I'm up here? What would that do to the Rushmoor name, Philip? My family would be devastated, and so would yours, for that matter." After letting the words sink in, her tone abruptly softened. She reached out to caress his face, tracing the outline of his lips, allowing him to suckle her finger. "Philip, my love, you can't possibly ring for the wine. You know how servants talk. No, darling, you'll have to go fetch up some bottles yourself."

Her suggestion did not sit well with him. Her seductive voice, the way she'd lightly touched herself . . . he'd be a fool to leave her now. What if she changed her mind?

With a loud growl Philip reached out to grasp Claire's hand and pull her closer to him. Crudely he pressed his hand against her breast and caressed it as if he was kneading dough. With his fingers he pinched the nipple in what he thought would be enticement enough for her to change her mind. Unfortunately for him, it did not.

With stubborn determination not to show her revulsion, Claire moved away from Philip and stood at arm's length from the bed.

"Why, you devil," she teased, wagging a scolding finger at him. "Don't go trying to make me forget about it, because it won't work." Then she thrust her lower lip out in her best pouting imitation, vaguely recalling Lavinia once mentioning it was a gesture men found irresistible.

"Go on, Philip, really. I'm terribly thirsty, and besides,

you're always saying how learned you are in the ways of wine. Now go down to that cellar and pick us out a truly fine bottle. Something," she licked her lips with eager anticipation, "appropriate enough to celebrate our first evening together."

The gesture worked. Although he was still averse to leaving the seductive comfort of the bedroom, perhaps she was right, after all. It would be more than just a mild annoyance to deal with quelling idle servants' gossip, particularly when it was both their reputations at stake. And anyway, with the way she was talking and moving her lush body, his drunken mind was certain there was no acting going on. Claire Rushmoor was nothing but a little wench, and tonight she would prove it to him.

"Very well, I shall go. But mind you, I won't be gone long. And when I get back I expect to be handsomely rewarded for my efforts." He winked at her. "If you know what I mean."

She didn't, exactly, but presumed he'd let her know in a hurry. With assurances of being ready as soon as he walked back through the door, Claire watched with relief as Philip finally left.

Immediately, she sprang into action. The shirt, if it were here, could realistically be hidden anywhere. But Claire decided to start with the most logical place—his armoire. As quietly as she could she swung the doors open, then ruffled through the shirts hanging there with lightning speed. As was typical of Philip, everything was neatly in order, and though the shirts reflected his shockingly bad taste, they were nevertheless all new and unblemished. Although it seemed to Claire that the armoire's floor was somewhat high, it was, nevertheless, empty, with neither a shirt nor crystal figurine stuffed into the corner. Not allowing time for disappointment, she moved on to inspecting the chest of drawers. Inside were his undergarments, stockings, and socks, again all

folded neatly into place. She lifted up a pile of Philip's
crisp white stockings, hoping that the underside would
expose either the paperweight or torn shirt, but there was
nothing. As carefully and quickly as she could she replaced the socks just as she'd found them, slid the drawer
shut them made a swift inspection of her surroundings.

The four-posted bed was the centerpiece of the room.
Against the opposite wall sat two matching wing chairs
with a round table between them. Along the same wall
was the armoire, and beside it stood a vanity. The bed
was flanked by identical end tables. Everything was so
neatly in place, Philip really ought to be commended for
his astute choice of servants. They must come in here
daily to clean the room, it was so . . . that was it! With
almost tangible force her mind reeled from the answer
to her search. Philip's servants were in here daily cleaning, dusting, making sure everything was neat. Therefore,
wherever Philip hid that shirt and crystal swan had to
be a place the servants would never look. Someplace
where they never went, either because they didn't know
about it, or were given instructions that it was off limits.
But in this room of almost maniacal organization, where
would such a place be?

Again she took a hasty look around, and again her
eye was caught by the freestanding armoire. There was
something about it, something she'd noticed during her
first inspection of it. Carefully she scrutinized the length
of the giant clothes cupboard, until all at once she realized what had bothered her. The floor! The armoire's
floor had seemed to come up awfully high, and Claire
was certain it could mean only one thing—a false bottom. She raced over to it and once again swung open
the doors. Crouching down on her knees, she quietly
knocked against the armoire's bottom and was not in the
least bit surprised that the wood sounded hollow. Just as
though there was open space beneath it. Frantically

Claire felt around to discover how one opened the hidden false bottom. There must be some sort of lever or latch, she thought, but precious seconds ticked by without the answer revealing itself. Certainly the furniture maker was clever, but his ingenuity was at the moment not appreciated, for Claire knew that Philip's return was imminent, and she doubted she'd get a second chance to explore his bedroom alone.

Desperate to allay her rising panic, she now used both hands to feel underneath and around for signs of access. Damn! she swore silently, for the first time in her life. She was certain of her knowledge; why couldn't she find the answer? There had to be a way of opening the bottom! Beads of perspiration had formed on her brow; her palms, too, were becoming sweaty. It was becoming harder and harder to maintain her grip; she was going to have to stop and wipe them clean. But just as she began pulling her left hand from underneath the armoire, the slippery palm slid and landed upon the tiniest lever carved right into the bottom. Attached to the end of it was a small, delicate ring, and when Claire grasped upon it and pulled, the drawer cracked open.

Oh, dear God in heaven, thank you, thank you, she breathed with relief, but the prayers were uttered a second too soon, for bumbling up the stairs, singing drunkenly to himself, was Philip.

Twenty-two

She had just enough time to shed most of her clothes and dive into bed before he entered the room. In his arms he carried two bottles of his finest French champagne, 1795 Veuve Clicquot, along with two crystal flutes and a silver bowl filled to the brim with fresh strawberries.

"This ought to keep you happy," he growled, setting everything upon one of the end tables. When his arms were free he wasted no time in disrobing, then eagerly crawled back into bed.

"Now I've got you where I want you," he said with a hiccough, then gathered her in his arms. Without warning his mouth descended and smothered her lips. Resisting the urge to shove him away, Claire endured the assault for as long as she could, then finally turned her face away. Philip took the gesture only to mean that she needed some air, and his behavior continued unabated. Pressing her firmly against the bed, he slid down her body to nip and kiss her neck. For a moment Claire felt panic well inside her, for Philip had her pinned beneath him. But she refused to let this vile beast get the best of her, not when she was so close to having the evidence she needed to put him away.

Leaning her head back to feign enjoyment, she uttered low groans of approval while thrusting both hands in his jet black hair.

"Oh, my darling!" she gasped. "I can already tell how

accomplished you are, for you give me such pleasure!" Her cheeks burned with embarrassment as she whispered the false praise; still, she had to do whatever was necessary.

Wiggling with fake delight she pulled free from his grasp and scurried to the edge of the bed. He tried grabbing hold of her hand to pull her back, but he was drunk, and his movements were slow. Just what Claire wanted.

"We can't let this wonderful champagne go untouched, my lord," she purred, standing before him. "Come, enjoy some of it, while I entertain you." Without waiting for his agreement she poured him a glass of the champagne and prepared a plate of strawberries. She then thrust both items into his hands and stepped back from the bed.

"What's going on here?" Philip demanded, suspicious of her actions.

"Nothing more than a woman wanting to pleasure the man who would be her husband," she responded silkily.

"So, you've finally agreed," he said with a wink, pleased by her words.

She said nothing further but only smiled, then with smooth, subtle movements, began to gyrate her hips.

Philip's breath caught in his throat at the sight of the sensuous creature before him. She had taken off her dress, stockings, and shoes, and now wore only the thin, transparent tunic that originally covered her gown. Because its length was just to her mid-calf, he had a tempting look at her small, delicate ankles and feet. In addition, the candles behind her made it possible to view her entire body through the translucent satin material. She was ethereal, exquisite, and she was dancing for him. His loins began to burn, and the warmth crept through his body. He shifted his position in bed to accommodate the bulge between his legs, then leaned back on one arm to enjoy the show.

At first Claire felt silly and awkward performing, as

it were, for Philip. But she had to do something to get him to drink more champagne and stall for time, and this was the only solution that came to her mind. Still, it wasn't easy pretending to please him when what she really wanted was to see him rot in jail. If only it were Devon lying on that bed instead of Philip, she thought, I could do this so much more convincingly. But reality sat there, staring her in the face, mouth slightly open. Suddenly Claire realized that if she closed her eyes, she could block out the repulsive sight before her, and pretend it was Devon for whom she danced. Philip would never know the difference; in fact, he would think her eyes fluttered shut from sheer enjoyment in what she was doing.

"Enjoy your champagne, my lord," she encouraged as her arms reached up to undo the pins in her hair. When she pulled the last one free her golden locks cascaded downward like water spilling off a cliff. She imagined the intense gaze Devon would be giving her at this moment, and her hips rocked lushly back and forth in response. The satin tunic swayed gently around her moving body, swishing across her nipples and causing the little buds to harden. As if in response to her body's arousal, Claire moved both hands along the sides of her waist, starting at her hips and sliding upward. As she reached the swell of her breasts, she brought her hands forward and delicately stroked along the edge of the creamy globes. She rolled each nipple between her thumb and forefinger, then continued moving her hands upward until they swept underneath her hair and lifted it like a provocative courtesan.

Philip's mouth went dry from watching the show, and with his customary greed he drank his first glass of champagne in a single gulp, then promptly refilled the glass and continued drinking. He was to the point where there were two Claires before him instead of one, but what kind of fool would not bless such good fortune?

The dance continued for several more minutes, then turned into a seductive strip show. By then Philip could stand the teasing no longer. His loins were on fire and he needed relief!

"Warm my bed now, wench," he demanded, and Claire knew she could deny him no longer. Reluctantly she walked toward the bed, but not before she reached for the champagne bottle and made certain Philip's glass was full.

"Were you not pleased with the dance, my lord?" She pouted.

"Pleased? Bloody hell, woman, you've set me on fire until I can take no more. Now stop your teasing and get into this bed."

Slowly she pulled the covers back and slid in beside him. With clumsy haste Philip mashed down on her mouth and forced his tongue through her lips. His breath was sour from both the food and champagne, but she managed to convince him that he pleased her immensely. Besides, despite the vigor he initially displayed, already he was showing signs of slowing down. With cautious hope Claire positioned their bodies so that Philip was lying on his back and she alongside him. Tenderly she kissed his forehead and cheeks, knowing the gestures would prompt his eyes shut.

"Tha's it," he mumbled, sleep now looming very close at hand. Slowly Claire drew herself downward to place kisses at the base of his throat and against his chest. She used her hands to massage his shoulders, knowing that any gesture to relax him was to her advantage. With casual ease Philip placed one hand against the back of Claire's head, steering her to where he wanted her to go. But the silent instruction did not last long, for within a few short minutes Claire heard the methodical rise and fall of his breathing; Philip was fast asleep.

Her heart hammered wildly in her chest. She was afraid that his drowsiness would be short-lived and he'd awaken to demand her sexual favors. For three agonizing minutes she lay still as a mouse, needing to make sure he would remain in slumber. Finally, she rejoiced upon hearing the rumble of his snores; a sound that made her as happy as a bride on her wedding day. It meant Philip was out for the night.

With excruciating slowness she eased her way out of bed, being sure not to make a sound. Stepping away from the bed, she realized that her nakedness was to her advantage. Skirts and undergarments might dangerously rustle.

The candles had not yet burned down, and there was just enough light for her to continue the inspection. Again she crept in front of the armoire but this time did not have to waste precious moments figuring out how to open the false bottom drawer. With precision her nimble fingers felt along the wood until they again touched the tiny lever. She pulled on the ring, and the drawer slid open.

She cast a nervous eye toward the bed, but Philip was still sound asleep and showed no signs of wakening. She pulled the drawer out as far as it would come, then reached inside. At first she felt nothing, but when she stretched a little farther her fingers lit upon a soft silken fabric that could only be Philip's torn shirt.

She tried sliding it out, but there was some resistance. Was it caught upon a nail, perhaps? No, it appeared that something was holding it down, something rather heavy . . .

The cool, smooth crystal of the swan figurine was the most satisfying thing she'd ever held in her hands, and the final piece of evidence she needed to free Devon. It had been placed atop the shirt and was the weight restraining the garment. As quietly as possible Claire lifted first the paperweight from the drawer, then the torn silk shirt. It was too dark for her to thoroughly inspect the shirt, but she knew without doubt that it was the one he'd worn the night Joshua was murdered.

It was premature to celebrate victory, but Claire couldn't extinguish the tiny glimmer of hope that had begun burning in her heart. If all went well, Devon would be free and Philip locked up. The shirt and crystal swan, along with the matching button that Devon had, were surely enough to convince the magistrate that Devon had been wrongly imprisoned. I'm coming for you, my love, she whispered to him, wishing he could hear her.

She laid the valuable objects on one of the nearby chairs and retrieved her clothing. With haste she donned her stockings, petticoat, gown, and tunic, but decided to delay putting her slippers on until she was outside the bedroom. She could be her most silent if she crept out barefoot.

She gave a second glance toward the bed to be sure Philip was still sleeping, and had a moment of frozen horror when she saw him turning. Was he still asleep? Did he see her standing there? Her heart thumped in her chest, but her fears were for naught. Philip continued to sleep.

Quickly she gathered up her things and made for the door. Later, when she looked back on the entire incident, she knew it had been her haste that ultimately led to her grievous mistake.

In her right hand she carried the slippers; in her left, the shirt and figurine. The objects had not seemed awkward to carry, but in her rush to get out of the room, she failed to get a proper grip on the crystal swan. She took several steps forward before realizing the object was slipping out of her hands. By then it was too late. Knowing the noise it would make on the floor, she had valiantly tried to break the fall, but to no avail. It dropped to the ground, landing solidly on top of her uncovered foot.

Pain seared instantly throughout her body, and unable to help it, she let out a sharp cry of agony. The rest of her load dropped to the ground as well, and reflexively she raised her foot so her hands could inspect the damage. It was an impulsive movement, and her ultimate undoing. Despite the noise and her anguished cry, Philip had still not awoken. But raising her foot threw Claire off balance, and before she could rescue herself she stumbled several steps and crashed into the armoire.

Now she was doubly in pain, and the noise she'd created had woken her adversary.

"What in God's name?!" he blustered, shaking his head to clear away the effects of sleep and drink.

Automatically he reached over and lit his bedside lamp, and the sight that greeted him made his blood boil. Sprawled across the floor was Claire, massaging her foot while at the same time scrambling to gather up damning evidence against him. Somehow she'd discovered his torn shirt and her family's figurine, and was now acting as though the possessions were hers.

With barely contained rage he towered above her. "Just what do you think you're doing, you little fool?" he sneered.

He momentarily intimidated her into silence, but her reason soon took over and put the situation into perspective. He was the one who had murdered Joshua, he was the one who had stolen from her family, he was the one who had framed Devon; she was the one who should be furious.

"I'm taking back what you stole from my family," she shot right back, anger replacing her earlier fear.

"I don't believe that shirt was ever yours," Philip said, making a lunge to grab for it.

He was too slow, and she was closer to it. With a lightning-fast move she plucked it from the ground and held it firmly to her bosom. "Maybe not, but I'm using this shirt to free our family's servant; something else you stole from us by having him thrown into jail."

Philip raised an eyebrow as he listened to her accusations, but aside from that raised eyebrow his face betrayed no emotion. "Is that what you think? That I had an innocent man put behind bars?" He laughed at her allegations, his face turning angry and dark. "What kind of idiot do you take me for, you silly little whore. I have no more intention of letting you leave this room with that shirt than I have of letting your pathetic boyfriend out of jail."

She opened her mouth to protest, but his words silenced her.

"And don't think you've been fooling me about your relationship with that dreck of society," he scoffed. "I know how he's heated your loins with his muscular body, how he's stoked fire in your bed night after night. Don't try convincing me that you want him out of jail because he's an excellent footman. Face it, my love. The bastard's been servicing you, and you want him back."

Why that vile, disgusting . . . Claire stopped herself before the words poured out. That's exactly what Philip wanted. He was trying to make her furious, trying to get her to admit something he may have suspected but had no proof of. And she had almost fallen for his ruse. Remain calm, she commanded herself, and somehow you'll get out of this mess.

"Go ahead and say whatever you want, Philip," she retorted. "But no matter what, you'll not distract my attention from the truth. You are a murderer, a thief, and a liar. You'll do whatever's necessary to save your hide, and that's exactly what you're doing right now. But I've got the evidence to put you in jail for the rest of your life. No matter what you say, you're finished."

Philip's eyes snapped dangerously dark, and even with the lack of good lighting in the room, Claire could see how enraged he was.

He moved toward her as an animal stalking its prey, and with the armoire behind her, Claire could not back up. She grabbed the figurine and held fast to the shirt, then as Philip made a lunge toward her, she scurried to the side and headed toward the door.

With the agility of youth on her side, and Philip's intoxication working against him, she might have had a chance. But nothing could prepare her for the excruciating pain that shot through her body when her weight came down upon her injured foot. Unbeknownst to Claire, the ten-pound crystal swan had shattered several delicate bones, and despite her courageous determination to get away from Philip, the broken foot prevented her escape.

She fell as soon as she took the first step, and it was easy enough for Philip to grab hold of her and pull her to the bed. He shook her like a dog with prey in its mouth, then threw her down and slapped her, hard.

"Now listen to me, you ungrateful bitch," he snarled. "You're not going anywhere with those things. They, and you, are spending the night here. In the morning I'll sneak you out of here and take you home, with the promise that if you spread any of those nasty lies you've hurled against me, I'll make certain the entire upper society knows you spent the evening with me. Your reputation would be ruined, your family's reputation would be ruined. And naturally, I simply couldn't marry you after such a scandal, so it looks like you'd be spending the rest of your days as a used spinster." Philip clucked his tongue as if imagining the horror of the situation he'd

just described. "That would be a shame," he pretended
to lament, "and something you must consider."

There was nothing she could say, as his hand was
clamped firmly down on her mouth, but neither did she
nod agreement. Philip would not get the best of her,
no matter what he did. She would fight to the end—for
Devon.

Disgusted that she failed to submit, he gave her head
another good shake. "I'm warning you, Claire," he said,
"do not try resisting my orders. Neither you nor your
family can afford it. And would you really throw everything away on a good-for-nothing servant? You know
your family wouldn't." He snorted. "Why, your mother
would be furious if she even knew what you were thinking, much less trying to do, on behalf of a servant."

He took her wide-eyed stare as tacit agreement, and
decided that she was ready to be released.

"Before I take my hand away," he warned, "you must
agree not to make a sound. Not a cry, shriek, or call for
help will utter forth from your lips. Is that understood?"

She understood his words, but had every intention of
disobeying them. Still, the firm clamp he had over her
mouth was making her feel faint. She needed deep gulps
of air and would get them only after he removed his
hand.

She nodded, and bit by bit the pressure of his hand
eased until finally he removed it completely.

With relief Claire gulped life-giving oxygen deep into
her lungs. Since Philip no longer was pressing against
her she lifted herself into a sitting position. But the
slightest brush of anything against her ankle reminded
her that sitting was something she'd be doing for a long
time to come.

"Very good, my pet. Now we can talk as two adults
would."

Claire scoffed at his words and tersely replied, "My

ten-year-old twin sisters are more adult than you are, Philip. And do not make the mistake of pretending that all is well between us. I shall never forgive you for what you've done to me, my family, and especially to Devon. You are lower than anything that ever has or ever will walk the face of this earth. Your vileness cannot be described with words. You are without remorse or regret for anything you've done, and you have the blackest soul of anyone I've ever met."

Philip pretended to wince from the force of her words, but in truth he found them merely amusing. "I certainly hope such venom won't be displayed on our wedding night, my pet. I dare say it would put a damper on the evening."

His sarcasm was not lost on her, but she refused to give him the satisfaction of acknowledging it. "I can assure you they won't be said on your wedding night, Philip. At least not by me, for I've no intention of ever becoming your wife."

Oddly, this seemed to irritate him more than the insults she had earlier hurled. She saw his face cloud over with anger once again, and he grabbed hold of her wrist to bend it painfully back.

"You'll be my wife before the year's out," he growled, "and in the morning everyone who matters will know it."

"Philip!" Claire cried out with alarm. "You're hurting me!"

"This is nothing compared to what I'll do if you don't shut that mouth of yours," he spat back. "Remember what I said, and keep quiet. If the servants come, your reputation will be ruined, for what explanation could there be for them finding you in my bed?"

He was right, of course, but suddenly Claire realized that it mattered not a whit to her. The only man she wanted in her life was Devon, and sadly, she did not have to sustain an immaculate reputation for him. Ironically, if the servants found her in Philip's bed and started gossiping, it would work to her advantage in trying to get Devon for her husband. Her family would think her ruined for any "respectable" man and probably relent to a betrothal to Devon. Her only concern now was making sure she escaped with the items she came to get in the first place.

Gingerly she stuck her tongue out to lick away the blood that had pooled in the corner of her mouth after Philip's slap. His hand had smashed her cheek against her teeth, and already she could feel that area starting to swell. The injury did nothing, however, to diminish her determination. Her dilemma was deciding on the best possible timing. With her broken foot and slight disorientation from the shaking Philip had given her, Claire knew her only chance out of there was by alerting the servants to her plight by screaming—exactly what Philip had warned her not to do. But it was not the ruination of her reputation that concerned her. It was the fact that she'd only get one chance to scream, and it had better be long enough and loud enough to alert the servants. If she blew it, she was not only stuck in the room with Philip until morning, but more importantly, when he finally let her go it would certainly be without the items she needed to free Devon. Even if she went straight to the magistrate's office after Philip finally left her, by the time she convinced anyone to search his home Philip would have destroyed all evidence against him. Her only hope was to alert the servants so she could escape with the precious shirt and crystal intact.

An idea suddenly formulated in her mind. Perhaps it wasn't the best plan of action, but it would have to do. Gently, so as not to alert him, she turned and looked him straight in the eye.

"Philip," she began, her voice timid, letting him believe he'd scared her into obedience.

She waited for his response. At first he said nothing, but when it became apparent that she would not continue until he acknowledged her, he growled, "Well? Out with it!"

She folded her hands in her lap and cast her eyes downward. "I . . . I think my foot is quite badly hurt. Perhaps even broken."

Thankfully, it was not sympathy she expected from him, because he certainly gave her none. "Serves you right, as far as I'm concerned. If you hadn't been sneaking around where you've no business, it wouldn't have happened."

"You're right, of course," she replied, catching him off guard. He cast a questioning eye toward her and raised his left eyebrow. "What are you bumbling on about?" he demanded, annoyed by his own confusion.

"It was just my own foolishness that made me come here in the first place, and I deserve this injury. I should have known better than to question you. Now I realize that everything you've done was for my own good." Slowly, slowly, he was warming to her compliments.

"You were right about everything, Philip," she pressed. "I must admit that I did have senseless notions about Devon. But you saw through the absurdity of it all and did what it took to show me." With a theatrical flourish, she tossed her hands up in exasperation and then buried her face within them. "I'm so ashamed, Philip," she moaned. "Imagine what would have happened to my reputation, not to mention the unblemished Rushmoor name, had you not saved me from my own foolishness."

It was just the right amount of melodrama to make him believe her. With a crude show of affection he pulled her into his embrace and fondled her.

"Shhh, calm down, pet," he murmured, and when she quieted immediately he believed his caresses had worked. In truth, they had. Claire was so repulsed by his touch that she'd been unable to continue.

She pulled her hands away from her face and looked at him again. "I want to ask you for just one more thing, Philip."

The alcohol was still working through his bloodstream, and had managed to calm his anger. Though he was far from falling into the soporific state that had claimed his body earlier, he was relaxed enough to consider her request.

"And what might that be?" he said.

"My foot has begun stiffening up and is quite uncomfortable. Before we sleep, may I please just walk around the room for only a short time, just enough to loosen the ankle so that I can lie comfortably by your side?"

The idea of that sweet, warm, naked body servicing his every need was enough to entice him into doing almost anything. Still, he had one reservation.

"Since I know you'll not try running away on that ankle, I'm granting your request," he said. "But neither am I taking any chances. Before you begin your journey around the room you'll fetch me that shirt and crystal swan which you left on the floor. Then you may walk."

Perfect, Claire thought. With Philip holding the very items pointing to his guilt, the evidence against him would look that much stronger.

With quiet obedience she hobbled back to the armoire to retrieve the spilled items. But keeping quiet hadn't been easy. When she first stepped on the broken foot the white-hot pain that seared through her body had sent a scream racing toward her lips. It was only with a determination fiercer than she had ever known before that she had held the scream back. Unless done properly, one noise out of her would ensure certain failure. The time for screaming would begin soon.

Now, however, she handed the shirt and crystal to Philip, who had lain back down while still keeping a watchful eye in her direction.

"Thank you, pet," he murmured as she gave him what he'd asked for. Claire nodded, then turned away. Best not to cause any alarm until the last possible minute.

Slowly, she limped away from the bed, stopping periodically to stand on her good foot and give the other a rest. Philip's bedroom door seemed miles away, but it was where she had to go. Her idea was simple, really. She'd make her way over to the door. It was as far away from his bed as she could get, and it was also the closest she could be to the servants while still inside the room. Then, with all the force she could muster, she'd start screaming. Hopefully, before Philip raced across the room to clamp shut her mouth, her screams would be long enough, and loud enough, to wake the household. No matter what happened she'd be in for the fury of his wrath, but she prayed the servants would come to put a stop to it.

It took nearly ten minutes for Claire to reach her goal, and when she finally stood before the door she was truly miserable. Her foot throbbed with excruciating intensity, and she could feel her head swimming in a dizzy haze. She waited for the feeling to pass, but it persisted. With growing panic, she blinked several times and shook her head in an attempt to clear it. Philip was going to wonder what she was doing standing by the door if she stayed there much longer, and anything unusual would arouse instant suspicion in him. Then again, if the dizziness didn't pass she doubted she'd be able to summon forth a tiny yell, much less a piercing scream. Suddenly, with terrifying clarity, she knew what she had to do. It was the only solution.

With a rare courage, Claire set down her broken foot and rested her entire weight upon it. The pain brought tears to her eyes, but it was nothing compared with what she did next. Bracing her hand against the door to maintain her balance, she lifted up her good leg as high as she could raise it, then with every ounce of force she could muster, she drove the heel down and crushed it on top of her broken foot.

The savage pain that roared through her body brought every sense agonizingly alive. But this time she had no intention of holding back or keeping quiet. This time the scream that ripped from her throat was released with unbridled fury.

The piercing force of the scream brought Philip flying out of bed. That scheming wench! She'd pay for trying to outwit him, and she'd pay good. He was by her side in seconds, and aided by his momentum, crashed on top of her with brutal strength. Immediately he slapped both hands across her mouth, silencing her ear-splitting screams.

"Shut up!" he roared, forgetting that his yells, too, would be heard by the servants. Too late. Before Philip could do anything further, the entire household, it seemed, was pounding on the door.

"What's going on in there? Let us in!"

There were at least five men right outside the bedroom, and yells from the women could be heard in the background.

Philip's mind raced trying to figure a way out of this mess. If he said nothing, the servants would think something had happened to the both of them and force open the door. If he tried assuring them that everything was fine, they'd doubt his words until Claire chimed in. It was her screams, after all, that had brought them running. His only choice was to threaten her into compliance and hope she'd obey.

"Now, listen!" he demanded of her, digging his fingers into her arm to ensure she realized his power. "You're going to tell Albert and everyone else out there that all is fine. Say you spotted a mouse and just had a start. Demand that they all go back to bed, and that you're sorry for causing such a fuss. Do you understand?"

Although she was unable to speak, Philip thought Claire gave the slightest nod of her head to indicate her agreement. Well, at least he hoped she was, for at this point there was nothing else he could do. The relentless pounding and yelling continued on the other side of the door, and he was forced to acknowledge it.

"Calm down, calm down, everyone," he called out. "I'm afraid we just had a bit of a scare by a mouse. But I've killed it and now everything is fine. Go on back to bed."

He was hoping that his servants, who he'd always viewed as hopelessly dim-witted, would be pacified by his impromptu explanation and authoritative voice. Perhaps most of them were. But Albert, who'd always had a bit too much confidence for Philip's liking, now began speaking on behalf of the group.

"We heard a lady's voice in there, Lord Townsend, and we have to hear from her that everything's all right."

Damn that Albert! First thing tomorrow he'd send the bloody lout packing. In the meantime, however, his demands appeared to have stirred up the rest of them, and more shouts were asking for Claire's reassurance.

Philip shoved his face against her ear and fiercely reminded her of his earlier command. "You say one wrong thing and your cute little sisters will pay for your disobedience," he snapped, hoping that threats against family members would force her compliance.

He took away his hands, lifting them just above her mouth in case he needed to force her mouth shut again.

"Help me!" were the only two words she had time to scream, but they were more than enough. Despite Philip's best preparations, he could not clamp his hands down in time to silence her.

Worst of all, Albert recognized Claire's voice. In seconds their violent shoves against the door cracked the wood, and with a couple more heaves it came flying open.

"Lady Rushmoor!" exclaimed Hannah Crandall, appalled at finding such a noble woman lying battered and half-conscious on Lord Townsend's floor. Immediately the head housekeeper rushed over to fetch the pitcher and washbasin and began attending to Claire's bruises.

When he realized that the servants' arrival was imminent, Philip had raced over to his bed in a desperate attempt to hide the shirt and crystal. But the quick actions of his own servants, coupled with Claire's shrieks, defeated any chance he had of success.

"Grab those things on his bed!" Claire demanded, "and hold him down. Your master is a murderer, and those items prove it!"

The atmosphere in the room was a study in confusion, as men ran in every direction in an attempt to grab Philip and rescue the items Lady Rushmoor seemed so desperate to have. Like a wild, confused animal, Philip leapt atop his bed and in a single sweep grabbed both incriminating items. He managed to dodge the cook who'd lunged toward him, and left the man sprawling across the bed.

But despite that small success, he had no real chance at escape. By now there were seven men vying for the chance to hold Philip down. One look at Lady Rushmoor told them something terrible had happened, and they had witnessed their master's fierce temper often enough to know what he was capable of.

It was ironic, Claire often thought as she looked back

on the incident, that the very servants whom Philip had mocked and laughed at so many times were ultimately the ones who ruined him. As he attempted using the crystal swan to break the window and leap outside, his burly groomsman grabbed both Philip's arms and pulled them behind his back. With his vice-like grip, he forced Philip to drop both the shirt and the swan. One of the footmen then lunged forward to retrieve the items, while Philip was forced facedown atop the bed and held immobile by three strong groundskeepers.

The cool water Hannah had been sponging on Claire was enough to revive her, and as all eyes turned to her for further instructions, she explained what was going on.

"The crystal figurine you're holding belongs to my family. Lord Townsend stole it. But much more important is the torn silk shirt. That shirt is proof that your master is a vile, low-down murderer who brutally kicked a man to death in the East End less than four months ago."

A shocked silence filled the room, until a tiny scullery maid found her voice and spoke aloud the question on everyone's mind.

"But 'ow would ye know such a thing, Lady Rushmoor?"

The crowd waited expectantly, and Claire knew she owed them the truth after all they'd just done for her.

"The murdered man is the best friend of one of my family's footmen. This same footman has been framed by Lord Townsend, and right now is sitting in squalor at Newgate, doing time for a crime he did not commit." She looked at the doubtful faces surrounding her, and understood their uncertainty. Through his continuous demeaning behavior, Philip had long ago forfeited any chance at earning his servants' loyalty, and now they were skeptical about any upper-class person appearing to support one of their own.

"Although we still have a long gap to bridge, not all noble or wealthy people distance themselves from the working class as your master has. I ask that you trust in my words and believe what I'm telling you. I am truly here so an innocent man will be freed and the guilty one imprisoned. Despite their respective positions in society, I will see justice done."

For a moment, no one moved; not a sound was heard. Claire knew she'd done her best to try to get Philip's servants to trust her. But the ultimate decision was theirs to make. There was nothing more for her to say, and she knew now that unless she got out of there and made her way home, she'd succumb to the exhaustion that was threatening to overtake her.

She propped herself up to a sitting position, then waited for the ensuing dizziness to pass. And while she sat there, Albert spoke up on behalf of the group.

"Just tell us what we need to do, my lady, and it will be done."

That simple statement said it all, and Claire flashed a grateful smile at him.

"I need that shirt," she began, and it was passed over to her at once. "The crystal stays here until the police arrive. It can be used as additional evidence against Philip, for they'll want to know what this Rushmoor heirloom is doing in his house." Claire smoothed down her skirts and gestured for Hannah to help her up. "In the morning I'm going to Newgate to speak with the officials. Until then, when I can get the proper officials to take your lord away, he must be restrained and guarded. Is there rope around here?"

The servants were initially shocked at the idea of tying up their lord, but Claire directed them like a seasoned military commander, and her calm demeanor settled their nerves.

"Jeffrey," Albert spoke up, "go on out to the stables

and fetch the rope that Lady Rushmoor requested. And make sure to get the good, strong hemp."

The boy ran off as if wings were on his heels. "When he returns use the rope to secure Lord Townsend to the bedpost," Claire instructed. "Then make sure he's guarded by at least two strong men for the rest of the evening. We can take no chances of him getting away. Albert, you arrange for the shifts to be set up. When daylight comes I'll go to the prison and explain everything to the officials there. If all goes well I expect to return here, escorted by the police, who will then take Lord Townsend into custody."

For the past several minutes Philip had been forced into silence, having his face pressed into the bed. But now he managed to turn it to one side, serving the dual purpose of allowing himself to breathe, as well as voicing aloud his protests.

"This is utter lunacy!" he yelled. "Albert, tell these oafs to get off me this minute! The both of you are fired, and I'll make certain you'll never work in this city again!"

For one horrifying moment, Claire feared the servants would believe Philip's threats and actually release him. But Albert had anticipated their reaction.

"Stay put!" he commanded them. "Lord Townsend will do no such thing, for come tomorrow morning he'll be in jail. You will indeed work in this town again; in fact, you'll surely find an employer with a much kinder disposition than the one you've put up with over recent years."

His tone calmed them, but it was Claire's final statement that put their fears to rest. "If you'll help me now, I'll personally make sure that each and every one of you finds good, lasting jobs with decent employers. It's a promise."

They nodded their agreement, then a couple of them

smiled, and then even some chuckles were heard. It was clearly the tension of the crazy evening releasing itself, but they all knew for certain that what had started out as a horrible shock was suddenly turning into gratifying revenge on a most distasteful employer.

"Please, Hannah, help me up."

"Of course, my lady, but you really shouldn't be walking."

The housekeeper's concern was unexpectedly funny. "Believe me," Claire assured her with a giggle, "I couldn't walk, even if I wanted to. And with the pain in my foot, I definitely don't want to. Now, may I ask that someone go out and summon my driver? He's likely sleeping and will need to be roused. I'll also require help getting downstairs and into the carriage."

"Oh, my lady, don't go home now," cried Hannah. "The guest room's all fixed up; you can go on in there and get yourself some rest. In the morning we'll help you over to the prison."

"Thank you, Hannah, but I'm afraid I won't do any sleeping with the way my foot feels. I'll have Daniel take me to the doctor and then head home. My family would be frantic if I were away from home all evening. I'll be fine."

There was no arguing with the sight of that foot, and Hannah agreed that if Claire could get help at such an hour, then she must go right away.

"We'll be waiting for you in the morning, Lady Rushmoor," she said, as Claire was carried downstairs.

She assured them all that she'd be back in the morning with the police by her side, and then offered up a silent prayer that her promise would come true.

Twenty-three

Dr. David Wreston pursed his lips in a mixed expression of annoyance and concern. He was not accustomed to being woken in the middle of the night, and was astounded when he was made aware of the reason. In all his years of practice he'd never seen a foot so badly broken, and he could not believe what torture Claire had inflicted upon herself to put her foot in this condition. Never mind the reason behind it; to his way of thinking, the girl was heroic beyond good sense.

He finished wrapping a comfrey and goldenseal root poultice around her foot, then gently laid it upon the softest feather pillow he owned. He stepped back, made sure that Claire was as comfortable as could be, and made his way toward the door to signal Daniel. Together the two men helped her outside and into the carriage.

"I'll leave you be now, Lady Rushmoor," said Dr. Wreston. "Get plenty of sleep and keep applying that comfrey root. It will help the healing. I'm close by if you need me, but regardless I shall call on you in a week to see how you're doing."

Claire smiled her thanks and assured him she'd be fine. But as the carriage headed for home and she was left alone with her thoughts, she wondered. Would she really be fine? Would everything work out as she hoped? Her mind whirled in a hundred different directions, sometimes cheering her bravery; sometimes chastising her recklessness.

She knew the enormous risk she had taken by attempting to free Devon while tarnishing Philip's name in the process. Only a fool—or someone in love—would have been crazy enough to try it.

But was her love all for naught? Would Devon have anything to do with her once he was free? He'd originally come seeking to find Joshua's killer. Now that his mission was complete, was there any room in his heart for her?

At last, after an evening that seemed to have lasted an eternity, she was back home. Daniel helped her inside and up the stairs to her bedroom door before she dismissed him for the evening. She was lucky that she'd managed to escape the prying eyes of her family and the servants. Even dutiful Marie had not been able to stay awake long enough to assist Claire to bed. Admittedly, it was difficult preparing for bed without the servant's help, but Claire was glad of being spared the need to give an explanation for her foot until the morrow.

After removing the last of her garments she washed her hands and face, then climbed gratefully into bed. It had been an evening to remember, though its final outcome was yet unknown. In the morning she would make her way to Newgate to free Devon, and with any luck have an arrest warrant issued for Philip and convince the police to go with her to his town home. After that . . . well, she'd just have to wait and see.

The great stone prison loomed ahead of them like an impenetrable fortress. A cold, gray mist swirled forlornly about the grounds. Claire pulled her wool cloak tightly about her and peered out from the carriage window. They were nearly there. Her nervous stomach flipped, and apprehension threatened to consume her. With resolve, she pushed the feeling aside and concentrated on what she had come to do. To reassure herself, she locked her hands tightly around the object that was the key to her success. Providing May was right, and the officials still had all the items that had been in Devon's possession, she would match Philip's shirt with the button Devon had, proving Philip's guilt. She'd also received an unexpected boon. With the arrival of daylight, spatters of blood on the shirt became apparent. Undoubtedly they were Joshua's, and though the sight of them made Claire's heart ache for the man she never knew, his blood on Philip's shirt would help ensure that his killer went to jail.

All too soon, the carriage pulled up to the gate. On purpose Claire had taken the one bearing the crest of Bedington, as she knew its symbol of nobility would work to her advantage. And indeed, the gate guard barely gave pause before waving them through.

After they pulled up to the main entrance, both Daniel and James jumped down to help Claire out. It was difficult to avoid touching her foot, and Claire winced a couple of times as it was bumped against the side of the carriage, or against one of the men. Finally they had her out and properly situated with her crutches. James stayed by her side to escort her in, while Daniel rode off to take care of the coach.

She was arriving later than she'd hoped to, but it had been quite impossible to hide her broken foot from her family, and she owed them an honest explanation of the night's events.

They had all sat in rapt attention while Claire spelled out the details of what had transpired. Their faces had displayed an array of emotions, from astonishment at Claire's brazen behavior, to concern and sympathy for her broken foot, to anger at being duped by Philip. At first Claire could also sense her mother's doubt, because, for whatever reason, she had truly been fond of Philip. But as Claire produced the shirt and told them the crystal swan was still over at Philip's, all reservations in believing her were dissipated.

No one but Lavinia suspected the real reason Claire was so adamant to free Devon, and she was reluctant to tell the others. Besides, she'd reasoned, perhaps there would never be a cause for them to know the truth. She had no idea what would happen after Devon was set free, nor was she willing to speculate. It was best right now for them to think Claire was simply a champion of justice and did not like seeing an innocent man in jail.

At first her father had insisted on going with her to Newgate. "No daughter of mine will be going to that cesspool alone," he stated, expecting no argument.

"But, Father, please," Claire pleaded. "This is something I must do myself. And I won't be going alone. I'll have both James and Daniel with me."

"That's not the same as an escort, Claire," Louisa pointed out. "Your father is right; he must accompany you."

She had been so sure of completing what she'd set out to do on her own that she had given no thought to an alternate scenario. The only way Devon would know how sorry she was for not standing up for him before would be if she did everything she could to free him now. But having her father along lessened the impact of her actions, for that would be the traditional thing to do. Only by going against convention could Claire prove to Devon that she had opened her heart to him. Now she must convey to her family her yearning for independence without revealing the true reason behind her desire.

"Father, Mother, please. I beg your indulgence just this once. I feel responsible for putting our servant in jail because I was not attentive to Lord Townsend's behavior. He was always insulting his own staff, and I should have realized what a cruel man he was."

"But how could you have known he would do something to one of our servants, Claire? What possessed him?"

Louisa, and everyone else around the table, waited for Claire to answer her mother's question. Claire's mind worked at a frenzied pace. She could not reveal that Philip had been jealous of Devon. They would wonder what she had done to cause it.

"I can only speculate on why Philip did such a thing," she began, "but he had expressed concerns over Devon becoming one of our footmen. I suppose he felt that a groom's assistant was not qualified for the job. He had told me once that he would advise Father about the error he had made with Devon's appointment."

Kendal Rushmoor showed little outward reaction over this bit of news, although those who knew him well were aware of his irritation.

"Of course I informed Philip that Father was capable of making such decisions without Philip's guidance, but I have felt ever since then that Philip had the need to prove Devon's incompetence so that he, Philip, would appear all the wiser in my eyes." Claire took a deep breath, knowing that to prove her point she must tell the whole story. "He had, after all, proposed to me."

There was an audible gasp around the table. Kendal was the first to speak up.

"And you're telling us this now, daughter?"

Claire gathered her courage. "I would have told you before. Truly I would have. But there were doubts in my mind about Philip. He sometimes said such cruel things. He was an incorrigible gossip. And he had such genuine distaste for poor people."

"I had no idea," Louisa said softly.

"Nor did I," Claire responded. "When Devon told me

his suspicions about Philip's involvement in the death of his friend, I didn't want to believe it. But Devon seemed to have some proof, and when I thought about the horrid comments Philip had made to me, I realized that if he was capable of kicking a man to death he was more than capable of framing someone."

"So you arranged to see Philip in an effort to find your mother's crystal and Philip's shirt?"

"Yes, Father," Claire answered meekly, certain of meeting his strong disapproval. Instead, he surprised her.

"And you want to finish all you have set out to do by proving Mr. Blake's innocence?" he asked.

"Yes, Father."

A low chuckle rumbled in her father's throat, and when Claire summoned up the courage to look into his eyes, she was thrilled to see him beaming with respect.

"I never thought to see such determination in my ladylike young daughter," he said, "but I would be a liar if I said I wasn't a proud man."

"Thank you, Father," Claire replied.

"This is a dangerous task you've undertaken, daughter. But since you will not be returning to Lord Townsend's home but only sending the warden to fetch him, you may finish what you have started. James is a stronger man than I. Have him go inside with you and you'll not have any trouble."

It wasn't only Claire who was surprised by his decision. After she and her sisters had left the table, Louisa demanded to know what had gotten into her husband's head.

"It's crazy to let her go there alone, my lord. She'll be in danger!"

Kendal took a final drink of his breakfast tea before pushing himself away from the table and rising to leave. "If I thought for one minute that she would be in danger I would not let her go," he said sternly. "But she will be safe. James will make sure of that. And she needs to do this, Louisa. She gets that stubborn streak from me." He wiped his hands and excused himself, but as Louisa watched him go she couldn't help but notice the proud way he strolled through the door.

Despite having her father's approval, thus far the trip had been a nightmarish experience. Prisoners detained within Newgate's dark, clammy walls were enveloped in filth and devastation. The noxious odor of human waste permeated every crevice of the building. When Claire had first stepped inside she feared spilling the contents of her stomach, so foul was the stench that assaulted her nostrils. Water dripped everywhere, creating a perfect environment for a variety of molds. A chaotic din prevailed as inmates and guards traded insults and foul language. The imposing structure even appeared to frighten away the sun, for no matter the time of day, there was an ever-present darkness within the prison's walls.

The reception wards escorted Claire and James into the head warden's office, then without saying a word promptly left them there. Finally, after keeping them waiting for nearly twenty minutes, the man they needed to see at last strolled in. Puffed up with self-importance, he gave a curt nod to both Claire and James, and settled his bulky frame into the chair behind his desk.

"Now, what's this all about, young lady?" he demanded of Claire, purposely phrasing the question in a way meant to demean her. But she had no intention of letting this pompous clod get the edge.

"I've come regarding a prisoner of yours, Mister—er?"

"Cleats, madam. Dunhill Cleats. And what prisoner are you speaking of?"

"I might first introduce myself, sir. I am Lady Claire

Rushmoor, eldest daughter of Lord Kendal Rushmoor, Earl of Bedington. This is James Finch, one of my grooms."

Her title was duly noted, and the warden righted himself in his chair.

"We've come regarding one of your prisoners, a Mr. Devon Blake."

One of the guards, who had entered the office along with his superior, handed the warden the prison register. The prison head scanned the list, and his eyes lighted upon Devon's name.

"Ah, yes. Devon Blake. Brought here August third, in the year of our Lord eighteen hundred and eight, awaiting sentencing on charges of theft, bribery, and slander."

The list of false charges infuriated Claire, for Philip must have used his influence to inflate them. But she managed to hold her tongue.

"Do you wish to pay Mr. Blake a visit, Lady Rushmoor?"

"No, sir, I do not. I wish to free him."

The warden belched out a guffaw of laughter, with the door guard feeling compelled to join in the merriment.

"Free him, madam?" Warden Cleats sputtered. "On what grounds?"

"On the grounds that he is an innocent man, sir. I have the evidence to prove it."

Clearly the man did not believe her, and for a moment Claire thought he would have her dismissed without another word. But she had worn one of her finest day dresses, demonstrating her family's wealth and prominence. That, along with her title, were the only reasons he hadn't had her ejected immediately.

"Now, listen, miss," he began, but by then Claire had decided she'd had enough.

"No, sir, you listen to me," she interrupted, bristling

with anger. "Mr. Devon Blake is our family's footman, wrongly imprisoned for a crime he did not commit. I've come to get him back. I have also come to serve charges against a man who is a murderer and who, as of yet, is walking freely about."

The mention of murder captured Dunhill's attention. "Murderer, you say? And who might that be?"

Claire held her trump card for a moment longer. Smiling with all the inbred gentility she could muster up, she requested that Devon's things be brought to her so she could retrieve an item that would prove her charges.

As was prison custom, all the personal possessions Devon had with him upon arrival at Newgate were all tossed together in an envelope bearing his name. With a heavy heart, knowing Devon was locked away somewhere within these wretched walls, Claire picked through the envelope until she found the button. Holding it tightly within her palm, she felt fortified by the mere possession of it. No matter what it took, she'd use this and every ounce of influence she had to put Philip where he rightly belonged.

She unwrapped the small bundle she'd been holding against her side. "This, Mr. Cleats, is a shirt belonging to a prominent member of nobility. If you'll notice, it's speckled with blood."

Dunhill leaned closer to examine the item and saw that what Claire said was true.

"Not long ago," she continued, "the man owning this shirt kicked another man to death. The blood drops are those of the murdered man. Before he was killed, he put up a good struggle for his life, and managed to tear off a section of his adversary's shirt and put it in his pocket. When his friends found him lying nearly lifeless on the ground, they also found a section of the shirt that included this very fancy button." Claire held it up so the warden could see it, then she placed Philip's shirt right next to it.

"As you can see, sir, the buttons are identical."

Dunhill Cleats understood at once. "So whoever owns that shirt is likely the murderer." Claire nodded agreement. "And you know whose shirt it is, I trust?"

"It belongs to Philip Westbury, the Marquess of Townsend, sir. He is the one who should be imprisoned, not Devon Blake."

The warden shook his head in confusion. "But, my lady," he implored, holding up his hands as if to stop Claire's words, "your Mr. Blake is not in here for murder. He's in here for theft."

Claire nodded with conviction. "I'm aware of that, sir. And it is that charge which I'm here to dispute. Mr. Blake is accused of stealing a valuable crystal figurine belonging to my family. The charges were brought by Lord Philip Townsend. The very same Lord Townsend who owns this shirt. You see, Devon Blake confronted Lord Townsend about the murder, and in retaliation Philip turned around and framed Mr. Blake for taking the figurine that he, Lord Townsend, had stolen."

Once again the warden was skeptical. "But how would Mr. Blake have known Lord Townsend was the owner of that shirt?"

Here Claire paused, not wanting to reveal the scope of Devon's past. Still, she knew that to free him, she had to tell everything, so she related all she had learned from May.

A stunned silence filled the room, but the warden was bristling with anger. Why, the nerve of this woman! "Do you expect me to believe the idle rambling of a prostitute over the noble reputation of a marquess?" he stated, with the air of one not used to being challenged. "Really, Lady Rushmoor. The prostitute you speak of was no doubt slighted by Lord Townsend and out for revenge."

Now it was Claire's turn to get angry. She held back an urge to shout her indignation, knowing it would most certainly result in being escorted through the door. However, she would not let this pompous man think he could so easily dismiss her story.

"Perhaps your notions about the validity of a prostitute's words preclude you from having an open mind, sir," she said, "but you seem to have no problems believing the titled gentry. Particularly those who can influence the number of coins allotted to your pocket every year?"

Her meaning was clear, and Dunhill Cleats knew when he'd been bested. "Certainly, my lady. I beg your most gracious pardon."

Ignoring his plea, Claire continued. "I found not only the shirt but the missing crystal heirloom in Lord Townsend's home last night. Lord Townsend has been calling on me, and had proposed marriage. I paid a visit to him last night on the pretense of discussing his proposal. In reality I was searching for the missing crystal swan and the shirt. And I found them both."

"Good Lord, woman!" the warden exclaimed, admiration creeping into his voice at Claire's obvious show of bravery. "Is that banged-up foot the result of your endeavor?"

Claire smiled wanly. "Indeed it is, sir. However, there is no further time for delay. Has the magistrate sworn you in to carry out arrest orders?"

"He has."

"In that case, although I realize it is beyond the normal scope of your duties and is a highly unusual request, I ask you and your men to please go straightway to Lord Townsend's home. He's being held up by his servants at my command. It's crucial that you get over there at once and arrest him. Once there you'll find my family's heirloom, so you'll know I tell the truth about not only him, but Mr. Blake, as well."

For the first time since their meeting, the warden took action. Leaping out of his chair, he shouted commands at his guard to round up some men and prepare for departure. After the guard was on his way, Dunhill turned back to Claire.

"You'll leave that shirt and button here for evidence," he stated.

"As long as I have your assurance that it will land in the hands of the magistrate and not Lord Townsend," Claire said.

"You have my assurance, Lady Rushmoor."

"Very well. Then you may keep these things. See to it that nothing happens to them."

Claire pushed back her chair and signaled to James to help her up. The warden gathered up the evidence against Philip, then made to leave. Before exiting, however, he paused in the doorway.

"Lady Rushmoor, I need to know one other thing."

Claire looked up, startled. What now?

"Why in the world would you go through such trouble for a servant? Why not simply employ another one?"

Instead of growing angry with the man, Claire found herself smiling. After all, she realized, she would have wondered the same thing less than six months ago.

"Why, Mr. Cleats," she said primly, "you know how difficult it is to find good help these days. And Mr. Blake happens to be an excellent footman."

The warden still appeared doubtful, but decided that Lady Rushmoor must be telling the truth. After all, what other reason could there possibly be?

When he left Claire felt that a great burden had been lifted from her shoulders. She knew then that she'd done all she could. Devon's fate now rested in the hands of the law, but she had supplied them with damning evidence against Philip. Evidence that should be enough to put him behind bars and set Devon free. But the unfortunate reality was that there was no guarantee of justice where money was concerned. Philip could, and would, try using his wealth and influence to make the charges against him quietly go away. The only question now was, would he be successful?

The assembly of guards charged forward to Philip's home as if on a mission from King George himself. Leading the way was Warden Dunhill Cleats. As they approached the house he slowed the party down, not wanting to startle the occupants inside and take a chance of creating an opportunity for Philip's escape.

All twelve men reined in their horses to a walk, then stopped completely as they stood in front of the house's main entrance.

Dunhill dismounted, signaled his lead guard to do the same, then approached the door. Banging upon it, he waited only seconds before the door flew open and they were greeted by a very distressed Hannah Crandall.

"Oh, thank heavens you're here," the head housekeeper exclaimed, not bothering to confirm who was at the door. "We've had quite a time holding on to Lord Townsend and enduring his relentless bellowing. This way, if you please."

A small army of guards followed Dunhill Cleats and Mrs. Crandall inside and gathered in the lobby. The other servants not guarding Philip also joined them; now, as a fortified group, they walked up the stairs to Philip's bedroom.

The sight that greeted Dunhill was so preposterous that had the circumstances not been serious it would have seemed comical. Tied around every post of the bed was a stout rope, and connected to each of them was one of

Philip's limbs. Indeed, he was sprawled on his back across the bed, tied up as if to be drawn and quartered. But he was by no means a cooperative prisoner. Instead, Philip blustered orders as if his present condition was not of concern.

"Albert, you are to untie me at once!" he bellowed. "Let's not forget who's in charge around here. Do you realize who you're dealing with?" On and on he raged, never once tiring from the sound of his own voice.

"Silence!" roared Dunhill. His command was obeyed at once, as all heads within the room swung round to see from whom the order had come.

Without bothering to explain himself, Dunhill strode into the room and next to the bed where Philip was tied. Glancing down, he noticed the crystal heirloom Claire had spoken of.

By then Philip had regained his composure. "Sir, as you are obviously a member of the proper authorities, I ask that you see to it that I'm immediately untied—"

"Enough! I'm here to examine some serious accusations made against you, my lord, and I'll not be stopped by your inane protests. Now keep quiet."

As indignant as Philip was at this man's demeanor, he knew he was not in a position to do much about it. After swearing that he'd ensure the man's dismissal as well as that of his servants, he kept quiet. Noting the number of guards stationed by his bedroom door, Philip had enough sense to realize he had no choice but to cooperate.

Picking up the crystal swan, Dunhill noticed the ornate engraving of the Rushmoor name on the object's side.

"Explain to me, my lord, what this heirloom is doing in your home when clearly it belongs to the family of Lady Claire Rushmoor. She has stated you stole it. What's your story?"

This time Philip decided to switch gears and try appealing to what he hoped would be the man's respect for nobility. "You are aware of my position, are you not, sir? Now if you'll just untie me I can explain everything."

Dunhill raised an eyebrow in Philip's direction, but beyond that stood still. "I'd no more release you than I'd blaspheme the king," he answered. "There have been some very serious charges made against you, my lord, and I'll be needing an explanation."

Philip sighed, as if making the reluctant decision to obey the warden, regardless of the fact that he had no choice. "Very well. In answer to your question, no, I most certainly did not steal that figurine."

"Then how do you explain its presence in your bed-chamber?"

"Very simply, sir," Philip beamed a knowing smile. "It was a token of affection from Lady Rushmoor, who is my fiancée. She's madly in love with me, and often expresses her feelings with gifts."

In his years of dealing with criminals of every kind, Dunhill Cleats had learned a thing or two about spotting liars. What he had before him now was a perfect example of one.

"Very well, sir. I have noted your explanation for the record. The other charge against you, however, is not quite so benign. Your fiancée accuses you of murder."

"Murder?" Philip sputtered. "Preposterous! She'll say anything to ruin my good name!"

"She's doing much more than simply talking, sir. She has evidence."

"Surely you're not referring to that shirt she has," laughed Philip. "Why, the thing's not even mine."

His denial of ownership caught Dunhill off guard. He had expected another of Philip's absurd stories to explain away the shirt, but he hadn't thought that the man would deny owning it. Could he be telling the truth?

Being careful not to reveal too much doubt, Dunhill

pressed on. "How do you explain the actions of your servants?"

At the reminder of his predicament, Philip became visibly annoyed. "Again, it's all connected to Lady Rushmoor's deep feelings of affection toward me."

Dunhill barely contained the snort of laughter that lay just behind his lips as he responded, "She appears to have an unusual way of expressing her feelings, if I may say so, my lord."

Philip shrugged. "She's been pressuring me for a wedding date and, with plenty of coin, bribed my servants into doing this until I consented to her demands."

Though Philip had intentionally whispered to avoid having anyone but Dunhill hear him, he had not quite succeeded. "That's a lie, sir!" boomed an unexpected voice, and all eyes swung toward a blistering Albert Monroe, who had stepped forward from the assembled group. Rage contorted the servant's usually placid face as he turned toward Dunhill and gave his account of the events.

"It's true that we're holding Lord Townsend on Lady Rushmoor's command, but not because she wishes to marry him. On the contrary, we had to break into this room last evening after hearing the lady's screams for help. When we came in we found Lady Rushmoor on the floor with a broken foot, and my lord running toward his bed to retrieve the Rushmoor heirloom and his shirt."

"Silence!" Philip tried commanding his servant, but the order was ignored.

"Take a look at the broken bedroom door, sir," Albert instructed Dunhill, "and you'll see I tell the truth."

The warden walked across the room and examined the shattered door. So the servant's story was true, he mused, now convinced beyond a doubt of Philip's lies. Still, he was in an uncomfortable situation. Imagine arresting Lord Philip Townsend and then having the charges proved false. What a scandal it would cause! Dunhill's career would be ruined, not to mention his reputation. He wished there were a way to settle this beyond matching one story against another.

As if reading his thoughts, Albert again spoke up. "Why don't you have him try on the shirt, sir?"

The statement shook Dunhill out of his reverie. "I beg your pardon?"

"The shirt, sir. The one that Lady Rushmoor says is Lord Townsend's, and Lord Townsend says is Mr. Blake's. Have both men try it on. Then you'll know for sure whose it is."

"Absolutely not!" Philip bellowed. "This is absurd! I will not subject myself to such scrutiny. I've committed no crime, and refuse to be treated as a criminal."

Dunhill peered down at the blustering man, and felt his earlier anger beginning to swell. "I'm afraid you don't have a choice, Lord Townsend. If, as you say, the shirt isn't yours, then you should welcome the chance to clear your name. After all, Mr. Blake is a considerably larger man than you are, so the chance of you both fitting into this shirt is virtually nonexistent."

Philip felt the sweat trickle down the middle of his chest. It was evident that Dunhill Cleats knew the shirt belonged to him, and now was proceeding to publicly ruin his reputation. Well, he'd see about that. This no-good warden would rue the day he'd met Philip Westbury. After all, he had connections. He had ties. He was a member of the gentry!

"Come along, Lord Townsend. If you'll agree to be a gentleman about this matter, then I'll not restrain you. But be warned, my men will be watching your every move."

Knowing Dunhill Cleats spoke the truth, Philip reluctantly obeyed. The ropes that bound his wrists and ankles were removed, and he was allowed to stand and stretch before being led away.

One of the prison guards had earlier instructed Philip's groom to prepare his horse. He now mounted it and rode off with Dunhill Cleats and his soldiers, apprehensive about his future. His heart slammed against the cavern of his chest, and blood roared through his eardrums like crashing ocean waves. Unfortunately, it failed to smother the sounds of collective triumph—the cheers and laughter of his own servants that echoed after him, like those of taunting children, until he and Cleats's men rounded a corner and rode out of sight.

Twenty-four

The door banged open with unexpected force, and standing before him was a somber-faced guard.

"On your feet, Blake," he commanded, not raising his voice. He knew the order would be obeyed without question.

As Devon lifted himself from the dirty straw pile upon which he lay, he couldn't help but wonder why he was being summoned. Though he knew better than to voice any questions (two harsh beatings had made sure of that), it was impossible not to inwardly speculate.

As custom dictated, he held out his hands for the metal links to be locked upon them, but this time the guard shook his head.

"You'll be needing full use of your arms in a minute," he said. "But try anything stupid and I'll beat the bloody pulp out of you."

Devon gave the guard a curt nod, then followed him outside. They were met by another guard, and together the two of them escorted Devon to Dunhill Cleats's office.

As usual, the warden was seated behind his desk. But Devon's great surprise came when he saw who was seated in the opposite chair. Surrounded by guards, looking decidedly un-noble, was his nemesis, Philip Westbury. The normally regal man had dark circles under his eyes, mussed hair, and wrinkled clothing. Looking far from the aristocratic man he fancied himself to be, he was downright disheveled. He sat with a scowl etched deeply upon his face, and glared at Devon as he walked through the door.

"Have a seat, Mr. Blake," the warden instructed him. "We've some business to discuss that involves you."

For the first time that day, Devon found his voice. "I'm wanting to know what this is about."

"In a moment," Dunhill answered, before instructing his guards to step out of the room and take up posts by the doorways.

The guards did as they were ordered, and Dunhill rose from his chair. Devon saw that he held a shirt in his hand, and a closer look at the buttons confirmed it was Philip's. Devon also noted the spattered blood drops on the shirt, and he felt his stomach clench with such violent loathing toward Philip that it took all the restraint he possessed not to reach over and strangle the man.

The expression on the warden's face was serious. "Mr. Blake, the charges that hold you in this prison have been called into question and instead leveled against Lord Townsend. In addition, Lord Townsend has been charged with the crime of murder. He adamantly denies everything and instead places the blame upon you. We are now here to put Lord Townsend's accusations to the test."

"So ye're accusing me of murder as well?" Devon asked, the depth of his fury tempering his voice to an eerie calmness.

"We're not accusing you of anything. So far."

"Then what am I doing here?"

Dunhill held the shirt before Devon. "It seems this shirt was worn by a man who kicked another man to death. The buttons on this shirt match the one we found in your pocket the day you were brought here. Although the shirt was found in Lord Townsend's bedroom, he claims it belongs to you. We're here to find out whether that's true."

Devon sat back in disbelief. Claire. She had to have been the one who found the shirt. No one else who knew about the murder was in a position to be in Philip Westbury's bedroom. At the thought of her with the evil cad Devon was awash in jealousy, but now was not the time for such feelings.

Instead, he scoffed at Dunhill. "Are ye crazy, man? Ye know that's not my shirt. What would a poor bloke like me be doing with silk?"

It was a thought that had occurred to Dunhill; still, he had to continue with the test to make sure there was nothing Philip could use to try getting himself freed.

"I'll have no further words from you," he stated firmly. "Let's proceed. Remove your shirt, Mr. Blake."

Slowly Devon stood to do as he was instructed. After unbuttoning his shirt he slipped it off and tossed it on his chair. Taking the shirt from Dunhill's hands, he put his right arm through the sleeve, then his left. He couldn't help but admire the silken smooth feeling of the expensive material—not unlike the incredible softness of Claire's creamy white skin.

Although the sleeves were tight, especially around his shoulders, he was able to get both arms through them. When it came to buttoning the front across his expansive chest, however, it was all but impossible. The shirt was several times too small for Devon's size, and forcing the material together in order to close the buttons would have ripped it to shreds.

Unable to suppress a victorious grin, Devon looked calmly at the warden. "Well, sir, what do ye think?"

The man's attitude bordered on disrespect, but Dunhill Cleats felt no animosity toward his prisoner. It was obvious to everyone that he had not committed this crime.

Dunhill looked around at the guards standing in the

doorways. "You're all hereby to serve as witnesses," he announced, "so take a good look at this man. Are you all in agreement that the shirt does not fit?"

The question bordered on lunacy to the guards, but they knew their warden was only making his investigation official. They solemnly nodded, agreeing with the statement.

"Fine. Now, Mr. Blake, you may remove the shirt and hand it over to Lord Townsend for his turn."

Despite every card on the table being stacked against him, Philip still had the audacity to feign his outrage.

"My turn? What the devil are you talking about? I'll not be trying on that shirt for you or anyone else here!"

A prickle of annoyance crept into Dunhill's voice. "Keep quiet, Lord Townsend. These are serious charges against you, and I'll not allow you to dictate the way I conduct business. You're not in one of your Pall Mall clubs now where you can throw around your title and get instant respect. This is a prison, my lord, of which I am the head official, and you are charged with a crime. Now have the decency to conduct yourself as the gentleman you claim to be. Remove your shirt."

The words had effect. As ordered, Philip removed his shirt and silently took the one Devon handed him. He was more humiliated than he'd ever realized possible, for he knew the shirt would fit him perfectly. Like all his clothing, it was custom made, and the exorbitant amount of money given to his tailor every year assured the exactness of his clothing's measurements.

With a deep sigh of resignation he slipped on the shirt, buttoned it with ease and turned to face the warden. The two men's eyes met and locked, silently exchanging their mutual understanding of what the moment meant.

For the second time Dunhill looked about the room. "Are you all in agreement that this shirt appears to be a perfect fit for Lord Townsend?" At the guards' silent nods, Dunhill turned to Philip and made his official pronouncement.

"Philip Westbury, Marquess of Townsend, you are charged with the crime of murder. Because of your position, your case shall be heard by the House of Lords, who will decide your fate. Until such time you are to be held in Newgate Prison. Have you anything to say?"

Knowing he had been trapped by a member of the dreaded lower class unleashed a rage in Philip that was akin to that of a rabid beast. He snarled and railed at everyone in the room.

"That putrid, low-down offal tried robbing me!" he screamed, spittle flying from between his thin, cracked lips. "I felt his slimy hand slip between the folds of my frock coat. He was about to lift my money purse and I defended myself as any respectable gentleman should! For this I'm treated like a common criminal? For this I'm thrown in jail? It's preposterous!" His face had turned scarlet; corded veins bulged along his throbbing temples. "How was I to know the filthy bastard died? I was defending myself, I tell you! Anyway he deserved what came to him. What's wrong with ridding the earth of a little stench? Far as I'm concerned I did London a favor."

Philip pointed a stubby finger at Dunhill Cleats, emphasizing his point, but the warden was unsympathetic. He cleared his throat and fixed Philip with a steely gaze. "And as far as I'm concerned, Lord Townsend, Lady Rushmoor returned that favor by putting a rotting piece of condescending garbage in his proper place—Newgate Prison. Now shut that insolent trap of yours and listen. You're going to jail for a very long time. Murder is no matter for jest my lord, regardless of who you are. You'll be treated just like everyone else. The vermin aren't partial about whose cell they're in."

At last it was becoming clear to Philip that he might

not be able to get out of this predicament as easily as he earlier thought. He was going to need some help.

"I want my solicitor contacted at once!" he shouted, trying to sound imposing. Instead his voice revealed paranoia.

"Your solicitor will be contacted, Lord Townsend," Dunhill answered. "But do not expect to be giving orders around here. You're not the one in charge."

Philip bristled at the warden's statement, but there was little else he could do.

"Take that shirt off, Lord Townsend, and hand it over to me. It's evidence."

Dunhill looked over at Devon. "Mr. Blake, you were charged with the theft of a crystal heirloom that was also found in Lord Townsend's bedroom. Lady Claire Rushmoor claims it was taken by Lord Townsend and not you, in conjunction with the other crime of murder. Taking into account the evidence against Lord Townsend, it would appear she is correct. Therefore, by the authority given to me by the magistrate I declare you cleared of all charges. Go with the release guard to fill out the necessary paperwork. Then you are free to leave."

Devon expelled a deep breath he'd been unaware of even holding, and felt the first surge of victory coursing through his veins. To be cleared of false charges was satisfying indeed, but his real joy came from the realization that Philip Westbury would pay for his crime. Revenge had been exacted upon a heartless, cruel killer, and for that Devon rejoiced.

After signing the release register, he walked with the guards to the prison's main entrance, then stepped thankfully into the freedom outside. Despite the swirling mist, the air felt crisp, clean. He breathed in deeply, filling his lungs, then began to walk. His spirit was absolved of the heavy weight he had carried for the past several days, and his feet now felt as though they walked on air. The more he truly realized that the ordeal was over, the happier he became, and the longer were his strides. Suddenly he had an overwhelming urge to run, to release the pent-up feelings of anger, resentment, and helplessness that he'd been carrying with him like an eternal cargo load. His feet flew over the paving stones, unmindful of their slickness. Before he even consciously realized where he was going he was running in the right direction, for every stride brought him closer and closer to familiar territory. He began seeing the costermongers, the fishmongers, the rat catchers, the beggars, the matchgirls—horrible, yet comforting sights that were as welcoming to him as toys to a child. Up ahead he at last spotted his destination, and with a final burst of speed he ran up the steps to The Night Star—and into the arms of his mother.

Twenty-five

"Claire?" No answer. Another knock. "Claire, can you hear me? Mother says you must come to dinner now. Everyone's waiting for you, and Lilia will be so disappointed if you take this meal in your room. After all, it's her birthday."

More silence, but then, "Come in, Linny. The door's not bolted."

With more than a little trepidation, Lavinia pushed the door inward and slipped into her sister's bedroom. It was unusual for Claire to invite her in. For the past week she had been living like a hermit, only coming out when there was an event for which she simply could not make excuses. She had even begun asking for trays to be brought up instead of joining the family for the regular meals. And more often than not, Lavinia had spotted the tray coming back untouched. Her sister was enmeshed in misery, and only Lavinia knew the reason why.

She spotted Claire in her usual place, sitting outside on the balcony. Without saying a word she stepped out there as well and sat down beside her sister.

It was clear from her puffy eyes that Claire had been crying—again. But for the first time, instead of looking so woefully hopeless, Lavinia spotted a spark of determination shining beneath the sorrow.

"We're getting ready to eat, Claire," Lavinia said

softly, although she knew that hunger was the last thing on her sister's mind.

"I'll be down in a minute," Claire answered, unaware that she had even spoken, so absorbed was she in other matters. Then her focus seemed to clear, and she turned to face her sister.

"I've been sitting here for days, doing nothing but thinking and worrying and wondering what will happen to me now."

"Now . . . ?"

"Yes, now," Claire said calmly. "Now that I realize I can't live without him."

Her words were greeted by stunned silence, but Claire appeared not to have realized the effect they had on her sister. Either that, or she chose to ignore it.

"I can't think what to do, Linny. My mind has played out various scenarios, but none of them seem to work."

At last Lavinia found her voice. "Claire, are you crazy? You're talking like a half-wit, like . . . like some foolish schoolgirl gone out of her mind. You can't be actually thinking there's a future for you and Devon."

"That's exactly what I'm thinking, Linny. I'm head-over-heels in love with him. Thoughts of him fill my mind and heart every waking minute. What else would you have me do?"

"I would expect you to get yourself together and re-member who you are. You're a Rushmoor, Claire. You're titled gentry. Our family dates back for centuries, and our history is filled with nobles. How can you possibly even pretend that Mother and Father would approve of a union between their eldest daughter and a footman. It's utter nonsense."

Her sister's words filled Claire with rage. "And that's just the reason I need to be with Devon. He treats every-one the same, be they gentry or common. He makes no false show of respect toward people who are hateful or unkind, like Philip." Her last words were almost inaudible, she'd uttered them so quietly. It was obvious that the memory of the man she had nearly wed was still painful.

"Philip was a horrible man, Linny." Claire continued, "He murdered someone. But because he's gentry it didn't seem to matter. Meanwhile, an honorable, decent, hardworking man like Devon is falsely accused of a crime he didn't commit, just because he's poor."

Lavinia blew out a breath of exasperation, knowing that Claire's mind was made up, and there was no changing it. That in itself showed the difference in her attitude. She now looked at the world through different eyes. She saw suffering and poverty and prejudice where before she hardly knew such things existed. Lavinia was not yet convinced that she liked the change in Claire, but she knew there was no way of going back.

"You'll devastate Mother and Father, you know."

The words made their intended impression, for Claire cringed and swallowed hard before she spoke.

"It can't be helped," she said resolutely. "I simply cannot go through the rest of my life living with someone whom I care nothing for when my heart belongs to Devon."

"Is love so very important to you, then?"

Claire looked at her sister with eyes that spoke volumes, and Lavinia had her answer. "It's the most important feeling a person can ever have, Linny. Without it, you're empty inside. With it, your whole body and spirit feel as if they're celebrating. You feel helpless, yet powerful. You feel like sharing everything with the one you love. You feel that your heart will burst, it is so filled with emotion. You can never imagine what it's like until it happens to you, Linny. But once it does, it's magic."

Never before had Lavinia seen such a glow of happiness surround her sister, and in that moment she knew that she, too, wanted to be in love. How could one not crave the inner happiness that Claire appeared to have? There was no further discussion. Lavinia wanted to help her sister, not try uselessly to change her mind.

"It's settled, then. You must have him."

Claire clasped her hands together, turned her head toward the heavens, and closed her eyes. "I pray every day that it could be so. But it does not appear that my prayers will be answered."

"What do you mean?"

"It's been nearly three weeks since Devon was freed. The gossip over Philip has even begun to die down. And yet . . . nothing."

Lavinia shook her head in confusion. "I don't know what you're talking about."

"Don't you see? Devon hasn't come. The only thing he ever wanted was to find out who murdered his friend. Now that it's all behind him, he's forgotten about me." A large tear had formed in the corner of one brown eye, and now it slowly rolled down the middle of Claire's cheek. Hastily she wiped it away, as though the tear had no business existing.

"It's not as though I blame him, of course," she continued. "After all, I'm the one who landed him in prison."

"You did no such thing!"

Claire ignored the protest. "I tried making up for what I did, but it's no use. I had reminded Devon often enough of our class differences, so why should he think I'm any different now?"

The sorrow overtook her, and Claire buried her face in her hands and no longer tried brushing away the tears. And Lavinia, not knowing what else to do, simply pulled her sister into her arms and held her.

* * *

"Hell's teeth, Devon! I'm telling ye, 'tis an easy job."

"And I'm telling ye I'm not doing it."

Clive scratched his head in disbelief and glanced over at Jonathan for guidance. Ever since Devon had left that West End job for good, he'd been a different man. He now refused to take part in any thefts they pulled, and wouldn't even lend his expertise on the best way they should go about doing it.

Gareth gave it a try. "Look, Dev. Sooner or later ye got to start joining us again. A man's got to eat, ye know. And ye can't have that much money saved up. After all, ye gave most of it to us."

Clive was right about one thing. Devon didn't have much money left. It was becoming a source of concern for him, but he knew that going back to his old ways was impossible. He'd had a taste of what life could be, of the good things it had to offer. And though he knew he'd never be as rich as Kendal Rushmoor, he also knew that he had enough brains to make something of himself besides a criminal.

"Look, lads, ye know ye're my best mates, and nothing will ever change that. But I'm telling ye for the last time, I'm not pulling any more jobs with ye."

Gareth snorted from the corner. "Not good enough for us anymore, I suppose?"

Clive and Jonathan both shot him a warning look to be quiet. The subject Gareth dared broach out loud to Devon was one they'd discussed amongst themselves. But all three had come to the conclusion that Devon would never turn his back on them, despite his exposure to the wealthy.

Gareth's comment, however, angered Devon. "I did what I did for Joshua, and ye know it," he said coldly. "Don't ever accuse me otherwise."

Then he turned and walked out the door, giving it a hard slam as he left.

"Now ye've done it, ye dolt!" yelled Clive. "I don't expect he'll be coming back to us anytime soon."

"We might as well lay the cards on the table," Gareth shouted back. "And since ye're too cowardly, I figured 'twas best that I said something!"

Jonathan ignored their arguments as he stared at where Devon had just been standing. There was indeed something different about their friend, he noted, and it wasn't just his reluctance to renew his life of crime. Devon's mood had been dark and brooding since he had been released from Newgate. The injustice of the situation had angered him, but Jonathan knew that Devon's present state of mind had nothing to do with a dank, dreary prison. And it would be interesting to see what he intended to do about it.

May looked at her son with the concerned eyes of a loving mother. He was thoroughly downtrodden. He wasn't eating, he wasn't sleeping, and he kept to himself almost constantly. The source of his troubles, she knew, lived mere miles away, but for Devon the solution to the problem seemed unreachable.

The remarks of Gareth seemed to have put him in an even darker mood than the one he'd been carrying around lately. But, May speculated, perhaps it was good. For the first time since he'd been released from Newgate, Devon seemed in the mood to talk.

"My mates are asking me to come back and work with them," he was saying, "but I told 'em I won't do it, and I mean it. I can make more money as a servant, though I won't do that, either. I got me some other plans now, Mum. I know a lot about grooming and caring for horses. I could get more work in a livery. Maybe someday open a place of my own. I don't know. But 'tis possible that I could make a go of it."

On and on he went, and though May enjoyed hearing some spark in her son's voice, she knew he was avoiding speaking about what was really on his mind.

At last he appeared to have exhausted the subject of his future employment, and a comfortable silence fell between them. Though she was reluctant to break that silence, May felt she would get no better opportunity to bring up the subject neither wanted to discuss.

"There's nothing stopping ye from going to see her, ye know."

Devon looked up sharply, then looked away, realizing at once to whom his mother referred.

"I don't want to talk about her, Mum," he said in what he hoped was a dismissive tone. May Blake, however, was not so easily put off.

"Ye should at least thank her for what she did," she said.

"Thank her? For putting me in jail? Since when do people receive gratitude for that?"

May's eyebrows shot up in surprise. "Then ye don't know what she did?" she asked.

"She did nothing as far as I'm concerned," Devon responded bitterly. After having avoided speaking about Claire for so long, the mere mention of her name brought forth a maelstrom of emotions he had bottled up inside.

"Ye'd still be in jail if it wasn't for her," May said.

"I'd never have been in jail if it wasn't for her!" His voice was strained and quiet, but he jumped to his feet and paced around the room. "She always thought she was too good for me, and she made sure I was aware of our differences. I was the servant, and she was the princess. No matter what happens, 'tis the way it's always going to be. Nay, Mum, she'll never think of me as anything more than someone who trims the lamps and serves the dinners. Never."

Now May felt her temper rise, along with her son's.

"What about her work at St. Matthew's?" she challenged him.

His pacing stopped, but only for a moment, as his mind offered an explanation for why Claire might have done that. "It means nothing," he snapped. "It was only one day. She was just trying to pretend that she knew something about the way other people lived. That's all."

"And risk the reputation ye say she cared so much about? Come on, Devon. Ye're not daft."

Damn it! His mum was making sense, and that angered Devon all the more. He didn't want to accept any other explanation for Claire's action. It was easier that way.

"Maybe she doesn't care so much about reputations," he retorted.

"Well, if that's the case, why not go talk to her?"

"Be silent, Mum!" Devon shouted, in a rare display of losing control.

"Ye only want me silent so ye don't have to hear the truth, Devon, because the truth will be harder for ye to deal with. Ain't that what's bothering ye so much? That ye're trying like a desperate fool not to admit how much ye love her."

As usual, his mother was right, and Devon slumped back down in his chair like a deflated balloon.

"She loves ye too, Devon."

He could not have been more stunned had a cannon ball come crashing through the door. But his mother's words were even more powerful than that. It was several moments before Devon could speak.

"Loves me?" he finally croaked.

The depth of his emotion touched May's heart. "Aye. I know it for a fact, Devon. She told me herself. The girl is in love with ye."

The girl is in love with you. Could it be possible? Was his mother telling the truth? But . . .

"How could ye know that, Mum?"

His mother took a deep breath, knowing she had some explaining to do. She had avoided telling Devon about the conversation she'd had with Claire, reluctant to break the promise she had made. But her first loyalty would always be to her son, and May Blake finally decided that she could not stand seeing the bitterness and sorrow etched upon his face. He had to know the truth of how Claire felt. It was only right.

She held back nothing, wanting Devon to know everything Claire had done. She told him word for word all that Claire had said. Devon listened intently, never once interrupting. There was a subtle glow that illuminated his face; other than that, his features were unreadable.

His mother's explanation finished with the telling of how determined Claire had been to get Devon out of jail and correct the wrong she felt she had done him.

She finished her story and waited while he digested her words.

"Everything I've told ye is the truth, Devon."

"I'm wondering why ye didn't tell me sooner."

Although May knew he didn't mean it that way, Devon's words sounded more like a challenge than a question. But she knew he was hurt, and she wanted to help.

"She asked me not to say anything."

"Because she was ashamed to feel anything for me." He sounded almost triumphant, as if suddenly realizing the answer to a mysterious puzzle.

"Nay, Devon. Not because she was ashamed of how she felt toward ye. It was because she was afraid of being rejected by ye."

The enormity of what he was being told suddenly overwhelmed him, and he begged his mother to say no more. He needed silence; he had to think. Rejected by him? Did Claire really believe she'd be rejected by him?

If that was so, then everything he had just accused her of was patently untrue. She could not be the regal, arrogant, self-serving creature he'd just been spouting about if she feared rejection from someone society deemed 'beneath' her.

It occurred to Devon, as he contemplated those ideas, that he was acting toward her in exactly the same manner as those he criticized in the upper class. He was judging her because of her standing in society, not what she really was as a person. He had decided that she must think a certain way based on stereotypes about her class of people. All this time, since being released from Newgate, he had refused to entertain the idea of a future with her because he imagined he knew how the gentry would feel about it. But never once did he think to ask Claire herself.

Before he allowed the internal questions to go further, he raced over to the bed and grabbed his coat.

"Going somewhere?" May asked, a giant grin plastered on her face.

"Aye, Mum. I got to be off now."

"I suspect there's someone ye need to see."

Perceptive as always. "That's right. Someone I need to see."

He leaned over to give his mum a kiss, then swiftly walked to the entrance way and swung the door open wide.

"Give her my best."

Devon paused for only a moment, then turned back around.

"Aye, I'll do that," he said, as he whisked away.

Twenty-six

She gave herself a final check in the looking glass, then picked up her reticule and walked, haltingly, through the door. The bones in her young foot were healing rapidly and Claire could now get by with using only a cane. And since she'd made up her mind to leave, she was determined to do so as quickly as possible, before the logical side of her mind prevailed.

Before descending only a few steps, however, her progress was impeded by Emma Leeds. The housekeeper looked hesitantly at Claire, sensing that she was about to leave.

"What is it, Mrs. Leeds?"

"I beg your pardon, my lady, but Mr. Blake is in the parlor to see you."

Claire was so startled by the news that she temporarily lost her composure. "Devon?" she gasped.

"Yes, my lady. But you appear ready for departure. Shall I send him away?"

No! her mind yelled, for he was the very person Claire was on her way to see. Instead she pulled herself together and answered, "That's quite all right, Mrs. Leeds. I'll receive him."

"Very good, my lady. I'll inform him that you'll be down straight away."

"No, let me tell him!" Lilia exclaimed, having heard the conversation as she came from her bedroom. The young girl dashed down the steps and toward the parlor. Emma made an attempt to catch up with Lilia, but Claire stopped her, knowing the effort was futile. Lilia had always held a special place in her heart for Devon and was excited to see him again.

"It's all right," she called out. "Let her have a visit with Mr. Blake. She's always been fond of his company."

Emma Leeds frowned at the impropriety, but Claire disregarded the housekeeper's objection as she walked back up the stairs and returned to her room.

Once inside, she took a couple of deep breaths to steady herself. Devon was here! Although she'd been on her way to see the very person who was now in the parlor, his unexpected arrival caused her nerves to jangle. What in the world could he be doing here? Why did he want to see her? Her mind chased the questions around and around, like a dog going after its tail.

Claire knew she had to face him. Lilia would keep him occupied for only so long. She laid her reticule back down upon the bed, pulled the pins from her hat, then placed it beside the handbag. She took just a moment to smooth down her hair before walking back out the door and down to the parlor.

She stood for a moment just inside the parlor door, able to observe Devon without being noticed. It had been several weeks since she had seen him last, and she was struck, as she'd been so many times before, by how undeniably handsome he was. His green eyes sparked with laughter from the amusing anecdotes Lilia told; his lean, masculine face was graced by an engaging smile. The taut, muscular lines of his body were accented by the close-fitting black breeches and snug waistcoat he wore. His brown, sun-streaked hair flowed back to just brush against the tops of his shoulders, giving him the rakish look Claire adored.

Though it felt as if she had gazed at him for several

long minutes, in truth she stood there only a few seconds before he raised his head and looked straight into her eyes. In that moment the pronounced smile on his face became something more akin to an expression of contentment, and Claire, too, realized how comforting it was to set eyes on him again.

He stood up at once, but for a moment said nothing, as if waiting for her to give him reassurance that his visit was acceptable.

"Hello, Mr. Blake," Claire began formally, unable to brush off a lifetime of proper etiquette, despite knowing Devon cared not a wit for it.

"Is my coming here an intrusion?" he asked, casting aside traditional greetings.

"Not at all," she answered, then turned toward her cousin. "Lilia, please excuse us. I need a moment of privacy with Mr. Blake."

Lilia hesitated only a moment, realizing that this was not the time to broach an objection. "Very well." She sniffed, walking toward the door. "But don't leave before saying good-bye," she reminded Devon.

When they were at last alone, Claire invited him to resume his seat as she took one across from him. For several moments neither of them said anything, causing Claire further anxiety. Here was the moment she'd thought about, waited for, then decided to do something about, materializing before her very eyes, and she could do nothing but stare down at her hands and pray for a thought to enter her mind.

Devon was apparently just as anxious, for he could not even tolerate sitting. In an instant he was on his feet, pacing the room, not quickly as would a new father waiting for news of a birth, but slowly, as if the gesture would buy him extra time.

His hand trailed along the mantelpiece, the very same one that held the treasured Rushmoor heirloom. The gesture evoked memories in both of them of the fateful day Philip had Devon hauled off to Newgate. At last Claire remembered what she wanted to say to him, but just as she drew in a breath to begin speaking, Devon's words broke the silence.

"I wanted to come here to thank ye," he said simply. "I know what ye did for me."

His show of thanks was like a dagger in Claire's heart, for she never would have had to do anything if only she'd stood up for him in the first place.

She held up her hands as if to block further words, then pleaded with him, "Please don't thank me. I don't deserve it."

His brows drew together in evident confusion, and wrinkles formed across his usually serene forehead.

"What do ye mean? I'd still be sitting in prison if it weren't for what ye did. Of course ye deserve my thanks."

Now it was Claire's turn to stand up. "No!" she said sharply. "I deserve nothing. Don't you see? You would never have been in prison if it weren't for me. I knew you didn't steal that figurine. But the night you were accused, I said nothing. I held my tongue, and you went to jail."

The anguish in her voice touched Devon deeply, and in that moment he knew his heart would belong to her forever. In the few words she'd just uttered, she had hurled away societal barriers, thrown off countless generations of rules and restrictions. She'd defied any semblance of genteel behavior and had shown feelings for a man society had decided was below her. Devon's mum had told him of Claire's love; now he had proof.

She'd sat back down after her brief outburst, and buried her face in her hands. In three long strides Devon was by her side and knelt down before her. Gently he grasped hold of one of her small, delicate hands and engulfed it within his own. With unconcealed tenderness he kissed her palm, then held her hand against his face.

"Ye've done so much more for me than anyone ever has," he insisted. "Ye risked yer life, yer reputation, yer very future for me. Knowing what a wretched bloke Westbury is, I suspect even that broken foot has something to do with ye helping me. How could ye now deny me the opportunity to thank ye for what ye've done? I owe so much to ye, Claire."

His words penetrated through her harsh self-reproach, but instead of being appreciative of the effort he had made in coming there, Claire felt curiously empty inside.

Her hand slipped away from his and she once again stood up. It was her turn to do the pacing, and she limped across the room feeling the need to get away from him. Why did she feel so disappointed? Wasn't it kind of him to thank her for what she did? Of course it was, she insisted to herself. Yet, the feeling remained, as if she was hoping for something . . . intangible . . . a profession of something other than gratitude to issue forth from his lips.

"It's so kind of you to have come to thank me," she said formally, falling back on the personality that masked her vulnerability. "But it was quite unnecessary. I would have done the same for anyone who had been treated unfairly."

What was the matter with her? Devon wondered. Why was she acting as if they were meeting one another for the first time? A barrier had suddenly been erected around her, shielding her from . . . from . . . of course! Now Devon had his answer. She was in love with him, yet didn't realize he shared her feelings. She probably thought he was only here to thank her for what she did. And why not? It was the only thing he had said so far.

Slowly, purposely, he walked toward her. He could sense her agitation, not knowing what he was doing, unsure of the situation between them. But she allowed him to stand before her, never minding the fact that they were inches apart. She raised her eyes to meet his, and he saw within their brown depths a myriad of unasked questions. But as he placed a sure hand upon her cheek to tilt her head upward, he knew in an instant that he'd remove all her doubts.

His mouth landed on hers with the softness of a feather descending to earth. But the familiar sensation crashed through her body with all the force of an exploding cannon. In an instant she was no longer the stiff, formal Claire of a minute ago, but instead the sensual, earthy woman whom Devon had grown to love. Her body melted against his as every nerve came achingly alive, begging for his hands to soothe and caress. His lips yielded more insistent pressure, and the tip of his tongue dove its way into her mouth, basking in the sweetness it held.

She met his kiss with a frenzied passion, as a starving person would do when finally offered food. He felt her body trembling against his, and he held her tighter to assure her she was safe. All their emotions, bottled up over the past several weeks, now rushed forth with a frantic intensity.

A moment of sanity poked through the madness as Claire realized how vulnerable they were to discovery. But the whole family was upstairs, on the other side of the great house, preparing for an outing, and the servants were scrambling to help them get ready. Privacy would be theirs, at least for a few moments. Time enough to lose herself to Devon.

Claire thrust her head back with sensuous abandon, knowing Devon's lips would devour her neck. He responded with a fervor unlike anything she'd known, and she clung to him while her body shook with pleasure. Suddenly she knew that her legs would not support her.

The sensations firing through her body from Devon's lavish attention made her dizzy, and weak. Her legs gave way and she knew with a certainty that she would crash to the ground, but the fall never came. Devon was there to catch her, to support her, and in a single motion he swept her up and carried her over to the divan. He laid her gently upon it, as if she were a fragile package, then without further words between them, removed her clothing. When she was fully exposed he caught his breath in a sharp gasp. Her stunning beauty would always have that effect on him. With impatience he removed his clothes, too, then eased his way on top of her. Again he began kissing her, making sure she was ready, but there was no doubt that her desire for their union matched his own. With unashamed boldness she spread her legs before him, welcoming his entry. He plunged inside her.

She was so hot, so inviting, that Devon feared he would lose control from the moment he joined her. With a mighty will he held back, needing to make sure her pleasure matched his own. He moved against her in a frenzied rhythm, and soon heard her cries of release. In seconds he joined her, sharing the ecstasy of their reunion.

It took several minutes for either of them to find a voice, but finally it was Claire who roused herself.

"I must get dressed," was all she said, but there was apprehension in her words. Silently Devon followed her lead, wondering what would happen next.

When Claire had finished dressing, she, too, seemed at a loss for something to say. Their physical need had been temporarily sated, but what now? It occurred to her that their lovemaking had simply been Devon's way of showing her his gratitude. He had come here to thank her, and perhaps he thought that pleasuring her with his body was a means of expressing appreciation. At once she felt silly and ashamed. She was in love with this man, but she had no indication he felt the same for her. And why would he? She'd made it clear that there was no future for her with a man such as him, so why would he allow himself to fall in love, if ever the thought had even crossed his mind. Certainly their lovemaking was no indication. Where he came from, it was used as a tool for many things, even a way to show thanks. She shouldn't assume it meant anything else.

"Your gratitude is noted," she said stiffly, "and I shall consider myself properly thanked."

Her words had the effect of someone slamming a fist into his stomach. Is that what she thought? That he had made love to her as a way to say thank you? He was devastated that the thought had even occurred to her, much less that she accepted it as fact. With alarm he saw that she was headed toward the door. But as he saw the slight tremble of her lower lip, he knew that she was not as indifferent as she tried to appear.

"Claire, wait," he commanded, placing his hands upon her shoulders. " 'Twasn't only to thank you why I came here today."

She looked at him with wary curiosity, as if holding her breath until he spoke the next sentence.

"Ye also need to know how much I love ye."

She looked as if she didn't hear him. Either that, or she didn't understand. Her mouth dropped slightly open; her eyes became wider. Her face held a curious mixture of serene calm and wild confusion. Suddenly she realized she was holding her breath, and she blew it out in one great gust.

"Love me?" she echoed, unable to figure out anything else to say.

Devon smiled from the effect his words had on her. She was all at once the most beautiful, the most wonderful, the most desirable woman he had ever met, and the fact that his love for her left her speechless made his heart leap with joy.

"Aye, 'tis right," he said, drawing her close. "I love ye. I love ye more than anyone on this earth. I love ye more than I thought possible. And I want ye to know it."

Her lips lifted up in a small, quivering smile, and her eyes shone with tears.

"I can't believe it," she said shakily, doing her best to get control of the tears. "I was on my way to see you, just before you came. I was going to tell you the very same thing."

"And so ye have," he said, smiling, then drew her against him.

He was so strong, so sure, making no excuses for who he was. Perhaps what Philip had said was right—that Devon used to be a thief—but Claire would never again judge other people for who they were or what they did. He had done what he had to do in order to survive, and she would be ever grateful for that. She felt so right in his arms, as if it had been her place all along.

A knock on the door startled their solitude, and Louisa's voice then smashed it to pieces.

"Claire? Are you in there? It's time to leave for Lady Lyden's tea."

Without waiting for an answer Louisa opened the door, and for the first time in her life was startled into silence at the sight that greeted her.

Standing in the parlor, wrapped in the arms of their former footman, was Claire. She looked neither startled nor ashamed, but instead stood there as if it was the most natural thing in the world.

Louisa stared at them open-mouthed, and would have continued to do so if Lavinia hadn't walked through the door.

"Oh," was all she said, but her face could not hold

back a victorious smile. She alone had known what Claire felt for Devon; it seemed Claire had finally let Devon in on the secret.

"Lavinia!" Louisa shrieked. "Go get your father."

"I'm right here, Louisa," Kendal Rushmoor was heard saying from a few feet away.

"Kendal, I think you should come in here."

Knowing that she was in for a huge confrontation, Claire broke away from Devon so as not to agitate her mother any further.

Her father entered the room. "What is it—oh. Hello, Mr. Blake."

"Good afternoon to ye, sir," Devon responded politely.

"Kendal, I caught these two . . . well, that one had his arms on Claire!" she gasped, puckering her face against the horrid thought.

"Mother!" Claire said, angered that Louisa should give the impression that Devon had been doing something base.

Kendal looked at his daughter with a mixture of apprehension and curiosity, and Claire was relieved that he was at least acting calmer than her mother. For now, anyway.

"You may as well know the truth," Claire began, realizing she had an audience. The entire family, including Lilia and Aunt Bella, even the twins, had been planning on attending Lady Lyden's tea; now they all stood gathered before her in the parlor. Claire decided she may as well be blunt.

"I've finally found the man I love, and it happens to be Devon."

"Oh my Lord," choked Louisa, growing shaky in the knees. "Kendal, help me."

Lord Bedington assisted in getting his wife situated on the divan, then called to her sister, "Bella, have one of the maids bring in some water and a cool towel. Your sister looks faint."

Bella ran off to call a maid, and Kendal turned his attention back to his eldest daughter. "You're in love with Mr. Blake, daughter?" he said in his usual mild fashion.

"Yes, Father," Claire answered, her voice not wavering.

Kendal turned his eyes toward Devon. "And you, Mr. Blake. Have you anything to say?"

Devon cleared his throat and answered, " 'Tis true. I'm in love with yer daughter, sir. And I ask ye for her hand in marriage."

Now Louisa was not the only one who was shocked, though her loud cry sounded throughout the house. Claire was nearly as astonished as her mother, for she and Devon had discussed nothing beyond declaring their love for one another before they'd been interrupted. But before she knew what was happening Devon was on his knee in front of her, sincerely taking her hand in his and asking her to marry him.

"Two people who are in love generally get married," he said quietly, "and though I haven't the financial means to support ye yet, I can promise I will get them. I love ye more than anyone on this earth, Claire Rushmoor, and I want ye to be my wife."

"How beautiful," Lavinia tearfully uttered.

His words were more wonderful than anything she'd ever heard, and though they were surrounded by people, Claire blocked everyone out except for Devon. He knelt before her as gallantly as a medieval knight, laying his heart on the table as he braved all odds and asked her to be his wife. Claire felt that if she were to die this very day she would never be happier than she was at this moment. Whatever the consequences, she would be Devon Blake's wife.

The room seemed inordinately quiet, despite Louisa's

loud protests, Lavinia's sniffing, and Claire's two young sisters asking everyone what was going on. Those were extraneous noises that her mind blocked out. The only sound she heard was the exceptionally loud beating of her heart. She was so overjoyed by what was happening to her that she allowed herself to sink to her knees so that she could look straight into Devon's eyes as she gave him her answer.

"Yes! Yes!" she joyfully exclaimed. "Yes, I'll be your wife!"

Unmindful of the audience surrounding them, Claire and Devon embraced one another with a rush of overwhelming love. Claire's heart was pounding so loudly she was certain it could be heard by the others. Never before had she even been aware that such profound joy existed; now she gathered strength from it. Unabashed tears streamed down her face while she held on to Devon as tightly as she could. She wanted this moment to never end, but her mother interrupted their bliss.

"Take your hands off my daughter and leave this house at once, you filthy Irish rake," she commanded Devon from her place on the sofa. "I don't want to ever see you here again."

At first the threat was easily ignored, as if it were no more than a puff of air passing through the room. But when Louisa repeated her words, amplifying her voice tenfold, Devon reluctantly detached himself from Claire and rose to his feet. He felt his old anger toward the wealthy boiling up to the surface of his mind, constructing sarcastic comebacks that he longed to hurl at his would-be mother-in-law. But he had learned a lot over the summer about dealing with the wealthy, and he now knew that a good routing would do no more than get him permanently removed from the house. It would also prove highly ineffective in persuading Claire's family to allow their marriage.

He restrained his anger and looked straight into Louisa's eyes. "Begging yer pardon, m'lady," he said quietly, "but 'tis my understanding that the man of the house is the one to make such decisions." Then, without waiting for the protest he was sure Louisa wanted to make, he turned toward Kendal Rushmoor and rested his fate in the hands of his former employer.

"Ye heard what I have to say, m'lord. I love yer daughter, and she loves me. I'm not a titled man, nor do I have any money. Yet. But now that the misunderstanding about my honesty has been cleared I mean to make some, enough so that I can properly provide for her. I'd like Claire to be my wife, and I'm hoping ye'll see yer way to allow us to be together."

Every eye in the room swung toward Kendal, and without warning he was the center of attention. Though he was a Parliament member, he was generally thought of as a thinking member, not a vocal one. It was known among all his friends and colleagues that Kendal Rushmoor was not a man to bluster out foolishness or speak without completely thinking through a situation. He was frequently the one looked to when ties had to be broken or disputes resolved. He listened to both sides of the story, then made his decision. But now he had to make one of the most important decisions of his life, and he felt uncustomary apprehension about the position he'd been thrust into.

"Really, Kendal," Louisa huffed, "put this man in his place and get him out of here. It's all very touching that he's fallen in love with our daughter, but who wouldn't, in his place? He's a servant, for God's sake, and according to Philip Westbury, no more than a common thief. It's a shame, really, the nasty business that happened with Philip. I was truly beginning to admire the man, and he'd have made such a lovely husband for Claire that I—"

"Silence!" Her husband's unusual tone of voice

stopped his wife cold. She stared at him with eyes as round as serving platters, dropped her mouth open, and took a sharp breath. Never had her husband so much as raised his voice; now he had nearly shouted at her.

"Are your wits properly about you, wife? Because you're carrying on like you may have lost hold of them. Lord Townsend is a murderer. He shamed himself, his family, and his name with what he did, and if he hadn't been caught we would have allowed the lout to marry our daughter. I don't know how you feel, Louisa, but it gives me no comfort thinking how close we came to having a murderer brought into the family."

He paused to let his wife absorb what he'd just said, and the shy glances around the room from other family members showed what an impact his words had made.

"Now you're acting faint of heart because this young man, our former footman, is asking for Claire's hand in marriage. Of course, he's right about one thing. He brings no title or money with him. In the eyes of our friends, Claire would be committing a bigger crime by marrying Mr. Blake than the crime that put Philip Westbury in Newgate." A fiery blush rose to color Kendal's face, and though he remained composed, it was clear to all how angry he'd become.

"But I do believe I've had all I can take of the insipid rubbish we deal with every day. What does it mean when a man who commits murder is held in higher esteem than one who works for an honest living? Why are wealthy men who spend their evenings gaming and whoring portrayed in a better light than their servants who live a faithful life?"

Louisa paled at her husband's use of such abhorrent words, but she sensed it was better to keep her objections quiet.

Kendal walked toward Devon until he stood directly

in front of him. Both men were nearly matched in height, and they were able to look each other straight in the eye.

"Mr. Blake, though you were here for a short time, you were the best footman ever employed in this household. You're bright, you're sharp; there's an intelligence about you that I rarely see these days. You've done a lot of thinking in your time, and you've got the experience of the streets to heighten your awareness of dangers and obstacles. Those qualities will get you far in life; you need only find the right opportunity to use them."

In all his life Devon had never had a father's touch to guide him, and he'd never had a man he looked up to give him words of encouragement. Now here before him stood the man he hoped would be his father-in-law, praising him simply for being who he was. Kendal's words touched Devon deeply.

"I know you love my daughter, and it's clear that she loves you. We always promised Claire that she could marry the man she loves, so I give you my permission and my blessing to become my daughter's husband."

The words were momentous, and Devon could only smile and thank Kendal again and again. When Claire heard his words she let out a cry of joy and rushed into her father's arms. She flung her arms around his waist and hugged him as though she'd never let him go. Though Kendal was unused to such affection from anyone, he savored the moment he shared with his daughter. He could feel his throat constrict as the emotions welled inside him. He welcomed the way his heart and soul felt so alive. And from the sniffles he heard throughout the room, he knew others were just as touched. Except for his wife.

She had been listening to all that was going on with barely restrained anger, but when Kendal granted his permission for their daughter to marry this dreck of society, she lost control.

"Kendal!" she cried out. "Have you gone mad? Think of the scandal this would cause! The family would be shamed forever and the talk would never stop. Claire could never step foot anywhere in the city anymore. She'd be a complete outcast. I fear, dear husband, that you may have forgotten those little details."

His wife's sarcasm was not lost on Lord Rushmoor, but with calm reserve he addressed her concerns.

"Indeed, dear wife, I have not forgotten nor ignored those potential problems, but I believe I have a solution for us all."

At the unexpected announcement everyone in the room pressed forward, not wanting to miss a single word of what Kendal would say next.

"I know you may think me not attuned to the goings on of this family, Louisa. But, in fact, I have known for some time that this day would come. Perhaps it is my silence that makes me more observant. The less I talk, the more I see."

Louisa had the good grace to blush at her husband's gentle reprimand of her penchant for gossip.

"At any rate, despite your best efforts to hide it, dear daughter, I knew that you had fallen in love with Mr. Blake. And fallen hard. I can't say that I blame you, of course. He is, after all, dashing to look at, and much more interesting than your usual callers."

Claire was astonished, and a little embarrassed, at her father's words. How could he have known? What had he seen? She cringed as she remembered the torrid situations she'd been in with Devon, but she was absolutely certain they had not been observed. No, it was more than likely a new look she'd had on her face, perhaps different gestures or mannerisms, things that only a very observant person who knew her well would have noticed, that had given away her feelings toward Devon.

"I also knew, however," Kendal continued, "that the

situation would pose certain challenges for the family. But upon thinking it over, I believe I've come up with a way for it to work."

He turned to face Devon directly. "I'm about to invest in a joint shipping venture with another fellow. He owns a fleet, but needs capital to back him up. He's sailed several times to Africa, and says there are treasures to be brought back from there if only he can get an investor to fund the trips. I'll get a cut straight off the top of whatever he imports, plus a percentage from the sales. It's a solid investment, but it needs someone who can keep track of the operations. Oversee the unloading and distribution of all imported goods, monies collected from sales, expenses incurred during the trips. I also need a problem solver, and a leader. Someone who can give orders and command respect, but who's fair and rewards loyalty and hard work. If truth were to be told, I simply haven't the time for it. Nor do I have the inclination to leave England."

If he'd meant to cause confusion by that last statement, he'd more than accomplished it. Everyone in the room looked at each other as if to confirm whether or not they'd heard him correctly. But when Kendal said no more, Claire finally prompted him. "Leave, Father? But whatever are you talking about?"

"The dock to where the ships will be sailing is on the southeastern coast of Ireland."

Astonished silence held everyone's tongues, until finally Devon broke the spell.

"Did ye say Ireland, sir?"

Kendal's expression remained serious, but Claire was certain she saw a twinkle in her father's eyes. "Indeed I did. The ships will be importing goods to Ireland. And to judge by your accent, Mr. Blake, it's your homeland."

"My mum's homeland, m'lord. She was born and raised outside Dublin, but came to England when she was a teenage girl. I've not been there myself, but 'twas my mum who raised me, taught me to speak, and all my best mates are from Ireland. I suppose that would account for the accent."

Kendal nodded in agreement, then continued. "You've no doubt seen our family crest, and know that two-thirds of it represents our family name. But the bottom of the crest depicts a castle, and I know that neither you, nor anyone in this family, knows that that castle is located in Ireland."

"But Kendal!" Louisa gasped. "You've always told me your family's from North Yorkshire!"

"They are, Louisa, they are," Lord Bedington replied, speaking in soothing tones to calm his wife. "But my great-great-grandfather Cecil was somewhat of an independent spirit, and the story goes that he had an Irish mistress named Sara who captured his heart. They were lovers for some three years until she became enceinte with his child. Much like the situation still is today, Sara was considered socially 'beneath' Cecil, so it was impossible for them to be together. And anyway, Cecil had been promised since infancy to his eventual wife. But he refused to let his true love and babe live in squalor, so he secretly used family funds to oversee the building of a place for them to live. And not just any place. To show the depth of his feelings, Cecil built his beloved a castle in Ireland."

"Why Ireland, Papa?" little Emily piped up.

"Because having Sara in Ireland shielded her, and Cecil's family, from the scorn and gossip that would have surrounded them had she remained in England. Cecil and Sara devised a story for the locals in Ireland that she'd wed an Englishman and carried his child, but that her husband had been killed in the Civil War. In her devastation she could no longer remain in the country that had made her a widow, so she came back home to birth and raise her babe."

"What a beautiful story, Father," sniffed Lavinia.

"Kendal, I had no idea—"

"There's no need to say anything. I never told anyone about the location of that castle because of the unfortunate attitude we English have toward the Irish. But it's time the truth came out. That castle hasn't been inhabited for nearly a hundred years. I've an overseer who makes sure the property is kept up, but it's high time it be lived in again. Like it or not, that castle in Ireland is part of this family's heritage, and I want it treated as such. Now, it happens to be located in southern Waterford, quite close to where those ships will be docking. I'll be needing someone to act as overlord there. You'll need to hire staff to help you, Devon, but you mentioned something about having friends here? Men you can trust, I'm assuming?"

He said no more, but it was obvious what he was asking, and in that moment, Claire's heart felt as if it would burst with the love she held for her father. He was giving Devon the chance he needed to turn his life around, and for them to be together without living in shame or embarrassing the family. Instead of looking the other way, he was looking to help them. Claire knew her father would never have proposed the idea if he hadn't felt Devon could do it, but she realized that he was also doing it for her.

"I . . . overlord, sir?" Devon stammered, unable to believe the good fortune showering upon him.

"That's right."

Devon inhaled a deep breath, savoring, just for a moment, the idea of what such an opportunity would bring him. But as the air slowly expelled from his lungs, so, too, did the idea. "I'm happy about the offer, m'lord, but I'm afraid I'll have to decline."

If someone had slammed a hammer against Claire's chest, her heart couldn't have stopped any faster. She was so certain Devon would leap at the chance, and why not? This was the opportunity of a lifetime for him, and he'd never get another offer like this one. Why, then, was he refusing?

Even Kendal was taken aback. At first he even thought he'd misunderstood, but when Devon unhappily looked away, he knew there'd been no mistake.

"The work doesn't appeal to you?" he asked, hoping he could do something to change his mind.

"Oh, it's not that, m'lord. It appeals to me just fine."

"You don't fancy living in Ireland, then?"

Devon shook his head emphatically. "I'd give my right hand for the chance to go back to my roots."

"Well then why are you turning down the offer?"

" 'Tis simple, really, m'lord. I got no book learnin'. I don't know how to read nor write."

"But you could learn, Devon," Claire rushed to point out. "Sally told me you have amazing skills at numbers."

"Who's Sally?" Lilia asked, and Claire's mind raced trying to think up an answer.

"She's a friend of my mum's," Devon said, and though no one bothered asking how Claire knew her, Lilia seemed satisfied.

"My daughter's right. With your intelligence you would learn quickly, and the first ship won't sail for nearly a year, so there's time. Time for you and Claire to get married, move your belongings to the castle, hire indoor and outdoor staff, and get settled." He paused, then added, "I bet your mum would make a fine head housekeeper."

Devon continued to shake his head, but Kendal pressed forward, acting as though he hadn't noticed. "Having someone to act as overlord means more than figures and paperwork. It's mainly about trust. I must be able to completely trust the person I employ. There's a great deal of money and responsibility involved in the position. My overlord must be honest and trustworthy. That's the reason I've asked you."

His words convinced Devon that he could do it. But what of Claire? Was she willing to leave her homeland and travel to parts unknown? Though his question remained unvoiced, he searched her face for the answer, looking deep into her eyes. Claire knew what he silently asked her and, with joy in her heart, gave him the answer he sought.

"As long as we can be together, I'll go anywhere with you, Devon. To be honest, I've grown weary of this life. I dislike the restrictions and rules, what can and can't be done. And I dislike anyone telling me whom I can and cannot talk to. Or be with. Or love."

A great smile spread across Devon's face, as he slowly nodded his head and accepted Kendal's offer. "Ye won't be disappointed, m'lord. Thank ye."

"Thank you, Devon. And welcome to the family."

Both men solemnly shook hands, paused, and then hugged one another with the enthusiasm of two long-lost friends. Father and future son-in-law clapped each other on the back and laughed as happiness spread throughout the room.

With the enthusiasm typical of most young children, Claire's ten-year-old twin sisters began clapping their hands together and jumping up and down. Lavinia rushed over to hug Claire, and then Lilia ran to join them. Even Louisa became affected by the contagious good cheer, and though she was still a bit reluctant to wholeheartedly accept Devon, she did enjoy seeing her daughter so happy.

At that moment, Emma Leeds came into the room, drawn by the unusual noise level they'd all created.

"My heavens," she exclaimed, "it looks like a party in here."

"And a party is exactly what we need, Mrs. Leeds," Kendal called out to her.

"Then a party you shall have!"

"Kendal!" Louisa called out, shocked by her husband's buoyant behavior.

"Oh, Louisa, calm yourself. I'm celebrating our family's first marriage."

"But we're late for Lady Lyden's tea!"

For a moment Kendal felt angry at Louisa but then realized he mustn't be too harsh on his wife. She'd been brought up in the proper way of all London gentry, without ever stopping to question whether their teachings were right or wrong. He couldn't expect her to suddenly become a different person after generations of noble breeding had formed who she was. Perhaps in her own time Louisa would accept Devon; for now it was enough that she had stopped berating him.

He walked over to the sofa and sat down next to his wife, taking her hand in his. The small gesture seemed to pacify her, and she looked into his eyes as if asking what to do.

"We'll go to Lady Lyden's tea just as we planned," he said, already managing to bring a smile to his wife's face. "But when we come back I think it's only appropriate to have a celebration meal to welcome Devon to the family. I know you don't approve, Louisa. But for once don't think of what other people will say; just look at your daughter and see how happy she is. That should be enough for you to realize that we've made the right decision."

Indeed, Claire was happier than she'd ever seen her, Louisa admitted. Her daughter's cheeks looked like roses in bloom. Her eyes sparkled with joy. It reminded Louisa of herself when she and Kendal had first become married, although Louisa hadn't been allowed to openly show her feelings. And perhaps, she realized for the first time, that wasn't good. What harm is there in expressing joy, especially when that joy stems from love.

"Come along, everyone," she called out at last. "We still need to get to Lady Lyden's tea."

Claire's face fell when she heard the news, but her mother quickly put her fears to rest.

"You needn't worry about going, Claire. I'm certain that attending a tea is not something you wish to do right now. We'll make the excuses for you, and see the both of you when we return for dinner."

Though she hadn't officially welcomed Devon to the family, both he and Claire realized that Louisa's acknowledgment of seeing both of them later was a step in the right direction.

"Thank you, Mother," Claire said, as the rest of the family slipped out of the room. Louisa nodded toward the couple, then left them alone.

When the carriages had finally trotted off leaving the house quiet except for the servants, Claire and Devon walked over to the sofa and sat down upon it with shaky legs. They were both so overwhelmed with what had just happened that they needed several moments before either could speak.

"I hope ye didn't mind me asking yer father if I could marry ye before I asked ye," Devon ventured.

"It was the kind of proposal girls dream of," Claire answered breathlessly, assuring him that everything was all right.

"I never thought I'd get a chance like the one yer father just gave me."

"My father is a wonderful man who understands our situation. More than I ever knew."

Claire leaned over to embrace the man she loved, needing to show him just how much he meant to her.

As always, the minute their mouths came together passions sprang to life, but this time, for the moment, Devon held himself at bay.

His soon-to-be wife pouted naughtily at being stopped, but he had to tell her one more time how happy he was.

"Ye're the most important person in the world to me," he whispered huskily. "Ye've taught me the wrongs of unconditional hatred. Taught me how unfair it is, that it doesn't have to exist. Taught me that not everyone with money is evil."

"And you've taught me about unconditional love," Claire whispered back in a shaky voice. "That you love someone for what they are, not who they are. I'm so very grateful to you for that, Devon. And I'll go on proving it to you for the rest of our lives."

Her honesty and adoration touched him deeply, and he gathered her into his arms and pulled her next to him.

"Perhaps now would be a good time to start."

Claire wrinkled her brows in confusion. "Start?" she asked. "Start what?"

"Start proving to me how grateful ye really are. After all, we're here alone, and 'twould be a shame to waste such an opportunity."

The wicked look in his eyes made her realize what he was after, and she was only too happy to comply.

"Then here's your proof," she whispered, barely getting the words out before his lips descended upon hers and drew her into paradise.

DO YOU HAVE THE
HOHL COLLECTION?